INK & AMBITION

Campus Love Series

EMILY R. BELLAS

For Eric

Chapter One

Margot

"THIS PLACE IS DISGUSTING," I grunt.

Flashing lights and deafening music assault my senses the minute we walk back into the house from the backyard. The bottom of my shoe sticks to the floor and it takes more effort than it should to pull myself free.

"Disgustingly beautiful. Where else will you see people lined up to do a keg stand? It's a magnificent display of humanity," my roommate, Sydney responds.

A cold wet line of sticky amber liquid creeps down my arm as a drink is spilled above me. "Truly glorious," I deadpan. Sydney grabs a napkin from the nearest table and starts wiping the beer off my shoulder but I take it from her hand to do it myself. "Seriously, can we go now? I promised an hour. It's been an hour."

"Not yet," she replies, taking the wet towel and throwing it on the floor, just adding to the grime and filth. "We have to find Danika first."

"Yeah, that keg stand line? I think I found her." I point in the direction of the chaos and spot our other roommate in the midst of a gymnastic feat she is in no way qualified to do.

"Ah, shit," Sydney mutters and we both shove our way through the crowd surrounding Danika. A tall, muscular boy in a homemade muscle tee holds up our friend and keeps her steady as she chugs the beer flowing from the tap.

"Twenty-nine, thirty!" The crowd cheers, and Danika is placed gently on her feet as if she's floating down from a cloud, Mary Poppins style.

"Thanks, gorgeous," Danika winks at the boy who held her up and whose eyes cannot willingly leave hers. "Hey, ladies!" She grins as we come into focus for her.

"Ready to go, Dani?" I ask, not hiding the desperation in my voice.

"Just a sec. I got one more piece of business to take care of." Danika turns around and grabs the neck of the boy who was holding her up. He responds immediately, pulling her back up into his arms and locking their lips together. While she sucks his face, I look around the room one last time, knowing this will take some time.

Somehow, I got away with not having to go to any parties during our first two years of college but Danika practically begged Sydney and me to come out with her more this year. And while this is certainly the last place on Earth I'd like to be right now, knowing that it made my best friend happy is reward enough–for now.

Danika and the boy break apart with a loud lip smack that I can't help but physically recoil at. "Thanks for the assist," she says as he sets her on her feet again, this time with much more reluctance.

If I wasn't completely used to this behavior from her, my jaw would be on the floor but instead I'm checking my watch and wondering when she'll finally be ready to leave.

"Okay, ready!" Danika cheers, pulling herself away from the boy and pushing between us, linking our arms and guiding us to the exit. Sydney and I crane our necks to give each other a knowing look behind Dani's back as we move toward the door.

"Did you have fun?" Sydney asks, the sweetness in her voice never wavering. She genuinely wants to know if Dani had a good time tonight. Whereas, having known Danika since I was five, I couldn't care less if she enjoyed herself. She knows we only came with her because of our pact. And in exchange for us going to parties with her, Danika has promised to give us free health checks as soon as she becomes a real-life doctor.

Dani rests her head on sweet Sydney's shoulder. "The best time, Syd. What about you?"

I open my mouth to respond but am cut immediately off.

"Not you, nerd. I *know* you didn't have a good time. I'm asking Sydney."

Giving her a dig in the ribs, I don't even need to respond because she's absolutely right. There's nothing I detest more than wasting my time standing around a crowded frat house watching hundreds of drunken, half-naked people fall all over each other.

But Sydney smiles. "I had a great time."

Just as we separate to single-file out the door, a loud commotion sounds behind us. Suddenly, I'm jolted forward as a huge weight hits my back.

"What did I fucking tell you would happen if I ever saw you in my house again." A loud, deep voice growls close to my ear. When I turn around to face the chaos, I see a guy laying on the floor at my feet and a huge man, the owner of the voice, towering over him. I know I've seen his face before but I can't pinpoint exactly where I know him from. Clearly he's a Tomlin University student but I don't think I've seen him in any of my classes. Maybe he's an athlete? Not that I keep up much with sports but my job on the school newspaper keeps me pretty up to date on the happenings on campus. Maybe I wrote a story about him once?

The entire room has paused as if this is the event they are all waiting for. Eyes are glued to the mess directly in front of me and I feel Danika shimmy up beside me to get her own eye-witness account.

"Alex, man, listen–" The poor guy can't get another word out before he's being picked up by the front of his shirt like a rag doll and thrown back on the floor.

Alex? Hm, not ringing a bell. Probably for the best, this guy seems like trouble. Throwing someone out of a party? What right does he have to do that? I cringe at the insane display of toxic masculinity happening right before my eyes.

"Clearly you're having trouble with your ears," Alex says, his voice deadly. "Or you're just not listening. So, let me make this abundantly clear."

Abundantly? I wouldn't expect a brute like him to have such an extensive vocabulary. I chuckle at his use of the word, which draws the crazed man's eyes directly to me. My eyes widen while his narrow. He glances around me for a split second before grunting.

"You mind moving a little to the left, sunshine?" He says.

Looking to my left and then to my right, I come up empty before settling my gaze back at him. *Is he talking to me?*

Alex lets out a sound that could almost be described as laughter along with a smile that certainly doesn't fit the demeanor he was just portraying mere seconds ago. "Yes, you." He nods his head toward the direction he wants me to go.

Hesitantly shifting away from the doorway, I watch as Alex bends back down, grabs the boy by the shirt and throws him out the door and onto the dewy grass beyond. He grunts loudly in my ear before bringing himself back up to tower over me and the rest of the crowd.

"And that's the last warning," he yells to the roughed-up guy. Immediately the noise of the party starts up again, as if the last thirty seconds didn't happen.

I hear the gruff voice in my ear. "Sorry for the shove," Alex says, looking down at me from his impressive height. Gazing up at him, my eyes connect with his deep brown, almost black irises. I can't tell if this is his natural eye color or if his pupils are completely dilated from the adrenaline of what he just did.

Pursing my lips, I give a curt nod before attempting my exit again. If I didn't already hate this party, that violent scene certainly didn't help. Before I can take another step, a rough hand reaches out and grabs my wrist, stopping me from leaving.

"Are you okay?" Alex says. "He didn't hit you in the head or anything, right? No permanent brain damage?"

This guy just picked up a whole human, tossed him out the door without any regard for his well-being and is now wondering if *I'm* okay? Is he out of his mind?

Raising my eyebrows, I shake my head as I reply. "Nope. All brain cells still intact...not that I could say the same for you." I mutter that last part but it's louder than I thought, causing Sydney to gasp and Danika to giggle with glee.

Alex narrows his eyes, tilting his head a little to show his confusion. "Excuse me?" *Oops, guess he heard me too.* I should apologize but I find myself not feeling the least bit sorry.

I think spending so much time in a place I didn't want to be coupled with being spilled on has caused me to toe the line on an emotional meltdown. And seeing the way this orge treated that other guy tipped me right over the edge.

"Who do you think you are treating people like that?"

Pulling himself to his full, still impressive, height, he asserts, "I'm the president of this frat."

"And that makes you god?"

He leans down so he's whispering in my ear, "In some circles."

I pull my head back in disgust. First he shoves into me, then he has the audacity to try and flirt? His eyes twinkle as his gaze reaches mine again and I'm sure he's ignoring the disdain in my glare. While I'm no pushover, I've never been this outwardly rude to somebody, especially someone I don't even know. Danika has been training me to be assertive like her for years but it's hardly stuck.

"And who are you, anyway? I've never seen you here before."

We're standing directly in the doorway now, blocking anyone from entering or exiting–a situation made apparent when two drunk girls stumble into us, pushing me out the door and shoving Alex back inside.

Perfect. Without another word, I swing around, grabbing Sydney and Danika's arms and bringing them on either side of me. I hear the faint sound of Alex yelling something from the doorway but I can't make it out.

"Margot, what the hell was that?" Dani asks with pride in her voice.

I sigh. "All I know is, I'm never going to another frat party."

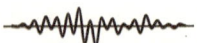

The overhead light flickers as I flip the switch.

"We really need to change that bulb," I remind Danika who shrugs as she kicks off her shoes. Our apartment is small but it works for the three of us. The entryway houses our impossibly long shoe rack, which is mostly overtaken by Danika's sneaker collection. Our coats are lined one by one along the wall, just waiting for fall to turn into winter. With the warmer weather this September, we haven't needed them just yet.

"Any pizza left over?" Sydney asks as we make our way into the kitchen. Danika collapses on the sofa nearby and I already know she's going to fall asleep there.

Shaking my head, I open the fridge. "We finished it before we left. But there's..." I search through the empty refrigerator to find something of sustenance. "Grapes?"

"Pass," Sydney sighs. "Sleep it is, then. Night, ladies."

"Night," I reply, draping a blanket over Danika's sleeping form. Her bedroom is only steps away from the couch–all of ours are–yet she always manages to make herself at home wherever she is.

Making quick work of brushing my teeth and cleaning my face, I head into my bedroom to finally pick up where I left off with my syllabus readings. While this first week of class was mainly introductory, it did give me the schedules for assignments and tests for the semester and I've been working non-stop on whatever I can to get ahead of the game.

The first two weeks of coursework for "Investigating Journalism" and "Journalistic Inquiry: The Written Word" are already done. I am so excited to truly start my journalism major courses this year that I might've gotten a little ahead of myself, but I didn't mind. From what I heard from my colleagues on the newspaper, junior year is the best in terms of true journalistic content learning. I can't wait to jump in and hit the pavement, as they say.

I wish I could take only journalism classes for the rest of my time at Tomlin University but alas, my advisor informed me that I needed to take three electives this year. In my haste to finish my course schedule on time and not get closed out of any of my core classes, I picked the first three electives I saw: Public Speaking, American Sign Language, and Psychology.

ASL and Psychology I can handle but Public Speaking? I am absolutely dreading it. I pull the syllabus up on my laptop and stare at the first assignment due on Monday.

"Prepare a one-to-two minute speech about something that scares you," I read aloud. *Does this class count?*

What scares me? Doing my taxes. Calling customer service lines. Dating. *Ugh.* I shut my computer and push it away from me on the bed. This will be tomorrow's problem, I decide and curl up under the covers to finally get some much needed shut eye.

Chapter Two

Margot

I WAKE WITH A start, as I sometimes do when rattled by a particularly startling dream. Grabbing the journal I keep on my bedside table, I furiously write out the insane scenario that just ran rampant in my head. After a few minutes, I sigh deeply and pull myself from the warm and cozy bed.

Clutching my dream journal, I head into the kitchen, immediately spotting Danika with a blanket around her shoulders, brewing a fresh pot of coffee.

"Good morning, beautiful people!" Sydney hops into the kitchen, clad in one of her twenty matching workout sets. Skipping the coffee, she grabs a water bottle from the fridge as she inserts her headphones into her ears. "Headed to the gym. See you in a bit." Danika and I groan our goodbye as the door closes behind her.

"Weird one?" Danika asks, looking at the worn down book in my hand. I hand it to her as I grab a mug of coffee. Behind me, Dani has flipped to the most recent page in my journal.

"Aliens? That's new," she comments as she reads. I plop myself down on the couch with my mug and Danika joins me.

"Green and blue aliens. Thoughts?"

"Well," Danika starts, humming as she thinks through the weirdness that invaded my head last night. "Being abducted by aliens is pretty cut and dry. You're not happy with where you are and you wish someone would come and transport you to a different place. Whether that be a physical location or some other change in your personal life."

She hands me the journal and takes another sip of her coffee.

"Maybe it's trying to tell me to transport myself out of that public speaking elective class I have tomorrow."

Danika gives me a sympathetic look. "You'll be fine. Journalists need to be good at public speaking. This is good practice."

"Since when?"

Danika only shrugs as she settles deeper onto the couch.

I sigh. "I think I need to log some hours in the library this morning. My study room is calling." I take a final sip of my coffee, and Danika hands me her empty mug as I walk toward the kitchen. "Care to join?"

"No, thank you very much," Danika replies, already hitting the power button on the TV remote. "I think I'll take this last day before classes really start as a day to rot." She scrolls through Netflix until she finds her favorite season of whatever dating reality show she's obsessed with this week and pulls the blanket over herself.

I laugh at her, wishing that I could join but I need to get this speech done and the only way I can truly focus is in Study Room G6–my sanctuary in the campus library. Getting myself together, I grab my things and head for the door.

"Enjoy rotting," I call to Dani's immobile form.

"I plan to!" she calls back and I chuckle as the door closes behind me.

While having an apartment off campus has its clear advantages, it also has an even larger amount of disadvantages, at least for me who has no mode of transportation other than public or begging. Today, I was too slow to hitch a ride with Sydney so onto the bus I go.

Fifteen minutes later, the bus pulls up to campus and I hop off with vigor.

I can write this speech. *Just pick an easy topic. It doesn't have to be that deep.*

"Hey Margot," Edith, the school librarian, says when I scan my ID. "It's nice to see you back. How was your summer?"

I shrug. "Uneventful," I reply with a smile. "How was yours?"

If she is allowed, Edith, with her tight gray curls and her lovable yellowing grin, can chat for hours on end without skipping a beat. Luckily for me, I have a couple years of practice on how to get her to focus on what's in front of her, which right now is me, trying to get the key to my study room.

Right in the middle of the word "Nantucket," I make my move. "Oh, Nantucket! I hear that place is beautiful in the summer time. I'll have to make a trip out there at some point. Anyway, I'm just going to head downstairs to G6, okay? See ya!"

As I'm already headed toward the staircase to the downstairs level of the library, I hear Edith call my name. *So close.*

"Actually, Margot, that room is taken," she says sheepishly. I stop in my tracks. Taken? But that's *my* study room.

While I do know that she can't permanently hold that room on reserve for me everyday—that would be ridiculous—still...I hoped she would at least steer everyone else toward different study rooms until that one was the very last resort! Is that too much to ask?

"The room was booked online this morning by a group."

"Wait, you can reserve rooms online now?"

Edith nods excitedly. "Oh yes, part of the new system this year."

I sigh. Online room booking will be very useful in the future but for today, it's done me dirty. "Good to know, thanks. Well, I guess I'll just take any available room then."

A look of anxiety flashes across Edith's face.

"You're kidding me," I balk. "The semester has barely started yet!"

A chuckle releases from Edith as she smiles proudly. "Apparently people are finally taking their studies seriously this year." My mouth flattens to a frown and I sigh, backing away from the desk, with a sad wave to Edith.

I could just sit at a table but the noise of passersby distracts me. Going to the newsroom is definitely out of the question. I usually love the quick atmosphere there, but not when I need to focus on school work. I could always just go home and work at the desk in my bedroom, but I came all this way...

"Morning, I booked room G6," a deep, somewhat familiar voice says, snapping me from my thoughts. There's a tall, tall man at the desk and while the voice sounded like something I've heard before, I can't exactly place him in my mind.

"Right, of course. I've got the key for you right here." Is Edith actually *blushing*?

The man doesn't speak again but I'm assuming he gave her a megawatt smile based on the way she all but melts in front of him. *Well now I have to get a look at him.*

As he turns around to face me, I can't control the way my jaw drops to the floor. Alex, the person-throwing ogre from the party last night, is here, standing in front of me. And he stole my study room.

"I can't believe I'm about to say this but, you should close your mouth. You might catch flies with it wide open like that," he smirks at me. *Smirks!* What an oaf.

I am stunned into silence. Even if I wanted to speak, I have no words to describe the feeling of seeing this man in broad daylight. I do have to give it to Edith though, he is wildly attractive. The sunlight shining through the windows brightens his dark brown irises and his even darker brown hair is tousled in that sexy "just got out of bed" look.

"Problem, sunshine?" I want to wipe that smirk clean off his face using the shirt from the guy that he threw out the door last night.

My anger returns and I'm finally able to muster up a response. "Nope."

He takes a step closer toward me but if I step back, I'd topple down the staircase so I hold my ground under his scrutiny. "You look surprised to see me."

"Just shocked you know where the library is," I reply, regaining my confidence little by little. I still don't know what it is about this guy that pulls the worst out of me but somehow I feel sure that he deserves it.

Alex chuckles darkly at my comment. "Another joke about my intelligence? Can't think of anything more original, sunshine?"

"Give me a few minutes, I'm sure I can think of another reason to insult you and why do you keep calling me sunshine?" I blurt out before I can stop myself.

Alex takes another step forward, definitely aware that I have no choice but to stay put. "You never told me your name."

Taking a deep breath, I look up directly into Alex's eyes, not letting the bottomless pit of brown lull me into a false sense of security. "You're right." I shrug and step around him to head out the way I came.

"Oh come on," I hear Alex laugh from behind me but I don't turn back around. I refuse to let this arrogant beast get under my skin anymore than he already has.

Once outside, I finally take a deep breath. Taking my phone out of my pocket, I call the only person who will be able to help me make sense of all this.

"Missing me already?" Danika says lazily.

"That guy I talked to at the frat party. Person thrower. Tall guy..."

Danika chuckles. "Is there a question in there?"

"Who is he?"

"Why the sudden interest?" I can tell her eyebrows are raised in that devilish way. One thing my best friend loves to do is make me squirm. I roll my eyes and dive into the sad library study room tale that ends with that arrogant troll getting a place to work in peace and my sorry ass out on the pavement.

Danika gasps. "Not study room G6! But everyone on campus knows that's *your* room."

"I am not finding you amusing right now," I deadpan. Danika's laugh loosens a bit of tightness in my chest.

"His name is Alex Prescott. He's the president of Kappa Alpha, the frat we were at on Friday. I'm not sure his major but I know he throws a great party. Thanks to daddy's money."

"Daddy's money?"

"His dad owns some big business, Prescott Cars or Motors or whatever." A loud crunching sounds from the other side of the phone and I know that Danika is indulging in her favorite lazy day snack—pretzels and peanut butter.

The news that Alex is rich doesn't surprise me one bit. Of course he is, no one with an ounce of humility would go around acting the way he does. I'll bet he's so used to getting what he wants. Which makes me all the more angry that he got that study room over me. I should go in there and demand he gives it to me. What's he even using it for? He doesn't strike me as the studious type.

As much as I wish I had Danika's confidence enough to go into that study room and demand it back, I can't do that. He booked it fair and square but over my dead body will he get it from me again.

"Well, now I've got nowhere to work so I'm gonna see if Sydney is almost done in the fitness center and then catch a ride home with her."

"Check this out while you're waiting. Might give you some insight on the great mystery that is Alexander Prescott."

Before I can ask what she means, my phone vibrates against my face and I pull it back to reveal a link to an Instagram profile. After a quick goodbye to Dani, I hang up the phone and click the link. My phone is flooded with workout videos and photos, all with Alex front and center. Quickly, I close my phone, suddenly remembering that I'm still directly outside the place I just ran into him and he could walk out those doors and see me cyberstalking him any second now.

Sending Sydney a quick text, I make my way toward the fitness center, hoping she's finishing up around now. As I plop myself down on a bench outside the gym, I pull up Alex's profile again. It really was impressive the way he handles the gym equipment. The videos look professional and the posts seem to have lots of good advice, even including things like nutrition and health. I guess this is what he devotes his time to, besides partying.

I'm not sure how much time passes as I get lost scrolling through the mind of Alex Prescott.

Chapter Three

Alex

MY SMILE LINGERS AS I watch her cute butt walk out through the library doors. If she was as shocked as I was to be seeing each other again, she didn't let on. In fact, she insulted me. Which shouldn't turn me on, but apparently it does. It's rare that I have to chase a girl and honestly, it's about time I get my running shoes on again.

Before I can stop myself, I find my way back at the help desk.

"Edith?" The older woman looks up at the sound of my voice.

"Yes, Mr. Prescott?"

I roll my eyes playfully. "How many times have I told you to call me Alex?" She blushes, as she always does and then nods. "What was the name of the girl who just left? I, uh, feel bad that she didn't get a study room." I say quickly as an excuse.

Edith doesn't miss a beat, as usual. "Oh, that sweet girl is Margot. I do feel bad her usual room was taken. She practically lives in this library during the year." Edith busies herself again with whatever she's working on and I look out the glass front door at the back of her head.

Margot. It's a beautiful name. A name that definitely fits a beautiful girl like her. Based on Edith's assessment of her, I seem to bring out the feisty side of her, which I could hardly complain about. I love a girl with some zest. I need a challenge. And I think my newest challenge is standing directly outside the front door of this building.

Making my way down the stairs to the study room I booked online this morning–because apparently you can do that now–I promptly ignored a call from my father. It is the third time he's called this morning, and knowing him, he'll probably show up to the house next.

Using the key Edith gave me, I unlock the room and make sure it closes tight behind me. The silence is immediate. While I'm not always a stickler for doing my assignments, I do enjoy coming here to relax and get away from the noise of the Kappa Alpha house. Don't get me wrong–I love my frat brothers. Drinking and watching sports in the living room with everyone is one of my favorite pastimes but sometimes it's just nice to get away from it all.

Noticing one more text from my dad, I silence my phone and shove it into the bottom of my backpack. He'll get to me eventually. Oliver Prescott doesn't let anyone ignore him, especially not his sons. He's been calling me to talk about the fraternity alumni gala next Sunday and I just can't be bothered.

As a Tomlin University alumni, my father takes every opportunity to flaunt his success on campus, especially on Greek Row. While I'm happy to have made him proud by continuing his legacy in KA, it still bothers me when he parades me around as his little trophy son.

Mom would've hated that.

Shaking my head, I turn my thoughts away from my father and grab my laptop from my bag. Since the semester started, I've fallen behind on my fitness posts on Instagram. I don't care much about graduating with honors but I do care about using information from my exercise science classes to help boost my personal trainer Instagram account. I'm no influencer by any means, but I've got a decent following. Enough where, if I don't post for a few days, people start to worry. That all seems ridiculous to me, clearly I have life outside of my fitness account, but I do enjoy creating routines and posting videos for my followers to use as tutorials in their own workouts.

While I don't have any plans to use my exercise science degree once I graduate in May, I entered the program for a reason. It's nothing more than a hobby at this point but it's nice to have something to do that's all mine, not touched by Oliver Prescott.

⎯⎯∿∿∿⎯⎯

After thirty minutes and about fifteen fitness post ideas planned, I send a text to a couple of my KA brothers. Now that we're seniors, it's time we get cracking designing an epic Greek prank, another thing my father won't stop hounding me about.

It's tradition that the senior members of the frats plan a prank on their rival house. It's all in good fun but it's slightly hush-hush on campus. The tradition has been going on since the school was founded and the administration has always turned a blind eye as long as no one was hurt, but there's always pressure to up the stakes from the year before.

My father loves to brag about how they got the Delta Epsilon house good when he planted a stink bomb in their pipes. And that was over thirty years ago. The stakes have risen much higher than that and this year, it's my job to pull out all the stops.

And soon. Before DE does something first.

Within minutes, the crew shows up at the door of my study room.

"Why did you want us to meet in the library? I didn't even know this floor existed," my housemate and pain in my ass frat brother Devon groans as he walks in, followed by Kai, one of the twins that also lives with us in the frat house. He shuts the door behind him and they both join me around the table.

"We're going to the gym anyway and I was already here." I shrug.

Kai groans, "Okay, so are you going to tell us the plan now?" Devon mutters his agreement.

"I would," I start, "but it's not fully formed yet." The boys gawk and I laugh at their expressions. "Relax, gentlemen. Things are falling into place. There's just one thing missing."

Kai speaks up in between bites of his croissant. What a prick for not bringing me one. "What's missing?"

"We need an outsider. Someone not in KA, who can't be traced back to us. Probably a girl, for good measure."

Devon scoffs. "That shouldn't be hard for you to get. Just ask one of the many on your roster."

"That's not going to work. It needs to be someone new. Someone that no one in the frat world knows."

Kai laughs, "Devon's sister just started this semester."

Devon is on Kai before he can even get another breath in. "Shut your fucking mouth about my sister, prick." Devon starts pounding on Kai who hasn't stopped laughing.

"Enough," I mutter, and Devon sits back down but not before giving Kai an extra shove for the fun of it. "Just keep your eyes open for an innocent, okay?"

The boys nod while the wheels in my head keep spinning and spinning.

Kai looks around. "Wait, where's Keith?"

"You only just noticed your twin brother isn't here?" Devon rolls his eyes.

"Right now, Keith should be checking the perimeter of the DE house, for hidden cameras and stuff."

"How come?"

I settle into my seat. "Well, for what I've got planned, we need to know what areas to avoid in order to not get caught."

Kai finishes his croissant with a flourish. Checking his phone, he nods a few times before crumbling up the pastry wrapper. Leaving his trash on the table, he heads toward the door. "This place is boring. Can't we wait on the quad?"

"Sit your ass down. Keith should be done any minute and then we'll meet him by the gym."

With reluctance, Kai sits back in his seat and Devon chucks the pastry wrapper in his face. It's hard to believe I've been best friends with this band of delinquents for over three years.

Kai and I met at freshman orientation and we vibed immediately, bonding over our love of exercising and our excitement to move away from home. Obviously with Kai came Keith, who is very different from his brother, but still we found hobbies to connect over. We became roommates in a suite for our first year at school and I convinced them to rush Kappa Alpha with me.

Soon after, we met Devon at frat rush and the rest is history.

I always knew I was going to be a member of Kappa Alpha, being a legacy and all. My father graduated from Tomlin University as the president of KA and he made it very clear since I started high school that I would be graduating the same way when my time came. I didn't mind. Being a part of something like a fraternity always appealed to me. Having my brothers around made me feel larger than life. It's one thing I have to thank my father for.

Can't think of much else though.

My phone buzzes in my pocket and I pull it out to reveal a text from Keith. Just one word. "Gym?"

"Let's go. He's done," I say, standing from the table. The boys jump up with me. We leave the library, paying extra special attention to Edith on the way out, and head toward the parking lot next to the fitness center.

Keith is waiting for us outside the gym doors. He nods his head once and I return the gesture but for a moment, my attention is drawn toward a familiar brunette sitting on the bench outside the gym doors. Her nose is stuck in her phone and there's an uncontrollable feeling in me that needs to know what has her so entranced.

"Pick-up game?" Kai asks, slapping Keith on the back in greeting.

"Let's do it."

The boys head toward the large gymnasium doors but I hang out a second. "I'll meet you in there," I say, heading right toward Margot before I change my mind.

"Twice in one morning. What are you, stalking me?"

Margot practically jumps out of her seat at the sound of my voice. Her phone goes flying into the air and on instinct, I reach out and catch it.

"Phew, close one!"

Margot reaches out to grab it from me but not before I see the screen. My instagram profile is front and center, and based on the post she was viewing, she is a ways back in my archive. The cheshire cat envies my grin.

"Whatchya lookin' at, sunshine?" I ask, smugness oozing out of every pore in my body. I almost felt bad for Margot with how beet red her face gets. Grabbing the phone from my hand, she mutters "nothing" before leaning down to grab the bag she left on the floor.

Before I can say anything else, ease some of the embarrassment she is clearly feeling, the gym door swings open and a blonde girl comes out looking peppy and familiar.

"Ready to go, Margot?" She asks the tomato next to me, who nods furiously before turning on her heels and heading directly toward the parking lot without another word or glance in my direction.

The blonde looks at me questioningly but I only shrug, grabbing the door she was holding open and heading into the gym myself. I have absolutely no idea why this mysterious, feisty girl was stalking my instagram but I now have every intention of finding out.

Driving down Greek Row is always a treat. You never know what you're going to see. From rushing freshman boys streaking down the street to gaggles of girls who look identical to each other. I keep my eyes peeled while I drive, taking in the sights but also ensuring I don't hit any unsuspecting drunk kids.

We pass the Delta Epsilon house on our way home, noticing some guys standing on the porch, beer in hand. The president, Ryan Walsh, stands front and center, surveying the street like his own personal fortress.

"Prick," Devon says, noticing the same thing as me.

I wouldn't exactly call Ryan and I enemies but we aren't besties either. Being president of our frats gives us a camaraderie of sorts but we are technically rivals and that trumps any kind of kinship we might have.

It also helps that our house is the main hub for campus parties, no matter how hard DE tries to get people to go to their parties. We form a sort of peace treaty on weekends when we allow DE and other frats to come to our parties. Brotherhood and all that. So far, it hasn't caused any problems. *Famous last words.*

Pulling into our driveway, I park the car and Keith parks behind me. The twins, Devon and I walk up to our porch, bypassing a group of girls on their way to some sorority event. Kai and Devon stop to look, which is appreciated by the group, while Keith and I just head inside.

I've never had to show any interest in girls. They just come to me. I've had my pick of the litter since I was a freshman and my reputation has only gotten more notorious. I don't really do half the things this campus thinks I do, but I also don't do anything to stop the rumors. If they want to think me a huge player asshole, go right ahead. I haven't lost a single wink of sleep over the rumor mill and I doubt I ever will.

"Clowns," Keith mutters nodding toward the guys we left behind. I grab Keith's neck and pull him into a headlock.

"Like you wouldn't react the same way if the baseball team walked by," I dig at him, nooging his head.

Keith laughs, shaking out of my hold. "Please, you know I'm into football players. Those scrawny t-ballers can't handle all this." Keith gestures to his biceps, flexing under his shirt. Behind us, Devon and Kai make their way up the porch stairs and Keith and I share a glance before shutting the door directly in their faces, locking it for good measure.

As they bang on the wood, shouting profanities, and searching their pockets for a key that we know neither of them remembered to grab, Keith and I saunter into the kitchen.

"Beer?" he asks.

"Please," I respond, completely ignoring the shouts of our brothers.

Chapter Four

Margot

PUBLIC SPEAKING CLASS ISN'T until two today so I spend most of the morning fretting through my other classes. By the time lunch rolls around, I can barely stomach the thought of eating anything and I head instead to the only other place I love on this campus besides the library: the newsroom.

Tomlin University has an incredible journalism program, which is why I chose to come here in the first place. Students on the paper move on to incredible careers in writing including working for major publishing companies and newspapers around the globe. My main goal is and has always been *The New York Times*. I've been dreaming about being a *New York Times* reporter ever since my dad gave me his newspaper to use as scrap for a painting project. I was drawn to the look, the feel, the importance immediately.

"Margot!" My editor yells the minute I walk in the room. A huge smile forms on my face as I rush over toward her desk.

"Jessy!" Grabbing her into a huge hug, I smell the familiar scent of vanilla and pen ink. Red, no doubt, to mark all the mistakes on our stories. "How was your summer?" I ask, releasing her. She leans back to prop herself up on her desk.

"It was nice, that internship at *The Washington Post* really took up a lot of my free time, but I absolutely loved it."

Jessy had been chosen out of thousands of applicants to do a summer program with *The Washington Post* and while I didn't apply due to inexperience, I was incredibly proud and insanely jealous of her for getting it. "We need a coffee date so you can tell me every single detail," I implore her and Jessy nods her head with a grin.

"Of course, of course. But first, I'm so glad you're here because," she starts, turning back toward her desk to grab a paper on top of her endless piles. I seriously have no idea how she keeps track of everything but somehow she does. "I have something incredible to show you."

"Tell me you got published this summer," I say, gripping her arm.

Jessy laughs. "Okay, not that incredible. But look."

She hands me the paper that resembles a printed out email. The first thing I do is note who the email is from. *Editorial@nytimes.com.* I look up at her with wide eyes but she urges me to keep reading with a giant smile on her face.

"Dear Ms. Sumers," I start to read aloud, not trusting my inner monologue to get the words right. "You are receiving this email as an editor of one of the top ten college newspaper publications. This year, we are offering a short winter internship program where we will choose college journalism majors to come to New York and work alongside our top reporters, getting the ins and outs of publishing and gaining immeasurable knowledge about the newspaper world." My jaw is on the floor but Jessy pushes me to continue reading. "Below you will find the requirements for our contest, and we request that you pass along the knowledge of this competition to your staff and encourage them to participate and apply."

"I'm not even showing anyone else on the staff. This is all you, Margot," Jessy says.

I shake my head at her with a grin. "Jess, come on. You can't do that."

"I'm the editor. I can do whatever I want," she insists and I roll my eyes at her. Walking over to the staff notices bulletin board, I tack the email onto the board for all to see. Behind me, Jessy protests but doesn't stop me.

I'm still staring at the paper, trying to gather as much information about this contest as I possibly can. "It says I need to submit an entirely original multimedia project that–and I quote– 'brings information to life' end quote. What am I supposed to do with that?" I panic. One thing I hate more than public speaking is ambiguous guidelines. *Maybe I should do my speech about that,* I think, giving myself a mental facepalm. I know the speech I've prepared is fine. Still, it's not my best work and I hate not always doing my best.

Jessy breaks me from my trance with a snap in my face. "Hey," she calls and I blink her face back into my vision. "We'll figure it out, just be excited!"

"I am, I am," I grin. Of course I'm excited this is an incredible opportunity. So why is the first thought on my mind that I'm going to fail?

I find the seat farthest from the front of the room, which is not my usual M.O., but for this class, I'd much rather be out of sight and out of mind. The classroom is medium sized, one of those theaters where the seats file down towards a stage with a desk and a white board. Only there's no desk this time, just a big open space that might as well have a flashing red sign pointing to it. *Here is where you will humiliate yourself, Margot Elaine Davis.* I shove myself further down into the seat.

A few more students file in, but the room is hardly filling up. In fact, there are probably only about twenty or thirty of us seated in the room before the teacher strides in and commands our attention.

"Welcome to Public Speaking 101," she says in an amplified voice. I can tell just by her demeanor that she is used to being on stage. "My name is Professor Walker and I'm happy to see you all here."

She looks around the room. "Not a big turnout this semester, huh," she sighs. While the lecture hall could easily hold one hundred people, there seemed to be about thirty seats filled. I feel a little bad about how happy I was at the lack of attendance–less people to embarrass myself in front of. "Well, no point waiting. Let's start the speeches."

My stomach jumps into my throat. *Already?* No lecture? No getting to know you icebreakers? Professor Walker means business, and while I usually admire that in a teacher, in this particular case, it terrifies me.

Professor Walker looks down at her roster and announces that she'll be starting at the end of the alphabet this time around, calling up a young student named Laura Thompson who bounds to the stage and immediately jumps into her speech about her fear of spiders.

The speech is short and sweet, and Professor Walker doesn't say a single word before, during, or after. All she does is scribble furiously on her clipboard the entire time and then calls the next name. The entire thing is very clinical, almost as if we're auditioning for a play or movie and she's the casting director.

Four more students go, and I've never been more happy to have an early alphabet last name. I feel myself relax more and more as each person goes. No one up there is perfect, evident by the boy who spoke about his fear of sponges. *This might actually not be so bad.*

Professor Walker looks at her list and announces, "Alexander Prescott, you're up."

If I thought my stomach was in my throat before, it's about to make its way onto the floor as I watch the towering man from the party and from the library, sitting four rows directly in front of me, stand up and walk toward the stage.

How had I not noticed him before? I guess I was so entrenched in my own discomfort that I didn't exactly look around to see if there was anyone that I knew in this class. I thought it was mostly freshman anyway, since this is an introductory class. Seems like I was wrong.

"Hi, my name is Alex," he starts and I sink even lower into my seat, willing myself to become invisible. "When I was six years old, my mother tried to kill me."

There are audible gasps heard around the room and even Professor Walker looks up from her scribbling to gaze at Alex. He continues, not as confidently as I'd imagined he'd be. I'm not sure if it's the nerves from standing in front of the class or if it's the content of the speech.

"If we're talking about things we truly fear the most, I think mine would have to be my mother. But that's crazy, isn't it?" He's looking at his hands, not into the crowd as the other presenters had before him. "How can someone be afraid of their own mother? Isn't there supposed to be some bond, some maternal instinct that says, 'That's your blood. Keep him safe.' I guess she didn't have that." He drops his hands and finally looks out. I wish I could melt even more into my chair, become one with the cushions underneath my body. He can't see me right now, not like this.

"When you're a kid, you're taught to trust your elders. Listen to them. They'll guide you toward comfort and safety. So, why wouldn't I trust my mom when she put my younger brother and me in the car one afternoon. Strapped us in so we wouldn't slide out of the carseats."

My heart is breaking for the man standing on the stage. The same man who threw another person out of a doorway onto the street. Who flaunted his library study room in my face. How could they possibly be the same person?

"She said we were going for a ride," he continues, and every single student is on the edge of their seat. "That was until she drove to Lake Grinold and pulled up right to the edge. I remember her telling us that she was sorry and I didn't understand it at the time but of course, I do now. She was sorry for being selfish. Sorry for taking her depression, her fears, her own fucking needs out on us."

I look over at Professor Walker. Surely cursing during a speech is inappropriate. I expect her to be scribbling away but she's still staring directly at Alex, her jaw slightly open in shock.

"She drove into the lake. If it wasn't for the courage of a couple passersby walking along the lake path, my brother and I would be dead. Thankfully, they pulled us out in time." Alex looks down as he finishes his speech. By the look of the audience, they would allow him to continue forever if they could.

"So, what do I fear the most? I fear my mother. But... can you truly fear something that's already gone? Someone that can't physically hurt you anymore? I guess you can't. So, then, I guess what I really fear is, one day...becoming her."

Alex looks over at Professor Walker who gives him a slight nod before he heads back to his seat. There is a silence in the room that is so loud I want to cover my ears to hide from it.

Professor Walker clears her throat and everyone turns their attention towards her. "Alright, class. That's all the time we have for today. We'll start fresh next Monday with," she looks down at her list. "Jason, Maya, and Margot. See you next week."

I should be on the floor with how low I am slouched in my seat. *It's fine, he doesn't know your name.* But for how stiff his shoulders get, I'm not sure that's the truth. As the students start filing out of the room, Alex glances up and down the aisles, clearly looking for someone, until he spots me and his eyes widen just a fraction as his gaze catches mine.

It takes almost a physical level of strength to pull myself from his gaze, grab my things and bolt from the room. I'm at the door when I hear his voice, clear as day a few steps behind me.

"Sunshine?" His voice sounds tense and against my will, I stop in my tracks.

He speaks again but I have yet to turn around to meet his eyes. "I thought this was a class of freshmen."

"And one junior who put off her electives," I reply, still facing forward. He comes around to stand in front of me, his jaw ticking intensely. Due to the sloped nature of the room, he's a step above me and as I'm looking up at him his eyes seem to darken when they capture mine. Something about the intensity of his stare causes me to shrink a little bit more in front of him, not that he needs any help gaining height on me.

Just as I think he's going to say something else, something to break this overwhelming tension, he draws in a sharp breath, turns on his heels and leaves me completely alone in the room. As he stalks toward the door, I can't help but think what the hell was that all about? And how did he know my name?

Chapter Five

Margot

SYDNEY NEVER FAILS TO serve an incredible meal and tonight is no different. I've never eaten so well in my life and I'm alway sure to tell her that.

"Dinner's on!" Sydney calls from the kitchen and Danika and I race toward the kitchen island to grab our usual stools. Dani makes it first since she chose to leap over the couch while I walk around it like a normal person.

Taking in the delicious smell of peppers, onions, and sausage, I salivate over the spread set out before us. "This looks amazing, Syd. Thanks for cooking."

"Of course," she replies, waving me off as she always does.

"Super amazing," Danika agrees, her mouth already full of half-chewed sausage. Sometimes I seriously wonder how Dani and I have been best friends our entire lives when we are so different in so many ways. But, I guess they say opposites attract and Dani and I couldn't be more opposite.

I take a bite and savor the incredible taste, finish chewing and then ask my daily question to the group. "So, how was school, darlings?"

"Well, Mom," Dani teases, "I started my biochem course today and I actually really enjoy it. There's something deeply interesting about DNA replication repair recombination."

I can't tell if she's being serious or sarcastic. While a party girl at night, Danika does really take her studies seriously and has dreamed about being a doctor ever since she was old enough to use a pretend stethoscope. It could also have to do with her grandma dying of breast cancer when she was a teenager, but she'll never admit that.

"I'm glad you're enjoying it!" I cheer, regardless if she meant it or not. Nodding toward Sydney, I take another delicious bite of her meal.

Sydney and I met during our freshman orientation and bonded over the fact that we both wanted to go out for the school paper. Even though Sydney is an exercise science major, she's always loved writing too and had planned to use the paper as a campus job for a little extra income, same as me. We clicked right away. When I introduced her to Danika, it was a friendship made in heaven. Since then, the three of us have been basically inseparable.

"That Music in Media elective I signed up for was actually super interesting, too." Sydney says before taking a bite of her own meal.

"Oh right, do you think that'll help you with your entertainment column for the paper?"

Sydney shrugs. "Here's hoping." She cleans off her mouth with her napkin. "What about you, Margot? How was that public speaking class?"

I want to tell them about seeing Alex in the class but for some reason I can't bring myself to tell them about his speech. There was something deeply personal about it. It clearly upset him when he realized someone he actually recognized was in the class instead of a group of nameless freshmen.

So, instead of going into detail about the ordeal, I find myself shrugging. "It was fine. I didn't actually do my speech, but I'm one of the first to start next week."

Dani groans. "Now you're going to be insufferable and anxious all week!" She teases me with a gentle shove and I roll my eyes.

"Yeah," I agree as wholeheartedly as I can but it doesn't connect. Before they can ask me any more questions about the class, I skillfully pivot the conversation. "Wait, but also I stopped by the newsroom this afternoon and Jessy told me about an incredible *The New York Times* internship she was told about. Sydney, did you see the board?"

She shakes her head. "No, I didn't get a chance to stop in there today. What's the internship?"

I dive into deep detail about the contest and how I have to do some sort of "multimedia" project. "It's judged in stages so every few weeks I need to send in an update on what I'm working on and the contestants get narrowed down as it goes on."

"Yikes," Danika mutters.

I nod, taking another bite. "I need to do something really eye-catching to make myself stand out against the other applicants."

"Hmm," both girls hum, and we fall into a comfortable silence as we think of potential ideas.

"A comic strip?" Danika offers.

I shake my head. "Hardly newsworthy."

Sydney takes a bite of her dinner before offering her idea of a "Dear Margot" column where people write in questions and I give advice.

"Not a terrible idea but it's not multimedia. Plus, who would want advice from me? I'm a nobody."

"True," Danika agrees.

"Thanks," I scoff.

"What about something audio? You can host a podcast on campus and interview people? Gather enough of an audience, the *New York Times* won't be able to resist."

"Back to my original question, who would care enough to be interviewed by me?"

Danika sets down her fork. "What if we combine the ideas? An advice column podcast."

"That's a great idea," Sydney grins.

I throw my hands up in exasperation. "Are you listening to me at all? No one is going to give a shit about what advice *I* have to give. Half the professors on this campus call me Margie." I roll my eyes.

Danika's face drops. "You're right." But she gets that grin on her face. That devilish grin that tells me she's about to say the best idea in the world and I'm going to absolutely hate it.

"They won't tune in just for you. But if it's you and say...frat boy royalty Alex Prescott, they'd have no choice but to listen."

"No. Way." I reply easily. Grabbing our empty plates, I start hand washing all the dishes, as per our agreement. Danika grabs the towel to dry but doesn't give up the idea.

"Oh, come on!" she whines, drying the clean dish I hand her and placing it onto the shelf. "You know it's a perfect idea. You just don't want to hang out with Alex," she says as if she's caught me on something.

I give her a pointed look. "Uh, yeah. Exactly," I reply, handing her another wet dish. Sydney chuckles from her seat at the island.

"No comments from the peanut gallery unless you're on my side." Danika points to Sydney who raises her hands in mock defeat.

"Although," Sydney starts and I whip around on her.

"Not you too."

Sydney giggles. "A video podcast is a really great idea. You know it's the way of the future for journalism right now. It probably would stand out in that contest for the internship."

"And the more successful the podcast, the better chances you have of winning!" Danika cheers and I flick some water in her face. And then I flick water in Sydney's face too for good measure. "You're just mad because we're right."

I roll my eyes but don't respond. Because they're absolutely right. It's a perfect idea. Just...not a perfect match.

"Let's get our heads back down to Earth here, people. Even if I did decide to go through with this idea, Alex would never agree to it. From what I've gathered about him, he seems like an egotistical arrogant jerk who only cares about himself." Even as I said it, I know it's not entirely true. Especially after the way he opened up in public speaking class. But the way he treated me after...the harsh brush off. It is more than a little confusing.

"He's actually a pretty nice guy. I've had a couple of classes with him," Sydney says.

"You have? Why didn't you mention that before?"

She shrugs. "You didn't ask."

"Yeah, I've seen him at parties, too. He really doesn't seem all that bad. You'll see at the party on Friday," Dani says, finally stacking the last of the clean dishes away.

I groan. "Do we have to go to another party this weekend? Can't we just...I don't know...chill at home?"

"We have a lifetime to chill at home, Mar. We're only in college for a few short years."

"Well, *we* are." Sydney comments. "You've got at least another four after this, Dr. Freeman."

"Exactly!" Danika exclaims. "And after you guys graduate, I'll be glued to the books every second. We need to live it up while we can. And

Margot," she turns to me with a terrifying gleam in her eyes. "This is your time to shine."

Passing a quick glance over to Sydney, I let out a deep sigh which is usually the sign that I've agreed to whatever crazy scheme Danika has come up with. I hold up my pointer finger. "Yes to the party." Then I hold up my second finger. "No to asking Alex."

"I'll take it!" Dani cheers and pulls me in for a hug, she's always been the affectionate type. Me, not so much, but I give in to her when I feel like she needs it. "Besides, you'll change your mind."

"Don't hold your breath," I mutter as I pull away from her to plop down on the couch, my Investigating Journalism textbook in hand. Sydney sits down next to me with her Music in Media book, ready to tackle next week's work.

Danika, still in the kitchen, just hums loudly in response.

The rest of the week flies by as uneventfully as I had hoped it would. Other than our awkward class departure on Monday, I haven't seen Alex on campus at all. I have, however, not been able to get that podcast idea out of my head. It would be perfect. He's so popular on campus. Girls would line up just to get the chance to talk to him, even virtually. It could be an advice podcast. People would write in with their problems and Alex and I could help them solve it.

But having to spend multiple hours a week alone with him? I'm not sure my fragile sensibilities could handle it. Especially since it's already been discovered that he doesn't exactly bring out the best in me.

I don't have a lot of time to dwell on it as Danika pulls me toward her closet Friday night to pick out the perfect party outfit.

"Can't be too obvious that you're trying to get his attention," she says, pulling out a black bodysuit and then immediately putting it back with a headshake.

"I'm *not* trying to get his attention," I mutter from behind her.

"Exactly," Dani hums, as if she's actually listening to me but I know she's not. In the doorway, Sydney leans against the frame, already dressed and ready as always. While she may not like the parties as much as Danika does, she loves an excuse to dress up.

"What about the red zip-up?" Sydney shouts her two cents at Danika, who promptly replies, "Red? With her undertones? Absolutely not."

Throwing my hands up in the air, my palms slap my sides aggressively. "Um, hello? Standing right here."

Sydney steps around me and into the room, taking up residence next to Dani at the door of the closet. Holding up a few pieces here and there, shoving them back in the closet or letting them fall to the floor, the girls finally lock eyes and both grab for the same hanger.

"This is it," Danika grins and Sydney nods her head approvingly as they toss the hanger and clothing item at me. "Go change. Living room in ten," she announces, promptly kicking me out of her space so she can get ready, too. Sydney takes the instruction in stride and heads to the kitchen to make a round of margaritas for the walk to the frat house, which is thankfully only five minutes away.

"Aye, aye, captain," I salute her before leaving the room and heading toward mine. When I emerge eleven minutes later—just to spite Dani—both pairs of eyes dart to my body immediately, taking in the mid-length maroon bodycon dress they demanded I wear.

"Acceptable?" I ask, giving the girls a little spin.

"Gorgeous, babe," Dani smiles and Sydney gives me a wink and a margarita in a red solo cup.

Taking a whiff of the beverage, I sense it's stronger than she usually makes and I'm grateful for it. If I'm going to get through this party, and possibly have to interact with "frat boy royalty", I'm going to need all the liquid courage I can get.

"Cheers, ladies," I say, raising my cup and meeting theirs in the air. The girls chorus with me and we all take a big sip. *Oh yeah, definitely stronger than usual.*

Chapter Six

Alex

THE BLONDE ON MY lap moves her ass back and forth trying to get my attention but it's not doing anything. In fact, it's more annoying than anything else. *Just sit still, geez.*

To my right, Devon's got some chick's tongue in his mouth, and Kai is chatting with a girl who looks way too young to be here. *What's going on with these parties?* I feel like every week it's the same old boring shit.

"Do you wanna head somewhere a little bit more...private?" The blonde asks me, her beer breath in my ear.

"Nah, I'm alright," I reply, trying my best to hold my breath so as to not inhale any of hers. "In fact..." I move to stand and catch her as she all but falls off my lap. She scoffs at the sudden affront but I don't really care. I don't even remember her name.

"I'm going to get a drink," I say, walking away from her shocked expression. The jaw on the floor face reminds me, for a second, of another surprised face I saw this week. A face I haven't been able to get out of my mind since I saw it peering down at me from the top of the auditorium in that public speaking class.

If I had known someone in my everyday life would be in that class, I never would've opened up so much about my mom. Not that Margot is in my everyday life. In fact, I haven't seen her since that day. And if I drop that class, like I intend to do now, I won't have to see her ever again if I don't want to.

I head into the kitchen and spot Keith cozying up with a football player, grinning as I recall our conversation earlier in the week. I don't want to disturb him so I quickly grab a beer from the ice bucket and turn back the way I came, content to just sit upstairs in my room and play Xbox until the party is over.

That is until the door opens and the porchlight shines through, casting a glow around the head of the girl that just walked in. The same glow that shined the first time I saw her. The glow that earned her the nickname *Sunshine*.

"Fuck," I breathe out and immediately duck back into the crowded kitchen, out the back door and into the backyard where there's already a crowd of smoke from the smoking corner.

Taking a seat by the empty fire pit, I finally release a breath and ask myself the question on the top of my mind. *Did I just run away from a girl?*

"Alex, hey," a female voice says above me and I look up to see the familiar face of my friend, Gia. I'm not known for my friendships with girls but Gia's a good one. We hook up now and then, she knows the deal and never asks me for anything more, which is why I keep her around. The relief that floods through me when I see her must be evident on my face because she says, "You okay?"

"Fine," I reply, hurriedly. "Come here for a sec?" I ask but don't give her a chance to respond before I grab her waist and pull her onto my lap, her long brown hair flying up as her legs rest together over my left side. She gasps in happy surprise but the sound doesn't linger before I grab her by the back of the neck and pull her face to mine, combining our mouths in a familiar way. Gia responds immediately to me, as she always does and I relax a little bit into the comfortability of it all...until I remember that the reason I'm even doing this is because Margot just walked into my house and now I'm all worked up and even more confused.

After a few minutes of intense making out, Gia pulls away and looks back and forth between my eyes. "Not that I mind at all, but is there something you need to talk about, friend?" She smiles and I again remember why I've kept her around so long. She's a great friend, always ready with a listening ear and a piece of helpful advice.

I sigh, resting my forehead against hers for a second before looking into her eyes again. "Probably. But I'm not sure yet." Gia seems to take that in stride, pouting her lips in thought before cracking a smile again.

"Well, I'm here if you need me. For anything," she says and the double meaning isn't lost on me.

"Thanks," I reply, almost sadly. Gia removes herself from my lap and gives me a couple pats on the back before saying her goodbyes and heading back into the house. I should follow her. I should drown myself in her like I've done many times before but for some fucking reason, I can't bring myself to move from this chair. All I can seem to do is stare into the flickering flames of the fire and picture another pouting brunette's face.

Chapter Seven

Margot

"Let's do a lap and end in the kitchen. I need to know what areas to avoid if I don't want to run into Nico."

Danika dated a soccer player named Nico for the better part of sophomore year, but the two ended on messy terms when she caught him hooking up with his lab partner from their shared biology class. She's way over it now, but it's always better to avoid him whenever we can. Nico still finds a way to ruin Danika's fun even a year later. At parties and such, we've gotten good at finding where he and his friends have posted up early and avoiding that area completely. It's worked well for us so far.

Sydney, Danika, and I make our way through the house, following crowded pathways until we end up in the kitchen.

"Drinks?" Dani asks and Sydney nods.

"I'm gonna get some water first. That margarita took a lot out of me, Syd," I tease and head over to the sink to fill up a cup with the tap water. As the cup fills, I glance up and peek out the window at the backyard. I do a double take as I see Alex sitting in front of the roaring fire pit with a girl plastered to his face.

Of course I expected to see Alex here. This is his house. What I didn't expect was to see him making out with a gorgeous brunette. Actually, no. I probably did expect that. What I *really* didn't expect was the way my stomach clenched when I saw it. I could not fathom why my body would have that much of a visceral reaction to seeing Alex Prescott kissing a girl in his own backyard.

"Uh, earth to—oh," Dani starts and I break from my trance to feel the cold water pouring down my hand. I shut off the tap quickly, pouring some of the water down the drain so the cup isn't so full. Turning to Danika, I'm ready to pretend like all of that never happened but she's too focused on staring at exactly what drew my attention in the first place.

"Typical," Dani scoffs. "Girls just can't get enough of that tall drink of water." I choke a little on my drink and her gaze catches mine. "All the better for your podcast!" She says as if the last thirty seconds of me watching Alex sucking face didn't just happen.

The door to our left swings open and the girl in question waltzes into the kitchen, not sparing any of us even so much as a passing glance. I mean, why would she? It's not like she knows we've just been watching her writhing her little toned body all over—

I feel Sydney's hands on my shoulders as I'm pulled back again from my dark thoughts. "Are you okay, Margot?"

"She's fine," Danika demands. "And she's found her opportunity to talk to Alex!" Dani walks around to my back as Sydney drops her hands. She pushes me toward the door the beautiful stranger just came in from and I can see Alex through the glass, his hands in his hair as he leans down over his knees, staring at the fire.

"Hold on just a damn minute," I cry, backing up away from the door, but Danika's body doesn't budge. I whip around to face her instead. "I agreed to come, I never agreed to talk to him. We made a deal!"

Danika laughs and my eyes narrow, suddenly feeling a little bit hurt.

"Will you ever get out of your own way?"

I pull in a breath, thinking about how to respond but nothing is coming to mind. Dani sighs before continuing. "Margot, you need to win this contest. Talking to Alex is the way to do it. I'm not telling you to marry the guy! What's the worst thing that could happen?"

"He could say yes?" I say, first as a joke but then I realize how true it actually is. He *could* say yes and then I'd have to talk to him on a daily basis. I'd have to collaborate, maybe even...relinquish a bit of control to him. Just the thought alone causes me to swallow uncomfortably.

I feel Sydney rub my back and I close my eyes with a sigh while a thought pops in my head– one I've been trying to ignore all week. *With Alex, you will win.*

With new resolve, I open my eyes back up and head toward the door again, pushing aside my reservations and fears as vehemently as I pushed the door open.

"Go get him, babe!" I hear Dani cheer as the door closes behind me and suddenly I'm alone. Not physically, the yard is full of party-goers and by the smell of the smoke, I can tell they're enjoying themselves. I'm alone in my mission for this *New York Times* contest. I want this internship more than I want my next breath. Dani's right: I need to stop being such a damn baby and just do something for myself for once.

With each step I take toward Alex's statuesque form, I feel myself getting more and more confident. Although, I do wish I had taken at least one more shot of liquid courage. I feel like, at the very least, I'll let him decline my offer and then I'll move onto plan B–whatever that may be.

Stepping up directly behind his chair, I clear my throat rather loudly to get his attention. But he doesn't move. *Is he asleep?* I walk around the chair to see his face, his eyes catching mine immediately and he jolts so incredibly I think he is going to fall out of the chair.

"Jesus Christ, sunshine. You can't sneak up on a guy like that," he says, leaning back into the lawn chair, pinching his eyes with his thumb and pointer finger to calm himself.

"I made a noise," I shrug.

He looks up at me, dropping his hand onto the armrest. "Well, next time, use your words."

I nod, slowly. "I'll be sure to do that." Alex's gaze pierces mine but he doesn't speak again. Instead, he takes his sweet time clocking my entire appearance from the tip of my head to the bottom of my heel. By the time his eyes reach back toward my face, I'm sure the expression on it causes him to snap back to reality.

"To what do I owe the pleasure?" he asks, his voice slightly huskier than before, or am I just imagining that?

"I...actually," I start, not quite sure how to get into this topic without completely stroking his ego. "I had something I wanted to ask you. A proposal, if you will..."

His eyebrows shoot up into his messy hairline, clearly shocked. He gestures to the chair next to his, a safe distance away. "By all means, the floor is yours, sunshine."

I roll my eyes at the nickname he insists on calling me, even though he basically confirmed that he knows my name because of public speaking class. Which still begs the question, how did he know? Was he asking around about me?

Sitting in the chair, I curl my legs up so that I'm comfortable and turn to face Alex. He's already looking at me, his eyes full of mischief and a hint of a smile ghosting his lips. He does have really nice lips, plump but not too—*Focus!*

"I want to work with you," I blurt out but Alex only cocks his head, interested to hear more. "I'm not sure if you know this but I'm a journalism major. In fact, you definitely don't know that, why would you? Anyway, there's a *New York Times* internship contest that opened up this year and I need to create a multimedia project that's creative and unique and well, I had the idea to do a podcast, well my roommates had the idea, but *we* thought I could do a podcast and well, you and me could do a podcast together and it'd be really easy and you wouldn't have to do work at all just show up at the designated times and we can make a schedule that's totally flexible and I'm just going to shut up now and let you respond."

I take a deep breath to refill my lungs after that completely jumbled speech.

For a moment, Alex is speechless. His mouth is closed, but I know it's only because he's schooling his features. He's genuinely shocked at my request. I allow that feeling to sink in for a moment, the feeling of stunning the school stud into silence.

He opens his mouth, then closes it. Then opens it back up again. Just as I'm about to demand he speaks, he finally replies. "Of all the things I thought you would propose to me, that certainly wasn't on the list. A threesome, maybe. But a working relationship?"

I scrunch my nose at his vulgar sense of humor. "In your dreams, frat boy."

Alex laughs at my dig and leans back into his chair, as if to really give the proposal the proper thought. "A podcast, huh?" He asks, looking over at me but keeping his head leaned back against the top of the head rest.

I nod, a little too eagerly. I'm so anxious for his response that I can feel my palms begin to sweat and I rub them against the tops of my thighs to dry them.

"Well, it's certainly an interesting idea," he starts, sitting up again and leaning over the armrest so he's closer, his breath, mint mixed with beer, brushing against my face. "It does beg the question, though: why would you want to do a podcast with me?"

I squeeze my eyes shut in defeat. I was really hoping he wouldn't ask me that but of course he would. Now, how do I tell him that his party boy status will give me my best listenership without completely inflating his ego?

"I just think...with the connections you have with...certain people...it'll make for very interesting podcast content," I respond, keeping the comment as vague as possible, but Alex's eyes darken as I finish my sentence.

"Ah. So this is about my father?" He says, apropos of nothing.

"Your father? No, I—"

"Because if you just need someone to bankroll your little project, sorry, you're barking up the wrong money tree," Alex pulls himself from the chair and starts to head back toward the house. *What the fuck?*

Jolting from my own chair, I run after him—yes, run because his over six foot strides are much longer than mine at just over five foot. Racing around to block him from entering the house, I step onto the bottom stair in front of him, bringing us *almost* face to face.

"I don't need you for your dad's money, Alex," I say with all the sincerity I can muster. I wasn't planning on asking him to fund any of the project in fact. I am planning to use as many of the newspaper's resources as I can, including use of the recording space on campus.

"Then why are you asking me to do this with you?"

"I don't need your money, I need your dick." Alex's eyes widen and I'm sure they match my own. I slap my hand over my mouth and mutter, "Oh my god, I didn't mean that," through my fingers.

"Please, sunshine," Alex's eyes swim with laughter as he pulls my hand from my mouth. "Please explain what you meant then because I am truly on the edge of my seat." He hasn't released my hand from his but I pull it free to help gather myself back to equilibrium.

"It's a known fact that you are pretty much number one on every girl's list of guys they want to get with at this school," He opens his mouth, but I don't allow him to interject as I continue, "and if they had a platform to try and get your attention, well..."

"So you really do want me for my dick?"

"I really do," I nod, serious for a moment but then both of us bust out into a comfortable laughter.

Alex pulls himself together first but the lightness stays on his face. "That must've been so hard for you to admit."

"It certainly wasn't easy," I nod, relaxing with him.

"Do you know anything about producing a podcast?"

No. "I've got a couple friends on the newspaper who are willing to help," I shrug easily. "So...what do you say?"

"Well...what's in it for me?" He asks, taking a noticeable step forward. I should've anticipated this reaction but for some reason, it didn't occur to me to have some incentive for him to help me. I thought he would just do it out of the kindness of his heart. *You naive idiot.*

My gaze locks with his and I know I don't have an answer to his question. Even if I did, I'm not sure I could even voice it with his lips so close to mine.

For the longest moments of my life, Alex remains silent again, his eyes piercing mine back and forth. Back and forth. He continues to hold my gaze for a minute longer and just as I'm about to open my mouth to say who knows what, Alex looks above my head into the windowed door. I'm watching his features change when all of a sudden, it's as if a light bulb has gone on in his head. Like some dots have been connected that he wasn't sure how to connect before.

"You know what, forget it. This was stupid of me to ask you for any–"

"I'll do it."

"You'll–"

"On one condition." *So close.* "I need your help to pull off the senior Greek prank." His eyes are wild, a very sudden shift from the levity of a few seconds ago.

I cock my head to the side, as if I'm not sure I've heard him correctly. "I'm sorry, the what?" He shakes his head.

"I'll explain it all later, just...do you agree to the terms?"

"The terms? Alex, what are you talking about?"

"I help you, you help me. Seems like a fair deal to me. So...?"

This sudden shift in demeanor stresses me out but all I hear is that he said yes to my proposal and that is the only reason I sheepishly say, "Let's do it."

Alex's face bursts out into the most brilliant smile I've ever seen and for a moment, I'm completely blinded by it. He grabs my shoulders and gives me a quick shake. "Great! I'll text you later to discuss the details," he says, moving me to the side so he can continue up the stairs and into the house.

The brush off is so abrupt, I have no time to register the fact that he doesn't even have my phone number until he's already gone. I'm left alone again in the backyard of Alex's frat house with the sickening feeling I've just made a humongous mistake.

Chapter Eight

Margot

"So, he said yes?" Sydney asks, excitedly.

I shrug with a lazy grin on my face. "He said yes." Of course I was accosted for details the second I walked back inside the kitchen. I left nothing out as I told them the whole story.

Danika squeezes the life out of me and Sydney hands me a beer, which I accept gratefully. Now that I've gotten the worst out of the way, I might be able to relax and actually enjoy myself for once at one of these parties.

Dani takes my free hand and leads us toward the living room, which is also the dance floor. As we walk, I get the lowdown from Sydney that Nico tried to corner Danika while I was outside talking to Alex, but he didn't get very far. In fact, from what Sydney told me, he got a swift knee in the goods and an expletive or two thrown in his face but that's about it.

Danika leads the three of us directly to the center of the dance floor and while I'm usually much more comfortable lounging against the wall, content to watch the revelry, tonight, I'm feeling bolder than usual. I faced a fear and put myself out there with Alex and it paid off. Now, I'm ready to let even looser if it keeps getting me the same positive result.

We laugh as the song changes to one I haven't heard since I was in middle school and I start to sway my hips back and forth. The music tied with the beer is intoxicating and I'm finally starting to understand why Dani drags us to these parties every weekend. That is, until I feel unfamiliar hands snake around my waist.

"Hey gorgeous," a deep voice speaks in my ear and my entire body tenses up. Danika watches the exchange from a few feet in front of me and eyes the guy for a second before leaning in to whisper in my other ear.

"Baseball player. He's cute and has never given me any trouble before. Let yourself have some fun," she says, pulling back with a wink. I trust Danika more than I trust myself sometimes so it's only with that glowing endorsement that I step a little deeper into his embrace and move my hips along with him. Danika and Sydney stay close to me as we all dance together.

Finally, after the song finishes, I turn and face the stranger behind me. Dani's right, he is cute. His friendly grin matches mine as he extends his hand toward mine. It's tight to his chest since the dance floor is rather crowded but still a sweet gesture.

"I'm Ryan," he says and I take his hand in mine.

"Margot," I reply. He doesn't let go as he continues the conversation and I let him keep holding my hand, which I quickly realize is a stark difference from how I pulled my hand away from Alex's grasp earlier in the night.

Ryan leans into my ear to continue the conversation in the middle of the crowded dance floor. "I don't think I've seen you around these parties before. I would've noticed."

I shake my head and pull his neck down to speak back into his ear. "I don't come often but when I do, I'm just usually in the shadows."

I hear his soft laughter in my ear. "That's no place for someone as pretty as you." I can feel the blush creeping up onto my face. No one has ever spoken to me like this before. Truthfully, I've never given anyone the chance to.

"Do you want to go outside and talk where it isn't so loud?" he asks and I nod. Ryan takes the hand he's still holding and pulls me along with him. I glance back toward Dani and Syd, who both nod encouragingly at me.

Just before we make it to the door, I feel a pull against my shoulder and I whip around to see a furious Alex standing in front of me. *Talk about deja vu.*

"What the hell, Alex?"

"You can't be here anymore. You need to leave." He says to me but his glance keeps shifting above my head to Ryan standing behind me.

"Excuse me?"

I sense Ryan step up behind me but something in Alex's stare keeps him back a step. Alex then unleashes that withering stare on me.

"Listen, I told you I'd tell you the details later but you can't be whoring yourself around–"

"*Excuse me,*" I step toward him, ready to battle, and his gaze softens only a little when he sees the hurt and confusion in my eyes. By now, some people have noticed the scuffle and Danika and Sydney have pushed right to the front of the crowd.

"Please, Margot. Just leave," Alex pleads with me, and it's not lost on me this is the first time he's used my real name. I have absolutely no idea why he's kicking me out of his party after that whole conversation we just had but, with the way I'm feeling right now, there's no way I'd want to stay anyway.

"You know what, fine by me. I never wanted to come here in the first place," I say, giving him a push to get his intoxicating scent away from me. I turn on my heels and brush past a very confused Ryan as I continue down the walkway. I don't even have to turn around to know that my roommates are only a step behind me, but I'm too furious to stop and wait for them.

"What the hell was that all about?" Dani asks as they both run up and flank me on either side. "I thought you said you had a good conversation with him?"

"I thought I did too," I reply, still entirely confused.

"Do you think he was jealous seeing you with Ryan?" Sydney asks and I burst out a laugh just at the mere thought of that.

"Please, there's no way," I reply, shaking my head, but Sydney only shrugs.

In the current furious state I'm in, my walking speed is double what it usually is so we end up at our apartment building in half the time it usually takes.

"What exactly did he say to you?" Danika asks as we head up the stairs to the second floor. Sydney unlocks our front door and we all kick off our shoes before heading into the living room.

"He said, 'you can't be whoring yourself around' or some repulsive, sexist thing like that," I say, laying down on the couch. I close my eyes to try and collect myself.

Danika grabs my legs, pulling them up to make space for herself and pulls them back down onto her lap. Sydney grabs us all fresh water bottles from the fridge before she cozies up in the armchair next to the couch.

"Sounds like jealousy to me," Dani shrugs and I give her a pointed look. Just then, my phone buzzes in my pocket, signaling an incoming text. As I pull it out, I see a message from an unknown number.

> Don't be mad at me

Immediately, I know who the text is from. But it doesn't answer the question of how he got my phone number in the first place. I don't even want to respond. I don't have to think about it too hard before more texts come in.

> I promised I'd explain, didn't I?

> Give me a chance, sunshine

I roll my eyes and send a text back before I lose my nerve.

> Sorry, you must be confusing me with some other "whore" who'd let you speak to her that way

> I didn't mean to call you that. It just slipped out.

> Even better

I hope he picks up on the sarcasm leaking through my words. As if it's okay to call someone that even by accident? What an idiot.

> I'm sorry, okay? I promise it won't happen again

> Don't go back on our deal. You need me, remember?

> Think about the New York Times...

> Ugh, would you shut up for a second? I'm thinking

> Atta girl

> I said shut up

He sends a zip-lipped emoji and I roll my eyes, dropping the phone onto my lap. "He has a point," Danika shrugs.

"He's repugnant," I counter, then I sigh. "What do I do?"

"At the very least you need to let him explain what you've signed up for with the prank. Then you can decide if you still want his help or not," Sydney pipes up from the armchair. I pull up my phone to answer this already incredibly annoying boy.

> You have five minutes. Explain

I can practically see the grin on Alex's face as he types this next text and the three of us wait anxiously for it to arrive. What could he even need me for? I'm not a prankster. I've never pranked anyone in my entire life.

The gray dots keep appearing and disappearing. At this rate, he's using all five of his minutes to send this message. Finally, after I've already downed half the water bottle and am visualizing what pajamas I'm going to put on, the text rolls in.

> Can't tell you via text. Too easily traced. Meet me at Cafe Royale tomorrow at 9am. I'll even buy you a coffee

"The boy has officially lost his mind," I say, showing the screen to Dani and Syd before turning to Danika. "Why have you set me up with this psychopath?"

Even she seems speechless for a moment before she cracks a huge grin. "This is all very intriguing though, isn't it?" She doesn't have a chance to dodge the pillow I throw at her head in response.

"This is completely ludicrous. I'm not going to entertain this any longer. It was fun while it lasted," I say, physically and mentally wiping my hands of this entire idea. I'll find someone else to do a podcast with.

Maybe I can ask a professor to host with me? That'll be interesting...for no one. My phone buzzes again.

> Don't chicken out, sunshine. Meet me tomorrow

"God, he's relentless! I'm so over this. And how did he even get my phone number?" Tossing my phone into the couch, I walk to the bathroom to brush my teeth. Sydney follows, but Danika takes a few seconds before meeting us at the mirror.

As we brush our teeth, Danika talks her usual gibberish that I can't understand but I know she's on her soapbox about Alex and giving him a chance. With her mouth full of toothpaste, she prattles on and on, knowing I have no idea what the hell she's saying but that doesn't stop her. Sydney and I give each other that look we always share when it comes to Dani.

We're both done before her and she finally spits out the remaining suds from her mouth. "All I'm saying is, you'll be glad that you went."

"But I'm not going," I say, wiping my mouth with the clean hand towel, waiting for Dani to say something else to convince me, but instead she's quiet...scarily so. Slowing, I look over toward her and her expression looks guilty as hell.

"You didn't."

She gazes at me with that sheepish grin and I can't run to my phone fast enough.

> I'll be there

"I'm going to murder you!" Throwing myself at Danika, I'm caught by Sydney, who is surprisingly strong for her short figure. "Murder!" I shout, now unable to make any more moves. Danika skirts by Sydney and me quickly, keeping herself close to the wall until she reaches her bedroom door.

"See you in the morning, ladies! Don't forget to set an alarm to meet Alex! Ok, I love you, bye!" She blows me a kiss and then slams the door behind her. As soon as it closes, Sydney lets me go and I sag against her, not realizing how much of my weight she was actually holding.

She hits me with that other shared "Danika" look. The one that says "we love her for a reason, remember that" and I find it harder to share in that one this time around.

"It'll be okay, Margot." Sydney says, rubbing my back once before heading to bed herself.

I'm left staring at the text exchange with me and the strange man that I agreed to work with for the foreseeable future. He didn't even respond to Danika's message. Just "liked" it and that was it. *Typical.*

I should just not go. Technically I wasn't actually the one who agreed to go so I have no actual obligation to go. Gripping my phone a little bit tighter, I think about everything that happened tonight. How hot and cold Alex was with me. Then I think about *The New York Times* internship contest. Then I sigh and set an alarm for eight thirty.

Chapter Nine

Alex

By nine fifteen, I'm convinced she's not going to show up. I'm halfway finished with my black coffee when the bell rings above the door and the sun shines through the doorway, adding a halo around the head of the girl that just walked in. Does that happen to her everywhere she goes or is it just for me? Every time, it shocks me.

Bolting from my chair, I step in front of her before she can get in line for her coffee. "On me, remember."

"How could I forget?" she says with a roll of her eyes. "Hazelnut oat milk latte."

I nod, repeating the order over and over in my head. I cock my head in the direction of the table I was previously occupying and Margot heads over to sit while I order her drink.

After a few minutes, I join her at the table, her latte in hand.

"Thanks," she says, holding the drink in both her hands and taking a huge sip immediately. It's actually pretty cute the way the normal-sized mug looks so massive in her small palms.

"I still don't understand why we couldn't just meet on campus."

I shake my head as I shift in the wooden chair across from hers. "Too many witnesses."

Margot's eyes widen as she sets the mug down. Taking a second to gather herself, she leans back in her chair and motions toward the table with her palms up. "Well, frat boy, the floor is yours."

"Lovely nickname, by the way."

She only scrunches her nose at me, seemingly determined not to speak until I tell her the deal. *Fair enough, sunshine.*

"First of all, I want to apologize for saying what I said. It was uncalled for and untrue. I was caught up and distracted but that's no excuse. I don't want you to think that's the kind of person that I am, because it's not." Margot blinks at me, apparently surprised by my apology. She remains silent, allowing me to continue.

"The reason I blew up the way I did is because of the prank. For the role I need you to fill, you need to be kind of invisible." Her eyes narrow and I raise my palms up. "Let me explain." I take a sip of my coffee before diving in.

"Every year the seniors in the fraternities set up one grand prank each to try and one up each other. It sounds completely childish *and it is,* but it's tradition. Delta Epsilon is my fraternity's rival and it's up to me to come up with the prank of all pranks to take them down."

"Why is it up to you?"

I didn't expect her to ask any questions just yet, let alone that one, so for a second, I'm silent. "What do you mean?"

"Why do you have to be the one to come up with the prank?"

"Because I'm the president," I say, as if it's common knowledge. I thought everyone knew that? I mean, every girl I ever interact with certainly does.

Just as I'm thinking at least this will impress Margot a little, she hits me with a quiet, "oh," before falling silent again, allowing me to proceed.

"Anyway, for this year's prank, we're doing a lock-in."

"What's a lock-in?"

"It's when we lock all the members in the house so that they miss an important event, that event being the Alumni Gala next Sunday."

"Why do you want them to miss the event?"

"It doesn't look good for a whole frat to miss an important event like that, and it's funny as hell."

Margot nods her head slowly. "Sure." She's quiet for a moment, then she speaks again. "How exactly am I supposed to help you with a lock-in?"

"Sunshine, you're actually the perfect missing piece of this puzzle. The idea formed completely in my head the minute you said you worked on the newspaper."

She's silent again, allowing me to continue.

"We need to make sure that all the guys are in the house and preoccupied while we sneak around and seal up their doors and windows." Margot opens her mouth. "Don't ask for specifics on that." She closes it.

"They're all dressed up, looking sharp, would be a perfect time for a member of the campus newspaper to come take a picture of them for the paper. Say, write an interview about the house? Distract them long enough for us to do what we need to do on the outside."

"So, let me get this straight," Margot says, sitting up in her chair. "You're willing to spend hours on end with me doing this podcast for who knows how long and all you need from me in return is to distract some guys for an hour?"

"Yes."

Margot shocks me by shaking her head. "That's hardly comparable. I owe you much more than that for all the work you're about to do for me."

"I promise you, this is all I want in return. Besides," I start, lifting the coffee mug to my lips with a slight smirk. "What makes you think that spending time with you won't be payment enough?" I hit her with my classic charming smile, expecting her to swoon, as they always fucking do but instead, I watch Margot's face transform into one of revulsion, as if she's just smelt an awful odor.

"Cut the flirty crap and you've got yourself a deal," she says, matter-of-factly and again I find myself stunned into silence. This girl truly shocks me at every turn. Just when I think I've got a handle on her, she surprises me again.

Margot holds her hand out for me to shake to make things official but just as I'm about to grip her palm, she pulls her hand back. "Just one last thing," her gaze jumps to mine and for a second, all I see is pure vulnerability. "This internship opportunity is the most important thing to ever happen to me. Don't shake my hand unless you are ready to promise me you're all in. I can't lose this contest," she says, with a sense of courage that I feel isn't entirely her own.

Reaching over the table, I grab her lifted hand and pull it down into a shake. "Sunshine, I would never let you down." And I mean it. As important as this prank is to me, I know this internship is a hundred times more meaningful to the beautiful girl sitting in front of me.

After Margot promises she'll follow up with me soon, she leaves, her half-drunk coffee left waiting on her side of the table. I'm tempted to take a sip and figure out what all the fuss is with oat milk lattes, but I decide against it. Instead, I take out my phone and text the boys that I'm headed to campus and hitting the gym. The sad excuse for a weight room in our house is just that–sad. The fitness center on campus is much nicer, albeit not as convenient.

Ignoring a text from my father, I swipe up on my instagram app as I'm walking. Already there's about twenty unread messages from various girls on campus. I hardly ever look at those anymore. If I wanted to find a hook-up, I wouldn't go looking through my DMs.

Holding my empty coffee cup out, I take a picture of the outside of the shop and the cup. With the caption: "Morning cup of Joe," I post the picture to my instagram story. Another couple of messages and reactions come in immediately but I silence my phone and put it in my pocket without looking at them.

I'm hoping some gym time can help me clear my head about this whole podcast thing. I think it'll be a fun experience for the most part, but I'm starting to get a little concerned about how much work she says it is. I'm not the most studious person on campus. I don't have to be since I know my fate is out of my hands the day I graduate from TU. No matter what I want to do with my life, the VP position at Prescott Cars has had my name on it since my dad founded the company.

Because of that, I never cared much about my studies. "Just get that piece of paper, Alexander, and I'll take care of the rest," my dad always said.

I always wonder what my mom would say about that. I don't have too many memories of her but I would hope that she would've advocated for me and Drew to do whatever we want with our lives. But at the same time, she was clearly not in her right mind. So, who knows what she would've done.

The ride to the gym takes enough time for me to distract myself from my dark thoughts. Blasting Kendrick Lamar can help you forget anything. Once I arrive, I pull into the lot and unintentionally park next to Margot's roommate's car, a fact I only know because she gets out of the driver's seat at the same time as me.

"Sydney, right?" I ask, pulling my gym pack onto my shoulder.

"Yeah, hey, Alex," she replies. We fall into step together as we walk toward the gym. The silence is a bit awkward, like we have no idea what to say to each other.

"We've got Exercise Physiology class together, right?"

Sydney nods and we walk again in silence. I should probably get some tips from her for women's workouts for my instagram. Maybe she would do some posts for me.

"Thanks for helping Margot with the contest, by the way," Sydney says. "I know she can come off a little strong about some things but she really wants this. And she deserves it."

Her comments shocks me a bit but I find myself nodding in agreement. "I'm happy to help. It sounds like a fun idea." As we get to the building, I hold the door open for Sydney to pass though.

"You guys are gonna kill it," Sydney says with a smile before walking over toward the treadmills. As I make my way toward the free weights, I think about what Sydney said.

I have to admire how headstrong Margot is. Clearly this internship means the world to her if she's willing to basically do anything I ask her to do for this prank. I just have to make sure that I put my all into this contest for her and she'll do the same for me. That shouldn't be too difficult.

Chapter Ten

Margot

THE NEWSROOM BUZZES WITH keyboard clanks and mouse clicks. Staplers and printers echo around the space and Jessy calls across the room for someone to bring her a coffee. *Ah, home.*

Before anyone needs to fuss, I hand Jessy the decaf black she's asking for, the one Sydney and I picked up on the way over because we knew she'd be asking for it by this time. Jessy looks at us gratefully.

"Angels. Both of you," she sighs, taking a sip of the hot beverage. Sydney walks over to her desk and drops behind the large desktop computer as I mosey my way over toward Nathan, trying to look as sheepish as possible.

"Hey, Nate," I say, standing over his desk as he sits behind his computer.

Nathan looks up, pulling his large headphones off his head to rest around his neck and shoulders. "Margot, hi," he says, with a smile. His teeth shine, and I don't think I've ever noticed how straight they are.

"How was your summer?"

Nate grins wider. "Oh, same old, same old. Nothing crazy. What about you?" He asks, leaning back in his chair and crossing his arms over his chest.

"Yeah, same here. Nothing special."

Nathan nods for a second, looking at me like he's done with the niceties and ready for me to leave so he can go back to his work. "Great," he says, raising his eyebrows a bit. A clear dismissal if I've ever seen one. Time to go in for the kill.

"Hey, Nate?"

Nathan laughs, "Yes, Margot?"

"Do you think you can help me out with something?"

Nate straightens his chair so that all four legs are on the floor.

"Sure, what's up?" He asks, but his attention is now split between me and whatever has just popped up on his computer screen.

I take a deep breath. Maybe it's better he's only half paying attention to me. Then maybe he'll say yes without actually knowing what he's signing up for. "I'm starting a podcast and I was hoping you'd help with the production of it all," I say in a rush.

Nate glances in my direction briefly but puts his focus back on the screen, clicking away at whatever he's working on. "A podcast? You're going to host a podcast?" He asks and then starts typing. At this point, I'm almost positive he's not paying attention to me. I could say anything and it would just breeze right by him. *Might as well rip the band aid off then.*

"Yes, I'm hosting the podcast. With Alex Prescott."

Nathan's fingers immediately stop their typing and his whole body freezes. I should've known that would be the thing that would get his attention, it seems to get every girl on campus's attention, too. Nate hastily clicks out of whatever was on his screen and gives me his full focus again.

"You're going to host a podcast with Alex Prescott?" He asks again with the addition this time. I nod briskly.

"Yep. And I need your help. Or at the very least, a crash course in podcast production." Nathan laughs and it releases some of my stress.

"I'll help you, Margot. It sounds, at the very least, like it'll be some entertaining days in the studio." I smile and nod again.

"Did you say Alex Prescott?" Jessy asks, stopping by Nathan's desk.

I nod, not wanting to get into too much detail with her at the moment. I don't want to get her hopes up until I know for sure that this is going to work out.

"I need a reporter to cover that Greek gala next Sunday, think you can score an invite from him? The Greek alumni are always so hush-hush about those events, it's almost impossible to get a press pass through those doors."

I thought for a moment. Lying to the Deltas about why I was in their house wasn't sitting right with me, my journalistic integrity was being questioned and I didn't like it. But if I actually was interviewing them for a real reason, I would feel much better about the whole thing.

Plus, it would be my first story of the year, and probably a big one since they hardly let press into their events. It could even make the front page.

"I'll ask him," I grin. Alex is the Kappa president, it shouldn't be hard for him to get me a ticket for the gala. Jessy claps me on the back as she walks past, clearly dismissing me.

Thanking Nathan one more time and promising him I'll let him know more details about the podcast soon, I wave to Sydney before leaving the newsroom and heading to public speaking class, having one knot in my stomach replaced by another.

———∿∿∿⋀⋀⋀∿∿∿———

As if I wasn't nervous enough at the mere thought of reciting my speech today, the feeling is now doubled due to the fact that Alex will be there watching me. Since Saturday morning at the cafe, I have been working non-stop to plan out this podcast and now that I have Nathan on board, I can finally talk the plan out with Alex. *Just get through this speech first.*

Ever since Alex opened up last week about his mother, I'd been feeling like my speech about open water just isn't deep enough–no pun intended. So, I worked through my Sunday, as usual, and came up with something much more interesting...at least to me. Not that I'm trying to impress Alex. I just don't want my speech professor to think I'm a vapid idiot with nothing between my ears.

When I enter the classroom, I opt for the same seat that I had last time, even though there really is no hiding in this class. Pulling my speech notes out of my bag, I sit a little bit straighter in my chair, knowing I'll have to get up there eventually today anyway.

I can't stop myself from peeking at the door every time it opens and students walk in. I'm not looking for Alex. Of course not. Even if I was, it's not like I want him to be here while I embarrass myself on the stage in about ten minutes. No, I hope he doesn't show up. In fact, I hope he dropped this class and–

The previously vacant seat next to me suddenly becomes occupied by a man who's familiar minty scent smacks me immediately.

"Sunshine," Alex says as a greeting.

"Frat boy," I respond, not meeting his eye but all too much feeling his arm graze mine on the shared armrest.

Alex lets out a dark chuckle. "You know, I'm not loving that nickname."

Still, not looking at him, I reply, "You haven't given me cause to replace it."

Out of my peripheral vision, I see Alex nod once. "Challenge accepted."

Turning to face him, my next rebuttal is cut off by Professor Walker commanding our attention at the front of the room.

"Alright, folks. Let's jump right into it today, shall we?" Again, no preamble in sight. Professor Walker calls the first boy up to the stage and he presents some speech about heights, I think. I'm not really paying attention, half my mind focused on my upcoming speech, the other half on the feel of Alex's arm brushing mine.

"So I've been thinking about this podcast thing," Alex whispers into my ear which causes an annoying chill to creep up my spine. "I have an idea of what we could call it."

"Shh," I silence him sharply, trying to keep my focus on the front of the room. Professor Walker has called up the next girl and I know, based on her list from last week, that I'm next after her. The girl, Maya, starts her speech about a trip to the Grand Canyon where she almost fell down off the side of the mountain range.

"Ah shit, that *is* scary," Alex comments after a minute or so and I shush him again. Loud enough that the people in front of us turn to get a view of what is going on. I push down a little in my seat but Alex barely seems to notice as he leans into me again. "So, the title...I was thinking–"

"Margot Davis," Professor Walker calls and I let out a high-pitched noise of surprise.

"Did you just squeak?"

"Shut up." Getting up from my seat, I feel my hands already begin to shake. *It's just a room full of people who mean nothing to you. Who cares if you mess up?*

I'll care.

Alex will definitely care. Well, maybe not care, but he will notice and more than likely make fun of me for it. My hands start to shake a little more and the paper I'm holding becomes more like a fan than a notecard. I put it down on the podium.

As long as I don't look in his direction, I can just pretend he's not there. But of course, the minute I open my mouth, the door to the classroom flies open with a late straggler and my eyes fly in that direction but instead land on Alex's intense gaze on the way. His concentration bothers me. He didn't give a shit about the two speeches before, why is he so laser focused on mine?

Trying my damndest to push away all errant thoughts of Alex, I take the deepest breath I can muster and dive right in.

"I wrote this speech twice. Last week, I had a speech prepared about how I was scared of heights, due to a hiking accident I had with my dad when I was three. But after having a week to think it over, I thought, while cliffs and the idea of falling is absolutely terrifying, it isn't what scares me the most."

I'm looking down at my hands and I know I should be looking into the crowd, or at the very least at my professor, but I can't seem to pull myself away from my cuticles, torn apart from a week of stressing about this class...among other things.

"I come from a poor family where the only food that was put on the table was either scraps left over from my granda's shifts at the restaurant or takeout when my dad took extra shifts at the factory. My older brother, Arden, and I got jobs when we were too young and helped the family as best we could. When my grandma got sick, we all had to pitch in on our part even more." I move my gaze from my fingers to the tip of the stage but I still can't bring myself to look up.

"Growing up in South Carolina wasn't that Southern dream that most people hear about. At least, it wasn't for me. When I left there to come here, it was under the condition that I make something of myself.

'Do better than your daddy did', that's what my father always said to me. So, the thing I'm most scared of in this life, the thing that keeps me moving the way I do is failure. It's not being the best I can be. Not doing the best I can do. Because if I fail, I'm not only letting myself down, but I'm also letting down my entire family."

I stop and after a beat, the applause starts. It's polite, the same applause that every presenter has gotten so far but I can barely even register it. Professor Walker thanks me as I walk off the stage and head back to my seat. Alex remains eerily silent as I take my previous spot next to him, sinking lower again to try and keep myself hidden. But I know I can't, I've already exposed myself. To the rest of the class and to him.

Alex doesn't say anything to me for the rest of the class but his arm stays pressed to mine on the shared armrest. I should be annoyed that he's touching me, but I realize I haven't moved mine away either.

"Excellent start, everyone," Professor Walker says as she takes her place back in the center of the stage. "Now that we've all gotten the scary part over, we can get into the real work. Next week, I'll be starting my lectures on speech content and how to prepare proper speech notes. Until then, have a good rest of your week."

With that dismissal, the students start shuffling out of the classroom. I'm relieved, at least. It seems like the speeches are over for the time being. I'm a much better notetaker than I am a public speaker but I guess this class is supposed to help me with that.

"You know, a little southern accent comes out in you when you talk about your family," Alex says, and his voice startles me. He had been so quiet the rest of the class that I thought he had already left when the professor dismissed us but no, there he was, standing over me with his backpack slung over one shoulder.

"I don't have an accent," I mutter, turning to walk down the aisle and up the stairs to the exit. Alex follows and I expect him to head in the opposite direction once we reach the door but he continues the same pace, walking next to me as I head toward the library.

"You do," he says. "Only a little bit. But I hear it now and then. It's cute."

I ignore him and continue my path to the library. I certainly learned my lesson last week and had already booked Study Room G6 this morning before heading to campus with Sydney and Danika. Edith just holds the key out to me as I walk in and I take it with a grateful smile.

I still feel Alex's presence next to me as I walk down the stairs toward the room. It's not until we reach the door that I whirl around and face him. He takes a step back, clearly startled by my affront.

"What do you want?" I huff with more attitude than necessary.

"Don't you want to talk about the podcast?"

"Oh," I say, mentally checking my "to-do" list. I do need to talk him through my ideas and I need to ask him for a ticket to the gala but after that speech, I'm mentally drained and already have a list of assignments I had planned on working on this afternoon. I didn't have the mental space blocked out for Alex until tomorrow since Tuesdays are my easiest days and I fully thought he would've dropped that public speaking class by now. *Thought, hoped, prayed.* To no avail.

"I don't really have the time right now. How about tomorrow?"

Alex chuckles and thinks for a minute before responding. "Tomorrow it is. Same time," he motions toward the study room behind me. "Same place."

"I thought you couldn't be seen with me," I clapback, folding my arms over my chest.

"A closed, private study room in the library is hardly a public sight, sunshine," he responds, folding his own arms in front of him in a mirrored gesture to mine. He looks much more intimidating than I do.

"Actually, now that I think about it," I start, something unsettling clicking in my head, "how are we supposed to produce a public podcast together if we can't even be seen with each other?"

"Don't worry about that. Once you fulfill your part of the prank, we can be seen together as much as you want. In all types of settings," Alex takes a step toward me, mischief twinkling in his deep brown eyes and I take a step back, the bag hanging off my shoulder hitting the door with a soft bang.

Alex notices our positions, notices the advantage he has over me and he also probably notices the way my heart rate has increased.

Not taking his gaze from mine, Alex simply says, "Until tomorrow, sunshine," and then leaves me all but panting against the door, a position I couldn't ever before imagine I'd be in...especially not because of Alex Prescott.

Chapter Eleven

Margot

> I was thinking something like "The Muscles and the Brains" or even better "Advice from a Six Foot Four Super Hot Genius and his Little Friend"

THE BOY IS RELENTLESS. Alex has been sending me podcast names all day, each one more ridiculous than the last. For all the work he's putting into just the title, one would think *he* was trying to win the contest, not me.

> "His Little Friend" could be easily misconstrued...

> What do you...

> oh HAHA ok you're right. Scratch that idea

I'm not even sure why I'm entertaining these texts from him. I already know what the podcast is going to be called.

> And anyway, I wouldn't exactly call it little...

> Bleh. Leave me alone now

Putting my phone down, I continue working on the upcoming assignment for psychology. After that class, I'll be meeting Alex in the study room to hash out the details about the podcast. Any more musings he has about it can certainly wait until then. My phone vibrates again and I get ready to chuck it at the wall if it's another ridiculous text from Alex, but instead I'm greeted with my older brother's smiling photograph.

"Hey, Ard," I say, answering with a smile on the first ring.

"Hey, Mars. How are things up north?" I notice for a second that Arden's accent is thicker than I thought, I never really thought about it before Alex brought my own to my attention during public speaking class.

"Oh, you know. All work and no play…" I sigh, closing the book in front of me and settling a little deeper in my bedroom desk chair to chat with him.

Arden laughs and it's like a melody I haven't heard in a long time. "You never play, Mars," he says. "But I hear you." I know I'm not imagining the sadness in his voice.

"How are things back home? Everyone the same as I left them?" I ask, trying to bring some light-heartedness to the call, but Arden only sighs.

"Yeah, everyone's the same. That's the problem, isn't it." It's times like these when I wish I could've stayed home and helped out more, but TU has one of the best journalism programs in the country and if I didn't earn all the scholarships I had, I wouldn't have been able to come here in the first place. I owe it to myself to do my best here and come out with all the skills I need to succeed in my field.

"Anyway, I didn't call to vent to you, Mars, you know that. I'm just calling to say a quick hi and let you know that we're all thinking about you and hoping you're doin' good."

The tiniest hint of a smile raises on my cheeks at the thought of the *New York Times* contest I'm entering. I want to tell him about it but not until I know for sure that I have a chance of winning. There's no use getting anyone's hopes up for nothing. "Yeah, I'm doin' good, Arden."

"Danika gettin' you in trouble?" Arden asks with a breathy laugh. My older brother and my best friend have always butt heads but they never fail to come together when it comes to things about me.

I laugh out a reply, "She's good, too." and then sigh. "I'm missing you guys though."

"Yeah, we miss you too. Anyway, I'll call again soon, alright?"

"Alright, love you," I reply. Arden repeats my words back to me and as quick as it started, the call ends. My older brother is many things but a wordsmith is not one of them. Still, it was nice to hear his voice. Sometimes that little reminder of home is all I need to keep me pushing forward.

By the time three rolls around, I've already staked my claim in Study Room G6. At the very least, if Alex doesn't show up, I'll still get some of my other work done. Just as I'm pushing aside my podcast notes and opening my psychology textbook, I hear a sharp rap on the wooden door.

"It's open," I call as the knob turns and suddenly the doorway is completely filled. I know Alex is tall, but when faced with a doorway, he overwhelms it. His deep brown hair is disheveled like ran his hands through it multiple times and he looks...tired.

Alex steps into the room, letting the door close behind him and then we are well and truly alone. There's a window that faces out toward the north side of the building but other than that, it's just us in this room. The minute he drops his bag and takes the seat across from me, I am painfully aware of that fact.

"Hello, sunshine," he says with that cheeky smile, and a hint of something else hiding behind it.

"Alex," I say with a curt nod, getting right to business by pulling out my podcast notes and placing them in front of me. My posture is straight, controlled and I think he can tell I'm trying to be professional because he straightens his own spine ever so slightly.

I clap the various papers into submission on top of the table. "Let's get started, shall we?"

"We shall," Alex says, with a hint of amusement in his voice. He folds his hands in front of him on top of the table.

Placing an identical stack of papers in front of myself and him, I hold his gaze for just a moment longer, showing him—hopefully—that I mean business and I am not to be messed with today. Alex meets my eyes and for a moment I actually think he's going to be good, but then his eyebrows jolt up in that infuriatingly challenge-like way and I roll my eyes before I jump into my spiel.

"So, it'll be an advice video podcast. Basically, we'll take listeners' comments and questions beforehand, and we'll craft a show around your responses to them."

"My responses?" Alex asks, his eyes scanning the paper in front of him.

"Yes," I say, matter-of-factly. "And the podcast will be called 'Ask Alex'."

"Why?" I feel his eyes shoot to mine but I don't meet his gaze.

"Because you're the focus, not me," I pause for a beat before continuing. "So–"

"Wait, no. This is a partnership. This isn't all about me," Alex pushes the papers in my hand down so that I'm forced to meet his eyes. The sincerity in his gaze gives me a momentary shock but I shake myself loose.

"I'm not asking you to do most of the work, if that's what you're thinking, it's just—"

Alex cuts me off again. "No, sunshine. It's not about the work. I'm happy to do whatever you need me too, it's just...this is *your* project. I want you to be featured in it just as much as I am."

I let out a dark laugh. "Please, no one on this campus gives a shit about me," I keep laughing, picking up my papers and continuing my speech. Alex is looking at me with trepidation but doesn't interrupt me again. Together we come up with a schedule that will work for both of us. We decide to meet for planning sessions on Monday's after public speaking class and then film the episodes on Saturday afternoons. I told him we wouldn't have to do the weekends if he'd rather have time to himself but he insisted Saturdays would be fine and I didn't push, my weekdays are full enough as it is.

"Any questions?"

Alex puts his papers down and looks at me again. "Who's going to produce this thing, by the way? You said someone on the newspaper staff is going to help?"

"Oh yeah, my friend Nathan already agreed," I say, starting to pile the papers back up. I move to take Alex's too, but he's clutching them pretty tightly. Looking up to tell him to hand them over, I am momentarily thrown by his darkened gaze.

"How well do you know this Nathan guy?"

"What?" I ask, completely confused. "He's my friend?" Alex nods with a distant look on his face. I have no idea why the air shifted so abruptly at the mention of Nathan helping us, but the idea clearly upsets Alex. Looking down at my watch, I noticed we've been at this for over an hour.

"Shit, I gotta go," I say, bursting out of my chair. "I told Sydney I'd meet her outside ten minutes ago to ride home together."

Alex looks up at me and then raises from the chair himself. "You don't have a car?"

"Nope," I state. "Anyway, thanks for meeting with me. I guess I'll see you again next Monday for our first planning session." I reach my hand out across the table to shake his, sealing our professional deal the only way I know how.

Alex looks down at my hand and rolls his eyes before taking it in his own. We shake twice firmly and then I move away, but Alex holds tight, moving his thumb up and down the back of my hand.

"You know, I've got a car."

"Congratulations," I say, yanking my hand away. Alex chuckles.

"I mean, I could drive you home if you need. And I could drive you to campus, too."

I pause while packing my bag, not looking him in the eye. "And why would you do that?"

"Because I'm a nice person, duh." I can sense the smirk in his voice, and I roll my eyes before looking at him again. Scrunching my nose, I murmur my sarcastic agreement while hitching my backpack over my shoulder.

Alex and I head upstairs to the exit where Sydney is waiting patiently outside the building for me.

"See you Monday," I say, getting into the passenger side of the car.

"See you, sunshine," Alex replies, watching me close the door and only walking away from the spot once Sydney has pulled away.

Chapter Twelve
Alex

THE SOUNDS OF A ball hitting a bat and a roaring crowd fill the room.

"Score?" Kai asks as he walks in from class, dropping his backpack onto the dining room table. He wanders into the kitchen and comes back with his hands full of beer.

"One, nil. Top of the fourth."

Kai hands me a cold one as he slides into the seat next to me on the couch. He nods, looking at the TV and taking a sip of his beer. I sip mine as well as I shift my gaze from the television to the computer screen on my lap.

"I think I'm actually liking these business classes this semester," Kai says. "Maybe I could work for a sports team or something one day."

"Yeah?" I answer but I'm distracted. Margot had texted me a link to the website that housed a comment box for people to write in questions they wanted to ask me. She was already promoting the podcast, name and all, and suddenly it all seemed to be happening so fast.

"What's that?" Kai asks, extending his beer toward the screen.

"The podcast I'm doing with Margot," I say, absentmindedly. I scroll through the pages but all I see is me, me, me. The cover page has a giant picture of me, not a bad one I'll admit, I just don't know where she got it from. There's an "about me" page with some seemingly random facts that everybody knows but not a whole lot else. It leaves more to be desired, but I guess that's the point of the podcast.

As I continue to scroll through the colorful, well-designed site, I notice something that causes an ache to grow in my chest. The only thing that's missing from the page is any information about the podcast creator herself. I told her I wanted this to be an equal partnership, but I guess she didn't take me seriously. I'll have to remind her again when we meet on Monday.

Margot had granted me access to the behind the scenes of the website so I could see the questions pouring in, many of them incredibly dirty. I am shocked at how many questions have already been gathered seeing as the site only went live about five hours ago. At this rate, we'll have material to last us for years. I groan internally.

"You good, man?" Kai asks from my right. I guess my groan was more physical than mental.

"Yeah," I sigh. "Just not really sure what I got myself into here," I reply honestly.

Kai peeks over and looks at the growing list of comments. His eyebrows raise. "Damn, you're really taking one for the team here."

"What do you mean?"

"I thought you were doing this because it was the only way to get that girl to help us with the prank, right?"

"Oh, right...that's—"

"Go, go, go, fucking Aaron Judge every fucking time." Kai's ass finds its way back to its cushion after standing up in support of the almost home run. He's not really paying attention to me, which is why I drop the conversation entirely, taking another sip of my beer as I shut down my laptop. There's definitely a lot of things I want to say to Margot about all this and at the rate she plans, I don't think I should wait until Monday.

> You're needed for official prank duty

> KA house. 9pm

> I'll come if you can swear you didn't giggle at the word "duty"

> ...

> Please come anyway

By the time nine rolls around, I've paced my room enough to carve a hole in the floor. It was risky to ask Margot to come over while there's a party going on, but I figured it was easier than her coming another time. Considering how her roommates like to party, she'd probably be here anyway.

I glance out the window for what's probably the billionth time and still see no sign of Margot or her two roommates. The task that I'm about to set before her for the prank is none too pleasant. I'm seriously hoping she doesn't run for the door and call the whole thing off. I guess I could hold the podcast and *New York Times* contest over her head but that seems like an asshole thing to do. I've been actively trying not to be an asshole these days, especially when Margot is involved.

The next time I glance out the window, I'm convinced it'll be my last time. I'm only proven right when I see Margot and her roommates walking up the path. From here, I can already tell she looks incredible. I need to get downstairs and snatch her up before other guys see her and start to take notice.

Heading for the stairs, I take them two by two until I'm at the door at the same time as Margot.

"Hey, Alex," she says, with more glee than I thought she would greet me with, especially considering the way the last party that she attended ended. "You've met my roommates, right?"

Danika nods. "We're acquainted." To be honest, I don't really know them well but I've seen them around at parties, the gym or class. They're both beautiful girls, though. Sydney's fit from the copious hours she's spent at the gym. Danika's fire red hair is a force to be reckoned with, but I've never felt the pull to her like some of my brothers have. Apparently I have a pull toward uptight, workaholic brunettes. Who knew?

"Nice to see you guys," I say, in a hurry to get Margot upstairs and out of sight so I can talk her through the plan. "Margot, mind coming upstairs with me to...talk?"

I don't miss the widening of her eyes at the suggestion of us being alone upstairs in my room. And I can't control my body's reaction to *her* reaction to the idea.

After a moment, Margot's jaw closes and she nods once in agreement and once toward the staircase, motioning for me to lead the way. I turn immediately and have a gut feeling that she's mentally communicating with her roommates about the situation. Even though this meeting is strictly professional, I can't help but feel a flutter of goodness float through me. Her roommates, especially Danika, wouldn't let her come upstairs with me if they didn't trust that I had good intentions. Hell, she wouldn't come up with me unless she knew I meant business. And I do, I definitely do...this time.

Once outside my bedroom, I open the door and gesture Margot inside, following quickly in her wake and closing the door behind me. I lock it for good measure and don't miss the quickening of Margot's breath.

She brushes it off and takes a slow glance around the room. There's nothing much to see, to be honest. A few Led Zeppelin posters and a small bookcase filled mostly with course textbooks and one or two Stephen King novels.

"Into horror?" she asks, and I can tell she's just trying to break the tension that came suddenly when I locked the door.

"I guess," I reply, shrugging. Truthfully, I don't read much. Those books have probably collected more dust than they've had pages turned, but she doesn't need to know that.

Margot just nods slowly, continuing her perusal of my room. I've had loads of girls in here before. Believe me, this room is not unaware of the female sex, but I can't say I've ever had one that I haven't immediately just taken right to my bed. The thought is...kind of jarring.

Margot goes to sit on the edge of the bed but seems to think better of it, opting instead for my surprisingly clothing-free desk chair. "So, you wanted to talk?"

I breathe out a sigh of relief. Yes, let's get down to the real reason I brought her up here. I end up sitting on the edge of the bed, not disgusted by my own bodily fluids that might be lingering there, as Margot clearly was.

"The prank is in place for next Sunday night, that's when the alumni gala will be going on. The guys should all be there early in the day, getting ready. You'll need to get in touch with Ryan Walsh, their president, to set up the interview for that time but I can't imagine he'd say no. Any press for DE is good press, they hardly have anything going on over there."

"About that..."

I tilt my head at her.

"You know, my journalistic integrity is not feeling too great about having to lie about this interview. In fact, I think it would make me feel a whole lot better if I was actually able to write something about them, then I wouldn't be lying."

"Oh, go right ahead if that's bothering you, sunshine. Just don't write anything *too* nice about them," I joke, mostly.

"Actually," she starts and suddenly I feel like she's about to grab my balls in a vice grip. "I want to cover the gala. You can get me in for that, right? Spare an extra ticket?" She looks equal parts hopeful and determined and I almost wonder how long she's been sitting on this request.

Truth is, I can get her into the gala, but not as event press. The Greek community is very specific about the people they allow at these parties so anyone unknown by other members would have to have a very special pass. So, I can get her in but...I don't think she'll like the circumstances. *Do I?*

I realize I haven't answered her request yet and she's starting to look more and more crestfallen. "I can get you into the gala." Her eyes perk up immediately. "But you'd have to be my date."

For a moment she's stunned into silence and I think this might be the first time I've made a girl truly speechless. She's looking back and forth into my eyes and I'm worried for a second that she might never speak again. Thankfully, she does.

"Why do I need to be your date? You don't have a press table at these kinds of things?"

"Not typically. Or if we do, it's very exclusive and, no offense, but the campus newspaper isn't the type of press the alumni board typically caters to."

"So, I'd be like...sneaking in?"

"You wouldn't be sneaking in. You'd be walking in, with me."

She's shaking her head. "But I don't understand, you said we shouldn't be seen together and now you want me to join you on the dance floor to boogie the night away?"

"Yes, well...minus the boogying part. Do you know what decade you're in?"

Margot rolls her eyes, pushing herself up from the chair. She starts to pace around the room similarly to how I did just minutes before.

"Fact is, we're going to have to seal the last door the second you leave their frat house so they're going to know that the Kappas pranked them and that you were involved, whether we want them to or not. Ryan and the Deltas aren't stupid. If you're going to be at the gala, it's better you're with us than on your own anyway."

Margot stops pacing, squints her eyes and lets out a deep breath.

"I need to think about it," she says, turning toward the door.

Wait. Don't go, my mind screams and I do the first thing that comes to my head, which is bolt off the bed and stand directly in between her and the door.

"What's there to think about? You want to write an article for the paper, we need them distracted for the lock-in, this whole thing is like killing ten birds with a bat."

Margot takes a step out of my personal space and crosses her arms. "That's not a thing."

"Also," I continue, ignoring her. "This will be better for your podcast. If they see us together at the gala, it would start some whispers on campus and they'd be more interested to check out our first episode." I raise my eyebrows at her, knowing I made a good point.

"Technically though, we aren't going to be seen together for the podcast. With the way I designed it, I'll be—"

"Yeah, that's another thing. I know you want me to be the center of attention for this thing, but I really need it to be a partner production. I can't just be sitting there answering questions and looking like I'm talking to myself. This is your project, sunshine. You need to be there too. On camera. Talking with me."

Margot opens her mouth to fight me, but I close my hand over it. "Another topic for another day."

Margot shoves my hand away and I reluctantly let it drop, missing the feel of her soft lips on my palm. "I hate you, you know that?"

I chuckle at the little lion cub trying to tussle with the alpha. "Sure you do."

Margot releases a deep breath. "I would need to change before the gala."

I nod. "Bring your clothes, we can run over to Kappa quickly before the gala."

It's only then that I notice we're still painfully close to each other, her arms having dropped in the heat of the conversation. If I take another step forward, I know she would undoubtedly take a step back to keep the comfortable distance, but I'm hoping to prove myself wrong. Stepping forward, I keep her eyes and watch as they widen softly, but she doesn't step back. Her neck cranes a bit to keep my eyes on hers.

"You can text me these details, right?" She asks, her words a little breathier than normal.

"Sure, sunshine," I nod, taking another step closer to her and farther away from the door. Her coconut scent fills my nose, momentarily catching me off guard. *Do I want to kiss Margot?* Before I could even entertain the idea, she looks up, meeting my eyes again.

"Great," she gives me a lazy smile. "Be sure to do that, then," she says suddenly, quickly stepping around me, unlocking the now available door and heading into the hallway without another word uttered, leaving my brain confused, my ego bruised, and my mind more than a little amused.

Chapter Thirteen

Margot

WHILE I DON'T NECESSARILY want to be lingering at the party after that talk with Alex, I know Danika just got her night started so I move to settle into an empty chair in front of the fire pit. It's a beautiful spot and yet almost always left empty during these parties. Not that I'm complaining, I think, as I pull my novel out of my bag. I get a sudden flashback of the last time I sat here with Alex and my cheeks start to warm but not because of the heat in front of me. Quickly, I shake the vision away, opening the book to where I last left off.

"This seat taken?" After a few minutes, my zen is interrupted by a somewhat familiar voice. Looking up, I see Ryan, the boy that I danced with last week. A small grin forms on my face as I shake my head and he sits down in the seat next to mine.

"I appreciate a girl who does what she wants," he says. When I look at him with confusion, he laughs, gesturing toward the book in my hands. "Reading during a party."

I giggle, inserting the bookmark back into place and putting the book inside my bag again. "Hey, sorry about just leaving you in the dust last week."

Ryan scratches the back of head in a nervous gesture. "It's all good. I didn't mean to step on any toes if you and Alex are–"

"Oh, we're not anything," I interrupt, probably a little more forcefully than intended but the comment hits its mark when Ryan's small grin becomes a full on smile.

"Cool," he says. "Alex isn't exactly my friend, but I don't want to get on his bad side either way."

I cock my head, giving him a questioning look. "If you aren't his friend, why do you come to his parties?"

Ryan laughs, nodding his head toward the packed house behind us. "Everyone comes to these parties. Unfortunately, I have to admit Kappa Alpha is more popular than my fraternity so these parties tend to be more packed than ours."

I've never been privy to fraternity life before meeting Alex but now I feel like it's everywhere in my life. "Which frat do you belong to?"

"Delta Epsilon," he replies, taking the last sip in his beer bottle. I freeze, having just heard that name upstairs in Alex's bedroom. Is that why he was so upset seeing me with Ryan last week at the party? Now that I know the logistics of the prank, it's probably best that I don't cozy up to Ryan, as cute and nice as he is. Alex is right, he can know I'm connected to the Kappas afterward but beforehand, I wouldn't want to give him any reason to doubt my reasoning for coming to their house for the interview.

Although, Alex did mention that I would need to reach out to Ryan to *ask* for the interview. Now would be as good a time as any to make that connection, especially after he just offered up all that information about his fraternity.

I perk up a bit as the idea forms in my mind. *But first, play dumb for a bit.* "Oh, you're in DE? Do you know who the president is?"

Ryan's chest puffs up a bit with self-importance. "I'm the president, actually."

"No way!" I feigned as much shock and interest as I could. "I'm actually on the campus newspaper and I've been trying to find the president of Delta Epsilon to ask if I could do an interview of your fraternity."

"Really?" he asks, skeptical.

"Yeah, actually, that's why I was here last week - to ask Alex for an interview for the Kappas. He said if I wanted a good picture of the group, I should come on Sunday before the gala when everyone's all dressed up."

"Oh, that's a good idea," Ryan mutters.

Like taking candy from a baby.

"Now that I know who you are, I can see why he wasn't really happy to see me talking to you last week. I bet he doesn't want me to interview both frats."

Ryan's eyes dance with deep thought. "That makes sense."

I nod, trying to hide my triumphant smile. I haven't sealed the deal just yet.

"So what do you think? You up for it? I could go to KA first and then come to DE right before the gala. That way everyone is looking their best for the...front page?" I raise my eyebrows, suggestively.

Ryan grins and I know I've got him. *Bingo.*

"Sounds great, Margot. Let's do it."

I beam for more reasons than one. There's a slight twinge of guilt in there as well but it's not like I'm really lying. I *am* interviewing them and I *am* writing an article for the paper. Just...not exactly what they are going to expect.

"Awesome!" I squeal. Ryan smiles and for a second we're both just standing there grinning at each other. It's...nice? Awkward? Both? I'm not sure.

"Maybe we should exchange numbers so we can coordinate the interview and stuff." I nod, handing him my phone where he puts in his number and then calls himself.

"Do you want a drink? I'm going to get a refill," Ryan asks. I shake my head as Ryan gets up. A few seconds after Ryan leaves, I feel my phone vibrate in my pocket. When I pull it out, a text from Alex greets me.

good chat?

My breath draws in and I look up toward the house, seeing the silhouette of Alex standing in the doorway, his phone clutched in his hand. Looking up at him, I tap the side of my nose twice with my index finger, indicating I did my part of the *secret* job. I can't see his face but the outline of his shoulders shake briefly in laugher before he disappears down the hallway.

Pulling myself up from the deep chair, I grab my bag and head back inside to find Danika and Sydney, hoping they'll be ready to head home soon.

"Mars!" Danika hits me with the nickname that's typically used by Arden only so I know she's really feeling the alcohol tonight. Dani drapes her arms around my shoulders in what I can only assume is meant to be a hug but really seems more like I'm carrying her. Sydney saddles up beside her, seeming out of breath.

"I tried to rein her in, but–" Sydney starts but doesn't need to finish as I nod in understanding.

"Ready to go, Danimal?" I say with fake enthusiasm, using our own special nickname for when she gets a little too out of control.

Danika kisses my cheek with a fat smack before turning toward Sydney and doing the same. "I love you guys," she sighs, resting her head on my shoulder. I've got one arm wrapped around her waist and the other pulling up my phone to call an Uber because there's no way I'm dragging her ass all the way home.

As I'm typing my destination, I feel the heavy weight of Danika pulled from my grasp. At first, I think she's fallen, but instead, I see her ass in the air and her body being fireman carried by Alex Prescott.

"Let's go. I'll drive you guys home."

"You've been drinking," I protest.

"No, I haven't." He calls behind him as he walks toward the door without a glance back to see if we're following. Sydney and I exchange a look before running after them.

Alex's jeep is parked directly in front of the house. Sydney runs ahead to open the back door, slide into the seat and help him maneuver Danika into a laying position since she's now completely passed out. I climb into the passenger seat and Alex walks around to the driver's side.

He starts the engine and for a moment, it's the only noise that fills the vehicle. I'm not sure what he's been up to the whole night, but for some reason, I trust him when he says he hasn't been drinking. Maybe that could be the reason why his jaw is so clenched right now. He didn't get to have fun at his own party.

"Nice car," I say to break the ice.

Alex lets out a chuckle, his jaw loosening a bit. "Thanks."

I can feel Sydney's sly smile from behind me as she watches Alex's and my every move. It's a small blessing that Dani is asleep, there's nothing that would stop her from saying whatever she wants and embarrassing the hell out of me. That's why Sweet Sydney balances us out. She's the perfect middle ground between Dani's crazy and my uptightness.

We arrive at the house in mere minutes by my directions and Danika stirs as Sydney shuffles her awake. I move to open my door, but a large, firm hand on my knee stops me.

"Margot, can you wait for a minute?" Alex asks, and he seems...nervous?

"Thanks, Uber man," Danika sputters and Alex just laughs, shaking his head.

"I'll be right in," I say to Sydney, who looks between us for a second before nodding and heading inside to put Dani into bed.

As soon as the back doors close, Alex sighs, running his hand through his hair.

"Is everything okay?" I'm not sure what's got him so worked up.

"I was out of line last week."

It takes me a minute to remember what he's talking about but when the lightbulb goes off, I open my mouth to protest. Alex doesn't let me get another word in.

"Ryan is a DE guy and for some reason seeing you with him..." Alex trails off, and I'm having difficulty putting together the pieces that are missing from his comment. Is he saying he's jealous that I was talking to Ryan?

"Alex, I—"

Alex draws in a breath before cutting me off. "It's just not a good look for you to be seen with a Delta when we're about to pull this prank. It could risk everything." His eyes suddenly shudder and it seems like he wants to say something else, something more, but he doesn't. He straightens his back, pulling his hand from my leg as if he just realized it was still there. I hadn't forgotten it was.

I blink. "You don't want me to talk to Ryan...because of the prank." It's not a question. It's a realization. Of course that's what he's thinking about. How naive could I possibly be to think it had anything more to it than that? We're in a mutually beneficial work arrangement. We should be focused on making sure both our plans go off without a hitch.

Alex doesn't respond but his dark eyes bore into mine. Even in the blackness around us, I can still see a slight twinkle in his gaze.

"You know the only reason I talked to him tonight was because it was the perfect opportunity to ask for the interview..." I say, resolved.

Alex nods, solemnly. It confuses me because I thought this was what he wanted but still...something in his expression looks sad.

"Is there anything else?" I ask, my hand reaching for the door handle but my eyes still on Alex. His jaw ticks when my hand hits the handle.

"No, sunshine. That's all I wanted to say." He looks over at me with a lazy smile that completely contradicts his demeanor from just a second ago. The whiplash is confusing, but I don't dwell on it.

"Okay," I say, opening the door and sliding out of the seat. "See you in class Monday then." I don't give him a chance to reply before I close the door. The temperature has dropped a few degrees since we left his house and I wrap my arms around myself as I rush toward the lobby door. I don't look back at Alex's car, but I know he doesn't drive away until I'm safely inside. In fact, I don't even know if he drove away after that or if he sat outside for a little while longer. Content to just sit and wait. Not quite sure what for.

―――ᚢᚢᚢᚢᚢᚢ―――

Opening the living room curtains, I'm greeted with a groan from the otherwise lifeless lump on the couch.

"Evil," the blanket mound moans. "Devil girl."

"Morning, honey!" I cheer, much more brightly than usual. What kind of friend would I be if I didn't completely rib my best friend while she's aggressively hungover? "You know you have a bedroom, right?"

Sydney's door opens and she laughs while Danika whines, shifting her pillow over her face to block out the sun.

"Headed to the gym. You need a ride to campus, Margot?" Sydney asks as she heads into the kitchen and pulls a water bottle out of the fridge, tosses it to me and then grabs another for herself.

"God, yes, please. Take her with you," Dani sighs under the pillows.

Rolling my eyes, I drop the water bottle onto Danika who grunts but then mumbles in gratitude. "Yeah, just give me a minute to change and grab my things." In another five minutes, Sydney and I are out the door and headed to campus. The drive is pretty short but a nightmare to walk, so I'm eternally grateful to my roommates who also act as my personal chauffeurs whenever I need them.

"Do you want me to drop you off by the library?" Sydney asks, pulling onto campus.

I shake my head. "The newsroom. I'm meeting with Nathan to talk through the podcast." Sydney pulls up to the Lincoln Building and we say our goodbyes before I close the door and she pulls away to park by the fitness center.

As I walk into the building, I bump directly into a large, muscular body.

"Nathan, hey," I say with relief. "I was just coming inside to meet you."

He smiles. "I know, but I figured it'd be easier to have this meeting in the campus recording studio so we can really map out how this is going to work. What do you think?"

"Oh good idea," I reply, and we walk in companionable silence across campus to the media building, which just so happens to be directly next to the fitness center. *Could've gotten Sydney to drive me all the way there*, I think for a second. As we walk by the gym door, Nathan tells me a story about something he did this weekend and I'm so engrossed in his tale that I don't notice the door swing open and a group of sweaty, chuckling men exit.

"Sunshine?"

Alex is drenched in sweat, his hair a deeper shade of brown than I've ever seen. He walks toward us, his freshly exercised muscles straining against his tight gym shirt. He looks back and forth between Nathan and I with narrowed eyes before his gaze finally lands on me.

"What are you doing on campus?"

I hitch my thumb toward Nathan, who's standing a little taller than he was a second before. "Nathan is my friend from the newspaper who's going to help us out with the podcast." I turn toward Nathan. "Nathan, this is Alex, our star."

"Nice to meet you, man," he says, extending his hand toward Alex who takes it quickly and shakes it once before they both drop.

"Nathan and I are going to look at the studio and make a plan of action for production. I'll tell you about it during our meeting on Monday." I dismiss Alex, grabbing Nathan's arm to pull him along. We make it another ten steps down the path before Alex shouts my name from behind us.

Nathan and I pause as Alex jogs up to us. "I'll just come with, that way you don't have to play telephone, sunshine."

I look at Nathan, who cocks his head toward me at the nickname. I only roll my eyes in response. I take a step closer to Alex and away from Nathan.

"Okay, listen. I actually think it would be great if you come because I probably won't understand a lot of this technical jargon but Alex, I mean all the offense when I say...you smell like absolute ass."

Alex gives me a blank stare and I think for a second that I might've genuinely broken him. But then he lets out the most boisterous laugh and I can't stop the grin that escapes my clutches as well.

"I'll head back to the gym and shower there quickly. Meet you guys in the studio in ten minutes." I nod, letting out a resigned breath through my nose and head back to join Nathan as Alex jogs back toward the fitness center.

"Is he coming?" Nathan asks as we continue walking in our original direction.

"Yeah, just going to take a shower first."

Nathan sighs in apparent relief. "Oh, thank god." We both laugh as we enter the campus media building and head up the stairs to the recording studio.

In record time, Alex finds us in the studio, showered and smelling minty fresh, which I greatly appreciate. The minute he finds us, he pulls up a chair right next to mine and listens to Nathan explain how the sound board works. If I didn't know any better, I'd think he was genuinely interested in this project and not just here to do me a favor.

The more Nathan talks, the more worried I get that it's going to scare Alex away. He shows no indication of wanting to bolt, but this is already turning out to be way more work than he's asking me to do for him. The guilt is eating me alive but I'm pulled back from my negative thoughts when Nathan calls my name.

"Huh?" I ask, blushing from being caught not paying attention.

"I was just asking if you're going to need camera space for two people or just one," Nathan asks, his eyes glancing toward Alex.

When I turn to look at him, his eyes are open and pointed directly at me. The conversation we had in his bedroom moves to the front of my mind. *You need to be there, too. On camera. Talking with me.* His words echo in my head. He should know from my speech in public speaking class how poorly I do in front of people. But, joining in front of the camera, giving him what he wants could help lessen some of the guilt I've been having about asking him to do this.

I glance through the glass wall over to the recording room that's already set up for two people. It could be kind of fun and since there won't be a real audience—besides Nathan—there'll be less pressure on me to perform in front of a live group of people. I might even be able to forget that we're recording and just enjoy talking to Alex. There have already been a few times where I've caught myself genuinely enjoying his company.

When I look back at Alex, his eyes are gleaming with challenge.

"Two."

"What's that, sunshine?" Alex asks, his hand behind his ear in a mocking way.

I shove his arm. "You heard me, jackass." His chair swivels around as he laughs.

Nathan glances at us both. "Two it is."

We spend another hour in the studio with Nathan who shows us the booth and how to sit close enough to the microphone to be heard but not too close that our voices get muffled. Alex makes more than a few inappropriate jokes throughout the morning but all in all, it's a productive work session. When Nathan gets a call from his roommate, he excuses himself with a quick goodbye and a promise to meet again next Saturday to record the first episode.

After Nathan leaves, Alex continues to swivel around in the chair as I put my notebook and papers back inside my backpack. I check my phone to see a text from Sydney telling me she left campus more than an hour ago. *Bus it is,* I sigh.

"You headed home now?" Alex asks, bringing the revolving chair to a stop.

"Yeah," I reply, putting my phone back into my pocket and hoisting my bag onto my shoulder. Alex stands from the chair and grabs his gym bag from the floor.

"Let's go, then," he says, casually walking out of the room. I follow him out of the building and give him a wave as I start to walk in the opposite direction but a pull on my wrist brings me back to face him.

"Where do you think you're going?"

"Home," I reply, confused.

Alex looks toward the parking lot behind us. "Is Sydney still here?" When I shake my head, Alex uses the grip he has on my wrist to pull me toward the parking lot where his jeep is parked. "Let's go, sunshine. There's no reason for you to take the bus when I live five minutes from you."

While my instinct is to politely decline his offer, taking the ride *would* save me about twenty minutes and be infinitely more comfortable, seating wise. With a sigh, I pull out of his grasp but continue walking with him toward the black car.

"How did you know that Sydney was driving me?" I ask as we both slide into our respective seats.

"I saw her at the gym. Figured you guys came together when I saw you outside with Nathan." Alex pulls out of the parking lot and onto the side street. At first, the ride is silent and I peer out the window at the scenery I've seen hundreds of times.

As we pull onto my street, Alex finally breaks the silence. "You know, I have to say I'm excited to start this project with you." The sincerity of the comment throws me off guard and I whip my head around to meet his eyes. He's looking at the road but a ghost of a smile dances across his features.

And, in that moment, I realize I am genuinely too. I'm excited to start this project and it wasn't because of the *New York Times* or because I wanted so much to win that internship. It was because of Alex. Because of the way he has put me at ease in situations that should've been stressful, the way he's made me laugh even when something shouldn't be funny, even the way he stares at me sometimes that makes me wonder what he's really seeing. Plus, that nickname. I couldn't help but smile when I think of it now.

He pulls up in front of my building, putting the car in park and finally meeting my eyes. "Me too, frat boy." Alex rolls his eyes but matches my grin with one of his own.

I thank him for the ride and we say our goodbyes. As I walk toward the door, I actually find myself feeling excited for public speaking class. *What is the world coming to?*

Chapter Fourteen

Margot

PROFESSOR WALKER OPENS UP her powerpoint and I sigh in relief that she's only planning to lecture today instead of having us make speeches again. Class started ten minutes ago, but Alex hasn't shown up. I don't know him well enough to know his punctuality habits, but he's never been late for anything that's included me. *Self-centered, much?* I focus on the professor's voice to drown out my ridiculous thoughts.

"Got a pen?" I jolt in my chair at the sound of the familiar, unexpected voice in my ear. I'm so enraptured by my own thoughts I didn't notice as Alex slid into the seat next to me. Alex lets out a breathy laugh, "Jumpy today, huh?"

Sighing, I roll my eyes as I hand him the pen I have in my hand and dig in my backpack for another.

"Thanks, sunshine." I'm sure he's trying to hit me with that megawatt smile but I don't give him the satisfaction of looking in his direction. He pulls a notebook out of his bag and opens to a fresh page. For a moment, he's quiet, seemingly focused on the front of the room and I'm actually shocked that he's going to pay attention and leave me alone.

"Don't you want to know why I was late?"

Shock over.

"No," I reply, copying Professor Walker's notes on "looney tune endings."

"This prank is becoming more elaborate than I thought it would be," he muses.

"And I didn't ask."

My inattention hardly deters Alex from continuing. "Devon and Kai think we should move in a different direction, but I think the plan we have now is going to work. Anyway, we were meeting about it. Lost track of time."

I keep my eyes focused on the front of the room and try my hardest to pay attention but the overpowering annoyance next to me is making it difficult.

"Devon says it's too risky putting you in the DE house next week. Says they might catch on to what we're doing and hold you hostage."

I draw a breath. *How did I not think of that?*

"Don't worry," Alex says, giving the top of my thigh a slight pinch before pulling his hand back. "I've got a plan." I finally meet his eyes and there is a deep earnestness settled there. And again, for some completely unknown reason, I trust him. "We'll talk about it more later." I nod, giving him a slight grin before turning back to the lecture.

Alex doesn't interrupt for the rest of the class time, but he also does absolutely nothing productive. The few times I glanced down at his notes, he'd doodled, "Eat my shorts" next to a terribly drawn picture of a clown. When Professor Walker dismisses us, Alex keeps stride with me toward the library where I've scheduled a study room for our podcast meeting.

"Okay so about this hostage thing?" I ask, my tone of voice slightly higher than normal.

"Would you relax," he says, giving Edith a smile as we walk in. She hands me the key, giving me a look I don't want to even try to decipher, and we head downstairs. "I'm not going to let anything happen to you."

"But how are you going to prevent that? You're not even going to be there," I rib him a bit, opening the door to Study Room G6.

"Where am I going to be?"

"I don't know!" We take the same seats we adopted last time we were in this room together.

"You think I would just throw you to the wolves and not be there to back you up?"

"Well, you can't come inside with me, obviously."

Alex shakes his head. "Obviously not inside. But I'll be right outside and I already talked to the guys, we can set up a code word if you start to get freaked out."

I pause for a minute. "You've really thought this through."

Alex looks at me like I have twelve heads. "Of course I have."

Rolling my eyes, something I feel like I've been doing so much more since I met Alex, I grab my notebook and laptop from the bag and open to the *Ask Alex* website page I made a week ago.

"We should get started, there's a lot to sift through here," I say, pushing the screen toward Alex and letting him scroll through the hundreds of responses we've gotten in just a week's time. I can't even imagine the responses we'll get once the show goes live.

"I've been doing a lot of research about podcasts—"

"Of course you have."

I continue, ignoring his rude interjection, "And I think we need to establish a rapport that we'll use when communicating and answering questions on air."

Alex looks over at me. "Why can't we just let that happen naturally? I mean, we seem to have a pretty easy rapport going as it is, sunshine."

"Yeah, frat boy?" I cock my head to the side. "You want to just bully each other relentlessly on camera?"

Alex laughs and it loosens something in my chest. "I guess not, although I do enjoy it."

Ignoring that comment too, I continue on. "I just think it's best that we establish our roles early. Like I'll be reading the questions that people send in and, obviously, you'll be answering them."

"Well, yeah, but there has to be some conversation afterward, right? No one is going to tune into me just spewing nonsense the whole time."

"You clearly underestimate the female student body of TU," I mutter and immediately regret it when that shit-eating grin transforms Alex's face. But he doesn't say anything, just looks at me with that expression until I give in from stress.

After thirty seconds, I've had it with the loud silence. "What?"

"You think I'm pretty." His smile continues to engulf his face and I would never admit it to him but it's an amazing sight. He *is* an incredibly attractive man and honestly, his personality doesn't suck either, but I would never tell him that.

"Can we get back to work, please?"

"That's not a denial." Alex kicks back in his chair, putting his feet up on the table and his arms behind his head. *Okay, maybe his personality can use some work after all.*

Taking the computer back with a huff, I click open a document I created with submissions that I thought were actually worthwhile. "How willing are you to give out your phone number on the air? There were dozens of responses requesting it."

"Not happening," he says casually, as if he's asked that every day. "What else you got?" He reaches into his backpack to grab his water, taking a sip.

Oh, what else do I got? Buckle up, pretty boy. Laughing, I leave my document and click back into the submissions page on the website.

"Well, one girl named *Kittyxo* wants to know if you'll come over and 'stroke her'." Alex chokes on his water and the sound of his reaction has me pulling up more of the ridiculous requests. "There's a comment here just referring to you as 'hot butt' oh, and someone named *Sexy69* is asking if you'll let her use her toys on you, specifically her ten-inch dild–"

"Okay, okay, enough!" Alex sputters, dropping his legs and sitting up in his seat. I get an immense amount of pleasure at watching his discomfort grow. The usually cocky and confident Alex Prescott reduced to a stammering fool. *I could get used to this.* "Please read some of the real submissions before I completely regret this decision."

"Whatever you want, hot butt," I giggle, pulling my document back up.

Alex leans his elbows on the table across from me. "I do not accept that as a new nickname," he mutters, his fingers slowly rubbing his eyes and his chin resting on his palms.

I laugh again, "Fair enough." Alex sighs in relief.

"I went through all the submissions and categorized them. The completely outlandish ones I didn't even include and then the rest are categorized by topic, relatability, and significance." I pause, giving him a minute to make fun of my category system but he doesn't. He just sits there, listening to me. I clear my throat as I continue, "With attention spans being what they are these days, I think we should keep each episode to about thirty minutes and that should give us time to discuss at least three questions with some banter before and after."

Alex is looking at me and I can tell he's actually listening to what I'm saying, instead of just feigning interest like Danika does when I talk to her about the books I read. He nods his head but still doesn't say anything, as if he's just waiting patiently for me to continue. So I do.

"In the first episode, we'll have to establish our brand, our conversation style and let the audience know what they're in for by jumping straight into the deep end. We need to make it clear that this is an advice podcast and not a free-for-all about Alex Prescott, but it's important to know...how much information are you willing to give?"

"What do you need?" He asks earnestly.

"Well, based on the types of questions we've been getting, I think it would really help our listenership if they can get a glimpse into your personal life if they listen to our show. But, of course, only what you're comfortable disclosing."

Alex thinks for a minute before responding. "I don't think it'll be a problem. We'll keep things light and I'll sprinkle in some seeds of interest about my life throughout the show. Whatever will keep them coming back for more, right?" He gives me a smile and I return it with my own relieved expression.

"Right."

For the rest of the hour, Alex and I parse through the categorized submissions and decide which questions will be best to answer in our first episode. We banter back and forth about what we might say and it's already like a glimpse of how the show will be. For a minute, I delude myself into thinking it might actually be fun, but then I think back to public speaking class and my excitement dwindles.

When the time is up, Alex and I pack up our things and head out of the library. Sydney and Danika are both waiting for me this time and it's apparent who's driving by the emphatic honks that keep sounding from the car.

"I'll see you Saturday, then," I say, giving Alex a wave as I head toward the car.

Alex's voice stops me. "You're not gonna come to the party Friday?"

I turn to face him but continue backing toward my impatient room-mates. "Can't. Gotta prepare for recording on Saturday."

"We just did that!" Alex shouts, sounding exasperated. The farther I walk away, the louder his voice becomes. "Plus we're not filming until the afternoon. Come on, sunshine. Just come!" His voice is loud enough that people passing by look over in his direction.

Without responding, I give him a shrug that hopefully says, *sorry, not sorry* and I climb into the backseat without another word in his direction. The truth is, Danika is probably going to drag us to that party anyway, for some reason, I like the idea of making him sweat about it.

"Not a peep," I say to the girls as soon as my butt hits the seat. Danika mimes zipping her lips and throwing the key, then Sydney mimes catching the key and unlocking Danika's lips.

"Margot and Alex sitting in a tree, k-i-s-s-i—"

"Children. You are both children." I buckle my seat belt and listen to Dani and Sydney sing for the entire ride home.

Chapter Fifteen

Alex

A CRASH SOUNDS FROM the kitchen, loud enough to be heard over the pounding bass of the music but I hardly register it.

"Everything's fine!" Keith shouts, and I chuckle at my frat brother. A minute later, he's back in the living room, sipping his beer and handing me a bottle of water. I mutter my thanks, twisting open the cap and taking a deep chug. We stand against the wall, surveying the masses. Devon is on the couch with the same girl he had draped across him a few weeks ago. At least, I think it's the same girl. It's hard to tell in that position. I look around for Kai, but he's absent again. He hasn't really been around the last few days and I make a mental note to pound his door down tomorrow and figure out what's been going on with him.

"Your girl coming?" Keith asks me, taking a sip of his beer.

I scoff. "Margot isn't my girl, Keith. She's a girl...that I know."

Keith looks back at the crowd. "A girl that you know." He nods slowly. "A girl that you've spent almost all your free time with. A girl you've brought up in conversation at least four times this week. A girl that–."

"Okay. Your point has been made but whatever you think, it's not that. In fact, it's so *not that* that I actually don't even want to hook up with her. We've got a mutually beneficial relationship and it actually appears that I like her company as a person more than just a chick who can give me half-assed sex whenever I want."

Keith looks over at me with an impressed expression. "Wow, Alex. You really are all grown up. I am...," he sniffs, wiping away a pretend tear, "so proud of my little boy."

"You want something to be proud of?" I ask, grabbing him around the neck into the crook of my elbow, holding his head in a choke hold. He laughs as he tries to fight me off but I've got a foot of height on him and just as much muscle, so he's got no shot.

"If you boys are done touching each other's butts, you can move out of the way," a familiar voice says next to us. I let Keith's head go at the sound.

"A pleasure as always, Danika." Danika smirks in response and I look over her shoulder to find Sydney who gives me a small wave and smile. But there's a painfully empty place where a third person should be.

"If you're looking for Margot, she's at home... 'sick'." Danika adds air quotes to the last word and rolls her eyes.

"That so?" I ask, taking another sip of water. By the time I've twisted the cap closed, I've made my decision. "We'll see about that."

I clap Devon on the back and nod toward the girls, one of which is staring at me agape, the other with a devilish grin mouthing the words *2A* to me with a wink. I head toward the front door, grateful to myself for always keeping my things on my person during these parties so I've already got my wallet and keys.

Getting into my car, I take one moment to pause and decide if I'm making the right choice. Then I look back toward the house at all the drunken ridiculousness going on. If I could spend a night hanging out with a friend or a night fending off drunken girls, I'm always going to pick the former. I just didn't realize that friend would be Margot.

—⁓⁓⁓〜〰〜⁓⁓—

Taking the stairs two at a time, I get to the second floor of her building in seconds. Not that I'm in a rush or anything. I'm just fighting off the adrenaline of showing up at her door unannounced. When I get to apartment 2A, I silently thank Danika for the information before knocking on the door.

There's a hushed jolt heard from inside and then a shuffling. "Who is it?"

I roll my eyes but smile, leaning my arm on the doorframe. "Open up, sunshine."

A gasp of surprise and the door opens immediately.

"Alex, what are you doing here?" Margot flips the light switch next to the door, as if she needs more illumination to make sure it's actually me. The bulb flickers relentlessly, but she doesn't seem to notice or care.

I can't help but notice her. Her brunette locks, typically worn down and loose around her face are up in a messy bun with a few pieces loose to frame her face. She's standing there in short shorts and a pink tank top, sans bra, I can't help but notice. *Focus, perv.*

"Well, I was looking forward to hanging out with you at the party but since you pussied out, I came here to get you." I stand up straight, throwing my hands in my front pockets.

She huffs a breath, her resolve returning. "That's nice and all but I didn't pussy out. I've had a long week of classes and honestly, I was just looking forward to laying on the couch and reading." She's quiet for a moment and then continues. "Plus, I'm meant to be 'laying low', aren't I?" She uses air quotes around the words "laying low" but I would've gotten her meaning by tone alone. I hadn't realized that my wanting to keep her anonymous for the prank would result in her hiding out in her living room wasting away with Shakespeare or whatever is it women read.

Whatever the reason she told me—and herself—, she did seem much more comfortable in her own apartment, clad in comfy pajamas.

"Such a nerd. Fine, show me your bookcase. I'll pick something to hold my interest." I gesture toward the apartment but she doesn't step aside. Instead, she looks at me with this intense gaze and then she takes a deep breath.

"I'm not going to sleep with you."

"Have I asked you to sleep with me?" I respond, not missing a beat and I wait for her to respond. Only after she shakes her head do I continue. "I came to the realization that I've never been friends with a girl like this. I actually like our friendship. It's different but I'm getting used to it."

Margot thinks for a minute, resting her head against the door she's still holding open. "So we're...friends?"

"Only if you want to be."

Margot thinks for a second, narrowing her eyes and then finding some resolve in herself because she opens the door a little bit wider.

I grin as I walk into her apartment. "Okay, but now that we're officially friends, can I request a more fun activity than reading? Please? Anything?"

She laughs and tosses the remote to me. "Pick a movie. I'll make popcorn."

I give her a grateful half-bow before jumping over her couch and settling into the pillows and cushions. *Girls, always got comfy shit around. I need more comfy shit.* Minutes later, Margot joins me on the couch with a steaming bowl of popcorn and two water bottles.

"I narrowed it down to three. You get to make the final decision but be warned: Your choice will affect how cool I think you are."

She grabs the remote from me with a huff, "I'll show you cool," she mutters, looking at the large screen in front of her. On the streaming app, I favorited three movies.

Fight Club. It. Little Women.

"You know, all of these movies are book adaptations," she says, popping a piece of the buttery snack into her mouth.

"You don't say," I reply, mimicking her snack movement with a smirk.

Margot looks over at me and finds something in my expression that causes her to smile. "Okay, let's break these down then. If I pick *Fight Club*, then I'm a tough chick that doesn't mind a little vulgarity and mind-fuckery."

"Is mind-fuckery a word?"

She ignores my dig as she continues, "If I pick *It*, I'm either into scary movies and will enjoy the horror and gore or I'm a scared little girl who you're hoping will cuddle up for *protection*," she rolls her eyes, placing them back on the screen. I laugh at her assessments, but also come to realize, she's not totally wrong.

"And if I pick *Little Women*, I'm a chick lit snob who will probably go on a rant about how Jo should've just picked Laurie from the start and avoided all this drama." Margot looks over at me again and I keep my expression as blank as possible.

"But the twenty-nineteen adaptation is so good," Margot pleads and I bust out a laugh as I grab the remote and put on *Little Women*. "Score," she hums, getting more comfortable in her seat.

Something I learn over the next one hundred and thirty-five minutes is that Margot Davis is a movie talker. If she wasn't trying to explain the plot to me, she was commenting on their clothes, their accents or how Timothée Chalamet really was cast perfectly.

"I didn't peg you as a Timothée Chalamet fan girl," I comment as the credits roll.

"I'm not," Margot responds. "I just think he's a good actor."

I nod, placing the empty popcorn bowl on the coffee table in front of us. Leaning on my side, I rest my elbow on the back of the couch and use my palm to hold my head up. "Who *are* you a fan of then? Better yet, who's on your elevator list?"

"My what?" Margot asks, her legs bent underneath her, her knees pointing toward me.

"You know, the list of three celebrities that, should you ever find yourself stuck in an elevator with them, you get a free pass to hook up with them."

Margot laughs. "That's ridiculous. When would I ever be stuck in an elevator with a celebrity and why would the first thought be 'oh, I get to hook up with them now. Rules are rules!'" She keeps giggling as she takes a sip of her water.

"You're thinking about it too hard, sunshine. Just pick three celebrities you'd want to hook up with. I already know mine."

"Go on, then," She caps her empty bottle, placing it in the popcorn bowl on the table. When she settles back onto the couch, her position mirrors mine exactly.

"Easy: Olivia Rodrigo, Selena Gomez, and Jenna Ortega."

"All brunettes," she comments, putting a stray piece of her brown hair behind her ear.

I purse my lips and shake my head with feigned confusion. "I don't see the correlation." Margot only raises her eyebrows. "Alright, fess up now. Who's on your list?"

Sighing, she grabs the empty containers from the table and brings them into the kitchen. "I need to think, I can't just make a hasty decision about this."

I chuckle in exasperation from the couch, my arm dropping as I careen my neck around to face her. "Oh, come on, sunshine. Just name the first three guys that come to your head!"

Placing the bowl in the sink, she turns to face me again, holding the edge of the kitchen island with both hands. "Okay fine." She thinks for another second before responding. "Hugh Jackman, George Clooney, and Gerard Butler."

For a second, I'm speechless. But only for a second. "Those guys are all, like, thirty years older than you!"

She shrugs, walking back around the island. "What can I say, I like distinguished men."

I get up from the couch to meet her on the other side. "Distinguished? What's distinguished about old balls?"

She scrunches her nose up in disgust. "Ugh, you are so gross."

"So is George Clooney's saggy, wrinkled dic—"

"Okay!" She shoves my arm to cut me off. "Enough insults about my taste in men. Isn't it time for you to go now?"

I pull my phone out of my pocket and look at the time. 12:41 am. "Huh, it is pretty late. I probably should," I reply, pocketing the device again. Margot walks with me and puts that god-awful flickering overhead light back on when we get to the door.

"I hate to admit this, but I actually had fun hanging out with you," she says, her head resting on the door as she holds it open for me to leave.

"I knew you would, everybody does."

Margot rolls her eyes and shoves me along so that I'm out in the hall. I chuckle as I turn around to say goodbye.

"See you tomorrow, then. Three o'clock at the recording studio."

For a second, I'm jolted back to reality. I forgot all about the fact that the only reason we're in this "friendship" is because we're helping each other out. And once the prank and the podcast are over, we'll probably go back to being nothing at all. The thought sends a pang of feeling through my chest but I can't quite decipher what that feeling is. Or maybe, I just don't want to admit it.

"Right." Giving her a small wave, I say my goodbyes. "Goodnight, sunshine."

Margot matches my wave. "Goodnight, frat boy," she says, before closing the door. As I walk down the hall, I can't help but think that tonight was the most fun I'd had in a long, long time.

Chapter Sixteen

Margot

THERE'S NOTHING LIKE TU campus on an early fall morning. Even though it's still the weekend, the quad is full of students hanging out, playing catch or just walking around. With my backpack full of our podcast notes, I head toward the media building.

It's usually easy for me to blend into the scenery on this campus, but for some reason this morning, everyone's got their eyes on me. Everywhere I turn, people are pointing, laughing and...taking pictures of me with their phones.

What the—, I look down at myself to see what all the fuss is about and that's when I see it.

I'm naked.

I'm completely naked on the quad.

My face is a tomato as I try to swing my backpack around to hide the goods but then I realize it's missing, too. When I try to run, my feet are glued to the ground. I whip my head around to try and find some salvation. I can't believe it can get worse, but then I see him. Alex. Standing there with his eyes glued to my body. He's taking me in, one slow inch at a time and there's nothing I can do to stop him. His expression stays static until he reaches my face and then he smiles.

With slow, methodical steps, Alex approaches me. He doesn't speak but his smile remains. As he nears, I realize it's not a taunting expression; he's not teasing me. It's that genuine Alex smile, the one he's given me when I say something funny or when I tease him. It's like he doesn't notice my embarrassment at all.

Alex shakes his head as he pulls a blanket from behind his back and drapes it around me. He holds it close in front of my body and leans in to whisper in my ear.

"Wake up, sunshine."

My eyes explode open. I drag my hand down my face as my heart rate dies down. *Just a dream*. I tell myself. The second dream that Alex has appeared in. Groaning, I drag my notebook off the bedside table and quickly write down everything I can remember. Pulling myself from the bed five minutes later, I find both Danika and Sydney in the kitchen cooking up some pancakes.

I slam the book on Danika's chest as I walk past her toward the coffee pot. She opens it with glee and immediately begins reading.

"Ah, naked on the quad. A classic."

"My epitaph, at this point," I sigh, pouring myself some of the fresh brew. "Keep reading, there's a new addition this time."

Dani is silent for a moment before she lets out a gasp. "A knight in shining armor!" She cheers in surprise.

"Who? Who?" Sydney asks, mid pancake flip. She cranes her neck to read over Dani's shoulder.

"Who do you think? Margot's new frat boy hottie boyfriend," Dani teases, holding the book open and pointing to the part about Alex for Sydney to see.

"One, he is not my boyfriend," I say, pouring almond milk in my coffee and taking my first sip. "And two, I know what the whole *naked in public* thing means, but what does it mean that Alex is there?"

Danika looks down at the book again. "I think it means you trust him. You're clearly nervous about putting yourself out there, but with the podcast it seems like even your subconscious knows that Alex won't let you crash and burn." She closes the book and places it on the counter. "That's actually kind of sweet."

Regardless of Alex's reputation on campus, my instincts about him haven't been wrong yet. He hasn't steered me wrong yet, about anything. Is it true that I really trust him to keep me afloat while my anxiety skyrockets during this podcast?

Sydney slaps a pancake onto a plate and hands it to me. "Are you gonna tell him about the dream?"

"Hell no," I scoff, taking the plate and moving to sit in my usual spot across the kitchen island. Within seconds, both of my roommates have joined me with full plates of their own. "Thanks for cooking, ladies."

Sydney nods with a smile and Danika mutters something like *you're welcome* with her mouth full of pancake.

"So, when are you meeting him?" Dani asks.

"At three," I sigh. It seems like a million hours away because of the early hour, but I know I'm going to be dreading when the time truly does come.

"What are you gonna do until then?"

"Something to distract me. Any ideas?" Danika takes a huge bite of pancake and then opens her mouth to speak. "Ah, ah," I hold my hand up to her face. "Chew, swallow, then speak."

Danika rolls her eyes at me but does what I asked. After a few seconds, she opens her mouth and sticks out her tongue to prove to me she's finished. I grimace but allow her to proceed with her thought.

"I have just the thing," Danika says, looking back and forth between Sydney and I with that expression that makes us regret ever saying yes to anything she says.

Half an hour later, Sydney and I share that look again as we strap the black vests to our chests and holster our loaded paintball guns to our backs.

"Leave it to Danika to take us to the last place I ever thought I'd be on a Saturday morning."

"How are we even gonna do this, though?" Sydney asks, placing the helmet on the crown of her head. "There's three of us, one will have to be on the opposite team all by herself," she pouts.

"Actually, we were thinking guys versus girls," a voice I had no idea I'd be hearing speaks from behind me. I whip around to see three smirking boys with their arms crossed across their chests. They encapsulated the very essence of 2000's boy band aesthetic and I bite my lip to keep from laughing. Alex's gaze drops to my mouth for just a second before jutting up back to my eyes.

"Right on time, gentleman," Danika says, pride in her voice. It's my impetuous roommate I whip around on next.

"You invited them?"

It's Keith who speaks up next. "Actually, we invited you." I look over to Danika and Sydney who nod with a feigned innocence.

Alex saunters up, grabbing his helmet from the table and holding it in the crook of his elbow. "Yeah, sunshine. You're actually crashing my Saturday morning activity. We don't do this every week, but when we can, we get our frustrations out on each other's asses with paintballs." In demonstration, Devon walks by Alex, whacking him in the butt with his paint gun. Alex gives me a wink before passing by me to grab his own rifle.

Dani comes up next to me. "Keith and I were talking last night at the party. He told me about their paintball game and it sounded fun." She shrugs. "If it makes you feel better, Alex had no idea he invited us, either."

I can't admit to Danika the feelings I had when I saw Alex in the doorway. Shock, first, obviously. Then anger at her for not telling me he'd be here. Not that I would've done anything different. I'm wearing a casual outfit with light makeup on. Not that I care what he thinks of what I look like.

The next feeling was indifference, so Alex was here? So what? He's my friend. Friends do fun things like this all the time. My last and most resounding feeling is determination. My roommates and I can be fiercely competitive if we need to. These boys don't stand a chance.

Sydney rattled up next to us, all the gear sounding off like an orchestra as she walks. "You okay with this, Margot?"

Grabbing my helmet from the table, I stare out at the three boys, the tallest of which eyes me with amusement. I place the helmet on the crown on my head and use my palm to push it all the way down so the plastic visor is over my eyes.

"Ladies. Let's roast 'em."

Nobody told me how badly paintballs hurt when they explode against your body. If I'm not completely bruised tomorrow, it'll be a small miracle. On our last round, Keith took Sydney down with a ruthlessness that astounded me.

Devon was hit by Danika and Alex shot her while I used my opening to get Keith out of play. That left only Alex and I on the playing field.

Hiding behind a large pile of hay, I catch my breath and assess my surroundings.

"Come out, sunshine," Alex taunts from what sounds like twenty yards away. Probably near the large wall painted to look like a school bus. "I just wanna talk!" He continues to shout and I know it's a tactic.

I skirt a little bit down the hay pile until I'm farther away from where I picture Alex to be standing.

"We can call a truce if you want," Alex's voice is more distant, confirming what I thought. I had mapped the playgrounds out as soon as I walked into the arena so I know that if I keep walking around this hay pile, I can skirt along the outskirts toward where he's standing and surprise him from behind.

Unfortunately for me, my aim isn't very good. If I want to win, I need to be in front of him. Or at the very least, close enough to get a direct hit from a short range. Alex says something else and the more he talks, the more it confirms to me that he has no idea where I am.

Smiling to myself, I hear him shout to the guys waiting on the sidelines to help him out with my location but Danika protests loud enough that they don't even consider doing it. I keep crouched as I walk around the outsides of the arena, keeping close to the out of bounds line but never crossing it.

For a second, I peek my head up and I see Alex standing exactly where I thought he'd be, looking back and forth for me, but I crouch back down before he gets a glimpse.

"I have a proposal, sunshine. Wanna hear it?" He sounds exasperated, but there's still a sense of amusement to his tone.

I keep moving, slow enough to not be heard, but fast enough that I'm on the other side of the school bus wall in less than a minute. I stand up to my full height and Alex stands directly in front of me looking in the opposite direction. I could shoot him right then and there but there's something about shooting someone in the back that doesn't sit well with me. *Not when I can shoot him right in the face*, I think menacingly.

"If you wanna hear my proposal, you gotta come out," Alex repeats, starting to turn in my direction and the second his eyes meet mine, I immediately pull the trigger, splattering his black jumpsuit with pink.

"I think we've heard enough," I say with a smirk and I resist the urge to blow into the barrel of my gun even though I *really* want to. Distantly, I hear the sound of cheering coming from Sydney and Danika, and I can't help the grin that erupts onto my face.

Alex's face is still so shocked, I take a mental picture of the expression to save in the back of my mind. After a second, the shock transforms into something else entirely. Pride? He steps forward, placing his gun in the side holster and holding his hands up in surrender.

"Very well played," he says with a bow of the head.

I give him a nod in response. "You too. Valiant effort." We take off our helmets and start walking toward the exit. "You know, I'm kind of surprised we were able to beat you considering you come here all the time."

"Maybe I let you win."

I stop, but Alex doesn't. He keeps walking, but he looks back at me with a sneaky smirk on his face. "Alex Reginald Prescott, you did not *let* me win!"

He stops, whipping around. "Reginald? That's not my middle name."

"I know, I don't actually know your middle name, but I needed one to make my statement more effective."

"And *Reginald* is what you came up with?"

I shrug, we continue to walk in silence until we reach the exit door where our friends are waiting on the other side.

"It's James, by the way. After my grandfather."

"Alex James Prescott," I say. "Sounds very dignified."

He scoffs. "Yes, that's me. The dignified-est." Alex opens the door and I'm immediately swept into a hug by Danika.

"You did it, babe! We crushed them." She tightens the hug before releasing me. I take a step back out of the embrace.

"Yeah, well, Alex let me win," I say with a defeated expression.

"Hey, hey. I never said that. I'd never let you win. I'm too competitive for that. I must not have been on my A game. Must've been distracted by something. I don't know," he mutters, walking off toward where Keith and Devon are standing buying waters.

I roll my eyes with a slight grin before turning back toward Danika and Sydney. "This was fun and all, but now I'm exhausted, bruised and completely dirty, so I think it's time we call it a day, yeah?"

They nod and we head toward the door that leads toward the parking lot.

"See you, boys. Thanks for the workout. Better luck next time," Danika blows a kiss in their direction and they hang their heads in playful shame.

"See you at three, sunshine," Alex says. "I'll pick you up." I nod with a wave to all three of them.

Walking toward the car, Sydney throws her arm around my shoulders. "He calls you sunshine a lot," she says, with a gentle teasing tone to her voice.

"He does," I say. "It was annoying at first but now I've gotten used to it."

"I think it's adorable," she says, releasing me from her hold and climbing into the driver's seat. Dani had already called shotgun when we left the building, so I climb into the backseat and buckle myself in.

Dani looks behind her seat at me. "Do we need to start singing again?" She looks at Sydney pulling out of the parking lot. "I think we need to start singing again."

"No, please god, no singing," I groan, getting ready to cover my ears with my hands if necessary.

"Fine, no singing. But for the record, I agree with Sydney. Very adorable."

I stick my tongue out at Dani, who returns the gesture right back before she turns around in her seat to face forward. She turns the radio volume up to twenty and starts belting out the words to *Dance, Dance* by Fall Out Boy.

Looking out the window, I see the three boys file out of the building, Devon's hand on Alex's shoulder, all three laughing about something. I'm glad that Alex and I are able to hang out as friends and there's no tension or any expectations. But I also have to agree with Sydney. The nickname is starting to feel adorable. I'm just not sure if that's a good thing or a bad thing.

Chapter Seventeen

Margot

A SHOWER HAS NEVER felt so good. After I peel the clothes off my disgustingly sweaty body, I assess the bruise damage. Thankfully, it wasn't as bad as I'd thought it would be. I'd only been shot a few times, mostly in the chest and stomach where I had the most padding. I did have a bruise forming on my right shoulder but I'd just avoid tank tops for a few days.

I notice I'm not the only one with a few bruises as I sit across from Alex in the recording booth later that afternoon. "Someone got ya good there, huh?" I comment on the purplish bruise on his left forearm.

"Yeah, someone," he replies with an eye roll and adjusts the headphones that Nathan gave him. "These aren't the most comfortable things in the world, are they?"

"Blame the campus media budget," Nathan says through the speaker connecting the recording studio and the soundbooth. "Okay, you guys ready to start?"

Alex had picked me up exactly at three and we went over the script on our way to campus. I know we are as prepared as we can be. Still, I can't stop the nervous twitch in my leg. I bite my lip to keep myself focused on the task at hand and not at the insane public speaking anxiety I'm feeling. *New York Times. New York Times. New York—*

Alex puts his hand on my shaking knee. I hadn't realized I shut my eyes until I opened them to look at his earnest expression. "We got this, sunshine. Piece of cake."

I nod vigorously. "Piece of cake," I say in agreement. "Piece of cake, okay. Let's do it." Alex pinches my knee with a wink and looks toward Nathan in the sound booth.

"You heard the lady."

Nathan's voice appears over the speaker again. "Okay, give me just a minute to make sure everything is set up correctly and then I'll start recording."

I look down at my outfit, suddenly regretting the striped sweater and skirt combo. I look like a sailor. I start to pull at the sleeves to bring them down over my hands.

"Hey," Alex says, pulling me back from the brink again. "You look beautiful, okay?" He says and it's not just a line he's saying to keep me grounded. I can tell he actually means it. "Everything is going to be great. Do you think I'd let you fall, sunshine?"

My eyes bolt to his as the memory of my dream floods my brain. Even my subconscious knows to trust him. Now all I have to do is let my consciousness trust him too. With a smile, I nod at him again. "Okay."

Alex whoops loudly in excitement and I giggle, looking toward Nathan to tell him to start recording.

Nathan gives us a thumbs up and above us, a bright red RECORD-ING light blinks on. Alex claps his hands loudly.

"Hellllllllllo, everybody! Thank you for tuning in to our show *Ask Alex* where you send in your questions and I answer them as best I can. I'm your host, Alex Prescott and here beside me is my lovely cohost, Margot Davis. Give everyone a wave, Margot."

For a moment, I'm stunned by his showmanship. Screw whatever he's majoring in, he's made for the big screen. But as he says my name, my attention snaps back into focus. I give the camera a small wave and smile meekly.

"Hello, folks," I say, my voice small. I see Nathan out of the corner of my eye mouthing at me to speak up. "Welcome to the show," I say louder.

When I glance over at Alex, he's grinning at me but not just for show. The pride shines on his face and it motivates me to keep going.

"Margot and I are super excited to start this podcast and connect with all you viewers slash listeners out there. You guys really came through already! We had hundreds of submissions on our website this week."

"Be sure to go in and add more questions after this episode if you're trying to be featured on our next one," I add with a smile. It is starting to get easier to just sit and chat with Alex. We do this all the time, it shouldn't be so different now.

Alex claps loudly in excitement and Nathan waves his hands up as if to say "Don't do that." Alex frowns. "Oh, was that loud? Sorry, guys. We're still learning all this stuff," he says, sheepishly.

"Let's jump right in, shall we?" I say, pull up my notecards and bringing the conversation back in focus. "Our first question is sent in from Kelly B."

"Thanks, Kelly," Alex says with a wink to the camera. He really can be a ham when he wants to be and it's all the better for me. If girls on campus want to get a personalized shoutout from him, they'll be more inclined to tune in.

"Kelly asked 'How do I get a guy to notice me?' Alex, take it away."

"The answer is simple, Kelly," Alex says, folding his hands onto the table in front of us. He's really a natural at this. I can't help but be mesmerized as he continues. "You gotta be yourself." He stops talking and a pit forms in my stomach. It can't just be that? I resist the urge to raise my eyebrows at him, to urge him to say something more.

Alex takes a deep breath then speaks again. "And when that doesn't work, you gotta make yourself unbelievably hot."

"What!" I burst out, not able to control my reaction. "That's terrible advice!"

Alex laughs. "No, it's not. There's no better way to get a guy's attention than to be the hottest girl in the room. Trust me, I fall for it every time."

"You just want girls to walk around dressed to the nines with pounds of make-up on their face twenty-four/seven?"

"I didn't say that," Alex says, his grin lingering. "I just said you gotta be hot. But listen, hotness can come through looks, but it can also be through personality. Being the hottest girl in the room could just mean you are exuding confidence like no other. Being confident is hot as fuck."

For a moment, I'm shocked by his answer. He somehow took an insanely pig-headed perspective and turned it into an actual piece of good advice.

"Do you agree?"

With a grin, I nod. "I like it. You hear that ladies, confidence is key. According to Alex Prescott." Glancing over in his direction, we share a look that says *We're killin' it.*

"In fact, that's how Margot and I met. She confidently told me to fuck off." Alex comments and shoves me playfully.

"It wasn't quite like that," I respond with a smirk before looking into the camera. "But more or less, yeah." Then it's my turn to wink.

I can't believe it but I actually think I'm having fun.

Alex and I answer two more questions and the banter continues effortlessly. We actually sound like we have been doing this kind of thing for years. Before we know it, it's time for the last question.

"And now, even though this is an advice podcast, we wouldn't dare let our listeners and viewers down by not also giving them what they want." I say, side-eying Alex. I know he's most excited for this part. "We got a record number of questions asking about specifics on Alex's life so here we go. Our last question, from Phoebe A."

"Thanks, Phoebe," Alex says with a wink again and I can't stop my eye-roll this time.

"'Tell us something that no one knows about you'. There ya go, Alex. Let's hear it."

Alex puts his hand on his chin in a pondering motion. "Something about me..." He continues to rub his chin dramatically. "Hmm..."

"Sometime this century, Alex."

"Okay, okay. Something about me is...I hate olives."

I pause. For a moment, we're both completely silent. Then I snap out of it.

"You hate olives?"

"I hate olives."

"And that's a big secret?"

"Never asked for a secret, she asked for something no one knows. I don't think anyone's ever asked me my opinion on olives. I hate them." Alex shrugs then leans back in his seat. I can only sigh.

"Alright, folks. It seems like you need to be a little bit more specific in your questions for Mr. Loophole over here," I say with an eye roll and a thumb toward my co-host. Alex only laughs as he sits back up to close out the show. "That being said, we hope you've enjoyed our first episode and we can't wait to get into more of your questions next week. Until then—"

"Adiós!" Alex cheers. With a side-eye of confusion, I just wave my hand in farewell until the overhead light turns off, signaling that we are no longer recording.

"Adiós?" I ask, gathering up my notes.

"I panicked," Alex says.

I chuckle. "Clearly." We grab our things and head back out toward the sound booth.

"That was a great show, guys, and I mean that genuinely," Nathan says leaning back in his chair.

"Thanks, Nate. Any chance you can teach me some editing techniques? I've never really done any video editing before."

"Sure, no problem. We can meet tomorrow and I'll walk you through it."

"You rock, dude," Alex says, clapping his hand on Nathan's shoulder.

"Uh, thanks, Alex," he says with an uncertain grin.

"That went much better than I expected," I say as we head toward Alex's car. The sun is setting, which means we were in that room much longer than I thought and that is confirmed when the clock in Alex's car reads 5:05. "Wow, that took two hours."

"Time flies when you're having fun," Alex says as he pulls out of the parking lot. "But seriously, that was so epic. You totally crushed it!" Alex drives toward my apartment and I can't help the blush that forms on my cheeks from his praise. I finally understand why his frat brothers love him so much, he is an incredible hype man. When Alex Prescott tells you you did well, he means it. And I hold onto that feeling all the way to the front door of my apartment.

Chapter Eighteen

Alex

AFTER GOING OVER THE plan with her more than two dozen times, Margot leaves the Kappa house and heads toward Delta Epsilon. I'm a bundle of nerves, but I'm trying not to show it. I don't need her any more nervous than she already is.

Devon and Keith spent the better part of the day using waterproof caulk on the first floor windows after Kai and I snuck over in the dead of night to work on the upstairs windows. As far as I know, no one saw us. While she's inside, we're going to super glue the back doors and lay in wait on the front until she's out the door and on her way across the street to change.

It's a foolproof plan. Of course it won't stop the deltas from showing up at the gala but it will slow them down and, more importantly, piss them off.

Through the dining room window, I watch with bated breath as she knocks on the door and Ryan opens up, beckoning her inside with a hand on her back. The noise that escapes causes me to stir.

"Dude, did you just growl?" Kai asks. I didn't even hear him approach the window.

"Shut the fuck up." We watch the door close and then we wait.

According to the plan, she's got forty-five minutes in there to interview the guys and then take the group picture, ensuring they are all in the house and not leaving for the gala early. I wish we could just go over there now and wait to seal the doors but it would be ridiculous to stand out there for that long and we would almost certainly be noticed.

The other guys mill around, slowly getting ready for the gala while sipping beer or water. With a sigh, I turn away from the window and see Kai looking at me curiously.

"What is it with you and this girl?"

I walk into the kitchen, grabbing a water bottle from the fridge and checking my watch. Three minutes have passed. I sense Kai following me into the room. "Nothing, man. I'm just worried we've sent her into the lion's den without a chair."

"She'll be fine. And even if she's not, it's not like they're going to hurt her. It's a harmless prank." Kai grabs a beer, twisting the cap off. "No, it's more than that. You've been distracted lately."

Suddenly, I remember that not that long ago, I was thinking the same thing about Kai. "I'm not the only one. Where have you been these past few weeks? You're, like, never here."

Kai takes a sip and looks away. "Guess I'm here when you're not." He walks out of the kitchen and I hear his heavy footsteps on the stairs. *Weird.*

Fighting the urge to look out the window again, I head upstairs to change into my suit. As much as I'm dreading this event, at least I'll get a visit from my father out of the way. Speaking of which, I should probably figure out if he's on his way here yet. It would fuck up everything if he showed up at the house instead of just meeting me at the gala. Why didn't I think of that? *Fuck.*

I jump into my dress pants with one hand and use the other to call my brother.

"What's up, shithead?" My brother says, the sound of a clicking keyboard and some kind of virtual combat in the background.

"Hey, Drew. Listen, has dad left for campus yet?"

"Fuck if I know. Fuck. Fuck. Shit. You killed me, Alex. Thanks a lot," Drew sighs into the phone, the clicking sound disappearing momentarily.

I roll my eyes, putting the phone on speaker and dropping it on the bed so I can button up my white collared shirt. "Can you just stop the game for a second to talk to your only brother?"

"I can," he starts. "But I won't." The disdain in his voice is apparent. While my brother and I get along fine, the age gap is difficult especially these last few years where he's been in high school and I've been away at college. In the beginning, he would come visit me now and again, but it's been a while since he's been to campus or the frat house. And when I come home for holidays, he hardly ever leaves his room. I know it's hard for him to see me and not think about our mom, hell it's hard for me, but I try to be as patient with him as I can.

"Fine, just can you check outside to see if Dad's car is there. I want to make sure I get to this stupid gala before he does." I hear Drew huff and the clicking stops again.

"Car's gone," Drew says quickly, no doubt returning to whatever game he's playing. *At least he's still on the line with me.* For the past four years I've felt guilty about leaving him behind, but I had to get out of that house before I was well and truly suffocated. My next step is to get Drew into a college as far away as possible so he can escape too.

Tying my tie, I look out the window toward the DE house to see if I can get a glimpse of Margot.

"Thanks for checking. He's probably on his–" I stop. "Fucking christ."

And there he is. Oliver Andrew Prescott. Pulling up in front of my house on fraternity row. He parks his black Mercedes in front of the driveway and ambles out of the car, walking up the house like it's his own. I hear the door slam underneath me.

"Alex?" My father yells from the entryway. Yells louds enough that not only can I hear it through my closed door, but so can my brother.

I hear Drew chuckle from the phone. "Guess you found him. Have fun at the ball, princess." I tell Drew to shut up before hanging up and pocketing my phone.

If I don't get down the stairs and intercept him now, he's just going to come up and the last thing I want is Oliver's assessment of my bedroom. Grabbing my dress shoes from the side of my bed, I hoist them on and then practically run down the stairs.

"Alex, good you're dressed. Let's go. I'm not going to be late." He demands. Of course he demands.

"Hi, Dad. Good to see you, too. Yes, I am doing well. And you?"

Oliver waves me off. "Cut the bullshit. Get in the car."

"I'm driving with the boys. I don't need your ride. You go ahead and I'll see you there," I say, walking past him into the living room. I feel a firm grip on my upper arm that stops me. I've got a foot on my father but he's got four decades of anger on me.

"This is an important night for us, Alexander. Don't fuck around."

I take a deep breath before ripping my arm out of his grasp. "Wouldn't dream of it," I reply. Looking in the living room, I see Keith, Kai and Devon, all ready to go across the street and finish the job. I need to be with them. I promised Margot I would be there, to protect, to help her. Not that I don't trust the guys, I just...I need to do it myself.

"Dad, we're actually about to do some prank business so it would be a lot better if I just went with the guys."

My dad's eyes softened a bit. The idea of me fulfilling the senior prank is something he's been proud of since last semester. But he also tried to control it and wouldn't stop giving me dumb ideas until I just eventually stopped taking his calls and answering his texts.

He looked into the living room at my brothers who were now just standing awkwardly in the middle of the room. *We should be over there by now.*

"Did you fellas take any of my ideas?"

No one says a word. Devon fakes a cough and Keith's shoes suddenly become very interesting to him.

I sigh. "No, dad. We decided to do our own thing. And we have to go do it right now or else it'll all be for nothing."

Oliver takes a step closer to me. "This alumni event is the one night of the year that I get to show everyone I graduated with how proud I am of my son." Then, through his teeth. "And if you chose that one night to complete your senior prank then that's pretty fucking stupid of you."

I close my eyes.

"I take it you boys can handle whatever needs to be handled for this prank without my son, yes?"

"Yes, sir," all three mutter.

"Excellent," Oliver grabs my arm again, pulling me toward the door. "Alexander, let's go." My heart is racing. I want to text Margot and tell her the change in plan, but I don't want to startle her and blow her cover. Hell, I want to run across the street and hide out until my dad leaves, but I know that's definitely not an option.

Before walking down the door, I only have a second to look over my shoulder. "Make sure there's no issues." *Make sure she's alright.* The guys nod and I have no choice but to leave the house with my father, hoping beyond hope that everything goes so according to plan that Margot doesn't even notice my absence.

I check my phone again for any update, but no text has arrived in the twenty minutes I've been sitting here. None of the guys have arrived yet, no Deltas but also my Kappa brothers are missing, too. I have no idea what the fuck is going on, but I don't know how much longer I can sit here without figuring it out.

When we arrived, my father carted me around to all his fancy, rich friends like he always does. Showing off the goods to his CEO comrades as if he wanted to sell me off like cattle when I graduate. I had been gearing up to introduce him to Margot, a situation I thought I couldn't avoid at this juncture, but she hasn't shown up yet. I had breathed a sigh of relief when everyone was called to sit at their tables and his seat was across the room with the alumni.

They should've been here by now. I take a sip of my beer and check my phone for the hundredth time before placing it face down on the table. Just as I'm about to bolt out of my chair, the back door opens and in sneaks Kai, Keith and Devon...but no Margot. My heart is in my fucking throat, but I try to remain as calm as possible while they take their seats beside me.

"What the fuck? What happened? Where is she?" I whisper yell at Kai who sits on my right.

"Fucking Ryan, man. He walked out the door with her. We had no choice but to stay hidden until they left the porch and then we bolted. She seemed okay though."

"She *seemed* okay?! Fuck!" I yelled and the room stopped, all tables turning in my direction. Ignoring the looks, I push out of my seat and rush toward the door, pulling my phone out of my pocket. Once I'm in the hallway, I call her.

My first call rings a few times then goes to voicemail. The next, right to voicemail. She's ignoring me? Is she safe? I told her I would make sure she was okay and I failed. I don't even know where she is right now. Ryan could've taken her anywhere. He could've—

As I'm about to call her again, I hear the front door open and I sigh in relief when Margot walks into the room. And then my fists ball in anger when I see Ryan walking in behind her. His hand is on her back as he guides her toward the ballroom door.

"Oh fuck that."

Margot's face lights up when she sees me, but there's an anxiousness to her expression. "Hey, Alex..." Her voice trails off as her eyes glance nervously toward Ryan, who's attention seems to be on the seating chart beside the door instead of the conversation happening next to him. The doors open behind them and a flood of Deltas come in, ready to party. As if they didn't have to pry themselves out of a locked house.

I hold in my rage as best I can. "Are you okay?" Margot nods once. I feel like she's trying to convey something to me that she can't yet say until this meathead walks away. "Let me show you your seat."

"Thanks again, Ryan," she says and Ryan finally brings his attention to us.

"Oh, no problem, seriously. Are you okay to stay with him?" he says with a concerned look toward Margot. *What the fuck?* Margot nods a few times and Ryan takes that as an okay to leave. "Alex," he says with a nod toward me. Taking his seat card, he walks toward his table without another word.

I don't give myself a second to consider that reaction I just had as I take Margot's hand and walk her toward our table. I want to interrogate her right this very second. I need to know everything that happened in the past hour when she should've been here. With me. But I can't, not yet. I need to show face before I can drag her away. Plus, I promised her she'd get to cover this event for the paper so in order for that to happen, she needed to be there. At least for a little while.

"Hey, Margot. About time you got here," Devon ribs her as she takes the empty seat next to me. She shoots him a look but also seems relieved to be sitting down with us. Still, there's a nervousness to her that supercedes her usual jitters.

Margot takes the napkin off her plate and shakes it out onto her lap. She gives me a tight smile but doesn't say anything else. *Oh no, this is bad.* I want to rip that napkin off her and pull her out of the room for some answers.

Leaning close to her ear, I whisper, "Do you want go talk...?" Her head whips to mine, our noses basically touching, while a fierce emotion flashes in her eyes. I move to grab her hand, but right before I can, I hear that voice I've been trying to ignore for the past twenty-one years.

"Alexander, it's time for us to head to the stage." Pinching my eyes shut, I lean back away from Margot, even though every instinct in me is screaming not to. I hear her let out a sigh as well and she situates more comfortably in her chair. I should introduce her to my father but I can't, in good conscience, bring her attention to the man that's taken my mother's psychotic episode out on me and my brother for the past fifteen years.

Without a glance at anyone else at the table, I push my chair back and follow him to the front of the room. A hush falls along the crowd as we take the stage, my father finding himself at home behind the podium in front of an audience with eyes only for him.

"Welcome, faculty, brothers, and guests, to our Seventy-second Annual Fraternity Alumni Gala." He pauses for applause. "It is my honor to welcome you all this evening alongside my son, Alexander." Waving his arm in my direction, he motions toward me but that's all I'm here for. A trophy for him to wave around and gloat to his friends about. *My son, chapter president. Had nothing to do with my influence or the amount of money I threw at the school to get him that position.* I have to physically restrain myself from rolling my eyes.

Oliver talks for another minute or so about whatever the hell he talks about. I don't catch a word. All I can see is Margot sitting in the seat next to mine, her long brown hair cascading over her right shoulder. I didn't really get a glimpse of her outfit when she came in, too relieved just at the sight of her.

Her dress is strapless, holding her up in all the right places and the turquoise flowers compliment the deep blue of her eyes. When I reach her eyes, she's looking directly into mine. Her mouth opens in a bit of surprise. *Fuck, I'm in trouble.*

My father claps me on the back with laughter and the crowd erupts in glee. I know I must be the butt of some joke, but I hardly care. I just want to get off this stage and talk to Margot. I need to know what happened before she got here. A moment later, the crowd claps and I descend the stage, walking immediately toward the table and leaning into Margot's ear.

"Meet me out front in five minutes," I whisper before continuing my path toward the bar. Requesting a refill on my drink, I stand and wait, not looking back, until the fresh beer is in my hand and I'm heading out the side door with it. I know this building, having had many functions here before. Down the hall to the left is another exit to the outside. I take it and circle around to find Margot waiting for me under a light by the main door.

Putting my beer down, with no real intention of picking it back up, I grab Margot's arm and pull her into the shadows along the side of the building.

"Jesus, you scared me," Margot screeches when she realizes it's me. She narrows her eyes at me. "Are you okay?"

The laugh I let out is merciless. "I should be asking you that question. What the hell happened and why did you walk in with Ryan?"

"Everything was going fine. I interviewed the guys, I got the picture and just as I was about to leave, Ryan decided he just *had* to walk me out. He wanted to walk me all the way home, but I needed to get my dress from your house, which was a whole other ordeal."

"He walked you out the door?"

"Yes, practically on top of me, there was no way for me to casually leave without him coming with me. I didn't look to see what the guys were doing but based on how the rest of DE left right after us, I'm guessing they didn't glue the door."

"No," I sigh, running my hands through my hair. "They couldn't."

"I'm sorry, Alex."

I whip on her. "Sorry? For what?"

"I had one job and I failed."

I meet her eyes again. "Margot, please. Don't even think about that. I'm just glad you're okay." I want to pull her into a hug but I don't know if that's appropriate. We are friends. And friends hug. Giving myself the permission to hold her, I reach out and pull her in. She gasps a little but lets me embrace her, only for a moment before we pull away from each other, slightly more flushed than before.

"What excuse did you give?"

"Excuse?"

"For getting your dress from my house. For coming to the gala?"

"Oh," I don't miss the way her cheeks turn slightly pink as she looks down, suddenly very interested in the pack of grass beneath us. "Well, I just told him the truth. I told him I was your date."

My heartbeat picks up just slightly. Of course she would say that. That is the alibi we agreed on. But still, hearing her say the words, knowing she said them to the president of my rival frat, a guy who obviously has his eye on her, I can't help but feel a swell of pride.

That feeling was quickly followed by a crash of regret when I remembered I left her behind for her to end up in this situation. And based on her expression, she's just remembered, too.

"What the hell happened, by the way? Why weren't you there?"

"I'm so sorry, sunshine. My dad showed up and demanded I go with him. There was nothing I could do. Believe me, I tried." Margot leaned back against the brick wall.

"Well, I didn't know that. So...I had to make something up." Her voice is small and I can't help but get the feeling that I'm not going to like what she is about to say.

"Sunshine..."

"I told Ryan that I was supposed to meet you back at the house and then I'd change and we'd go together. I tried to walk there myself but he demanded to walk me to your door. I couldn't avoid explaining to him that you must've left without me when he saw the empty house."

"You told him I stood you up?" I practically yell, trying my best not to but hardly succeeding.

"I didn't have much choice! Ryan offered to bring me here as *his* date and I told him I'd take the ride, but I still wanted to come and find you."

I shake my head before I realize I'm doing it. "I'll bet Ryan was more than glad to help you out."

Margot stands back up. "It was nice of him to do it."

"Of course he did it, he wants to play knight in shining armor and get in your damsel in distressed pants after." Margot shrinks back at my crassness and for a moment I feel guilty about taking this out on her. I should be happy. She got out of a bad situation—that I put her in—and now she's here. But for some reason, I can't get the image of his hand on her back out of my mind.

While I'm stuck in my thoughts, I don't notice Margot's building anger. "Hey, I did what I had to do for you and your stupid prank so let's just get back inside so that this night and our fake date can be over."

"Woah, woah, hold on. Wait—"

But Margot just shakes her head, refusing to listen to anything else I have to say right now. Honestly, I don't blame her. She walks toward the door and with a sigh, and I follow after her, not another word uttered between us, but the air full of unspoken emotions.

———⌇⌇⌇———

We sit in silence. We eat in silence. And just when I'm about to suggest we head out, I'm met with silence when I glance over to her chair and notice it empty. When had she gotten up? Scanning the room, I find her standing in front of the bar. With Ryan. He's laughing, she's smiling, and suddenly my blood is boiling.

I go to bust out of my chair and break up their little party but a small voice in the back of my mind stops me. It says *friend*. Over and over it says that word in my mind until it gets too loud to ignore. Margot is my friend. She did her part of the prank and now she's free to do whatever she wants. With whoever she wants. Even if that whoever is Ryan. Even if that whatever tears pieces of my soul bit by bit.

I swallow my pride, not an easy thing to do with how big it is, and I head over toward them. Ryan is laughing still and I want to smack the glee off his face, but Margot is touching his arm and I can't ignore that.

"Hey," I say to her, almost sheepishly. "I'm heading out with the boys. Do you want to come with us?" I leave the invitation open. It's a simple yes or no question for her. Yes, I want to come with you or no, I want to rip your heart out and stomp it on the ground.

Margot meets my eyes and I'm sure she can see the trepidation behind them. It's standard to leave a party with the person you came with and while Margot is *my* date, she did technically *arrive* with Ryan, so the choice is really up to her.

I expect a little bit of hesitation from her, the back and forth of which guy to choose. What I don't expect is for her eyes to brighten when they meet mine.

"Yeah, I'm about ready to go," she says with a smile that is not malicious or unkind to anyone. It's just a simple fact. The night is late and she's ready to leave.

Margot places her half drunk glass of wine back on the bar. "See you around, Ryan. Thanks again for the ride."

Ryan smiles at Margot but I can't help but sense the disdain he has for me written all over his face. When his gaze hits mine, I shoot him my favorite smile. *That's right fucker, she's mine.* He contains himself before looking toward Margot again.

"Anytime, seriously. I'll call you, yeah? We can talk more about hog-tying."

Margot giggles and nods before turning back to me and walking out the door by my side.

"Talk about what?"

She rolls her eyes at me and scoffs but doesn't respond. I can't help but notice her positive attitude has shifted slightly as we walk toward my brothers waiting at Devon's car parked in the parking lot.

"Hey," I stop her stride with a hand on her arm before we reach the car. When she turns to look at me, her expression is blank. "I don't think I thanked you for everything you've done for me tonight."

"There's no reason to," she says, crossing her arms in front of her chest, which causes my hand to fall away from her.

"No, there is. You did everything right. We can still follow through on the plan while they're sleeping and they'll just miss some of their morning classes instead of the gala. Same harm done."

Her eyes soften a bit at the sincerity of my voice. She looks up at me, and I take a step forward. As I do, her body shakes a bit, and I realize she's wearing a strapless dress on a cool September night. I immediately shrug off my jacket and wrap it around her back, pulling her body up against mine, whether purposely or not. I don't stop to examine it.

"Well then, you're welcome...frat boy." When she hits me with that little dig, I can't control the smile that breaks out on my face. She rolls her eyes but grins with me. We continue to walk toward the car, much closer than we were just seconds before and I take quick stock of everything that's happened tonight.

Our prank is almost completed, I made good with my father and I've got my beautiful...*friend* next to me. This might have turned out to be a perfect night after all.

Chapter Nineteen
Margot

MUCH TO THE ENTIRETY of the passengers' chagrin, I had Devon drop me off at my apartment instead of going back to the frat house with them. Even though all I had done was interview a few guys, take a picture, then sit and have a free meal, I feel completely exhausted. Waving goodbye to the boys, I head inside and upstairs to the apartment.

"Spill," Danika is on me within a second of the door closing. "Spill. Spill. Spill." She pulls me into the living room and pushes me down on the couch where Sydney is sitting with a book in hand.

"Hey, Syd," I say looking backwards at her. She laughs, "Hey Margot." Sydney closes her book as I adjust myself upright. Danika sits on the coffee table, placing her hands on my knees.

"I don't think you understand how deeply I need this gossip. Please, Margot." Danika is begging and the sight is almost unbearable.

"You're going to be pretty disappointed at the turn of events, Dani. After a slight hiccup, I didn't exactly pull off the prank, but it ended up being fine. I went to the gala, I ate, I drank, and then I left. The end."

Danika's hands grip my legs a little bit tighter. "The...end? That's it? No big upset? No dramatic fight? No romantic kiss?"

I squint my eyes at her. "What were you expecting, a netflix rom com?"

She releases her grip slightly but not entirely. "I was expecting at least *something*!" Danika looks to Sydney for backup but she just shrugs.

"Wait, you didn't complete the prank? What happened?"

"Ryan is too gentlemanly for his own good. He walked me out the door, so the Kappa guys couldn't seal it shut with him on the outside. But it's okay, Alex said they'll finish it tonight. Oh, and then Ryan took me to the gala." I lean back into the couch, closing my eyes for the first time in what felt like decades. I feel my phone vibrate in my bag but don't have a chance to check it before Dani's hands become a vice grip. "Oh my god, Danika. If you don't let me go—"

She immediately releases my legs and jumps up from the table. "Margot Elaine Davis. I'm grasping at straws here and you're burying the fucking lead!"

"You're mixing your metaphors," Sydney says and I choke back my chuckle.

Danika, of course, ignores her. "How did you end up with Ryan? And what did Alex think about that?"

"Ryan walked me toward the Kappa house, but when he saw it was empty, I had to tell him that Alex stood me up. He told me he was on his way to the gala too and offered to drive me."

"Hmm," Danika hums, finally relaxing into the arm chair across from the couch. Her eyes narrow and she holds her fist over her mouth but doesn't say anything else.

After a few too many moments of silence, I break. "What are you *hmm*ing about?"

"Nothing," Danika purses her lips. "Just *very* interesting, that's all."

"What are you getting at?" I ask, getting up from the couch to grab a water bottle from the fridge, suddenly very parched.

"Nothing, nothing," she says too casually. "Just...why do you think Ryan was so insistent on walking you out the door?"

After taking a large sip, I cap the bottle as I head back to my spot on the couch. "Because he's a gentleman?"

"I guess but..."

"I don't know, Danika, but I'm sure it's not what you're thinking. Ryan is a nice guy. He doesn't get caught up in all this prank nonsense."

"You sure about that?"

No. I'm not.

"Well, speaking of prank nonsense, what did Alex say about you coming in with Ryan?" Sydney asks.

"I mean, he wasn't exactly thrilled but he got over it," I respond, picking at the paper wrapper of the water bottle. I can tell they're both itching to ask me more about it but there's really nothing more to say. Alex has no reason to be upset with me talking to Ryan. I stayed away from him for prank purposes, but now that my part is done, I'm free to do what I want. And Alex and I are free to just keep working on the podcast together and cultivating the weird friendship we have growing.

My phone vibrates again and I remember the feeling from earlier. I take out my phone to reveal two texts, sent about ten minutes apart.

Ryan

> Thanks for keeping me company tonight

Frat boy

> Almost lock in time! The deltas have no idea what's coming. Thanks again, sunshine. Couldn't have done it without you

The texts make me smile but the trouble is that I'm not sure which one truly causes the grin. Without answering either boy, I grab my laptop and write up the article for the paper while everything is fresh in my mind. As confusing as this night was, at least I got a front page article out of it.

When I wake up, I'm surprised to have had a restful dreamless sleep. *Relieved, more like it.* Pulling my socks on, I venture out into the kitchen to start a pot of coffee. Sydney should be walking in any minute, her Monday schedule similar to mine with our first class starting at nine am.

I open the cabinet to find the empty coffee tin and sigh deeply. Sydney comes out of her room as I close the cabinet.

"Morning, Margot," she says, always the peppiest, even first thing in the morning.

"No coffee," I reply, like the caffeine-addicted robot that I am.

"Shoot," Sydney looks down at her watch. "If we leave in five minutes, we can hit Cafe Royale on our way to campus."

I don't need her to tell me twice as I bolt back into my bedroom to change into the first outfit I pull out of my closet and then zoom to the bathroom to brush my teeth and run a comb through my tangled locks. I'm back in the living room and ready to leave before that five minute alarm in Sydney's brain could go off. All she does is laugh as we head out the door.

In another ten minutes we're leaving the cafe, coffees in hand and smiles on our faces. At least there's definitely a smile on my face as I take another sip and let the warm, rich goodness flow through me. *I really am addicted.*

"You think she looks that happy while thinking about other things or only coffee?" The familiar voice breaks me from my coffee euphoria.

Alex and Keith stand in front of me, both smirking incessantly like they just made the most clever joke the world has ever heard.

"Too bad you'll never find out," I reply, pushing myself through them, creating a Margot-shaped hole that Sydney walks through after me, truly just for fun.

"You wound me, sunshine!" Alex calls from behind me. I refuse to look back at him. "See you later!"

I wave at him from over my head, still not looking back as Sydney and I get into the car to head to campus.

Once again, Alex is late to class, and I start to think I might have the wrong idea about his punctuality habits. He's not nearly as stealthy this time as he slides into his seat and drops his bag loud enough that people in the nearby seats look at the commotion. Professor Walker stands in the front of the room, discussing the importance of outlining our speeches. I'm taking copious notes, of course.

"Don't even think about it," I say without looking up from my notes.

"Think about what?" Alex feigns innocence.

"You aren't copying my notes. Come to class on time."

Alex gasps. "Sun–"

"Shush," I huff, straining to hear what the teacher said about speech times.

Alex shuts up for approximately ten seconds before he says, "What's got your panties in a twist?"

I roll my eyes but continue to ignore him. Well, as best I can ignore a massive frat boy who's trying to peek over my shoulder and copy what I'm writing.

"Oh I got it. You're freaking out about the podcast, aren't you?"

In all the craziness of Sunday, I was almost able to forget that Alex and I are going live with the first episode of our podcast today after class. I couldn't forget entirely though, especially when Alex wrote: *T-minus two hours!* on the top of my note page. When I looked at him with trepidation, I am met only with a brilliant smile.

"I'm not freaking out. I'm just nervous," I say, my voice small.

Alex puts his hand on my leg for a second before removing it quickly. "There's nothing to be nervous about, sunshine. We did a great recording this weekend and I think it's gonna be a huge hit!"

I scoff but not in a mean way. "Of course you do, campus hottie número uno."

"I'm sorry, can you repeat that? In fact, give me your phone, I'm changing my contact name." He holds his hand out to me, but I just slap it away with a small giggle.

After class, Alex and I walk in tandem toward the library where we've basically got a standing appointment in Study Room G6. I'm in there almost every day but on Mondays, Alex joins me. Edith seems used to this by now and has stopped giving me those knowing glances.

"You ready, sunshine?" Alex chooses the chair directly next to mine today so we can look at the computer together. Nathan helped us queue up the video on our website so all we have to do is hit *upload* and we are good to go. I suggested that we complete our planning session first and then hit the "publish" button right before leaving the library but Alex was having none of that.

Hovering the mouse over the "publish" button, I rest my fingertip, ready to hit it. All the confidence in the world. Ready to show everyone the funny, clever thirty minute episode of Alex and I talking and answering questions. Of Alex and I bantering and laughing. Of us being open and honest. Ready to show...

"Wait," I say, moving my hand away from the computer and gripping both palms under the table. "Once we do this, we can't take it back."

"And that scares you?" Alex asks, in a curious way. I only nod but he edges me on. "Because..."

"Because..." I start but close my mouth again. How do I explain to Alex that this is the most I've put myself out there, ever, and I feel the fear of rejection down into my bones. How do I tell him that I'm terrified that he'll feel differently about me if this fails?

"Because I can't fail." Myself. My family. Him.

Alex reaches under the table and pulls my hands apart with his larger one. He grips my hand in his palm and holds firm. "I told you once that I'd never let you fall and now it's time for you to take my word for it. Do you trust me?"

When I meet his eyes, I can't help but hesitate slightly, thinking about how he left me in the lurch last night. But I surprise myself by answering with a nod.

Alex smiles and it hits his eyes in a way that almost makes me draw an extra breath. "Hit that button, sunshine." He nods toward the computer. I keep my left hand in his as I move my right to hover over the "publish" button once more.

One deep breath.

One press of the keyboard.

Published.

Alex squeezes my hand, and I actually feel a sigh of relief. And then I immediately change the tab to my question document. I hear him chuckle beside me but he doesn't fight me on the move. I just know I can't sit there and watch the views rack up, or worse, not rack up.

⎯⎯᷍᷍᷍᷍⎯⎯

Alex and I spend the next hour scrolling through questions and outlining our podcast for Saturday. Just as I'm typing up the last bit of banter for our script, I hear the faint sound of scraping on wood. Next to me, Alex is using the pen I gave him in speech class to etch something into the table.

"What are you doing? That's school property!"

Beside me, Alex laughs as he finishes the last of his vandalism. Blowing the wooden shavings out of the way, he brushes his hand over the marking. *A & M.*

"See? Now it really is *our* study room."

I want to roll my eyes at the cringiness but I can't take them off the letters he's permanently marked on to the table. I need to blink a few times before I can face him again and when I do, his smile is contagious. I couldn't stop my own grin from forming even if I tried.

"You're such a dork."

Alex laughs and any tightness I had in my chest loosens. Leaning over the table, he closes my laptop screen, signaling the end of our meeting.

"The script looks good but you know, there's a chance we have to reevaluate this during the week if the show picks up speed. I bet there will be hundreds more questions rolling in before Saturday," Alex comments as I shove my computer back into my backpack and we start to head out the door.

"Hm, good point. I'll keep an eye on it and let you know if we need to rearrange some stuff." After reaching the ground level, Alex hands Edith the study room key with a wink and then pulls the door for me to exit before him.

Just as I'm about to thank him and then rib him for his chivalry, my phone rings loudly in my pocket. As I pull it out, the name RYAN flashes on the screen.

"Oh look, your boyfriend is calling," Alex says with feigned enthusiasm. I give him a shove before picking up the call.

"Hello?" I answer after the second ring. I continue walking toward the campus exit since Sydney is already home and I need to catch the bus. I expect Alex to head toward the parking lot but instead, he grabs my elbow and pulls me with him. I don't have the time to question him as Ryan replies, "Margot, hey. It's Ryan."

I chuckle. "I know, caller ID and all." Ryan laughs nervously on the other side of the phone.

"Right, duh."

"What's up? Everything okay?" I ask, still being manhandled by Alex. With an annoyed look at him, I pull my elbow away but the look on his face makes it clear that he wants me to continue walking with him.

"Oh yeah, everything's fine. I actually was calling because I wanted to ask if you wanted to get dinner with me on Wednesday night? I know it's kind of random in the middle of the week but truthfully, I don't want to wait until the weekend to hang out with you. If you're interested, that is."

"Dinner?" I squeak out. I don't miss the way Alex's jaw ticks as we keep walking, but he doesn't look my way.

I don't know how to respond. I've never been on a date before. On the one hand, I'm absolutely terrified to put myself out there like that but on the other...Ryan is a nice guy. He's been a perfect gentleman to me at every turn. I have no real reason to say no. I glance at Alex again and he's staring straight ahead. No...no reason to say no.

His car is in sight and I've caught on by now that he isn't going to allow me to take the bus home so I slide into the passenger seat as he gets into the driver's side.

"That would be–"

My words are drowned out by the increasingly loud volume of Alex's car radio, blasting *Rambling Man* by The Allman Brothers Band. I almost drop the phone from the shock of the noise, but Alex doesn't seem to even notice it. With a huff, I turn the volume down to an appropriate level.

"I would love that."

Ryan sighs in apparent relief through the phone, having not even heard the radio interruption. "Awesome. I'll pick you up at seven. Sound good?"

Alex pulls out of the parking lot and makes a sharp left turn.

"Sounds great, see you then." I smile into the receiver as I end the call.

I look over at Alex incredulously, but he remains silent, his eyes firmly on the road ahead. With my signature eye roll, I turn my body toward the window and watch the familiar scenery fly by. Danika is going to have an absolute fit when I tell her about Ryan asking me out. She'll probably want to do a whole makeover for the event. Hair, nails, clothes. I bet she'll even demand I–

"You know I was kidding about him being your boyfriend, sun."

Finally he speaks and it's to tease me. I want to give him a piece of my mind but when I look over to do just that, his gaze doesn't look mocking. It looks...somber.

"He's not my boyfriend. It's just one date."

Alex sighs but doesn't say anything else. Within a few seconds, we pull up to the apartment and Alex reaches across me to open the passenger side door.

"I know. I'm just yanking your chain," He grins but it doesn't reach his eyes. Not like it did before. "I hope you guys have a good time," he says, his hands back on the steering wheel and his eyes on the road.

I can recognize a dismissal when I see one. After thanking him for the ride, I slide out of the car and shut the door behind me. Alex pulls away the minute I'm safely away from the vehicle and the motion makes me pause. Normally he'll at least wait until I'm inside the building...

I don't dwell on that fact, there's no reason to. Instead, I head inside and tell my roommates about my date in two days. Of course, Danika reacts exactly as I expected, just with more excited arm punches than I really needed.

Chapter Twenty

Margot

THERE ARE SO MANY eyes on me that I have to check four separate times to ensure that I'm fully clothed. After confirming every single time, I have to think of the next logical conclusion as to why everyone on campus is staring at me as I walk through the quad this morning.

My phone buzzes in my pocket and I'm glad for the distraction. A text from Alex rolls in followed by a video link.

> It's a hit!

The podcast! With Ryan asking me out and Danika ripping every strand of hair out of my body last night, I nearly forgot that we went public yesterday. The video link takes me to our website where there are over fifty thousand views and counting. Hundreds of comments roll in and I switch over to the editing side of the website and notice even more questions from viewers, too. Alex was right. We might need to reassess Saturday's show.

Taking a seat on a bench in the quad, I click back to the video link and skim through the comments. Hundreds of them mention how hot Alex is, which he absolutely does not need to inflate his ego even more. Even more comments about how charming he is, which I can't deny either.

The grin doesn't leave my face as I continue to skim the page. Until I find them. The comments about me.

Who is this girl? Never seen her in my life.

Why is Alex Prescott doing a podcast with this nobody? I volunteer as tribute.

Petition for Alex to do this show by himself... or at least with someone more relevant. That comment had far too many likes for me. Closing my phone, I squeeze my eyes shut to block out the noise I just read and the eyes all around me. My phone vibrates in my hand, and I peek my eyes open just enough to see the name before sending it to voicemail.

Immediately, Alex calls again, but I ignore it. Noticing the time, I head to the library to hide in my study room until class in an hour. When I close the door to Study Room G6, I feel like I can finally take a deep breath. Even walking into the library, there were eyes on me. Whispers everywhere. It's like everyone on campus has seen the first episode. Plopping in the seat, I pull my phone out of my back pocket as it continues to vibrate. This time from texts.

> Sunshine, ignore those stupid comments

> Most of these people have no idea what they're talking about

> I say most because those comments about me being hot are totally spot on

I roll my eyes, but his humor can't break me from this mood. I knew this was a bad idea from the beginning. I knew I should've stayed behind the scenes. My phone vibrates one last time, and I read the text before shoving it into my backpack, all unanswered.

> Where are you?

I'm not ready to talk to Alex about this. He's going to be too overwhelmingly optimistic about it and I want to wallow. Taking out my laptop, I start working on the article about the alumni gala. I might as well take my mind off my failures by completing work I actually enjoy doing.

After thirty minutes of vigorous typing, a knock is heard on the study room door. *What the?* "Occupied," I yell as I continue writing. .

Another, louder knock and then an urgent voice calling for "sunshine." The knock persists until I get up out of my seat and open the door.

"What are you doing here? How did you even know I was here?"

Alex rolls passed me into the room. "I know you have a break in your schedule at this time on Tuesdays. Doesn't take a genius to deduce where you might be." *He knows my schedule?*

Closing the door behind him, I wander back over to my chair, content to ignore him. Even though he showed up and ramrodded his way into my study room, it doesn't mean I need to talk to him.

Alex closes my laptop screen, almost taking out my fingers with it.

"Hey!"

"I'm not letting you do this. I'm not letting you give up." He sat himself on the table, his feet resting on the chair next to mine.

"I'm not doing anything. But you have to admit, I was right. I told you I shouldn't have been in front of the camera."

Alex sighs and it sounds like he's been holding it in for decades. "That is bullshit and you know it. Fuck those people. All they've done is give us a new goal: Prove them wrong."

"That's easy for you to say. Nothing ever stops you, frat boy." I don't mean for the nickname to sound harsh, but I can't help the way it slipped off my tongue. Either way, Alex doesn't let the jest shake him.

"I understand you're upset and you're allowed to be. But what you're not allowed to do is let shitty people that are unhappy with their shitty lives make you feel any type of way. At all."

I can't meet his gaze, but I do notice the clock above the door and realize I should probably start heading to class. Packing my laptop in my bag, I stand from my chair and accidentally find myself and Alex face to face. As I move to get away from his personal space, Alex grips my chin and pulls my face to meet his.

"Are you listening to me, Margot?"

If there's one thing I've learned from all this time spent with Alex Prescott, he uses my government name, he means business.

I pull my face out of his grasp, but I don't move too far away, our eyes still linked. "I am listening," I reply, my voice small.

"Hiccups are bound to happen. It's how we react to them that makes all the difference. And we're gonna show these assholes that we can't be fucked with."

The more Alex talks, the more I want to believe him. He's so incredibly positive all the time, it's truly inspiring. Before I know it, I find myself nodding. "Yeah."

"Yeah what?"

"They can't fuck with us," I reply, a slight grin starting to form on my face.

Alex's smile is Oscar-worthy. "What's that, sunshine? Say it loud and proud!"

I can't help the giggle that escapes. "They can't fuck with us!" I yell loud enough that I surprise myself, but not too loud that I forget I'm in a library. Alex jumps off the table and pulls me in for a tight hug, his arms underneath mine as he sweeps me off my feet.

"Fuck yeah, that's my girl!"

I laugh as he spins me around, as much as he can within the tiny confines of the study room. Once my feet hit the floor again, Alex and I both take a moment, laughing as we catch our breath. Looking up, I see

Alex's face much closer than it was before. Not a *friendly* kind of close. A dangerous kind of close. His breath is minty and it hits my nose as he exhales sharply. He licks his lips.

I blink out of the trance, taking a step too far back. "Thanks, Alex." He blinks too as if he was caught in the same trance. Then he nods a few times. And then smiles.

Alex is right. We'll show these haters who's boss. And we'll do it together.

"Did he say where he's taking you?" Danika asks, her nose in her closet again, picking out the perfect outfit for my date with Ryan. "Location is a huge factor in outfit-decision making."

"Nope," I respond, although I'm only half paying attention. I know she's not going to let me make the final decision anyway so there's no point in even trying to insert my opinion.

I must be a masochist because, instead of leaving it alone like Alex suggested, I can't stop myself from scrolling through the comments again. For every ten mean comments about me, there's one semi-decent one so I guess there's that? On the other hand, for every ten nice comments about Alex, there's one incredibly dirty one. Not one ounce of hate for the golden boy. *Must be nice.*

Before I can finish reading the comment about my "nasally voice," my phone is ripped from my hand.

"Why are you still reading these comments?" Sydney asks, closing the tab on my phone and tossing it onto the bed next to me.

I have no reply but, truly, I don't know why I'm still making myself suffer. Maybe I'm hoping for a miracle and all the mean comments will change to nice ones?

Sydney takes my hands and drags me over to the vanity. Pushing me down in the chair, she puts her hands on both my shoulders. "We are not giving any more attention to internet assholes. Right now, we are going to glam you up and then you are going to have the best time on your date with Ryan. Is that clear?"

"Sir, yes, sir," I salute Sydney and she laughs. Sydney starts working her magic to make my face look unrecognizable while Danika finally pulls the right outfit for me out of her closet. Within fifteen minutes, I'm dressed in the tightest jeans Danika owns and a black halter that makes my shoulders pop, just in time too as Ryan texts me that he's downstairs.

Danika gives me a once over and then hands me her tan wedges. I really am lucky that she and I are the same size in basically everything. "Ok, Mar. Let loose, have lots of fun, and don't do anything I wouldn't do."

"That's not a lot."

"Exactly," she says with a wink. Sydney gives me a tight squeeze and then I grab my purse and head down to the lobby. I had expected to get into Ryan's car but instead I'm met with him standing in the foyer waiting for me.

"I would've come to your door, I just didn't know which apartment it was," he says as I approach him. "You look beautiful."

The blush creeps up my cheeks and is masked only by my wide smile. "Thank you," I say. "You don't look too bad yourself." Ryan smiles and holds the door for me to leave the building. His car is idling out front and he holds the passenger door open for me too.

"So where are you taking me?" I ask when we're both settled in.

Ryan smiles as he pulls away from the curb. "How do you feel about Italian?"

"I feel great about it," I say, but on the inside my stomach clenches. Italian meals can be expensive and if I want to go Dutch, I'm gonna have to make sure I don't pick the most expensive meal on the menu–not that I ever would.

Within minutes, Ryan pulls up to a cute little mom and pop Italian restaurant and my gut loosens a little bit. When we enter, Ryan motions two fingers to the hostess and we're seated immediately.

Ryan pulls out my chair and I sit as gracefully as I can. He really is quite the gentleman. It's a stark difference from how Alex treats me sometimes. *Why are you thinking about Alex right now?*

"I hear the penne ala vodka is amazing here," Ryan comments as he opens his menu. I hum in response. If I'm going to give Ryan a real chance, I need to not let thoughts of my *friend* Alex leak into my brain during this dinner. Especially not thoughts about that moment we had in the study room. When he picked up and then put me down...*Stop it!*

"I'm definitely going to get that then," I reply, closing my menu.

Ryan laughs. "You're not even going to peruse the menu?"

"Nope, I trust your judgment," I say, taking a sip of the fresh water the waiter poured when we sat down. Ryan closes his menu, too.

"I'm going to get the same," he says definitively. "Well, that was easy."

I chuckle. Yes, it was. So far everything about this date has been easy.

When the waiter comes back, Ryan orders our entrees and he's polite to the waiter (something I always look out for) when asking for extra bread in our bread basket. Ryan asks me about my family and growing up in the South. I give him the abridged version, saving the real juicy details for a later date–if there is one. Ryan tells me about growing up in California and how he made his way over to the Northeast to go to Tomlin.

"Once I got that baseball scholarship, I couldn't say no."

"Would you have wanted to stay in California if you didn't get this scholarship?" I ask, finishing the last of my fourth glass of water.

Ryan had been right about the pasta, it was amazing. We had just finished eating dinner when the dessert menu arrived on our table.

"I'm not sure. All I know is, I haven't regretted my decision to come here for one second." He smiles and I match his expression.

Ryan holds up the dessert menu with a questioning look. He's letting me make the decision to extend the night or not. While I am having a good time, the edits for Saturday's podcast taping start to creep into the back of my mind. And the fact that I have class at nine tomorrow morning. It was nice that Ryan wanted to see me during the week instead of waiting until the weekend, but it does mean that I'm not really in for a long night on a Wednesday.

I think my indecisiveness is showing on my face because Ryan makes the decision for us. "Next time, we'll go for ice cream," he says and I grin in relief.

After a quick but non-confrontational fight over Ryan paying for the check, we grab our coats and head out. We ride in comfortable silence back to my apartment and I can't help but feel good. This date was really nice. Ryan is really nice. The whole evening I've felt comfortable and safe. So why, when he pulled up to my building, did I find myself shying away?

A goodnight kiss is standard for first dates.

"I had a really good time tonight," Ryan says, putting the car in park but leaving the engine running.

"I did, too," I agree.

There's a pause. A silence in the air. Ryan doesn't lean in. But neither do I.

After a second, I smile. "Goodnight, Ryan."

"Goodnight, Margot," he says. It's a clear dismissal of the date but not a dismissal of the possibility of another one. Ryan idles outside the building until I get in the door and then he pulls away from the curb. I take a deep breath. Nice. That was...nice.

Chapter Twenty-One

Alex

IT'S TIMES LIKE THESE I wish I had a dog, just to have an excuse to walk by her building as she's getting home from this date. I shouldn't care that she's on a date. In fact, I don't care. All I care about is that she's ready to work on this podcast since now my reputation is entwined with this thing.

Plopping on the couch, I make myself comfortable next to Kai who's typing away on his laptop. "Hey, man."

Kai only grunts in acknowledgement, not looking away from the screen. I can't help but peek over his shoulder and when I do, Kai shuts the screen before I can get a glimpse.

"What's up?" He says, his voice sounding and failing to sound natural.

If this were anyone else, I would just leave it alone but Kai is one of my best friends and he's been MIA for weeks now. Something's going on. "Are you okay?"

Kai scoffs, "Yeah, man, I'm fine. Why?" He drops his laptop on the coffee table before getting up from the couch. I follow as he walks into the kitchen and opens a beer. He offers me one, but I shake my head.

"You just seem off. You've seemed off for a while, actually," I say, leaning back against the sink and crossing my arms.

Kai thinks for a minute as he takes a sip of his beer. "I don't know what you're talking about," he says, pursing his lips. "Just got a lot of classes, I guess. Busy." Kai shrugs and walks out of the room and up the stairs to his bedroom. I should keep trying to get to the bottom of this, but if he doesn't want to tell me, then there's really nothing more I can do.

Instead of harping on it, I pull out my phone and check the clock for the hundredth time. When I do, I'm pleasantly surprised to see a text from Margot. It must've come in while I was talking to Kai. Eagerly, I open the message, hoping for some kind of "SOS" or "Save me from this disaster" or anything that can get me to stop thinking about Ryan's hand on her back.

> I think we need to replan our script for Saturday. Are you free to meet tomorrow?

I pull the phone back and look at the time again. It's half past ten and she's...texting me? What happened to Ryan? Don't ask. Don't ask. *Don't ask.*

> Why are you texting me while you're on a date?

> I'm not on a date anymore. Ryan dropped me home fifteen minutes ago

If she were on a date with me, we certainly wouldn't be home before midnight. Well, unless we were home *together.* She also wouldn't be texting other guys right after. She'd have no reason to.

> That bad, huh?

> What? No, the date was fine. I just have early classes tomorrow

> Just fine, huh?

Believe it or not, it's actually none of your business

> Isn't this the kind of thing friends talk about? Dating and relationships and shit?

...

You seriously want to hear about my date with Ryan?

No. Yes.

Fuck.

> Let's meet Friday afternoon. We'll rewrite the script and you can tell me all about Rowdy Ryan and your Really Hot Date, ok?

Those three little grey dots appear and disappear for a few minutes before her reply comes in.

Fine. Cafe Royale. 3pm

I send her a kissy face back that I know she rolls her eyes at. I have no idea why I decided that I want to hear about her date with Ryan when in fact, it's probably the very last thing on this Earth that I want to hear.

I can't help but feel better though. There's no way she had that good of a time and then went home at a reasonable hour. But she is very practical...

I shake my head to get the thoughts out. Margot is my friend. That's it.

That.

Is.

It.

—⁓⋀⋀⋀⋀⋀⋀⋀⁓—

While I'm used to people looking my way when I walk by, even I can't get used to the attention on campus. By Friday morning, everyone and their mother had seen the first episode of the podcast and my phone was blowing up with texts about it. Some from my friends and brothers ribbing me about it and others from random girls–how they got my phone number, I'll never know–asking if we could...well, you know. While I've never been one to shy away from attention, this has been a little too much, even for me.

"Alex." I hear a voice call my name and thankfully it's a familiar one. As I turn, I see Gia walking up the quad path toward me. She gives me a smile and wave, which I return as I wait for her to catch up to me.

"Hey, G," I say as she walks to my side. Together, we head toward the library where I'm meeting Keith and Devon before our next class.

"I saw the podcast," she says with a slight smirk.

I roll my eyes. "Cutting right to the chase, huh."

"Hey, I thought it was good!" She demands, her hands raised in surrender. "You and that girl really had some great chemistry."

I ponder that thought for a moment. I hadn't watched the episode at all, too embarrassed to look at myself on screen like that, but it didn't really occur to me how others would perceive our friendship.

"You think so?" We enter the library and head downstairs toward the stacks and study rooms.

"Yeah, you guys had good banter. You seemed very comfortable together," Gia replies. "She your girlfriend?"

"No," my reply is immediate and a knot forms in my gut, almost as if I'm betraying Margot. No, she's not my girlfriend. She's made it abundantly clear she wants nothing to do with me in that way. Not that I want anything to do with her either. But still, I don't want Gia to think she's meaningless to me. "She's just a friend."

Gia nods thoughtfully. I can tell she didn't ask out of jealousy or anything like that. Just a friend catching up with another friend. *See, I can be friends with girls.*

As we hit the bottom of the stairs, I spot the guys working at a table by the window.

"Well," Gia starts. "If you're not dating her, you wanna hang out tonight? It's been a minute since we've...hung out." She looks up at me with those doe eyes that have the power to make me melt. *Okay, maybe not...*

Now that I think about it, it has been a while since I've *hung out* with anyone really. I hadn't hooked up with anyone since the semester started and definitely not since meeting Margot. I mean, when would I even have the time? When I'm not with Margot, I'm in class or at the gym. Not a lot of time for extracurriculars with a schedule like that.

Maybe I should just hook up with Gia. There's clearly something pent up in me right now, especially with how I acted while Margot was on her date. Maybe I need to just let loose and forget about her for a night.

But I do have plans with Margot this afternoon and I'm sure she'll be coming to the house party with her roommates. I wouldn't want to ignore her while she's at my house. That would be rude. And it would also no doubt put her right back into Ryan's waiting arms.

"Alex?"

I blink and am reminded that Gia is patiently waiting for a response from me. Luckily, being the cool girl that she is, she lets me off the hook.

"I'll be at the KA party tonight, maybe we'll catch up then." She touches my arm with a slight smile before turning and walking toward the other side of the library. With a confusing sigh, I head over toward Keith and Devon.

"Yo, what's Gia up to? That girl is seriously hot," Devon says as a greeting as I sit at their table.

"Yeah," I reply absentmindedly. I have no idea what I'm doing but I need to figure it out quick. I thought being friends with Margot would be easy, but this feeling in my gut is not going away.

⎯⎯⎺⎺⋀⋀⋀⋀⋀⋁⋀⋁⋁⋁⋀⋁⋁⋁⋀⋀⎺⎺⎯⎯

By the time three rolls around, I'm sitting at the same booth that Margot and I met at the first time, a black coffee in front of me and an oatmilk whatever waiting on her side of the table. Margot walks in, does a double take between me and the counter before she comes to sit down.

"I didn't expect you to be on time," she says, taking the empty seat across from me.

"Why not?"

"Well, you're always late to public speaking class."

I laugh, taking a sip of my coffee. "To be honest, I don't really care about that class."

"But you care about this?" Margot starts taking her laptop out of her bag.

"I guess I do."

She hesitates for just the slightest moment, but I catch it. Pulling her laptop out of the sleeve, she opens it up and pulls up the podcast website. She absentmindedly reaches for the coffee and takes a long sip. "Thanks for the coffee."

I nod with a small smile. There's a slight awkwardness to Margot. Almost as if she's nervous about something. I push the thought aside, knowing she'd be open if she had something on her mind. Margot is nothing if not forthcoming about her feelings.

She jumps right into her show notes, pulling out the new questions that she believes will be better than the ones we had planned. We rework the script for about an hour, working tirelessly until Margot is satisfied with the changes.

"Thanks for meeting with me to fix this up. I think it'll be much better now," she says, putting her laptop away.

"Hold on, sunshine. Where are you running off to?"

She pauses with her backpack slouching off one shoulder. "What do you mean?"

"I was promised date details. Go on. Spill," I lean my elbows on the table and put my chin in my palms, the picture of attention.

Margot breathes out a laugh and looks at her watch. "Fine, but can we walk and talk? I gotta get home."

I get up from the table, throwing my empty coffee cup out as we walk out the door. "What's the rush?" I ask, as nonchalantly as possible as we head in the direction of our homes. I should tell her that I drove to the cafe and I'd drive her home but that would be a two minute conversation, rather than a ten minute one. And for some reason I'm masochistic enough to want to hear all the sordid details so a walk it is. I'll pick up my car later.

"No rush, just, uh... Sydney is waiting for me to help her with an article for the newspaper." She's lying. I know that she's lying. I just don't know why she's lying.

"Well then, talk fast," I reply, trying to make light of the situation. I'm still not sure why I'm even pushing this conversation, but something in me needs to hear about this date. I need to know what they did, where they went, what they talked about. *Did they kiss?* Does she like him? Every question and potential answer makes my stomach clench more and more.

Margot rolls her eyes as she walks in step with me. "What do you want me to say? He picked me up, took me to an Italian restaurant. We had pasta and bread. It was nice," she says, her voice clipped.

"Nice?" I bump into her playfully.

"Yes, nice."

"Is that what you want? Someone nice?" Her eyes jump to mine. I meet her gaze for a second but keep walking, definitely noticing her steps faltering a bit. For half a block, she's quiet and it's clear she's in her head. At this point, I'm not sure how safe that place is for me so I stay quiet too.

We pass the turn for my block, but I continue walking with Margot to her apartment.

"You don't have to walk me to my door, frat boy," she says and immediately the tension leaks out of the air, leaving a smile on my face again.

"Maybe I just want the extra exercise," I shrug and Margot nods with a giggle. Her apartment building comes into sight in the middle of the street. "You guys are coming to the party tonight, right?"

"Yeah, Ryan is coming to walk us and—" Immediately Margot closes her mouth tight as if she accidentally let it slip that her and Ryan would be coming to my party together. Like it was a secret. Like I would care.

And all at once, I realize I do. I do fucking care. She wants to show up at my fucking house with another guy?

Like a goddamn miracle, Gia leaves the same building that Margot is about to enter and I seize my opportunity.

"Gia," I shout and she gives me a huge wave and smile as she walks toward us.

"Hey guys. Great podcast—"

She doesn't get a chance to complete her sentence before I sweep her up with my left hand and crush her mouth to mine with my right. I kiss her with the force of someone in love, and it takes her a second or two to catch on but when she does, she matches my motion with her own flair. I ignore Margot next to us, no idea what expression she has on her face right now and trying my fucking hardest not to care. If she wants to date Ryan, bring him to my house in front of all my friends, make a fool of me...she can do whatever the hell she wants. And so can I. At this point, I have no idea what the hell I'm doing, but the train has already left the station. All that's left to do now is let it ride.

After a moment, I release Gia and she catches her breath. "Well, hello, handsome," she says, her hand still on my arm for stability. "I was just heading over to yours actually, figured I'd get there early before all the good beer is gone."

Perfect. "I'll walk with you," I say to Gia before turning back to Margot, her expression blank as a newly purchased canvas. "See you later, yeah?"

She nods a few times as I wrap my arm around Gia's shoulders and lead her back the way I just came from toward frat row. I don't turn around to check, but when I'm satisfied that Margot is safely inside her building, I drop my arm, putting both my hands in my pockets.

"You got it bad, don't you?" Gia laughs next to me. I almost forgot she was there.

"Shit, G. I'm sorry. I shouldn't have done that to you."

Gia waves me off easily. "I get it. And I don't mind. I mean, as long as I don't get bitch-slapped, I'm down to help you with your cause."

I run my hand through my hair. "What cause is that?"

"Obviously you want to make her jealous."

Do I? It begs the question, why would I want to make my *friend* jealous? Is it because the thought of her and Ryan, her and any other guy, makes me physically ill?

I sigh loudly. "I'm in way over my head here."

Gia laughs as we ascend the steps to the house. "Yes, you are. But you know the best cure for that?" She grabs the door and holds it open for me. Walking into the kitchen, she grabs two beers from the cooler and hands one to me. "Alcohol."

I take the drink from her hands, gratefully. "To a good cure," I say, holding my bottle neck up to hers. She clinks her drink against mine.

"To not getting bitch-slapped." We laugh and take sips of our drinks. The door swings open and no less than twenty people enter the house. Let the party commence.

Chapter Twenty-Two

Margot

By the time the four of us arrive, the party is in full swing. Ryan picked us up a few hours after I got home from the meeting with Alex, those hours spent prepping and pampering for this second-ish date.

I felt bad lying to Alex about why I needed to get home earlier, and it turned out it didn't matter anyway since I let the cat out the bag that Ryan had asked to come to the party with us—with me—while we were on our date. Alex would've seen us together there anyway but for some reason, I felt guilty about the situation. No reason I can truly understand, but the feeling is there nonetheless.

But that girl. Gia? He kissed that girl right in front of me. Like it was nothing. Like I wasn't even there. I had no idea who she was, but she seemed *very* familiar with Alex and him with her. I know for a fact she's not his girlfriend, frat boy royalty made it clear he doesn't do relationships. But who is she then? Hook up? Friend with benefits? Whoever she is to him, she's completely beautiful. I wouldn't stand a chance. Not that there's a competition for his affections. Not that I would want to win that competition either way.

My thoughts are still spiraling as we enter the house and walk into the frat party chaos. One thing I've learned the past few years at TU is that fraternity parties start early and end late. Seeing as it's about nine by the time we walk in, I'd say the party's been in full swing for more than a few hours by now. A fact made all the more clear when Danika drags us to the kitchen where a cooler that was previously filled with beer stands empty in the middle of the room.

"Devon, what the fuck!" Danika shouts at Alex's housemate as he enters the room. She gestures toward the empty cooler in disbelief.

"Don't worry, gorgeous. There's a full cooler in the backyard. Come on, I'll show you guys." Devon leads the way toward the back door and we all follow. The first thing I see is the fire pit that Alex and I sat at and made the deal that started this crazy ride.

"We should sit there later," Ryan says in my ear, motioning his head toward the fire pit as he snakes his arm around my waist. Looking up at him over my shoulder, I give him a smile.

Devon grabs a few beers from the outside cooler and hands us each one. Just as I open my mouth to say thank you, a loud cheer sounds from the corner of the yard and all our attention is turned toward a highly active game of beer pong.

That's when I notice Alex, a bottle of beer raised to his smiling lips, the fire shining against his face. God, he really is beautiful. He rests his head on that girl's shoulder before turning his attention our way.

"Sunshine!" He calls, and I can tell he's not himself. His words are slurred and his eyes are glassy. He can barely manage to stay upright, resting his body on Gia's shoulders, but it doesn't seem like she minds. "Sun, come play! Bring your–" he hiccups loudly "–friends. Come, come here." He is insistent and while I have no interest in playing beer pong, I feel like I should do what he says before he comes over and drags me to the table.

Ryan's hand is still on my back as I sigh and walk toward Alex.

"Hey, frat boy," I say with a grin, and Alex's brilliant smile smacks me in the face.

"I love it when you call me that," he says and I cock my head in amused confusion.

Gia pulls Alex back toward their side of the table. "We playing or what?" It almost seems like she made the move to ensure he didn't say anything else he might regret in his inebriated state, but I might be overthinking it.

"Sun, RyRy, you guys are up," Alex says, motioning with his half empty drink at the other side of the table.

Ryan speaks into my ear. "We don't have to play if you don't want to."

When I look up at him, his eyes are tight, as if playing beer pong is the very last thing he'd like to be doing right now. But if I know Alex, and I'm really starting to know him well, he isn't going to let me walk away from this table.

"No, it's fine. I want to play," I reply to Ryan, giving him the most genuine smile I can muster before walking over to the table. Ryan lets his hand drop from my back as he follows me over. Sydney and Danika take up spots on the audience line, the former a nervous wreck and the latter excited as hell.

For a few rounds, we take turns throwing the balls into the little cups full of beer. It turns out I'm spectacularly bad at this game. Luckily, Ryan is actually good and pretty much carries the team. We split the cups we have to drink, but Alex is so drunk that he doesn't even seem to be aiming for the cups so our drinking is limited.

After Ryan wins us the game rather quickly, I'm relieved and ready to head inside and do anything else.

"Good game, guys," Alex says, sauntering up to us. Well, he probably means to be sauntering, but he's really stumbling drunkenly. He ended up drinking a lot of the cups that Ryan sunk and still held onto his own bottle to sip in between throws.

Ryan nods to Alex and then puts his hand on my back to guide me back inside.

"Hey, bud. Let's keep our hands to ourselves, yeah?" Alex says, stepping closer to Ryan and me. Immediately, I hold my breath, waiting for a blow out. Gia walks up to our tight circle and puts her hand on Alex's arm to pull him back a bit. The motion causes him to drop his bottle, which hits the concrete floor and shatters.

We all step back from the spray, but Alex reaches down to clean up the mess.

"Alex, wait, don't—"

"Fuck," he cries, lifting his hand and letting the steady line of blood drip off his finger tips. I bend down to examine his cut and the second my skin touches his, his eyes shoot to mine.

"Do you have a first aid kit?"

Alex nods, his gaze not leaving mine. "Upstairs."

I nod, too, before standing back up and looking over at the girl he's been spending the entire evening with.

She holds her hands up. "I don't do blood," she says with a shrug before going inside the house. If she is his girlfriend, she's an awful one.

I look back down at Alex, his eyes now glued to his bleeding hand, and I just hope he doesn't need stitches. I go to help him up, but Ryan pulls me back a bit.

"Margot, let him fix his own messes. Look at him, he's drunk."

I narrow my eyes. "I'm not going to just leave him like this. Just let me get him cleaned up and then I'll meet you back inside, okay?"

Ryan looks back and forth between my eyes a few times before sighing. "Fine, let me help you."

He goes to grab Alex by the shoulders, but he jerks himself away. "Fuck you, I don't need your help." He says before storming into the house and I can't tell if he meant it for Ryan or for me. Regardless, I'm not going to let him stammer around a packed house of drunken idiots. Without a thought, I follow after him, hurriedly.

I see him standing in the kitchen, looking in the fridge for another drink. Without a word, I grab him by the shirt and pull him away from the fridge, out of the kitchen and up the stairs to his room.

Before I close the door behind us, I search the bathroom across the hall for the first aid kit and a towel. Then I walk into Alex's room to find him sitting on the bed, blood still dripping from his hand. Wrapping the towel around his hand, I try to soak up some of the carnage before I can get to work on cleaning him up.

Kneeling before him as he sits on the bed, I grip the towel wrapped around his hand and I look up at him.

"Well, this is a nice sight," Alex smirks and I reach up and punch him in his good arm. Hard. "Ouch! What the fuck!" Alex yells.

"What is wrong with you? Why did you almost start something with Ryan out there and why are you so drunk?" There's no point in beating around the bush. I want answers and I'm just hoping he's not too drunk to give them to me.

"I don't know what you're talking about." He tries to pull his hand from my grasp, but I hold it tighter, causing him to wince in pain.

"Here's what's going to happen. I'm going take this towel off, clean up your hand and assess the damage. While I do that, you're going to tell me what the hell is going on. Got it?" I keep holding the towel tightly.

Alex sighs. "Fine."

Slowly, I unwrap the towel and put it underneath his arm just in case more blood starts to drip out. Taking an antibacterial wipe from the first aid kit, I clean up the excess blood on his hand, paying close attention to the cut itself and trying to go slowly.

"How'd you get so good at cleaning wounds?"

"My brother and dad both work in a factory. Came home with more than a few cuts that never really got tended too while they were on the clock." Once it's all clean and I can tell he doesn't need stitches, I pull out the antibiotic ointment and apply a healthy portion to the cut before adding a clean, large bandage on top to seal it all in. "Good as new," I say, moving to stand up from my kneeling position. I'm still waiting for Alex to speak on the events of tonight but he hasn't. Instead, when I look down at him, I see his eyes are drooping, about to close.

"I'm tired, sunshine..." He falls backward onto the bed, letting his wounded hand dangle off the bed. I sigh, standing over him. *What am I going to do with this boy?* I move toward the end of the bed. "No, don't leave," he says in his sleepy state and I can't tell if he's said it on purpose or if he's talking in his sleep. "Everything is better when you're here."

I don't have the mental capacity to unpack that statement right now. Pulling off his shoes, I place them on the floor one at a time before grabbing a blanket from the closet. Looking down at this sleeping form, I can't help but remember what it is about him that makes me care about him. As a friend.

"Sleep, you idiot," I say with a smile, placing the blanket down on top of him.

Alex smiles too. "Sunshine..." he sighs before the snoring starts. I giggle quietly as I head for the door. I know he said he wanted me to stay, but he was probably confusing me with the girl from downstairs. Either way, I couldn't stay up here with him even if I wanted to. I've got my friends waiting downstairs. And Ryan. I think of Ryan as I close Alex's door gently behind me. Ryan is a nice guy who wants to be more than just my friend. Shouldn't that mean I should give him a real chance?

—⁓⁓⁓⁓—

Alex doesn't come downstairs for the rest of the night. Not that I expected him to, he was out cold when I left him all tucked into bed. We stay for a couple more hours, watching Danika flirt with the poor defenseless freshmen. A few times Ryan wandered off to say hi to friends, but he mostly stuck by my side, whispering jokes and comments in my ear every now and then.

It's different, having a boy show genuine interest in me. I'm not used to it, but I'm trying to adapt. It helps that every time Danika looks our way, the heart eyes emoji flashes across her face.

By the time we're ready to leave, Sydney is linked with Danika who is singing her famous rendition of *Don't Stop Believin'* while Ryan and I trail a few steps behind them.

"You know you don't have to walk us home, it's the complete opposite direction of your house."

"And miss the show?" Ryan gestures toward Danika who just completely butchered the high note at the end. She and Sydney collapse in a fit of giggles as we continue the walk.

"Fair enough," I reply with a smile. As we walk, Ryan tentatively slips his hand in mine and when I open my palm to invite him in, he latches on, interlacing our fingers tightly. We walk like this for another block before my apartment comes into view.

Danika grabbed onto Sydney's hand and took off running toward the building.

"See you inside, Margot and thanks for walking with us, Ryan!" Sydney yells as she's being pulled away, knowing exactly what Danika is doing. Even while drunk, Danika still has her motives.

I laugh and roll my eyes at their antics. "I would invite you in, but I'm not sure what exactly you'd be walking into."

Ryan laughs. "Nah, that's okay. It's late, I should be getting back anyway."

I nod, going to pull my hand from his, but he only holds it tighter. When I look up to meet his eyes, they're boring into mine with an intensity I wasn't expecting. I know without a shadow of a doubt that he is going to kiss me. Where the doubt comes in is if I want him to or not.

Ryan leans in and his breath hits my face. It's not minty like Alex's. Why am I noticing that? Why am I thinking about Alex right now? Instead of doing that, I close my eyes, leaning closer into him.

Everything's better when you're here.

I blink my eyes open and pull back. "Thanks for the walk. I'll call you, okay?"

Ryan steps back, letting my hand drop softly. He gives me a tight smile, and I turn away toward the door. "Is there something going on with you and Prescott? Something more than just this weird friendship you have?"

He has every right to ask, he is the one who's been giving me the attention that Alex hasn't. But still, I don't know if he deserves to know the full truth about us. I don't even know the full truth about us.

"No, Ryan. He's just my friend. That's it."

"Because I like you, Margot. I really like you and if I can avoid a painful situation down the line, I'd prefer to take that option now rather than later."

When I left Alex's room, I had vowed to myself to give it my best shot with Ryan. Alex and I are nothing more than friends and it's time I proved that to myself. And to him. Even if it's not so clear to me which *him* I'm referring to.

"I like you, too," I tell him, closing the distance again. I should let myself have this. Danika is always telling me to let myself live, well...no one else is trying to live with me more than Ryan is.

Reaching up on my toes, I place a light, gentle kiss to his lips that clearly takes him by surprise. He seems to buffer for a few seconds before snapping out of his trance and wrapping his arms around my waist, pulling me tighter. His neck cranes down so I don't have to stretch and his lips move against mine again, more hurried than before, more urgent.

The kiss is simple, easy. Like a walk through the park on a spring morning. With a gentle caress, his hands move down my body like he's trying to make sure every inch of my back is touched. There are no tongues, the softness of his lips is enough for now. After a few seconds, I pull back and Ryan smiles.

"Goodnight, Margot."

"Goodnight," I reply, grinning widely before turning around and finally entering the building. I press my fingers to my lips to hold in the feeling of Ryan against my skin. It really was a nice kiss.

Is that what you want? Someone nice?

I shake my head furiously, getting Alex's words out of my head. I need to go to sleep, but I know Dani and Syd are waiting impatiently on the other side of the door, so I put on my best face and gear up to tell them the bedtime story they're waiting for.

Chapter Twenty-Three

Margot

ROLLING OVER IN MY bed, I feel a soft kiss on my nose and I open my eyes to see Ryan smiling at me. He pulls me close, wrapping his hand around my neck to kiss my lips and I sigh into his embrace. Feeling more risque than usual on a Saturday morning, I kiss him deeper before pushing him onto his back and straddling his hips. Ryan grabs my waist and sits up to pull me to his chest. I let my head fall back, my hair cascading down my back as I do my best to hold in the moan that's threatening to escape from my mouth.

When I lower my head, it's now Alex who holds my gaze with a look that would have me soaking if I wasn't already. His lips are at my ear. He's calling me sunshine and a slew of other *dirtier* things and my head falls aside to allow him more access to my neck. I feel him smile against my pulse before he starts peppering the space with kisses.

With a jolt, I snap back into reality. There's a sheen of sweat across my brow, and I blink a couple of times before grabbing my notebook and reluctantly writing everything down. I know Danika is never going to let me live this down, but I have to show her so she can help make sense of this mess in my mind.

There's a knock at my door before I can get out of bed and Sydney pops her head. "Heading to the gym. Need a ride to campus?"

I look at the clock on my phone, also noticing a good morning text from Ryan waiting for me. I do need to get some work done, but most of it I can do from my desk here, so I shake my head. I pull myself out of bed as she leaves the doorway and walk out to find Dani still sleeping on the couch.

"Morning, huns," I say loudly, dropping the notebook on her stomach. Danika grunts from the impact and mumbles something about "bitches" before rolling over onto her side. I anticipate the sounds of the book falling to the floor but instead I look to see Danika cuddling it like a pillow as her snores pick up.

"See ya later," Sydney says with a chuckle as she leaves. I walk into the kitchen and grab a cup of coffee that sweet Sydney made before she left. Seriously no idea what I would do without her.

Grabbing another mug, I fill it the way Danika likes and sit on the coffee table in front of her. I place the cup in front of her and move it back and forth, wafting the rich smell under her nose. Danika sniffs and then blindly reaches out for the cup, which I immediately pull away from her and place on the table next to me.

Dani peeks one eye open and sees her mug out of reach. "You're a mean, cruel person, Margot Elaine." I remain silent as she sighs and sits up. "Can you just read it to me? My brain isn't firing on all cylinders this morning."

"Absolutely not," I say firmly, causing Danika to sit up a little straighter.

"Oh this is gonna be good," she says, taking a fortifying sip of her coffee. She places the mug back down and cracks open my journal to the most recent page.

Immediately her jaw drops. It stays dropped as she continues reading. And then it drops more.

"You saucy minx!" She finally looks up at me and gives me a little smack in the arm. I know my face is as red as a tomato but I don't shy away. "Well this one is super obvious, you don't need me for this." She hands me the notebook and grabs the mug from the table.

"I've never had a sex dream about two guys before."

After taking a sip, she lowers her mug to her lap. "Have you ever had a sex dream about one guy?"

I think for a moment. "No."

Danika shakes her head with a giggle. "Girly pop, you've got it bad. And now you've got a choice. The hottie you're dating or the guy you've decided is your *friend*." Danika adds air quotes around the word friend. I roll my eyes.

She puts the mug down and walks toward the bathroom, plopping onto the toilet. I follow her like a lost puppy. "Alex *is* my friend, nothing more."

"Then the choice should be simple," Danika replies easily. After washing up, she sticks her toothbrush in her mouth and hands mine to me. She tries to talk while we brush but she knows I can't understand a word she says so I just ignore her, making sure I hit every nook and cranny of my mouth with the minty brush.

We both spit and Danika continues her monologue as if I could hear everything she had said. "There's just something about Alex. He looks like he'd talk you through it, you know?"

"Oh my god, I'm going to my room. Goodbye, psycho." I head back past the kitchen, grabbing my backpack off the island stool.

"Hey!" she laughs from behind me. "You asked for my advice!"

"I take it back!" I call before shutting my door and welcoming the quiet. I can't think about Ryan or Alex or anything else besides my psychology homework. And for the next few hours, that's what I do.

—wwwwwwww—

Swinging the lobby door open, I'm shocked to see Alex standing outside, leaning his body against his jeep. There's an iced cup of coffee in his hand, the condensation leaking through his fingers.

"This is cold," he whines like a child.

I take the coffee from his out-stretched hands. "How long have you been waiting here?" Wiping the excess condensation on my sweatshirt sleeve, I notice the ice is almost entirely melted.

"I figured you'd leave a little early to catch the bus so I wanted to beat you to the punch." He shrugs nonchalantly.

I take a sip of the drink, the same I always get. "Thanks," I grin and he opens my door before swinging around to get into the driver's side.

"I owed you for the patch job last night," Alex says as he pulls away from the curb. He holds up his hand to show a fresh bandage.

I laugh. "I'm surprised you remember that."

"I remember everything," he says quietly. The rest of the ride is a blur of familiar scenery as we quietly make our way to campus. Pulling into the fitness center lot, Alex parks as close to the media building as possible.

When he shuts off the engine, I move to open the door but am stopped by Alex's hand on my leg.

"I'm sorry about last night. I acted like a caveman."

I shrug. "You were drunk."

"That's no excuse."

I pause for a moment. He's right, it's really not. But I didn't expect him to own up to it like this. "You're okay?" I ask, motioning to his hand.

"Yeah, I followed what you did yesterday with the cleaning and the ointment before putting on a fresh band-aid." He waves his hand to show me and then places it right back down on my knee. "How was the rest of your night?"

"It was fine. Good, we just hung out." I say casually, making an intentional decision not to tell him about the kiss with Ryan. And especially not tell him about the dream. He loosens his hand, and I take it as an all clear to leave the car and we do, gathering back together on the other side of the doors and walk toward the media building. Nathan had texted me that he was waiting in the studio so we walked right there so as to not lose any of our time.

"Hey, guys," Nathan greets us with a warm smile as we head into the sound studio. We smile back at him, as I take my sweatshirt off revealing the tight top I choose to wear for today's session. Well...the one Danika helped me choose, in an effort to be more likable. As I pull the hoodie over my head, the shirt rides up, revealing a sliver of my stomach. When I look at him again, his gaze is directly on my body, specifically that part and I pull the shirt down quickly and twist around, dropping the sweatshirt and hiding the blush that's crawling up my cheeks.

Alex drops his bag and hangs his jacket on the studio chair. "You ready, sunshine?"

I let out a deep sigh, "As ready as I'll ever be."

"Let's do it," Nathan says and I grab my notes as Alex and I head into the recording studio, taking the same seats as last time.

After we settle in, Nathan gives us a thumbs up and the red recording light turns on.

"Helllllllllllo, everybody!" Alex says, his signature greeting now. "Thank you for tuning in to our show *Ask Alex*, where you send in your questions and I answer them as best I can. I'm your host, Alex Prescott and as always I'm partnered with the ever lovely Margot Davis."

He's really laying it on thick and I can only assume it's because he's trying to get ahead of the mean comments that I'm sure are going to come in about me. If it seems like he likes me, then maybe the commentators won't have a leg to stand on.

"Hey, folks," I say in greeting. "We've got a really great episode for you today so let's jump right in." Gathering my notecards, I find the first question.

"Alright, Alex. First question. Are you ready?" I say with feigned seriousness.

"I am ready, Margot," he replies in a tone that matches mine.

"Sarah P. asks: 'How do you balance school work and a social life in college?' She says she's drowning in work and hardly ever gets time to go out with friends."

"Well, first of all, thanks, Sarah." Alex winks at the camera and I roll my eyes. Standard procedure. "And secondly, the answer is easy. You don't."

"Care to elaborate?"

"Honestly, sunshine, I think you're better equipped to answer this question. You're the workaholic here."

It was the first time he called me 'sunshine' on camera. I don't even think he did it on purpose, I think it just slipped out like he always does. Still, the nickname isn't going to do me any favors with the internet trolls.

"Well, I wouldn't exactly call myself a workaholic—"

Alex scoffs. "What would you call it then? You're in the library more than your own apartment."

"Just because I spend a lot of time on my schoolwork doesn't mean that I don't make time for my own things. You should know that, I go to your parties, don't I?"

This conversation is getting a little too personal for my taste, but I keep it going. We can always edit out anything we don't want to use afterward.

"You do but you've been known to bring a book with you," Alex laughs.

"Those books are for pleasure, you ass," I push him and he just laughs harder. "We're getting off topic. If I have any advice for balancing school and social life it's just to prioritize. Don't drive yourself crazy, just budget your time well and you'll find that you'll get done what needs to be done and still be able to go to a party or two over the weekend."

I shrug, because that's the best I can do.

"Yeah, and you know that the Kappa parties are the best so you should make sure to prioritize going to those parties," Alex jokes and I scoff. "You don't agree? Whose parties are better, then? The Deltas? Please."

He's skating on thin ice right now. There's no reason to bring up personal things like this. This podcast isn't about me. When the banter gets too close to home, it's time to switch up the topic.

"I wouldn't know." I shrug. "I've never been to one. Time for another question?"

Alex looks like he wants to keep this conversation going but the tone of my voice informs him that I'm ready to move on. He shuts his mouth and nods for me to continue.

We get through two more questions from listeners about life in the frat house and how to keep from gaining that "freshman fifteen" before it's time to get to the Alex-specific question.

"This question comes from Hannah L—and if you wink again, I'll strangle you."

Alex looks hesitant for a moment as he thanks Hannah for writing in but I know he winks once I look down at my notecard.

"Hannah wants to know your biggest deal breaker in a relationship." Putting my notes down, I give Alex my full attention. Not because I'm very interested in his answer, mostly because I...am very interested in his answer.

"That's a great question," Alex says genuinely. He takes a couple of seconds to think about his response. "I'd have to say my biggest deal breaker is dishonesty. There's no reason to be with someone if you can't trust them completely. If you're a dishonest person, I want nothing to do with you."

For some reason, I didn't expect him to take the question so seriously, but I'm glad that he did. It's a great response. One I completely agree with.

"Margot, what about you?"

My gut instinct is to say that these people don't care about my answers, but I don't want to add more fuel to the internet hate fire. "I agree with you. Honesty is very important." I want to elaborate more but again, this isn't *Ask Margot* so I leave it at that.

Alex and I give our send off goodbye and the recording light overhead shuts off just as Nathan gives us a thumbs up.

"Another great session," Nathan says as we open the studio door.

"Thanks, man," Alex replies as he clasps hands with Nathan. *Huh, when did these two get so chummy?*

"Great work, as always Nathan." Nathan nods in thanks.

"Do you wanna get some dinner or something? I'm starving." Alex asks as we head toward the car. It's a normal friend thing to do, grab dinner and hang out, but for some reason, it just feels like a betrayal to Ryan. I don't like the way my stomach clenches at the idea and I can't decide which thought bothers me more–the thought that Ryan would be upset or the thought that I care what would upset Ryan.

Either way, I decide that it's not a good idea.

"Maybe another time. I've got some—"

"Work, yeah. You know, you should take your own advice sometime."

"I do," I say as we leave the parking lot and start the drive toward my apartment. "I spend a lot more time with you when I should be doing work."

"Do you?" He asks curiously, as if he's really wondering if it's true. And it is. Whatever free time I don't spend with my roommates, I often spend with Alex. Whether it be at his parties, his gala, the library, or recording sessions, we spend a lot of time together.

Before I know it, we've pulled up in front of my apartment. "See you," I say as I climb.

"Bye bye, sunshine," Alex says and I can't help but smile.

Chapter Twenty–Four

Alex

I SHOULD'VE KNOWN THEY would retaliate. Fucking shit-stirrers really did a number on us this time. I guess having to unseal every window and door of their house could be tedious, but painting dicks all over the exterior of ours is taking it too far. This is going to take every man we have and then some to clean up and it has to happen fast before the school president sees this and gives us a citation.

"This is bullshit," Kai says, slapping the soaking wet sponge to the outer wall. There's paint everywhere, on the windows, walls, even the gutters. The deltas must've used brushes in the dead of night because one of us would've woken up to the sound of spray paint, but none of us heard a damn thing last night.

Keith grunts in agreement as he travels up the ladder to remove a crudely drawn ball sack from the second story window.

"You know we need to get even now," Devon says, using a long mop to hit the top corner of the first story wall.

"One could argue that this is them getting even with us," Keith shouts down to us.

"This is not fucking even," I say, taking the sponge to the brick staircase. "Blatant vandalism is not the same as using a little bit of glue."

"Damn, fellas, that's a real low blow." A voice shouts from the sideway and we all turn to see a few DE boys standing on the curb, holding in their laughter. The comment comes from Ryan, the clear leader of the pack. "I can't believe someone would shaft you like that." The group erupts into laughter, and I physically hold Kai back from jumping at them. Without another antagonizing word, the group continues down the street toward their own house.

It takes three hours to scrub the front of the house as clean as we can. The rest of the freshman brothers spend longer on the rest of the exterior but the pressure wasn't as heavy because you can't see it from the street.

Exhausted, we collapse on the couch as Keith gets us all beers from the fridge.

"So what are we going to do now?" He asks, handing us each a cold one.

Devon opens his bottle and takes a long sip. "We can put rotten eggs in their heating vents."

Keith shakes his head. "Too easy to clean. We need something equal to how fucking long it just took us."

Kai looks over at me. "What about emotional warfare?" I raise my eyebrows at him in question. Kai continues. "Clearly, shithead Ryan did this. What's important to Ryan right now?"

The wheels turn and click instantly. "No. Leave her out of this."

"Come on, man. Take your personal feelings out of it. We all deserve revenge. She's our best option."

"I fucking said no, Kai. That's the end of it. Think of something else." Leaving the unopened beer on the table, I walk upstairs to my room. As much as I'm pissed that Margot's shithead boyfriend pulled this shit on us, I can't exactly blame him. That's what happens between rival frats. I just didn't realize he would stoop so low as to vandalize our house.

We need to do something. If we just let this lie, they'll think they've won. And they haven't fucking won. Not even close. But I can't involve Margot. Not again. And not now that we're so invested in the podcast together. And the friendship...

I need to think of something good enough to get my brothers off my back that doesn't include any innocents this time.

Sitting on my bed, I pull out my phone to try and google some inspiration. But instead I find myself pulling up my text thread with Margot and sending her a message. Maybe it's petty but I need her to see what her *boyfriend* just did to us. I text her a picture of the outside of our house with no context. She answers within a minute.

> Omg what happened??

> Your boyfriend

> Ryan did that? Why?

> Just some frat prank war bullshit

> But that's too far. That's vandalism! Are you sure he did that? It really doesn't seem like him...

Is she serious right now? Of course, her angel boyfriend Ryan would never stoop to my immature level and pull a prank like this. My anger builds as I think about her standing by his side, supporting him against me. *Some fucking friend...*

> Of course you'd take his side

> What the hell, Alex! I'm not taking sides. I'm just saying it doesn't seem like something he would do

> And you know him so well

> By not taking sides, you're not taking mine. Just forget it

She calls my phone, but I ignore it, throwing the device down on my bed and heading back downstairs. If she wants to support him, fine. She can help him pick up the pieces after the fallout.

The boys are still sitting on the couch, no doubt brainstorming our next move. I stand directly in front of Kai. "What do you have in mind?"

A slow smile curls onto his face and I take a resigned breath. This is probably a terrible decision but at this point, all I see is red.

Chapter Twenty-Five

Margot

ALEX DOESN'T SHOW UP to public speaking class, nor does he answer any of the calls or texts I sent after he sent me that picture yesterday. I know he's pissed at me for what I assumed about Ryan but I don't feel bad about that. In all the time I've spent with him, he hasn't given me any indication that he could do anything so vile. But that doesn't mean that I don't believe Alex. The whole thing is very confusing and all I want to do is talk to Alex about it. I can only hope he's not so pissed that he'll flake on the podcast.

After class, I head toward the library to wait for Alex in the study room. When I walk up to the desk, Edith gives me a smirk. "Your gentleman friend has already picked up the key," she says with a wink.

I can't help the relief I feel as I walk down the stairs toward the room. I know Alex and I are in for a difficult conversation but at least he showed up to have it.

The door is wedged open a crack to allow me to enter without knocking. I open my mouth to apologize to Alex right away but what I'm met with instead causes me to shut it, just as the door closes behind me

Alex is sitting at the table but he's not the only one. Devon, Kai and Keith are also sat with him, all four of them looking directly at me.

"Hello?"

"Have a seat, Margot," Alex says, his voice oddly cold. It's then that I realize that all four of them are sitting on the same side and there's only one empty chair across from them. Like an interrogation.

I hesitate at the door. "I'm not sure I want to..."

Alex rolls his eyes and cracks a hesitant grin. "You're not in trouble."

Not really any more appeased, I cautiously take the empty seat across from them. "What is this about?"

"We need your help," Devon says immediately. "You saw what DE did to our house right?"

"Yeah, Alex sent me a picture."

"It's some bullshit and now we need to get them back," Kai continues Devon's thought. Almost like they planned this. It's actually kind of funny to me for a moment, until I remember I have no idea why they've gathered me here.

"I don't know what that has to do with me..." I already paid my prank dues. I didn't realize this would turn into an ongoing situation that I was to be forced to be a part of.

It's finally Alex who speaks next. "We need to reevaluate the terms of our deal."

Taking a deep breath, I make a demand. "Alex, can we talk about this without the back up?"

Alex looks back and forth between his friends before nodding once. "I got it from here." The rest of his crew stands and leaves out the door without another word or glance in my direction.

"What the hell is going on? You didn't tell me this prank thing would be ongoing."

"I didn't think it would. And I wanted to leave you out of this one, but you made it personal when Ryan and the deltas dicked up our house."

"*I* made it personal?"

"Ryan made it personal. And you are personal with Ryan."

"Cut the bullshit, Alex, please. Just what are you asking me to do?"

"We need you to help us get them back. And we want to go after Ryan."

"Why are you so sure that Ryan did this? There's a lot of guys in that frat. It could've been anyone."

"I know it was him."

I stare at him from across the table, my anger brewing. We sit in silence for a minute or so, neither one of us breaking the tension.

Alex sighs first. "Why don't you ask him then?"

He's challenging me. He doesn't think I would ask. I pull my phone out of my back pocket, dial Ryan's number, put the phone on speaker and set it on the table.

"Hey, babe," he answers after two rings.

Alex rolls his eyes but remains silent.

I lean down over the table to speak close to the phone. "Hey, can I ask you something?"

A car horn honks behind Ryan's voice. "Sure, what's up?"

"Did you have anything to do with the KA house being vandalized?"

Ryan sighs. "Ah, man I saw that. But no, of course not. I would never stoop so low with my revenge plots." His voice is casual, not a hint of regret or guilt.

"Why are you out to get revenge on the kappas?" As far as I was aware, they didn't know that their lock in was from Alex and his friends. And I definitely didn't want Ryan to know my involvement in it.

Ryan chuckles. "Everyone knows they locked us in the night of the gala."

I choose to ignore that comment, hoping he won't find out how integral I was to that plan, even if it didn't go as smoothly as we'd hoped, thanks to Ryan's chivalry. "Okay, so you're sure you had nothing to do with the graffiti?" I give him one last time to tell me the truth and I'll believe whatever he says. He's given me no reason not to.

"I'm sure. I wouldn't do that."

"Okay," I sigh in relief.

"Did Alex tell you I did? Because he probably just—"

Alex hits the large red button on the screen, disconnecting the call instantly.

"Hey!" I cry, snatching the phone off the table and out of his reach. "You got your answer, okay? He didn't do it."

"And you really believe him? Everything he just said was pure bullshit, Margot."

"Why wouldn't I believe him? Why would he lie?"

"Because he wants to get in your fucking pants! God, how naive are you going to be?"

I'm shaking my head, shutting out his hateful words. What have I ever done to him to make him so cruel to me? All I've done is try to be his friend. I should've known better than to let him in enough to have any control over my emotions. Lesson learned.

Alex's fingers are pinching the top of his nose. "I didn't mean that." His voice sounds pained but for once, I don't really care. The only thing keeping me from storming out that door is the fact that I did make a deal with him and he is helping me with the internship contest.

"I'll help you with the prank. Only because I made a deal with you and I need you to keep upholding your end. But I refuse to do anything personally against Ryan. Figure it out." I stand up and head toward the door.

Alex stands too but doesn't move toward me. "Wait, please. Don't go. What about the podcast meeting?"

I open my phone, find the website and click publish. "I'll plan the next episode myself and email you the script this week. See you Saturday."

Pulling the door open, I leave before he can say another word. I don't look back as I continue up the stairs and out the library doors. After a quick text to Sydney, I only have to wait about three minutes before she's pulling up in front of the library.

I see Alex leave the library as I get into Sydney's car. He spots me in the car and starts to walk toward us, hurriedly.

"Go. Go, go," I say to Sydney, and she confusingly moves the gear shift into drive and pulls away from the curb.

"Any particular reason why we're running away from Alex?"

I sigh, watching Alex's tall form disappear in the mirror. "Let's pick up a bottle of wine on the way home. We need a girl's night."

"Get me another slice," Danika says as I pull a piece of pizza from the box on the counter. Grabbing another for Dani, I place it on my plate as I walk back over to where they're sitting. We're about three-quarters finished with the bottle of wine and nowhere near close to figuring out what I should do about this whole Ryan and Alex thing.

Sliding the slice onto Dani's plate, I plop back onto the couch next to Sydney. "Can one of you just tell me what to do, please?" I ask, taking a sad bite of my third slice of pizza.

"What are you thinking?" Sydney asks.

I sigh. "I honestly don't know what to believe. Or who. On the one hand, it would make sense that Ryan would lead the charge for his frat house in retaliation for the KA prank."

I place the plate on my lap and lean my head back against the couch. "But on the other hand, vandalism like that is so disgusting, I can't picture a nice guy like Ryan doing anything like that. And then lying about it?"

Shaking my head, I look back over at Sydney and Dani who are looking back at me with twin sympathetic looks.

"It's definitely a tricky situation," Syd says, tapping my knee a few times before looking over at Danika for back up.

"I think it all comes down to who you trust more."

I narrow my eyes. "What do you mean?"

"Alex was your friend first. In terms of seniority, he should have your allegiance over Ryan. But you and Ryan are involved romantically and that can trump friendships."

I blink, listening to insightful words.

"So, I think the real question is: Who do you trust more? Because it can't be both, especially not in the case where they're telling you different things."

"Who should I trust?"

Dani lets out a breathy chuckle. "We can't answer that for you, Mar."

I lean my head back again with a groan. Squeezing my eyes shut I hope to shut out the demons in my mind.

Sydney rubs my shoulder. "Who do you want to trust?"

Alex. The name echoes in my brain. I open my eyes.

"Alex."

Sydney whips her head to look at Danika who smiles. "Atta girl."

A knock sounds on the door, and all three of us whip our heads around. Hesitantly, we tiptoe toward the door, Sydney in front who looks in the peephole. Pulling her mouth into a tight smile, she winks at me and then pushes me in front of her.

"Who's it—"

"Sunshine?"

I draw in a breath. Giggling behind me, the girls walk back toward the living room and go into their respective rooms. Turning back toward the door, I take in a deep, stabilizing inhale.

"Please, sun. I just want to talk. I'm really sorry about before. Just—"

I open the door swiftly, catching Alex entirely by surprise. I'm not sure what my expression says, but Alex seems to sigh in relief just at the fact that I opened the door. We stand there motionless for a few seconds.

Alex runs his hand through his hair. "Can I come in?" He asks nervously.

I nod and switch on the hall light to help guide his way. It flickers as usual and Alex looks up as he walks in, the door closing behind him. He takes a few steps forward until he's in our living room.

"Listen, let me just—"

I quiet him with a silent finger on my lips. Eying my roommate's doors, I cock my head toward my bedroom, motioning for him to go in there. He follows my silent instructions, and I shut the door behind us both, leaning back against the knob.

"Sorry, I just know my roommates have a cup wedged between their ear and those doors. We'll have more privacy in here."

Alex nods before turning to scope out my room. I'm having deja vu from the time I did the same thing to him a few weeks back. He glances at my bookcase, my closet, his gaze lingering on my unmade bed before he turns around and faces me again.

"I hate the way we left things back there."

"I do, too."

"I don't want you to think that I'm just using you for this prank shit. I've actually really grown to appreciate our...friendship." He hesitates on the word before continuing, "And I just don't want this dumb bullshit to get in the way of that."

"I feel the same way." I keep my replies short, not sure how much I want to reveal in this conversation.

Alex sighs and sits down on my bed. He looks down at his hands as he speaks. "I know you don't believe me. But I know for a fact that Ryan did the prank. Whether it was him or his house, he was involved somehow and I just—"

"I believe you."

Alex's eyes bolt to mine.

"I decided that I want to trust you so...I believe you."

Alex's eyes light up as he jumps from the bed and rushes toward me. Grabbing me around the waist, he lifts me up in a huge hug, and I'm a giggling mess laughing in his ear.

"Put me down!" I laugh and he does what I've asked but as his hands release my waist, he uses them instead to cup my face on either side. His face is inches from mine, and I hope to god my breath doesn't reek of pizza and wine. His smell is minty and fresh, as usual.

Alex looks back and forth between my eyes for a few seconds before he dips the tip of his nose to touch mine. "Thank you. Seriously, you don't know what that means to me."

I blink, not knowing how to respond. His lips are plump and so so close to mine. Just the slightest movement of my toes and I could be touching his lips with my own. I think he notices that too as his gaze leaves my eyes and looks down at my mouth.

"Sunshine..." he sighs and leans down a bit more. I close my eyes.

A bang on my bedroom door rips us apart.

"Margot?" A male voice. An angry male voice.

Pulling away from Alex, I open the door to see Ryan standing there, his face furious, a worried Danika and Sydney behind him.

"What are you doing here?" I step closer to him.

He looks over my shoulder and then back down at me. "What am *I* doing here? What is *he* doing here?" He motions with his hand toward Alex and I can feel Alex behind me, just as close as he was before but in an entirely different way. He puts his hand on my arm, not as a sign of affection. Almost as if he's ready to pull me out of the way if he has to.

Ryan doesn't give me a chance to explain as he steps back from the door and into the living room. "You haven't been answering any of my calls tonight and you hung up on me before–"

"We've been having a girl's night, dick," Danika says, her voice full of venom.

Ryan looks over his shoulder at her. "Yeah, looks like it. Didn't realize you had a sex change, Prescott."

Alex steps up closer to me, the rage wafting off of him in waves. I push him back a step as I move closer to Ryan. "Can you calm down? You're acting super immature right now."

"Oh, I'm immature?" Once again, he looks over my head toward Alex. "You know, I was planning on using her against you but I guess you beat me to the punch."

Everyone falls silent at his words, taking them in. The only thing we hear in the room for several moments is the sound of Ryan's heavy breathing. It's then that I notice the smell. He reeks of beer, his eyes glassy. He looks similar to Alex at the last party but more coherent.

When he looks at me at last, my eyes are like daggers.

"Get out." My voice is stone. Leaving no room for interpretation. Yet Ryan tries it anyway.

"Margot, wait, let me just—"

"Get the fuck out of my apartment or, I swear I will call the police."

Ryan blinks a few times. He looks over at Alex again before his gaze lands on me, lingering long enough that I have to look away.

"Fine." Ryan raises his hands for a second and then points a finger over my head at Alex. "He's not as innocent as you think he is. You're making a mistake choosing him over me but fine. I'll go." Turning on his heels, Ryan leaves the apartment, the door slamming behind him. It's not until that sound that I feel like I'm able to take in a full breath.

From across the room, Danika lets out a loud awkward laugh.

Turning around, I finally look Alex in the eyes. His expression still looks somewhat murderous but it's relaxed a bit now that Ryan is gone.

"What did he mean by that?"

Alex raises his hands, his expression the picture of innocence and turmoil. "I have no idea, I swear." He takes a tentative step closer to me but I find myself stepping back.

"'He's not as innocent as you think he is.' What...what does that mean?" I'm stuck trying to make sense of all this and Alex is being surprisingly quiet. As if he has the answers but he's not ready to tell them.

"Margot, listen, I..." His face looks distraught but I'm not ready to move on from it. Instinctively, I take another step away, landing closer to Danika and Sydney and farther from Alex.

Danika takes note of this and jumps into action. "Maybe you should go, Alex," she says, her voice soft but firm.

A flash of something crosses Alex's features but it doesn't linger. He knows it's best for him to leave and let me think through the events of the last five minutes but he's clearly reluctant to leave like this.

He takes a hesitant step toward me but I shake my head once. With a sigh, Alex exits the apartment, leaving an air of confusion in his wake.

Chapter Twenty-Six

Margot

DANIKA AND SYDNEY FOLLOW me into my bedroom where I sit on my bed and pull the pillow into my lap. With a blank expression on my face, I stare ahead, unsure of how to piece together what just happened with Ryan and Alex.

"So..." Danika starts, sitting next to me. Sydney has taken a seat on my desk chair but pulled the chair as close to the bed as she could.

"So," I reply, still not able to meet anyone's eyes. "That was something."

"Definitely something," Sydney agrees, putting a gentle, reassuring hand on my knee. "What are we thinking about all that 'something'?"

"I don't know." I blink, finally making eye contact with the girls. "Did I make a mistake?"

Danika shakes her head fervently. "No, Margot, you haven't done anything wrong."

"But what was Ryan talking about? Is Alex just using me? For what?"

Sydney sighs. "That's what's confusing me the most. What could he be using *you* for? I mean, if anything, you're using *him* for the podcast."

"But what if he's using you for the prank. What if Ryan was right and Alex was only getting close to you to use it against Ryan in the prank war?" Dani adds.

I'm already shaking my head. "But that doesn't make sense either. Alex was adamant I stay away from Ryan at first. That wouldn't help his plot."

The three of us sit in silence for another few minutes as we try to piece together the puzzle.

"I think Ryan is lying, and Alex is telling the truth," I say, having come to a realization. "Ryan was planning to use me against Alex. But that doesn't answer the question of why he would even think that would work. That would mean Alex would have to care about me."

Danika and Sydney sigh louder than I've ever heard.

"Mar, obviously he cares. Alex likes you. It's written all over his face every time he looks at you," Sydney says.

"No, he–" my sentence is stopped as I'm shoved back onto my bed.

"Would you just admit it already so we can get to the next episode of this melodrama!" Danika proclaims. "He likes you, you like him! Admit it. Say it. Right now." Dani is standing on my bed looking down at me while I'm looking up at her in shock.

"Danika, get down—"

"Say it!" She starts jumping and I'm afraid she's going to take out an eyeball, either mine or hers. There's only one way to get her to calm down.

"Alright, alright!" I put my hands up and Danika immediately plops down where she's jumping. Meeting Sydney's eyes, then Danika's, I take a deep deep breath in.

"I like Alex."

Before I can even get the 'x' out of my mouth, Sydney and Danika both are jumping up and down on my poor discount mattress. They pull me up so I'm jumping as well. Soon, we're a fit of giggles and we fall on the pillows in laughter.

"Okay so what are you still doing here?" Danika jumps off the bed and grabs my arms, pulling me off as well. "Go get your man!"

"Dani..." I roll my eyes, glancing at the clock on my laptop. "It's almost midnight, I can't go anywhere at this time of night. No, tomorrow I'll just—"

My words trail off as a loud knock sounds on our apartment door. I already know exactly who it is, and it seems like the girls do too because Sydney gives me a quick kiss on the cheek and Dani winks over her shoulder before they both scamper out of my bedroom.

Taking a deep breath, I smooth out my clothes and go to answer the door.

"Pst," Dani whispers from her doorway. "You deserve this."

I grin and then continue my walk toward the door. *You deserve this.*

The second I open the door, Alex whips by me like the wind, clearly on a mission. I close the door and turn to face him, the blinking light of our foyer making his expression look even more frenzied.

"Look, I know you wanted some time and space but I can't just leave things like that. I have to explain, I—"

Without a second thought in my head, I grab the front of his t-shirt and pull his body to mine. Our lips connect before he has time to understand what is going on, which was exactly my intention. No thinking, just doing.

Alex lets out a shocked sigh as our lips touch but he doesn't pull away. There's a hesitance to his movements. Surprise, more than disinterest but that surprise doesn't last long.

Within the next second, Alex has backed up us against the door, his kisses becoming deeper, more passionate. This is not the nice kiss that Ryan gave me after the party. This is a desperation I don't know I've ever felt before but would kill to feel again.

My hand releases Alex's shirt as he leans down to lift me from under my butt, my body held up by Alex's strength. He doesn't disconnect our lips as he walks us backward and I put up a silent prayer that he doesn't trip on Danika's shoes. Alex makes it to my bedroom with no issue and our fervor continues to grow as he kicks the door shut behind us.

His lips find my neck, and I tilt my head to give him more access, my long hair cascading down my back. Alex murmurs against my skin, and I feel goosebumps erupt across my whole body.

Before I can do anything else, I am dropped from the air onto my bed, my butt bouncing against the disheveled pillows and blankets. Alex is across the room, pacing a hole into the floor with his hands racking through his hair.

"Woah," he breathes.

"Yeah."

"We just kissed."

"We did," I reply, a small grin forming.

"You and Me. Kissed."

"Mhm," I murmur, holding back a chuckle.

"Alex and Margot. Kissing."

The laugh breaks free. "Are you going to keep saying it or would you like to continue it?"

Alex stops his pacing to look at me. "What the hell happened in the last ten minutes because I'm having trouble connecting the dots here."

"In the last ten minutes, I came to a realization."

Alex is still looking at me like a deer caught in headlines, but at least he's stopped walking. His hands have dropped from his hair as well. All good signs.

"What realization?"

Taking a deep breath, I let myself have what I want. "I've realized that the feelings I thought I might've been feeling for Ryan were really suppressed feelings I have for you."

"Me?" He squeaks out and I'd make fun of him for it if my heart wasn't in my throat.

"You, Alex. I like *you*."

I watch from the bed as Alex takes in one, two, three very deep breaths. The time that passes causes me to panic. I'm about to take back everything I've said and blame sleep deprivation until Alex cracks a smile the likes of which angels could surely sing about and saunters over to me. Yes, this time, he actually manages to saunter.

He takes two large steps and kneels in front of me, wedging himself between my bent knees. Gripping my waist in his large hands, he pulls my torso against his.

"Thank fucking god," he says and that's it. There's no going back. Alex claims my mouth in a way that I'll never be able to replicate with anyone else. And I don't want to. His hand moves to grip the back of my head and against our faces together; as if I'd ever let anything break us apart. My hands reach down to the hem of his t-shirt and I tease the bare skin underneath with my fingertips.

Alex smiles against my lips but doesn't break the hold as he allows me to push the t-shirt up toward his armpits. In a flash, the shirt is pulled clean over his head and his lips have found mine yet again, his tongue teasing its way through my pouty lips.

With a strength I had no idea he had (but should've guessed with how much time he spends at the gym), Alex picks me up again, linking my legs around his waist. My feet hit his butt and I drag my hands down the back of his head to hold onto his neck for stability. I know he'd never drop me and the weightless feeling is the sexiest thing I've ever experienced.

With my foot by his firm ass, I feel Alex's phone vibrate in his pocket a few times to indicate either a phone call or texts coming in rapid fire.

"Do you want to get that?" I ask, in between kisses on the neck and earlobe.

"Absolutely fucking not," Alex replies breathlessly, pulling my neck back toward his face to connect our lips. He's a man starved, and I'm his own personal buffet. I smile and allow him to continue traveling down my body with his hands. He's moved his knees onto the bed and laid me down on the pillow.

Before I can disconnect my linked feet from his waist, I feel the vibrations again.

"Fuck," Alex groans in exasperation and pulls back to grab his phone. Looking at the screen, he mutters the profanity again but this time, it's more worrisome.

"Everything okay?" I ask, feeling suddenly self-conscious even though I'm still entirely clothed.

"Yeah, I just...fuck," he pockets his phone again and looks down at me, his expression completely distraught. "I'm so sorry, sunshine, but I have to go."

With a sigh, he pulls himself up off the bed and grabs his shirt off the floor.

"What's going on?" I ask from the bed, still laying down in shock of the sudden change of emotion.

"I'm not sure. Something I need to handle at the frat house." His expression is guarded, and I know he's keeping something from me but it won't do me any good to ask him to elaborate. Grabbing the door handle, he turns it and I feel a sudden empty feeling take over my entire body.

Until he turns around and rushes back toward the bed, grabbing my face in both hands, he kisses me like there was never an interruption at all. Like he isn't about to leave my apartment and go 'take care' of some mystery problem.

Breaking the kiss, he rests his forehead against mine. "Don't overthink it. This is a good thing." I know he's talking about what transpired between us. And the fact that he knows my brain is immediately going to jetpack into overthinking mode the minute he leaves.

"Sunshine," he calls, bringing my eyes to his. "Promise me you won't overthink it."

"I promise," I whisper.

Alex smiles and kisses me again. "Liar." With a kiss on my forehead, Alex leaves my room, leaves my apartment, and leaves me alone with an ever pounding heart.

Chapter Twenty-Seven

Alex

"One of you better be fucking dying, Devon."

Devon's heavy breathing on the other side of the phone causes me to pause in Margot's hallway. "Just about, man. Keith got roughed up tonight."

I start running. "I'll be right there."

Within four minutes, I'm sprinting up the stairs of our house, pushing past busybodies surrounding the living room couch.

Keith's laying there, his right eye already black, bruises forming on his jaw. I'm not sure what other damage has been caused but he stirs awake as I kneel down next to him.

"Hey, bro. What happened?"

"Couple Deltas," he groans out, "surprised me while I was walking home."

"What the fuck," Kai's voice is loud behind me. He's standing over my shoulder, looking down at his broken brother's body with his arms crossed and steam pouring out of his ears. "Fuck this," he says, grabbing his keys from the mantle and making toward the door.

I jump into action, grabbing his arm before he can open the front door. "Hold on, Kai. We should get him to a hospital."

Kai whips his arm out of my grasp. "Take him then. I need to take care of this." He moves toward the door again but I stop him with a hand on the hardwood.

"Kai, think for a second." I try to reason with him but I know he's only seeing red.

"This is my fucking brother. I'm going to handle this."

"We don't even know who it was that did this to him. You going to fuck up the entire DE house?"

Kai scoffs in my face, "I will if I fucking have to."

Devon comes up beside us. "Keith said it was a couple guys led by Ryan."

"Motherfucker," I whisper. "Motherfucker!" I scream, pounding on the door.

"So this is your fault," Kai turns to me, venom in his stare. "You and your fucking girlfriend did this to my brother."

I know Kai is connecting dots that don't necessarily connect, but he's probably not that far off. Ryan was pissed as hell when he left Margot's apartment. Clearly he was upset, but I didn't think he'd take it this far. Physical altercations are the absolute last resort and should be avoided at all costs. It's also a low fucking blow to go after one of my brothers when his real issue is with me.

"Kai, wait—"

Before I can get another word in, Kai rounds a right hook directly to my cheek. I didn't see it coming so it made contact with a sickening crunch. Devon's got Kai's arms held behind his back before I'm able to even blink my vision back into focus.

"This is all your fucking fault!" Kai spits as Devon drags him upstairs.

Kai's sputtering quiets when his bedroom door closes, leaving the room with an eerie silence. All eyes are on me as I try to piece together what just happened. Kai hit me. He hit me hard. He hit me like he wants to hit Ryan.

Keith groans from the couch, breaking me from my trance. I don't have time to deal with Kai, I need to take care of this brother before I deal with that one.

Two other brothers are standing around Keith. "You guys help me get Keith into the car, I'm taking him to the hospital." The guys jump into action, gently pulling him from the couch as I hold the door open for them. No shot in hell did I imagine my night would turn out this way. I should be cuddled up with Margot right now, not nursing an aching face, a broken brother, and a wounded heart.

<center>~~~\/\/\/\~~~</center>

Seven hours, two broken ribs, two black eyes, one concussion, and one bruised jaw later, Keith and I collapse onto our own beds to finally get some sleep. Even though it's morning and I've got class in about an hour, I can't see myself going anywhere else today. Especially with this shiner on my face.

I know I need to talk to Kai and sort this out but I just can't deal with it right now. I have no idea where his head is at, he's been out of it for weeks.

Margot has called a few times and texted even more. I know it's not fair of me to leave her in the dark, especially after what transpired between us last night but I need to get to the bottom of the whole situation before I tell her anything. I need to know exactly what happened and how to take care of it and I would like to do it without bringing her into it at all.

I look at my phone and see her latest text.

> Not that I care but can you just throw a flag to let me know you're not dead

Chuckling, I send her a white flag emoji before turning my phone on "Do not disturb" and promptly passing out for six hours.

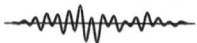

The midday sun crests through the window when I wake up again and I know it's past noon. Checking my phone, I see that Margot has "liked" my emoji message but sent no more after. She's probably pissed about my leaving and then sudden disappearing act, and I'll explain it all to her once I get it sorted out in my own head.

In the meantime, I need to find Kai.

Taking a deep breath, I open my bedroom door and walk smack into Keith, who grunts in pain.

"Hey, you just waking up too?" He asks, his face in a grimace.

I nod. "How are you doing?"

Keith lets out a breath. "Sore but mostly okay. Confused."

"Yeah, I think it's time we sort it all out." Clapping Keith on the back, he winces and I apologize quickly as we make our way downstairs. Just as I'd hoped, Kai is sitting on the couch, a basketball highlights reel on the TV and his nose buried in his laptop. He does a double-take when he sees us both coming down the stairs but doesn't move from the couch.

Slowly, Kai closes his laptop as we approach. "You good, Keithy?" He says the nickname with a gentle smile but it doesn't reach his eyes.

It doesn't wound me that he asks after his brother first. They are twins, after all. But, from the way he hasn't yet been able to meet my eyes, I can tell this is going to be a longer recovery for him and me.

"Yeah, I'll live," Keith replies, gently sitting down on the other end of the couch. There's a space left open in the middle, but there's not enough money in the world that would encourage me to sit there right now. I opt instead for leaning against the mantle across from the couch.

"I remember more of what happened," Keith says, his voice small. Neither one of us speak, giving him the floor and as much time as he needs.

"I was walking from campus, lost track of time in the library..." His code for hanging out with that football player he's into. Again, we both allow him to take his time telling the story. "I was just at the corner when a car pulled up next to me. It all happened so fast. I was knocked in the back of the head and then hit in the face so hard, I saw stars."

Keith takes a deep breath and looks over toward Kai whose face is scrunched up in anger. "I fell to the ground. They kicked me a few times in the stomach then once more in the face and that's all I remember. I woke up on the couch when you came in." Keith nods his head toward me.

"Fucking Delta scum," Kai spits.

"And you definitely know Ryan did it?"

"Of course he fucking does. You think he's gonna lie about it?" Kai puts his laptop on the table but doesn't stand from the couch.

"I definitely saw Ryan's face. It was the last face I saw," Keith adds. "There was a lot of taunting and yelling. No idea what they were saying, but it was loud and only got louder before I passed out."

Pinching the top of my nose with my fingers, I sigh deeply.

"How did I get to the house?" Keith asks.

Kai reaches out, gripping the top of Keith's knee. "I found you on the front lawn all battered up. Took three guys to drag your fatass inside."

Kai laughs and Keith smiles. I suddenly feel like I'm intruding on an intimate brotherly moment.

"Well," Kai says expectantly, finally looking me in the eye. "What the fuck are we going to do about this?"

I blink but don't respond. Because I have no fucking idea.

———∿∿∿∿∿∿∿———

Kai and I seem to form an unspoken ceasefire as we brainstorm how to handle this situation. Devon had come home during our planning session, bringing a six pack of beer and two pepperoni pizzas. It took the smell of melted cheese to remind me that I haven't eaten since before I went to Margot's apartment last night.

I can't believe that was last night. I can't believe that last night I was kissing Margot Davis. That I was about to do so much more with Margot Davis. It seems like a lifetime ago. I still haven't been able to process it all with what happened once I got home.

But something else that I realized while all of this was going on, I miss her. Usually I go half the school week without seeing her and I hardly bat an eye about it...hardly. But this? It's been less than twenty-four hours since I've last seen her and I already want to see her again. Hold her again. Touch her unreasonably soft skin again. Hear her wild thoughts about nineties rom coms and have her explain to me yet again the difference between MLA and Chicago style formatting. I just want to kiss her—

A smack to the back of my head breaks my reverie.

"Your girlfriend is here," Devon announces before sliding over on the couch and laying down behind me, effectively shoving me off. I give him a dead leg before I go get the door.

"Jesus Christ," Margot says as a greeting, her hand covering her mouth.

"This ain't church, baby," I say with the swagger of a long dead Elvis. Leaning against the doorframe, I cross my arms and wink, with some effort.

Margot, of course, sees right through me. Stepping forward, she gently touches my face with her fingertips. "What the hell happened to you?"

I take her hand, kiss her palm gently and then drop her arm back down. "Come upstairs, I'll explain."

Margot follows up blindly through the house, passing most of the brothers, including an apologetic looking Keith and a mean looking Kai. When we get upstairs, I close my door behind us and lock it for good measure.

"Did you get in a fight with Keith?" Margot asks immediately.

I shake my head but don't elaborate on that point. "No, I didn't." With a sigh, I sit on the edge of my bed and motion for Margot to take the spot beside me. With hesitance, she crosses the room and takes the seat.

"Alex, you're freaking me out."

"Something happened last night and we're still trying to piece together parts of it but it seems like Keith got jumped by some DE guys."

Margot's hand shoots up to her mouth again. Her eyes widen, and I can't help but notice how deeply blue they are. And as they start to water, they resemble oceans. I don't make her ask anymore questions as I continue.

"Devon had texted and called and that's why I left your apartment so abruptly. When I got home, I found Keith beat the fuck up on the couch and I took him to the hospital where we spent most of the night waiting on exams and tests and all that bullshit."

Margot blinks a few times as she takes in the information.

"But wait, how did *you* get a black eye? And where was Kai that whole time? Why didn't he go to the hospital with Keith?"

"Kai was here, but he was too upset about it to really think straight..." I trail off, motioning briefly toward my face. Margot gasps again and I almost chuckle at the dramatics she's bringing to the situation.

"Kai punched you? Why?"

I put my hand on her thigh, to relax her. To relax me. "It's a long story that we don't have to get into now. I'm sorry that I ran out on you last night and kept you in the dark all day. That was shitty of me."

Margot rubs my arm and scoots ever so closer to me. "It's okay, Alex. I can't believe you were going through all this and I sat in class wondering if you were regretting everything we did last night."

Her voice gets smaller and smaller by the time she finishes her sentence and she turns her face to hide but I don't let her. Gripping her chin, I pull her toward me and place a not so gentle kiss on her lips.

"Don't ever think that. I told you not to overthink it, didn't I?

"Yes, but—"

I kiss her again. "Didn't I?"

She smiles against my lips. "Yes."

I kiss her again before pulling back to meet her eyes. "Good, so it's time you start listening to me, woman."

Margot rolls her eyes but leans against me, allowing me to wrap my arms around her like I've been yearning to for hours.

I can't see her face but her voice is small again when she speaks. "Did Devon call me your girlfriend?"

I freeze. "He was just yanking my chain."

"Right, of course," Margot responds far too quickly. "Obviously." She sits up, a brilliant smile on her face and you'd think I'd just told her it was Christmas morning. The look confuses me but I don't push it for now.

"Look, I didn't mean to just drop by unannounced, I just wanted to see if you were okay and now that I have the proof that you are, I can head back to the library," she stands to get her bag, "It's time to submit the first part of the Times internship contest. I need to do a write up of our project and then send in the first two episodes. According to the website, I'll know by the end of the weekend if I've made it to the second round."

"You will."

"You're so sure." She swats at me playfully but there's trepidation in her voice. Before she can move out of reach, I grab her arm and pull her to standing in front of me, locking her lithe body between my knees.

"Yes, I am," I say firmly, placing a kiss on the tip of her nose. Margot lets a little tension out of her shoulders, whether she realizes it or not. I calm her. The knowledge that something I do can make her feel even a little bit more confident sends a jolt of energy up my spine. I sit up straighter, kissing her with a passion she's not expecting but not opposed to, based on how her body reacts. She winds her arms around my neck, pulling me closer and I want to sink my teeth into the soft skin of her neck. Squeezing my eyes shut, I wince as I'm reminded of the shiner my so-called best friend graced me with last night. Margot pulls back.

"Are you sure you're okay?" she asks, placing gentle fingers on my bruised face. The concern in her gaze is clear. She's worried about me. I pull her fingers away, kissing the tips of each one before letting her hand fall to her side.

"I'm fine, sunshine. You don't gotta worry about me."

She doesn't look convinced but she nods just the same, clearly appeasing me.

"I'll let myself out," Margot says, rubbing her hand down my arm one more time and then moving toward the door. "I'll see you Saturday?"

I laugh, standing to grab her under her butt, taking her entirely by surprise and lifting her so her face is level with mine. With my available hand, I grip the back of her neck and kiss her again so fiercely it leaves us both breathless. Pulling back, I rest my forehead on hers for a brief moment before placing her back on the floor again.

"You'll be seeing me way sooner than that, sunshine," I reply, kissing her forehead and then giving her a swift smack on the ass as she walks out the door.

Chapter Twenty-Eight

Margot

I WANTED TO PRESS Alex more on the purple bruise on his pretty face, but he didn't seem like he was in the mood to share. And as much as I wanted to know what happened between him and Kai, it wasn't my place to pry. He'll tell me in his own time.

Alex didn't come back to campus for the rest of the week. A fact I knew almost against my will but because of the Ask Alex podcast page, almost every comment on our newest episode was #freealex. It's like his adoring fans can't go more than one day without a sighting. It's actually scary.

For me though, it hasn't gotten much better. I've gotten used to the staring as I walk through the quad or the whispers in the hallway. Every once in a while, a bold girl will approach me with some disgusting comment and then walk away snickering with her friends.

On Friday afternoon, one such encounter occurred as I made my usual route from the library to the newsroom, a path that takes me right past the outdoor seating area of the campus food court.

"Hey, podcast girl." *A lovely nickname.* "How much you paying him?"

I ignored the comment, as usual, and kept walking. Until I heard her shrieking voice again. "I'll bet you just give him handies under the table after filming, don't you?"

"Don't be ugly, Josie. No one likes rotten leftovers." Danika's arm wraps around my shoulders and we keep walking, much to the dismay of the heckler behind us.

"Whatever happened to being a girl's girl?"

Danika scoffs. "It's college, babe. Girls at this place only want one thing and that's your boy." She flicks my long braid over my shoulder, fluffing out the green ribbon Sydney added to the bottom this morning when she did my hair.

"He's not my boy," I protest, knocking her arm off my back and turning to face her. "I hope the real world is better than this..."

"Doubtful," Dani laughs.

"And what are you two lovely ladies doing on this fine afternoon?"

I hear Alex behind me, but he doesn't put a hand on me. I feel the lack of contact like a slap to the face. Not that we are any type of exclusive, but there is something going on between us. Something new and different and undeniable. But he's not my boyfriend. And he's not touching me in public. So maybe it's not that special after all.

Danika levels him with a stern look. "Keep your girls in check, Prescott." She leans over to kiss me on the cheek before walking to her class.

"What is she talking about?"

I refuse to look him in the eye as I continue my walk toward the media building, Alex trailing behind. A firm hand on my shoulder stops me in my tracks.

"Margot, what happened?"

I sigh. "Nothing happened. Just some girl asking me about you, not exactly in a nice way." I keep going and Alex walks beside me, uncharacteristically quiet. We stay that way until we reach the door of the media building. I know Alex doesn't have any classes here and is just walking me to be nice.

As I open the door, I look back to see Alex standing behind me, his phone at my eye level, which he quickly shoves into his pocket.

"Did you just take a picture of me?"

Alex squints his eyes and looks at me like I've suddenly grown ten heads. "Uh paranoid, much?"

"What?"

"Huh?" Alex answers quickly. "Have a good class, bye." And he's gone, leaving me with more questions than I started with.

—⁓⁓⋀⋀⋀⋀ℳ⋀⋀⋀⁓⁓—

Halfway through class, a text from Dani comes through with a screenshot of an instagram story.

> Oh, he's good

The picture wasn't clear, no identification of the person. A blurry brunette braid with a green bow. Clearly a picture of the back of my head but only if you knew. Near the bottom, it's written, "going feral for this bow."

Still entirely confused, I text Danika back.

> I don't get it

> Check the name

Looking at the photo again, I see the username at the top left corner. *@AlexPrescott.* This is Alex's story. Alex posted a picture of the back of my head? *Why?*

> This, my friend, is called a soft launch

Still completely confused, I ignore the picture and concentrate on the lecture but within the next ten minutes, that seems to be a fruitless effort as DMs start rolling in from people I barely even talk to or don't know at all. All the messages follow the same theme: "*You and Alex are dating??????*"

As I leave the building, I feel all wandering eyes on me yet again. The whispers have increased in size and volume. I truly underestimated the status this man has on campus if within one hour everyone has seen and talked about his instagram story.

Now that my classes are over for the day, my mission now is to get off this campus as fast as I can.

"Sunshine!" *Not fast enough.* Alex comes up from behind me and grabs me by the elbow, pulling me immediately toward his car. "Let's go."

The fact that he knows my schedule and knows I'm done with classes today should startle me but it fills me with a warm feeling in my stomach instead.

Without hesitation, I get into the passenger seat as he walks around to the driver's side. After starting the car, he pulls swiftly out of the parking lot, both of us sitting in comfortable silence.

"So, how was your day?"

I look over at him. "Confusing," I admit, and Alex cracks a grin.

"Interesting assessment," he comments but does not elaborate. Before I know it, he's pulling up in front of my apartment. The whole instagram post left me with more questions than answers and as I open my mouth to ask Alex those questions, I'm immediately cut off.

"Go to dinner with me tonight."

I close my mouth. Then open it again. "Are you asking or telling?"

Alex hits me with that megawatt smile. "Whichever is going to make you say yes."

Looking over at him, I resist the urge to roll my eyes. Alex Prescott is asking me on a date. Alex, the guy I've been quickly getting to know and even quicker starting to admire and care about. Alex, the guy who defended my honor, helped me out in my time of need and always puts me at ease. Alex, the guy who hasn't steered me in any direction except "right" since the moment I met him. I would be a fool to say no, and it's that thought alone that has me responding, "Pick me up at seven," before whipping the car door open and running inside without so much as a glance back at the laughing Adonis behind me.

"Explain it to me again."

Dani rolls her eyes as she swipes some blush on my cheek. "It's like he's letting the public know that he's with someone without the label or even saying who it is." Danika instructs me to close my eyes as she continues talking. "That's why it's *soft*. A hard launch is full-on girlfriend label under a picture of you two riding off into the sunset."

Sydney laughs from her spot on Danika's bed.

"I don't see that happening," I scoff.

"You're going on a date with him tonight, Mar, I don't think it's that far off," Sydney says, grabbing the outfit we decided I'd wear from Danika's closet.

While I'm excited to go to dinner with Alex, I'm refusing to let myself get too excited. I know all too well about his reputation on campus. I have no interest in being another notch on his bedpost. But I do think he knows me well enough by now to know I'm not that girl. Hopefully...

"Plus you kissed," Danika raises her eyebrows at me suggestively. "Multiple times."

I roll my eyes, immediately regretting telling them anything about what happened between Alex and me.

"He kisses a lot of girls. We've seen him kiss girls before."

"You're different," Danika says confidently. She steps back to admire her handiwork. "Gorgeous, as usual. Now get dressed. You've only got two minutes before he's supposed to be here."

Looking at my phone for the time, I can't believe they distracted me enough this whole time so that I wasn't completely freaking out. Underneath the time, there's a message from Alex from four minutes ago.

See you soon, sunshine

The brief message causes the dormant butterflies to erupt in my stomach. The silly part of this whole thing is that Alex and I have spent many, many hours alone together but this is so different, I want to puke.

Grabbing the clothes my roommates picked out for me, I run into my room to change. By the time I'm pulling my last shoe on, a hard knock sounds on the door.

"What a gentleman, actually coming to the door," Sydney says, raising her eyebrows to her hairline. She grabs my sweater from the hook and wraps it around my shoulders. "You're gonna have a blast."

"And we'll see you at the party after! We'll be the drunk idiots waiting very impatiently for every single minute detail of the evening," Danika winks and I roll my eyes but I can't wipe the silly grin from my face.

Facing the door, I take a deep breath, willing myself to calm the hell down. I stand staring at the door, waiting for who knows what but my feet decide that now's the time to take a stand and not move.

The knock sounds again, a little louder this time and a rough shove of two hands on my back catapults me toward the door. I open the door a smidge before pulling it wider when all I can see is a bundle of sunflowers. Alex's lowers the bouquet and greets me with a smile.

"Sunshine," he says as a greeting, handing me the flowers.

I take the stems. "Thank you, these are really pretty." Putting my nose near the top, I take a big whiff. They smell amazing. Like summer and sunshine.

Danika is behind me almost instantly, a mom hovering before junior prom. I'm surprised she didn't make us take a picture.

"I'll put these in water for you." She snakes the flowers out of my hand. "Good move, lover boy," she says, giving me another not as gentle push into the hallway and closing the door quickly behind me. I let out a nervous giggle and meet Alex's eyes briefly before looking away.

Snap out of it. He's just Frat Boy.

I turn to walk down the hall when a firm hand grasps my wrist, pulling me back toward the door. Alex places his hand under my chin and forces my eyes to meet his.

"Sunshine," he says again. His tone is more questioning this time. His eyes travel back and forth between mine a few times before landing on my lips.

"Hi," I say, a smile forming on my face. Alex kisses me ever so lightly and the rest of my nervousness melts away. *He's not like this with other girls.*

Alex smiles against my lips before pulling back, removing the hand from around my wrist and instead sliding his palm against mine, connecting our fingers. We walk down the hallway like this. We walk down the stairs like this. We even leave the building like this, shuttling our way single-file through the door.

"I hope you're wearing comfortable shoes because I was thinking we could walk for a bit," Alex says as we meander past his parked car in front of my building.

A grip his hand a little tighter. "Walking sounds nice. It's a beautiful night."

Alex murmurs his agreement and I can feel his gaze on me.

Together we make our way toward the end of my block, which leads to a huge park. I don't get much time to wander around here but I always want to. It gives some beautiful views of Northeastern foliage.

"You know, I used to come to this park with my mom and dad, and my baby brother," Alex says as we stroll the tree lined path. "I don't have many memories of it but I do have one in particular that's coming to me right now."

I stay silent, urging him to continue. Alex hasn't opened up to me about his family at all. All I know is what he said during public speaking class. So I've been dying to hear more but I didn't want to pry.

"One time, it was my birthday. I think my fourth," he starts. "We were having a picnic and my mom packed all my favorite foods, which at the time was probably beef jerky and string cheese."

"A very refined palette for a four-year-old," I laugh.

Alex chuckles. "Totally." He squeezes my hand a little tighter as we keep walking. "There was really nothing special about that day. But I swear, it's the last vivid memory I have of all of us together. Happy."

I want to console him. I want to do something but I have no idea what to do. Or what he needs. Alex can be so independent and the very last thing I want is for him to think I'm pitying him. I just have this ache in my heart for the little boy who deserved a perfect family and ended up with a mentally ill mother and abusive father. At least he has his brother.

"Tell me more about Drew."

A ghost of a smile creeps onto his face. "Drew's a good kid. He's annoying as hell. Mouthy, rude, addicted to video games. But he's also smart and innovative. He's caring even though he pretends not to be."

"Sounds like you raised him well," I say looking up at him. Alex looks down at me and I can see the look of deep affection in his eyes.

"I tried my best." I feel so lucky that he's opening up to me. It's making me want to do the same for him.

We walk a little further into the park until we come across a parking lot with picnic benches and six different food trucks. "Figured I'd let you choose the cuisine tonight," Alex says, his voice already a little bit lighter than just moments ago.

"Tacos!" I shout, spotting the Mexican truck immediately. Alex laughs as I pull him toward the smell of cumin and chili pepper. He orders us six tacos—one of every kind on the menu—then finds us a table to sit and spread out our dinner. As we eat, Alex tells me more about growing up with Drew and I tell him a few stories about my older brother, Arden. We share a laugh over the time I convinced Arden to jump off the neighbor's roof into their inground pool and he lost his bottoms as soon as he hit the water.

"Does your brother visit often?" He asks, taking the last bite of the tilapia taco.

"Not so much, I mostly just go home to see the family."

Looking up, I meet his soft gaze. He takes my hand and kisses my palm before gathering up our garbage to throw away.

"We should probably head to the party now, huh," I ask. Alex nods, grabbing my hand. We walk for a few minutes in silence until Alex speaks again.

"You haven't talked much about your own family," he says as we start walking back toward the way we came.

"There's not a whole lot to say. I live with my dad, my memaw and my older brother. My brother works at the factory where my dad used to work. He got injured on the job and now he's home but I worry sometimes about Arden there."

"That sounds stressful."

I nod. "It can be. But he's capable and strong. He'll be okay."

"I'm sure they're so proud of you for coming out here and chasing your dreams."

I can't resist the sigh that escapes me. "I hope so." Alex squeezes my hand in reassurance.

"What about your mom?"

I reply matter-of-factly. "My mom left us right after she had me so I don't really know anything about her. All I know is that my parents were very young when they had Arden and still too young when they had me." I haven't thought much about my mom. My dad and Memaw did an amazing job raising Arden and I that I never once felt any emptiness that mother might fill. They made my childhood in South Carolina as amazing as I could've hoped for and I'll always be grateful to them for that.

"And I'm not sad about that, so don't worry about bringing it up," I say reassuringly. Alex seems like he wants to ask follow up questions but I'm grateful that he doesn't. Not that I wouldn't mind talking about my mom, I just don't think there's anything more to say.

"I'd like to meet them, too. Your family," Alex says.

Looking up at him, I see nothing but contentment in his eyes. I only nod, unable to voice how happy it would make me to bring him down to South Carolina, watch him at the dinner table across from my dad, playing games with my memaw on a Saturday morning. Yeah, I'd like that very much.

We walk again in comfortable silence for a few minutes.

"Sunshine?"

"Yeah?"

"What's a 'memaw'?"

Laughter bursts out of me and I gaze up at Alex with a twinkle in my eye. "That's what I call my grandma," I giggle.

"Ah, gotcha," Alex replies, laughing too.

"What do you call your grandparents?"

Alex shrugs. "I dunno. Never had any." That thought made my heart ache but I didn't press him on it either. Tonight is about good memories, not drudging up old, sad memories.

We near the edge of the park and I can see my block ahead of us. Suddenly, Alex stops us, pulling me off the path a bit. He gazes down with a fierce look of determination on his handsome face. It makes him look all the more beautiful. "I want you to know, sunshine, I'm really really happy with the way things are turning out between us."

My breath catches. "You are?"

"I am," he says and my heart grows to an impossibly large size.

"I am, too."

Alex sighs in relief and leans down to place a brief, chaste kiss on my lips.

"Good," he says, leaning his forehead against mine. After a moment, Alex puts his arm around my shoulders, pulling me into his side. We walk like this the entire way to his house and I don't think I've ever felt happier in my whole life.

Chapter Twenty–Nine

Margot

ALEX HOLDS MY CHEEKS in his hands as he places a gentle kiss on my lips. As it would turn out, I was the one who would turn ravenous for his touch. I creep up on my tippy toes and grab his neck, pulling his lips back down to mine with a force that seems to equally surprise and delight him. Alex's hands move to my waist and he grips me tighter, pushing us impossibly closer. I can't get enough. Alex can't get enough. He pushes me backward against the tree-lined fence where a stray branch whips me in the arm.

"Ow," I whine, giggling.

Alex pulls me forward away from the fence. "Ah shit, sorry," he says, glancing toward the frat house that is steps away from our rendezvous spot.

"We should probably go inside anyway. If I get another text from Danika, I think my phone might overheat."

Alex laughs, placing his hand on my back to guide me away from the shadowy corner and up the walkway of his house. Once coming into the light of the porch, Alex is immediately greeted by stragglers sitting on the miss-matched porch furniture. His hand drops from my back as he reaches up to grasp hands with his friends in greeting. No one acknowledges me, not that I expected them to, but also Alex doesn't offer any introductions. I don't let any ill thoughts about it take root in my brain, opting instead to enter the house through the front door that Alex is holding open for me.

The minute we enter, my senses are bombarded with flashing lights, alcohol stench, deafening music and mystery smoke. Beside me, Alex curses.

"These fuckers love to have their way when I'm not here," he says, he jaw ticking as he searches the entryway for one of his frat brothers.

Pushing up on my toes, I speak in his ear over the loud music. "I'm going to find Danika and Sydney." Alex nods but doesn't meet my eyes as my heels hit the ground again. He's clearly on a mission to find whoever's to blame for this chaos.

Leaving Alex in the foyer, I walk into the busy living room, narrowly avoiding an empty cup being thrown in my direction. The way this party is playing out reminds me of the first night I met Alex in this very house when he was aggressively removing someone from his home. I still can't believe how different he is when you actually get to know him. Gone is the rough exterior, at least around me. It's hard to be tough when he's admitted that his favorite movie is *John Tucker Must Die*.

Smiling to myself, I give a quick glance around the room and notice it's sans Danika and Sydney. I head outside, hoping to find them sitting around the firepit or cheering on a beer pong game. After a cursory glance around the backyard, I notice they aren't there either. There's only one more place to check before I send one an SOS text. Heading toward the backdoor, I move to pull the knob open but my wrist is caught by a hand from behind.

"Can we please just talk?"

Ryan's eyes pierce mine from the bottom of the steps, the overhead light making his blue eyes look like a glacier. I pull my hand out of his grasp but continue to look down at him. I have absolutely nothing to say to him. Even though Alex didn't tell me which Delta Epsilon guys were the ones that jumped Keith, there's a pretty high chance Ryan had something to do with it. Especially considering it happened right after he left my apartment, drunk and upset.

"Margot, please. Just one minute, that's all I'm asking for." His eyes are bloodshot. I can tell that he's not going to drop this easily so rather than make a scene, I relent.

"One minute," I say, firmly, nodding my head toward the empty fire pit, the place where we first talked. The irony is not lost on me.

Ryan lets me lead the way to the pit and I purposely pick differently chairs than the ones we previously sat in. Also, I wanted to be sure not to sit in the chairs that Alex and I sat in for some reason.

Plopping down in the seat, I watch Ryan linger slightly above me.

"Do you want a drink or something?"

I level him with a glare that answers his question, causing him to promptly sit down in the chair next to mine. We're facing the house with the raging fire in front of us. It's not a particularly cold night but my disdain for the person next to me is filling my veins with ice, causing me to shiver.

"Look, things got out of hand the other night. First, I want to apologize for what happened. I shouldn't have busted into your apartment like that and I didn't mean to blow up the way I did. I was not in my right mind," Ryan says calmly.

I look over at him, seeing the sincerity in his eyes. "I appreciate the apology." Ryan sighs in relief before I continue. "To be clear, I'm not saying what you did is okay and I don't necessarily forgive you but I can acknowledge your sincerity."

Ryan closes his mouth, clearly swallowing what he was about to say, and nods. For a moment, we're both silent, staring into the blazing fire.

"Well, if that's all," I say, gripping the lawn chair arms to pull myself up when Ryan speaks again.

"Kai is not who you think he is."

I'm stunned into silence. This is what he wants to talk to me about? "What does that mean? I hardly know Kai."

"Okay, then, he's not the guy *Alex* thinks he is."

In exasperation, I run my hands down my face. "Ryan, just spit it out. This cryptic stuff is giving me a headache." I feel my phone vibrate in my pocket but I don't pull it out. It's probably Danika looking for me and I know I need to get back to looking for her but not until Ryan gets to the point of his outburst. And boy does he...

"I'm sure you know that Keith was roughed up a bit by some of my guys," Ryan looks me directly in the eyes when he speaks about how his friends hurt one of mine. I want to scream at him for his cavalier manner in speaking about it but he continues before I get the chance. "I want you to know the reason why that happened.

"Some of my guys have...problems. Gambling problems. They make bets without thinking, and they get themselves in trouble. One of my brothers, Logan, was at the horse track betting one day when he saw Kai. Logan convinced Kai to get in on some bets with him, mainly just to fuck with the Kappas. But Logan had no idea what kind of shit Kai was into."

Ryan breathes fast and continues.

"Basically, Kai wrote more than a few checks his ass couldn't cash. He owed some of us Deltas a lot of fucking money and Logan was tired of waiting for it. None of the promises Kai made ever came through."

The fire flickers in front of us and my phone vibrates again but nothing could pull me from this conversation. This revelation. *If it is the truth...*

"Without consulting me, Logan and a few others decided to take some of the debt off Kai, by way of his brother. By the time I showed up after leaving your apartment, Keith was already pretty battered. I ripped my guys heads off and brought Keith to his front porch but the damage was already done.

"I didn't want anyone to see me and as it is, I probably shouldn't even be here but I knew you would be and I wanted to explain to you, relationship or not, I wanted to tell my side before it gets torn apart by Alex and his friends."

As if on cue, the back door flies open, and Alex leads a pack of Kappas toward the fire pit. I've never been afraid of him before but I am suddenly, for the second time tonight, reminded of the first time I met him.

"What the fuck are you doing here, Walsh?"

As they get closer to the fire, I can see that Alex is flanked by Kai and Keith, the latter looking tired and the former looking like he could kill Ryan via telekinesis. It's when I look at Alex that I start to sweat. He's shooting daggers at me. *Alone with the enemy.* Yeah, it doesn't look good.

To his defense, Ryan doesn't meet fire with fire. In fact, he raises his hands in surrender, standing from the chair. "Not here for trouble, just wanted to talk to Margot."

"You have no reason to talk to her," Alex spits.

Ryan doesn't fight, he doesn't raise his voice when he nods and says, "I'm leaving now."

"The fuck you are," Kai mutters, launching himself toward us only to be held back by Devon.

"Margot, come here," Alex says, his voice a command. He clearly wants to show us as a united front against Ryan, but I feel like this whole thing is ridiculous, especially because of what Ryan just told me.

"I actually think you guys should just talk to each other," I say, motioning between Ryan and the group. Ryan looks over at me and I give him a nod of encouragement.

But it's Kai who speaks up. "I'm not talking to the son of a bitch that tore up my brother. But you go ahead, princess, go with him if you care so much about what he has to say."

I look over at Alex, hoping for some defense but his eyes are narrowed at me too. "I'm not leaving with him. I'm just saying, maybe you should hear him out."

"If you trust anything that dipshit has to say, you don't belong here." Kai is taking over the narrative and based on what I just learned about him, I understand why. He doesn't want the truth to come out. And I don't want to be the one to fill in the gaps either. This has nothing to do with me and everything to do with the Deltas and the Kappas. I've never been interested in frat problems before and I'm not now.

But when I look over at Alex, he's gazing at me like he's looking at a stranger. Like he has no idea who I am. I can feel Ryan's eyes on me from the side and Alex's glare from the front.

"Can we go talk inside?" I ask Alex, my voice annoyingly shaky.

Alex stays quiet, looking back and forth between Ryan and me, and I know he's already made up his mind. He's taking this at face value rather than listening to what I have to say.

"Forget it," I say, looking up and shaking my head. I grab my bag from the chair and move away from the group to head inside. If I don't find Danika and Sydney on my way out, I'll just text them that I left, not wanting to linger any longer in this house.

Alex lets me walk past him, and I don't look back to see how the rest of the group manages their staring contest. As I enter the kitchen, looking back and forth and not finding either one of my roommates, I decide enough is enough. I'm out of here.

I don't let the first tear drop until I'm out the front door and away from the drunken revelry. I make it to the corner before the second tear falls and that's when I hear the pounding footsteps behind me.

Whirling around, I see Alex running up the block, and I couldn't move from my spot even if I wanted to. And trust me, I want to. I want to avoid this fight as much as possible because I know he's not going to believe what Ryan told me about Kai. Hell, I'm not sure I believe it. But there was something so sincere about the way he spoke, something so apologetic, that he had me listening, against my better judgment. It just made sense.

I'm not sure what I expect him to say when he finally meets up with me but it's not: "You're not walking home alone, it's almost midnight."

He barely looks me in the eye, just continues past me toward the corner. My jaw drops and I'm stunned into silence. For about three seconds.

"You're kidding me, right? After all that?" I whip around to see him standing at the corner, still not meeting my eyes.

"What do you want me to say, Margot?"

Finally gathering up the courage, I stalk toward him. "I want you to say 'Hey, sunshine, I'm sorry I treated you like shit back there. Won't happen again'," I say, standing directly in front of him. My comment finally gets his attention, and his eyes whip to mine.

"Are you serious?" He steps impossibly closer to me. There's an intimacy to it but this is not a romantic moment. "I leave you alone for five minutes to find you cozied up by the fire with the guy that beat the shit out of my friend and *you're* mad at *me*?"

"He didn't beat up Keith," I say, quietly and against my better judgment. But just as I expected, Alex laughs directly in my face.

"And you believe the lies he's telling you! What fucking else could go wrong right now." Alex runs his hands through his hair, spinning around in exasperation. "Keith told us that he saw Ryan's face in the fight. It was the last face he saw before he passed out."

"Ryan said he came up on his brothers beating up Keith and he broke it up. He brought Keith to the house." I know everything I'm saying is falling on deaf ears but I have to say it. The more I retell Ryan's side, the more I believe it. There's no way he could've beat up Keith, hardly ten minutes had passed since he had stormed out of my apartment and then Alex got that phone call.

Alex crosses the street, continuing the walk to my apartment even though he clearly wants nothing to do with me right now. "You are un-fucking-believable, sunshine." His voice is like venom, but he still calls me sunshine and that fact has hope blossoming in my stomach.

I follow behind him a few paces, mostly because he's walking too fast for me to keep up. When I see my apartment complex come into view, I know I only have a few more seconds to say my piece before he disappears.

Running up a few steps, I grab Alex's arm, whipping him around. "You need to talk to Kai. He's been keeping something from you."

"Keeping what from me?"

I sigh. "Just...talk to him."

Alex blinks a few times and then nods. Once.

I take my hand off his arm, but he grabs my wrist before it drops to my side. Clutching it tightly, he uses the contact to pull me closer to him, chest to chest. My breath catches at the sudden contact and my heart contracts as he snakes his free hand to the back of my neck, pulling my hair slightly to bring my eyes to his.

"I'm really fucking pissed at you," he says, his words saying one thing but his eyes and touch say another.

"I'm not too fond of you either at the moment," I mutter, trying and failing to hold onto my resolve from just moments ago.

Without another word, Alex reaches down and connects our lips in a scathing kiss. It's not nice, it's not loving. It's hard and needy. It's desperate and addictive. I reach up on my toes to match his fervor and he deepens the kiss, our hands clutching each other even closer.

After what felt like an eternity of this intimate torture, Alex pulls away, leaving me breathless and bereft.

"I'll see you tomorrow," he says curtly, reminding me that we still need to film our podcast tomorrow. After all this.

I nod, shutting my mouth and lowering my heels to the ground. Alex lets me go and I feel every inch of untouched skin.

I don't say anything as I walk around his tall frame and into the building. I don't look back as the door closes and I walk up the stairs and into the apartment. But, the first thing I do is walk across the living room to peer out the window to see Alex still standing outside, just as I knew he would be.

Chapter Thirty

Alex

THE WEIGHT HITS THE machine louder than necessary but I couldn't care less. Leaning down, I add another ten pounds to the resistance and then start my reps again, raising the bar above my head and lowering it down over and over.

I had spent the morning looking over Margot's notes for the podcast, thinking about how I'd answer some of these questions. Usually we come up with a script during our Monday planning sessions but this week has been so fucked up that we have hardly been seeing eye to eye on anything, let alone the podcast.

I can admit that, right now, my heart isn't really into this whole podcast thing but, no matter what the situation is with Margot and me, I won't let her down. I made her a promise and I keep my promises.

As I finish my last rep, my thoughts wander to the events of last night. How could such an amazing date end up with me and Margot barely talking and her instead chatting it up with the enemy? She told me to talk to Kai, and I haven't yet had the chance but I am going to see what he has to say. I don't think Margot is naive enough to just blindly trust what Ryan was saying. There must've been some truth in his words that I need to uncover.

The weight drops again as Devon and Keith walk up to my machine. "We're going to get lunch, you coming?"

"Nah," I reply, wiping the sweat off my forehead with the bottom of my shirt. They nod as they walk toward the door. Even though we all drove together in Devon's car, I opt to run home to finish my workout. I still need to blow off some steam.

Wiping down my equipment, I leave the gym, starting my jog toward home. It takes me fifteen minutes to get home and my head is still a jumbled mess as I walk through the door. I was happy to not see Kai when I came in. I know I need to talk to him but I just don't think I'm ready for another fight. Not before I have to deal with this uncomfortable podcast taping with Margot.

I shower quickly and then get back in the car to pick her up.

───∿∿∧∧∧∿∿∿∿───

Her bemused expression pulls a reluctant chuckle out of me as I drive up to her apartment. She walks to the car but doesn't open the door. Margot just stares at me through the window, which I roll down.

"Getting in?"

Margot raises her eyes, clearly shocked at the sight in front of her. "I didn't expect you to pick me up."

"I always pick you up," I reply matter-of-factly, turning back toward the dashboard. I have one hand on the steering wheel and one on the gear shift. What's noticeably absent is the coffee I usually bring her. Which means my own afternoon pick-me-up was also skipped. I may be mad but I'm not cruel enough to get myself one and not her. So we both go without.

Margot hesitates outside the door, not knowing which path to take.

"Come on, I wasn't going to leave you hanging," I tilt my head over to her again, egging her into the car. She opens the door, finally, and I take off the minute it closes.

We ride in silence for the five minute drive to campus. Her window is still down, allowing her to take in the familiar sights while her long brown hair whips in the car, sending wafts of her signature scent in my direction. Something I didn't think would be difficult to handle but I was proven wrong. The hand on the gear shift flexes with the desire to reach over and touch her leg. Caress the bare knee she has exposed through the slit in her long brown skirt. I grip the shift tighter.

Parking in my usual spot close to the media building, we walk to the door in the same silence and suddenly I can't take it anymore.

"Look, I—"

"Listen, Alex—"

Margot and I speak at the same time, cutting each other off. I turn my palm out to offer her the floor to speak. We still haven't gone inside the building but we clearly both had the same idea that we should clear the air before we do.

"I didn't mean to stick my nose in your business last night. Ryan wanted to apologize to me about the other night..."

"Why do you need an apology from him?" I ask, not meaning to cut her off but needing to know the answer all of a sudden.

"I didn't need anything from him. He seemed to need to say his piece more than I needed to hear it." She sighs. "I didn't expect him to tell me what he did but that's why I stayed to talk to him for as long as I did."

The only thing that can happen from here is that I need to talk to Kai. I'm still mad at Margot for not taking my side on the matter but that will all have to wait.

"Let's just go get this done, yeah?"

Margot nods, swinging the door open enough for herself to walk through but hardly enough for me. *Nice.*

"Hey guys, wasn't sure if you were gonna show up," Nathan sat waiting for us at the soundboard. Margot greets him with a smile that is usually on reserve for me but not today. She drops her bag on the chair and takes off her jacket, revealing a white lace crop top that shows a sliver of her stomach.

"Let's get this over with," she says with a cheerfulness that doesn't match the expression on her face. Without another word, she steps into the soundproof recording studio and takes her usual spot. Nathan spares a glance in my direction and I level him with a look like, *this is going to be interesting.*

When I meet Margot inside the studio, she's already laid out the session notes for me. "I hope you had a chance to look at my email," she says, without meeting my eyes.

"Yep, went through it this morning."

"Good," she says, leaning back in her seat. "Then this should be painless." *Ha.*

Once I'm settled in, we both give Nathan a thumbs up as he silently counts us down from three on his fingers. The bright red recording button appears at the top of the wall and we're off.

"Hello, folks and welcome back to another riveting episode of *Ask Alex*. As you already know, clearly, I am Alex, your host and resident question answerer and with me is my darling, lovely, beguiling, cohost, Margot."

"Oh, please, don't even try to butter me up, frat boy, we've got way too much on our agenda for all that," Margot says with a smile but her teeth are gritted a little too much to be a pleasurable expression. "And on that note, let's jump right in!"

Margot pulls up an index card where she wrote out the question. "This question comes from an avid listener named Kelly K. The question is, Alex, are you ready?"

"Yes, I am ready."

"The question is: At what age is it deemed *appropriate* to lose your virginity? And then there's a follow up of: What age did *you* lose your virginity, Alex Prescott?"

Margot places the card down on the table and crosses her hands on her lap, looking at me expectantly. I had anticipated this question, having looked at the script, but I didn't anticipate how talking about sex with Margot would make me feel.

"Kelly, thank you for writing in," I give Margot a pointed glance before looking back at the camera with my signature wink. "I think it's important that you, first of all, and the person you're with are of legal age. That being said, it's definitely not appropriate to have sex before the age of seventeen. Eighteen in some states, make sure you look up the laws, okay folks?"

Margot rolls her eyes. "Very solid legal advice, counselor."

I ignore her jab. "As for me personally, well...let's just say I didn't follow my own advice." Raising my eyebrows suggestively at the camera before looking over at Margot.

She's huffing out a breath before shuffling the deck to find her next question. Before she can pull one out, I place my hand on top of the stack. "Well, hold on, sunshine, I answered the question, now it's your turn."

"This isn't Ask Alex *and* Margot, is it?"

"Fair is fair," I shrug. "I'm sure the people want to know," I continue, pointing toward the camera. I don't miss the blush that forms on Margot's cheeks. She's looking down at her hands, not willing to meet my eyes.

With a huff, she looks up. "I haven't," she says simply before shuffling through the deck again. For my own personal sake, I want to dive deeper into that answer but I can tell she's completely embarrassed by it so I choose to let it go instead. I do, however, pocket the conversation for a time when we aren't fighting, which will be soon if I have my way about it.

"Next question," Margot presses on, and I let her, the ice around my heart melting slowly with each minute we pass together. Margot asks me two more questions, one about my fitness regime, which was clearly sent in by a dude, and one about my advice on college majors, which I didn't have a whole lot of.

"It's come to that time, folks. Our last question," I announce and I can already feel Margot start to relax a bit knowing the end of her time in the spotlight is near.

Margot picks up the index card, opens her mouth to speak, but then thinks better of it. Lowering her hand, Margot places the stack on the table and looks over at me instead. I don't hide the confusion in my eyes.

"The final question, Alex Prescott, is: Who deserves your trust more? Your best friend or your significant other?"

I take in a breath. I know what she's doing. She's making the question relatable by using that term but I know she's talking about what happened last night.

"Well, I think it depends on the situation. It also depends on how long you've known each person."

Margot settles into her chair, content to hear me out.

"If you've been bros with your best friend for years and this significant other is a new situation, I'd say trust the best friend...If the roles were reversed, I'd say the opposite."

As I start to think about it more, my mind starts to shift. "But what reason would your best friend have to lie to you? As shitty as it sounds, your significant other could have motive to make you believe something that's not necessarily true."

"Why would you be with someone that has ulterior motives?"

"Now, that's a good question... but unfortunately, our time is up so we'll have to leave it at that for now." I can't meet her eyes even though I can feel hers boring into the side of my head. "Until next week, ladies...and maybe one gentleman, based on that fitness question. This has been us." I give the camera a salute and watch the recording button blink out in my peripheral vision.

Margot is out of her seat before I even have a chance to say anything. She pulls the door open, grabs her jacket, bag and leaves the studio without even a word to Nathan. Since my seat is farther from the door, it takes me a minute to get my long legs out of the small space and reach the door.

By the time I make it out of the building, she's gone.

———ᴧᴧᴧ\ᴧᴧᴧ———

Kai is sitting at the kitchen table when I get home, and I take the opportunity to sort this out once and for all.

Pulling up the chair in front of him, I sit. Kai continues to shovel food into his mouth, effectively ignoring me.

"What's going on, Kai?" He knows from my inflection that I'm not asking casually.

He finally meets my eyes, his mouth full. He, thankfully, swallows his food before continuing. "What do you mean?"

"You've been off, man, for a while now. Something's not right."

Kai remains silent. He has a split second to decide what to do. Is he going to tell me the truth or is he going to lie to my face? I keep talking before he can make a choice. "We've known each other a long time. And you know I have your back no matter what."

Kai sighs, not meeting my eyes. "I'm not sure if I'm going to be able to pay for the final semester of school."

I raise my eyebrows, taking in the very last thing I expected him to say. *What does that have to do with Ryan and Margot?*

"Your parents aren't paying?"

Kai remains quiet.

"Why didn't you tell me? You know I can help, I—"

Kai gets up, bringing his plate over to the sink and throwing it in. "I'm not a charity case."

"What the fuck, man. It's not charity. You're my brother." I follow him into the kitchen where he's now gripping the sink, his knuckles white. "This is a drop in the bucket for my asshole father. He won't even realize it's missing."

Kai sighs, meeting my eyes again. "I appreciate it, man. But it's more than that." I keep quiet, allowing him to talk when he's ready. Kai turns around and leans against the sink, crossing his arms over his chest. "I got into some trouble."

"What kind of trouble?"

"The money-owing kind," he says. "I used the tuition money my dad gave me to pay off some debts but it wasn't enough."

"Dude," I sigh, not knowing what to say. My ass finds the top of the kitchen stool as I sink into it. "How much do you owe?"

"Let's just say it's a lot."

"Who do you owe it to?"

Kai remains silent, answering the question without saying a word. It's the Deltas. It has to be. Suddenly it all makes sense. Why Keith was jumped. Why Kai was upset about it enough to take his anger out on me, trying to push the blame on Ryan and Margot instead of himself. This is what Ryan told her last night.

Kai must see the spark of recognition in my eyes. "Don't tell Keith, please, Alex." I don't think I've ever heard this man plead for anything in the four years I've known him. "I will handle this."

"But you're not handling it. It's handling you." I try not to sound judgmental but this whole thing is so fucked up, I don't know what else to do. Fuck, Margot has every right in the world to be upset with me, especially after that my answer to that last podcast question. Once I'm finished up here, I vow to run over to her apartment and beg on my knees if I have to. None of this is her fault and yet she found herself in the middle of a shitstorm that I only made worse by thinking the worst of her.

Kai has his face in his hands. "I'll figure it out."

I sigh, raising from my stool to place my hand on his shoulder. "I'm here for you, man. Let me help." Kai looks up, letting his hands fall, his red eyes finally meeting mine. And he nods.

Chapter Thirty-One

Margot

"MR. DARCY WOULD NEVER," Danika comments, popping another piece of popcorn into her mouth. As an attempt to take my mind off what's going on between Alex and I, Sydney suggested a movie night which I happily agreed to...until Danika made non-stop parallels between the leading man and my podcast co-star.

I hit her with my millionth scathing glance of the night but she continues to ignore me. "Do you think Mr. Darcy would be into podcasts if he lived in modern times?"

"No, he would think they're a frivolous waste of time," Sydney answers for me, her eyes glued to the screen, as well. Even though we've seen this movie over a hundred times (this year), it's always our number one pick-me-up movie.

Just as Elizabeth is denying Darcy by not returning his affections, a knock sounds on our door. Both of my friends whip their heads to me. Alex better not have shown up right now. I am nowhere near ready to talk to him.

With a sigh, I pull myself off the couch and trudge over toward the door. Taking in a deep breath, I steel myself before pulling the door open. The face that greets me on the other side causes a gigantic smile to erupt on my face.

I scream and immediately Danika and Sydney are at my side, ready to fight whoever they need to fight to protect me.

"Geez, Mars," my big brother smiles at me from my doorstep. "Can't say I was expecting that reaction." Arden laughs before stepping forward and pulling me into a hug. I hug him back before pulling away, looking into his eyes.

"What are you doing here?"

"What, a guy can't visit his little sis while she's away at school?" I squint my eyes at him but decide to interrogate him later, instead pulling him into the apartment.

"Hey, Arden," Sydney says with a smile, as he pulls her in for a polite hug. When he turns his gaze toward Danika, his grin falls.

"Danika," he says.

"Arden," she replies.

I roll my eyes, pushing him past them and into the rest of the apartment. I grab his bag from his shoulder, noticing the heaviness of it.

"How long are you staying?"

Arden looks around. He's come to visit me at school before, but he hasn't seen this apartment yet. We only moved in here last year and Arden was too busy with work to ever come out and see me.

"Just a day or two," he says noncommittally. Once he notices the movie on the screen, he immediately grabs the remote. "You, ladies, have a problem."

Much to our protest, Arden turns the TV off, throwing the remote onto the couch. "It's Saturday night, you're young and in college. Why are you not out on the town?"

Danika crosses her arms and juts out her hip. "For once, I agree with Peepants."

"We are *not* starting that," Arden warns Danika. She just scrunches her nose at him. "Brat," he mutters. His lovely nickname for my best friend. I truly have no idea how they haven't killed each other yet.

Sydney, having not had the pleasure of growing up with Arden and Danika fighting as if they were the siblings, looks adorably confused. I lean in to explain. "Cause he peed his pants once when we were camping in the woods."

Sydney smothers her laugh with the back of her hand.

Arden looks at his watch. "It's 9:30. You have fifteen minutes to get yourselves all pretty and then we're going out."

Danika doesn't need to be told twice, running right into her room to change and swipe on some makeup. Sydney is still laughing as she walks to her own room, much more slowly.

I only look over at Arden. "Is everything okay?" My brother hits me with a smile that is supposed to convince me that nothing is wrong but I know him better than that.

"Everything's fine, Mars. Let's go, the clock is ticking." Arden takes my shoulders and turns me around, shoving me into the only empty room which he deduced was mine. Clearly, something isn't right, but he needs to blow off some steam before he'll talk to me about it. So I let him push me into my room, closing the door to change and ponder what could've brought my brother seven hundred miles from home.

The bar is full of underage girls, many of which I have classes with. Cannons is notoriously lenient on IDs so all the undergrads will come here if they don't want to go to another frat party.

Normally, I dislike the bar scene even more than the party scene but I was too excited to see my brother to care where we went. Arden got us the first round of beers, and Danika and Sydney were making their way to the bar for the second time when I finally got a second to sit down with him.

"Alright, enough already. What's going on? What are you doing here and why didn't you tell me you were coming?"

"Do I really need a reason to come visit you?" Arden sips his beer, looking around my shoulder for a pretty college girl to make eyes at. I snap my fingers in his face to bring his focus back.

"A reason, no? A phone call beforehand, yes."

Arden raises his hands in surrender. "You're right, sis, I should've called."

Satisfied for the moment, I take the last sip of my cold beverage basking in the glow of having my big brother out on the town with me.

"Round two, folks," Sydney announces, handing me a fresh beer. Danika goes to hand one to Arden but pulls it back right before he can grab it. The staring contest that ensues is vicious and I have to look away before I see one of them burst into flames. My eyes glance toward the door where suddenly the large frame of a very tall, very familiar man takes shape in the doorway.

Sydney clocks him the second I do. "Did you tell him you were here?"

"Nope," I reply, popping my "p". I take a very long sip of my drink before turning my head back toward the people I actually want to spend time with. I'm hoping, with the crowd being what it is, Alex won't be able to find me.

He hasn't texted, hasn't called since I left him in the recording studio. Not that I wanted him to. But it would've been nice to know he was thinking about me. Clearly, I was thinking about him. Again...not that I wanted to.

My wishful thinking bubble bursts within a few minutes as Alex finds his way over to us. Arden is sitting on my left, cheersing his beer with mine as Alex walks up.

"Didn't take you very long, did it?"

"Excuse me?" I say, initially intending to ignore his ass but can't possibly after that comment. All eyes are on Alex and I now. Even Arden is stunned speechless which probably won't last long.

"One fight and you're running off with someone else," Alex gestures toward Arden, and Danika gags on the other side of the table. Alex whips his head around to her, clearly confused.

"Hey, fella," Arden says, cool as a cucumber with his hand outstretched toward Alex. "I'm Arden."

Alex looks at Arden, glances at his hand then looks back toward me. "My brother."

The look of relief on Alex's face shocks me. He genuinely thought I'd run off with someone else after one small thing. *That's going to bode well for our relationship.*

"Brother?" He asks, hope leaking out of his voice. He takes Arden's hand.

"Brother," Arden replies, shaking twice then dropping Alex's hand. "And you must be Alex."

Alex's gaze whips to mine, his eyes dancing with mirth. "You told your brother about me."

"Uh, no," I look over at Arden. "I didn't."

He swallows the sip of his beer before continuing. "Well, I've seen your podcast, obviously." I don't get a chance to ask him any follow-up questions about how he even knew about the podcast before an ice cold drink is poured directly down my front. Some drunken idiot falls over on top of me and soaks me completely.

"Watch where you're fucking going, asshole!" Danika shouts but that's not what intimidates the man. No, it's the two over six feet tall men that have stacked up in front of me, looking to punch anything that moves.

Grabbing some napkins from a nearby table, I start to dab myself dry. "Down, dogs. Heel." I scoff, rolling my eyes at their dick-measuring display. When they don't move, I push past, heading toward the bathroom with Dani and Sydney on my tail.

Thankfully, the line is short and by some miracle the three of us file in and start damage control.

"You're lucky clear alcohol doesn't stain," Danika comments, wetting a paper towel and dapping the wet spots on my shirt.

"I don't feel lucky," I reply, quietly. Sydney gets a dry towel and soaks up some of the wetness. "This is so weird, right? My brother is here and he just met the guy I'm kind of dating, kind of not dating."

Danika laughs. "Definitely weird, but in a good way, I think."

"What's good about this?" I gesture toward my wet clothes. Syd and Dani take a step back, admiring my outfit disaster.

I see the lightbulb go off in Syd's head as she peels off her flannel shirt, leaving her white tank top revealed. She throws the shirt over my head and ties the two sleeves together in front of my chest.

"Fashion, baby," she says with a wink, turning me toward the mirror. The look isn't going to get me into any fashion shows any time soon but it hides the stains well enough.

"Thanks, Syd." She winks and I ready myself to enter the fray again. In my panic to get clean, I didn't even realize I'd be leaving Arden and Alex alone together.

"Oh god, let's—"

"Yeah, we should—"

The three of us barrel out the door, expecting to have to break up a full on brawl but instead we find the two guys, enjoying beers and...laughing? *That can't be right.*

As we walk back toward them, both sets of eyes glance in my direction. Arden pulls me into his side. "Crisis averted?"

I nod and smile awkwardly. I have no idea what they were just talking about and I'm even more sure I don't want to know. Anything that my brother and Alex Prescott have in common can't be good.

"Another round?" He asks, holding up his empty bottle.

I grimace.

"You should know your sister well enough by now to know she's not down for late nights, peepants," Danika says, the disdain seeping out of her voice.

"I can take you home if you want, Margot," Alex says. "So the rest of you guys can keep the party going."

Danika and Sydney both nod their heads reassuringly and I trust that Arden will take care of them. Not that I really want to spend any extra time with Alex at the moment, the thought of pajamas and a cup of hot chocolate sounds heavenly to me right now.

"See you guys at home," I say, purposefully avoiding Alex's hand as he outstretches it toward me to guide me toward the door.

When we finally enter the fresh air, I am able to take a deep breath. The bar reeked of stale beer and hot dogs so being out in the open has helped clear my head a bit. Alex and I start walking in the direction of my apartment without saying a word. After a block of silence, he finally speaks.

"I saw you leave your building tonight." I look over to see his eyes facing forward, not wanting to meet mine. "I went to your apartment to see if you'd talk to me but I saw you leaving with him. And I was jealous."

I stare ahead, just as he does, letting him speak. "I was jealous of you being with another man. I didn't like that feeling at all."

"Well, it's a good thing you have nothing to worry about, then," I mutter.

"Don't I, though?" Alex stops walking and I stop beside him as we turn to face each other. "What about Ryan?"

"What *about* Ryan? Clearly I chose *you* over Ryan."

Alex runs his hands through his hair in exasperation.

"Why are you trying to start a fight with me right now?"

He sighs, "I don't know." Alex is quiet for a few moments before he speaks again. "I talked to Kai. He told me what I'm assuming Ryan told you."

"Is he okay?" I ask, continuing to walk toward home as we keep walking.

Alex nods. "He's in some trouble, but we're gonna figure it out. Anyway, I don't like how easy it was for something like that to get between us."

"Us?" I ask. "Is there an *us*, Alex?"

"I'd like there to be." And there it was. The most honest thing he's ever said to me. If I stood my ground, I'd have him go home and wait for my call. If I had more guts, I'd send him packing for good.

Instead, I find myself saying the words I've never said to a boy.

"Do you want to come inside?"

Chapter Thirty-Two

Margot

I KICK MY SHOES onto the rack as the door closes behind us. Shrugging off my coat, I flip on the switch to turn on the overhead light and then hook the coat up. Gesturing toward the open hook, I motion for Alex to hang his things, too. Above us, the light flickers as usual.

"Make yourself at home," I say, walking into the kitchen to grab two water bottles. Alex follows me and starts rummaging through the cabinets under the sink. "Um, it's just an expression."

Alex chuckles, pulling out a white box from underneath and heading back toward the entryway.

"What are you doing?"

Alex walks back over toward the doorway. "Changing your lightbulb."

Without the use of a ladder or even a step stool, Alex reaches up and unscrews the light fixture from the ceiling. He hands the top to me as I stand bewildered underneath him.

"I can see that. Why are you doing it?"

"Because it flickers."

"Alex."

"Margot."

He removes the sputtering light and replaces it with the fresh one he found under the sink, taking the part from my hand and placing it all back within seconds.

"How did you know we'd have lightbulbs under the sink?" I ask, still amazed by what just happened.

Alex shrugs. "That's where my mom always kept the spare lightbulbs."

I nod, a grin forming. "Well, thanks," I say, handing him the water bottle and we both make our way to the couch.

"Would you tell me about her? Your mom? Only if you want to."

I pull my knees up to my chest and Alex sits across from me, his leg crossed at the knee. "My mom was...eccentric. And I know most people say that when you can't say anything nice about the person but I mean it. She was happy and funny, warm and kind. She would spend her mornings making us pancakes with smiley faces before she drove us to school. She would buy us treats at the store just because she wanted to or sometimes she'd plan a spur of the moment trip to some town or other on a weekend and we'd pile into the car and drive for hours.

"One time, she said 'get in boys, we're going to the moon' and then she drove us about four hours north to some frozen cave in Vermont," Alex laughs at the memory. "We sat in the cave, drinking hot chocolate, and she told us stories about her adventures to space with her sisters."

Alex pauses, his face being more serious. "We never met her sisters though. She had two of them, I think. They didn't want anything to do with us."

He takes a shaky sip of his water. "See, because those mornings she would make us breakfast and drive us to school, those were also the days she would forget to pick us up and chain smoke a pack of cigarettes on the back porch while I threw some frozen pizza in the oven for me and my brother.

"The treats from the store always came with a chuck out the window if we so much as looked at her the wrong way in public and those weekend trips, well...you heard what happened during the last one."

Alex stops speaking and I have no words to say. I can't believe he is opening up to me like this. I can't believe he's had such a tragic home life. Before I can muster up the courage to say something, he speaks again.

"And you might be asking, but 'Alex, what about your dad during all this?'" He cocks his head. "Well, he was building an empire, of course. Prescott Cars. Cars for you. Cars for life." He waves his hands up into the air as he quotes out the motto of his father's company. "And he loved my mother. Truly, he did. The love radiated off of him whenever he was around her. But when she was going through an episode, when she wasn't her charming, charismatic self, well, how could he love that person? No, that person didn't deserve his time or attention. And by extension, neither did her sons.

"I can't wait until the day that I can get Drew out of that house." Alex takes a long sip of the water, caps the bottle and then throws it across the room. He runs his hands through his hair, resting his elbows on his knees.

"I'm sorry," I lean forward, gently rubbing the shoulder nearest to me. "That is so horrible. You and Drew do not deserve that." Alex surprises me by catching my hand on his arm, he looks up from his lap, his red eyes capturing mine. And then he kisses me.

This kiss is unlike the rest. It's a kiss that's meant to help him to forget the past, rewrite the bad memories with good ones, ones we can create together. I lean into his passion, allowing him to lose himself in me as he leans me back onto the couch, pulling his body on top of mine. His hand travels down to the seam of my shirt and then he grips his way underneath, clutching at my bare waist.

My hands are in his hair, holding him impossibly closer to me as our mouths mold together. The hand under my shirt moves upward toward my lacy bra and I thank myself for putting on a matching set.

I move my hands down to the bottom of his shirt and with very little force, yank it up and over his head. Our lips part for mere seconds before he's on me again, his smile against mine.

Our passion continues and I release a moan when Alex's hand wanders down toward the button of my jeans. I want him there, more than I've ever wanted anything. Alex pulls back to look into my eyes, a silent question. I give him a nod and he kisses me again, his free hand releasing the clasp of my pants. Slowly, the zipper moves down.

And then the key turns in the lock and our eyes bolt open. We're on the living room couch. Alex is half-naked and my brother is about to walk through that door.

My frantic expression tells him what he needs him to do and Alex follows direction well as he jumps off the couch and runs into my room, slamming the door behind him, just in time for the front door to open.

"Y'all are back early," I comment breathlessly, smoothing out my hair and clothes before standing up from the couch.

"Bar got lame once you guys left, turns out you're the life of the party, Mars," Arden says, kicking off his shoes and hanging his coat. As that happens, Danika and I have a silent conversation.

Danika: *Alex leave?*

Me: *He's in my bedroom.*

Danika: *Yes, bitch!*

Me: *Eye-roll*

I stifle a giggle and look down to hide my blush. It's then I notice that Alex's shirt is still on the floor. My laugh dies in my throat. Sydney, having clocked the entire silent exchange, jumps into action.

"Arden, can you get me some water from the fridge? These heels are so uncomfortable, I can't walk another step."

My brother, being the southern gentleman that he was raised to be, could never let down a woman in duress. He jumps up and immediately sets toward the fridge. Once his back is turned, I swipe the shirt from the floor and run for my bedroom door.

"Well, okay, goodnight!" I say as a final goodbye before slamming the door and resting my back against it. I have to cover my mouth to keep the shaking laughter inside of me. Alex is standing in the center of my room, shirtless, entirely delicious and I can't help the laughter that erupts.

"That was not funny," Alex laughs too and he walks over, running his palm down the side of my face. He leans down and scoops me up into his arms, his right arm supporting my weight while his left continues to caress my cheek. He kisses me lightly. "Nothing like a big brother to ruin the mood," he jokes, resting his forehead against mine.

"That was so close," I sigh into him.

"Would it have really been so bad if he caught us?"

I lean back to look him in the eyes. "Let's just say, he doesn't just hunt for sport." Alex immediately drops me, letting my body fall against his as I grunt in surprise. "It's a joke, you big baby!" Using both my hands and most of my strength, I push him down onto the bed, his laughing form bouncing once against my many cushions and pillows.

Reaching forward, he grabs my waist and pulls me up into a straddling position on top of his lap. He runs his hands up and down my back inside of my shirt and the feeling is divine.

"Do you want to stay here tonight?" I ask, my heart in my throat.

"Or leave and risk running into big bro out there? Yeah, I think I'll take my chances in here," he says, gripping my waist and pulling me impossibly closer. He kisses my neck gently, then not so gently. I let my head fall back as he continues to pepper my skin with caresses.

"But we aren't having sex." Alex looks up as I look down. "I don't know if you were expecting..."

"I have no expectations, sunshine," Alex says, kissing the tip of my nose and then laying us both down on the bed, face to face. "Can't even leave to brush our teeth, can we?"

I push away from him. "Oh, I can," I say, sticking my tongue out at him as I skip out of the room, grabbing my pajamas on the way out. The living room is quiet as I walk through to get to the bathroom. *Hm, that's odd. Did Arden go back out or something?*

I don't give it much more thought as I brush my teeth, wash my face and run a quick comb through my hair. Shrugging out of my clothes and into pajamas, I give myself a once over in the mirror. *I'm about to sleep with a boy.* The thought warms my cheeks in the very best way. Even if we aren't having sex, this is still the farthest I've ever gone with a guy but Alex makes me feel completely comfortable.

When I return to my room, ready to blow my minty-fresh breath all over Alex's face, I find him curled up asleep amongst my pink and white duvet set. I curl in next to him, letting my back hit his front but not in a way where I'm forcing him to spoon me.

But, boy does he. Alex pulls me into him, leaving very little space between us. His top arm hugs my waist as he snakes his bottom arm under my neck.

"Goodnight, sunshine," he breathes into my hair.

"Goodnight, frat boy," I reply and he's so close I can feel him smile.

When I wake up, Alex is gone. Before I can completely panic, I find a note resting on the pillow where his head was.

Wanted to make sure we didn't get caught by big bro so I left early this morning. Stop overthinking it.

Something has me holding back my smile. What if he really just couldn't wait to get away from me. He didn't get what he wanted from me last night so he's left to get it elsewhere. I pick up the note and sigh in defeat before turning it over.

I said stop overthinking, beautiful. Meet me for lunch.

My smile erupts and there's nothing I can do about it. A date with Alex. Another heavy make-out session with Alex. Another smile because of Alex. Who am I and why has this love-sick teenager taken over my body?

The smile is still plastered on my face as I leave my room, the smell of fresh coffee sending me straight to the kitchen.

"Someone is happy this morning," Danika taunts, handing me a mug. I shush her with a finger to my lips, gesturing toward my brother's sleeping form on the couch. She rolls her eyes. "Oh please, he's out like a light."

I fill my mug with the life-giving elixir.

"So, spill!" Dani demands and I hit her with that *shut up* stare again.

"There's nothing to spill. We slept."

"You slept?"

I nod, taking a sip of the hot beverage.

"Did you at least sleep naked?" I swat her arm, indicating to her this conversation is definitely over, at least until there are less inquisitive ears about. "Is he still here?"

"He left early this morning so Arden didn't see him."

"What a gentleman, sneaking out in the morning," Dani rolls her eyes but she doesn't mean real offense.

As much as I want to meet Alex for lunch, I don't know how long Arden is going to be in town and I need to get to the bottom of what he's doing here in the first place. Sending Alex a quick text, I let him know I'll just see him tomorrow in class instead.

"Did Arden go back out last night?" I ask, pouring him a fresh cup of joe.

Danika glances at me before looking over at Arden's sleeping form. "How should I know?" She leaves the kitchen without another word. *Weird.*

Brushing off that awkward exchange, I bring Arden his coffee, leaving it on the table for him when he wakes up. For the next hour, I get to every piece of school work I've been putting off. All this time spent with Alex and on the podcast has really taken a toll on my coursework. I vow to myself this week to catch up and get ahead of my syllabi to make up for lost time.

"You work any harder, you're going to run those keys straight through the board," Arden jokes from the doorway. He runs his hands through his bedhead, yawning once. In his hand is the mug of coffee I made him that's more than cold by now.

"I can make you a fresh cup if you want," I say but he shakes his head, taking a sip of the previously piping hot beverage.

"Don't worry about it."

Finishing up the last sentence of my Investigative Journalism paper, I close the laptop and take a sigh of relief. "Lunch?" I ask, glancing at the clock on my phone to see the time. There's a couple of texts that I missed while I was doing my work. Mostly from Danika and Sydney in our group chat. A couple from Alex. I'll check them later.

"More like breakfast," Arden scratches his head and pulls his sleep shorts up a bit. Chuckling, I push him out of my doorway.

"Shower, change, be ready in fifteen minutes."

"Aye, aye," Arden salutes me before turning on his heels and following my directions. Shooting a quick text to my roommates to tell them where I'm going. Turns out both of them had left the apartment already, Sydney to workout at the gym and Dani to gawk at boys working out at the gym.

Once I'm dressed and ready, I plop on the couch to wait for Arden. Alex's text looms and I open it.

> Why don't you want to have lunch with me?

> > Having lunch with Arden

> And you don't want me to come because…

> > It's not that I don't want you to, it's just that I didn't think you'd want to hang out with me and my brother

> Don't assume to know what I want or don't want, sunshine

> > Do you want to come?

Yes

Too bad, see you tomorrow

I send a kissy face then close my phone before he sends his response but I feel it vibrate in my pocket. He'll get over it. I need to talk to my brother without anyone around.

"Let's roll, Mars," Arden says, giving the back of my head a light pat as he passes by the couch. I turn on the overhead light by the door and am immediately reminded of what Alex did last night. And then I'm reminded of what we almost did on the living room couch. I feel my cheeks start to flush as the memory invades my brain.

Shaking my head to clear myself of the vision, I whip my coat off the hook and pull my arms through.

"How's Cafe Royale sound?" I ask as we head out of the apartment.

"Sounds like it has food so I'm in," Arden holds the door as we leave and the brisk autumn air hits me like a force.

I pull my jacket a little tighter. "So, you just couldn't wait until the holidays to see me?" I let out a laugh but it's not sincere. I need to know what's going on with him.

Arden doesn't speak for a little while. As we approach the front door of the cafe, I'm about to grab his arm and demand he talk but he beats me to it.

"The factory job isn't working out for me."

I blink a couple times. "What does that mean?"

Arden sighs, running his hand through his hair. Alex does a similar move when he's exasperated. "It means I need to get out of South Carolina. I need to do something better for myself. I can do something better."

He sounds like he's talking more to himself than to me. "You can do whatever you set your mind to, Ard."

He laughs, "Thanks, Hallmark." Arden holds the door for me to enter the cafe and he follows suit as I walk in and head toward the order counter. After ordering two breakfast sandwiches and two coffees–and after Arden demands to pay we're sitting at a table by the window, coffees in hand and sandwiches being made.

"Did something happen at the factory?"

"The boss started cutting my hours. No rhyme or reason to it just, didn't need me as much, he said."

"Can they do that?"

Arden takes a sip of his black coffee. "They can do whatever they want, they own the place."

"So you're not doing as many hours at the factory but why does that mean you need to leave South Carolina? What about Dad and Memaw?"

As much as it wasn't fair that I was off in college with Arden was home helping Dad take care of our memaw, that was the deal that we made. Dad told me to get out there and make something of myself so that when I came back, I could help more than I could before. We made that deal for the betterment of our family. Something must be really bad for him to want to just up and abandon them now.

Arden sighs. "I just need a change of scenery, Mars. A change of pace." He sits back in his chair. The waitress takes this time to drop off our sandwiches and Arden tastes a massive bite.

I can't seem to stomach my own sandwich at the moment. "So what are you gonna do?"

He chews, swallows then speaks. "I'm not sure yet. I just know I've got options to weigh, that's all."

I nod once, swallowing the words I want to say. The question I want to ask. How does he know it's all going to be okay? Did Dad get a raise? Is Memaw on the mend? Do I need to go back and take his place as helper of the house while he figures out what he wants to do? It's only fair, I suppose. Although I really would've liked to graduate from TU before having to do that.

Arden, sensing my hesitation, reaches across the table and grabs my hand. "It's all gonna be okay, kid."

I nod again, letting him appease me. Or at least letting him think he is. Taking a small bite of my sandwich, I think about what I need to do in order to go home and help out. I'll have to go to the registrar's office and unenroll from classes. I'll have to quit the paper, and that means no more *New York Times* internship contest. No more podcast. No more Alex.

I choke a bit on a piece of egg sliding down my throat.

Arden peeks up at me from his sandwich. "You're not going anywhere," he says. As if he can read my mind.

"But, if you need to—"

"Margot, no. That's not what's going on here. You're finishing school. You're living out your journalistic dreams."

"But, Dad and Memaw—"

"Are fine." Arden places the food down with a sigh. "Will you just trust me on this? Everything is fine."

I have no idea how I can trust his words considering the situation we have at home but I have no other choice. Maybe after he's gone, I'll call Dad and see if he can shed some more light on the situation.

My phone vibrates in my pocket. I pull it out to reveal a text from Alex.

Dinner then? Cmon, I wanna see you

We're ordering in

Pizza or chinese?

Pizza

I'm in

Before I can respond, Arden is gathering up the garbage on our table, distracting me from the text. I would love to have Alex come and hang out with my roommates and my brother. It does, however, make me question even more what we are. Are we friends with benefits? Co-hosts with benefits? Are we going to announce to the school that we're together on the podcast? Are we together? Are we in a situationship? Too many questions and absolutely no answers. I need to assess with Dani and Syd. They'll know what to do.

"What do you have planned for the rest of the day?" Arden asks as we head toward the door.

I shrug. "Nothing, really. You're here so we can do whatever you want to do."

"I want to sit on the couch."

"Excellent," I reply, linking my arm through his as we walk back to my apartment to do just that.

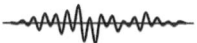

"Basketball or football?"

I tuck my feet underneath my butt on the couch, balancing the paper plate on my knee. Arden answers, his mouth full of pepperoni.

"Neither, baseball."

"What baseball teams are there in South Carolina?" Alex asks, shoving the last of his crust into his mouth. Reaching down to where he's sitting on the floor, I place my crust onto his plate. Alex catches my hand and kisses my knuckles.

If Arden notices the exchange, he doesn't let on. "None but I still like to watch. I'm a Yankees fan."

Danika scoffs.

"Problem, brat?"

She hits him with a withering glare but doesn't respond.

Alex apparently isn't done with his round of twenty questions to ask my brother. "What about cars?"

"Couldn't care less about them," Arden responds, undeterred. He'd sit there and answer questions all night if he could. It is actually a heart-warming sight. I enjoy seeing them bond, even though it only makes the questions in my brain about our relationship grow.

"What do you do in that factory in South Carolina?"

"I pack and load goods all day. Nothing fancy."

Alex grabs my empty plate and gathers it with his own. He gets up from the floor and grabs the rest of the garbage on his way to the kitchen. "That sounds like it would get pretty boring."

"It did."

"Did?" I ask.

Arden coughs. "Does. It does get boring but there are perks to the job."

"Like what?" Sydney asks from the chair across the room.

Arden takes the opportunity to flex his arms like a Greek god. "Got these amazing muscles to show for it." He winks at Danika who feigns vomiting before she gets up to join Alex in the kitchen. Grabbing a water bottle for everyone, the two of them join us back in the living room.

"I don't know what I wish I could do when I get out of college," Alex says somewhat absent-mindedly.

"You don't?"

"I don't exactly have a choice. I've been groomed for my career since I was a kid. I'll be next in line to run Prescott Cars." He sounds absolutely miserable about the idea of going into business for his father and I don't blame him.

"I'm guessing you don't want to do that," Sydney asks. Alex blows out a breath.

"It's actually the very last thing in this world I want to do and I've been fighting like hell to avoid it since I was fifteen years old but it seems like you can't avoid the inevitable."

The mood has shifted suddenly, and all eyes are on the sad college senior who seems to be receiving a death certificate rather than a diploma when he walks down the graduation aisle.

But Alex, being the ray of sunshine that he is, turns it into a joke to lighten the mood. "Another inevitability is a full bladder," he says with a chuckle, standing up from the floor to use the bathroom. The air is heavy as he walks out of the room but I know he'd rather have us on a different subject by the time he comes back. And I'm happy to supply that for him.

Chapter Thirty-Three

Alex

By the time I get back into the living room, the crowd has seemed to switch to a lighter topic, which I'm grateful for. I didn't mean to trauma-dump on Margot and her crew, and it also made me realize that I hadn't told her much about my dad or what's going on after graduation. And she has barely said anything about herself. If this was going to work, we needed to get to know one another better. I want to hear about her future plans and I want her to know mine. Shoot, maybe they could include each other.

Plopping back down next to Margot on the floor, I give her knee a tight squeeze, reassuring her I was fine after that conversation. I see a small smile form on her lips and I know she got the message.

We got onto a tangent about pineapple on pizza, something I am vehemently against while Margot seems to have a differing opinion. Something we'll have to argue about in the future. My phone buzzed in my pocket and when I pulled it out, I was reminded against my will of the conversation we just moved away from.

"Give me a minute," I say to Margot as I leave the apartment and take the call in the hallway.

"Hello?"

"What is this vandalism I'm hearing about? And fighting?"

I say. "I'm fine, Dad. How are you?"

"Enough with all that. You're supposed to be the leader of KA. How am I supposed to trust that you'll be a good VP of Prescott Cars if you can't manage your own frat brothers."

"What was I supposed to do? I couldn't prevent any of that from happening."

A glass clinks on the other side of the phone, a sound I know well. The top of a decanter being removed. "You need to be smarter. Get ahead of the other frats."

"Right," I replied, rolling my eyes.

"Alexander, I have a reputation at that school and I won't have you tarnishing it. You need to get your head out of your ass and get control of the situation."

"Yes, sir." The phone disconnects. "Love you, too." Running my palms down my face, I look up at the ceiling. I can't have control over my future but I need to be able to control the fraternities here? How am I supposed to do that?

Either way, I know I don't want to work at Prescott Cars. I don't want to eventually take over my father's empire. I don't know what I want to do with my life.

A laugh rings from the apartment, and the sound brings a reluctant smile to my face. I may not know what I want to do in seven months, but I know exactly what I want to do right now and that's go inside this apartment, kiss Margot right on the mouth and talk to her brother about his fitness routine.

By the time public speaking class rolls around, I am exhausted. I had spent most of Monday morning in the gym or in the library, catching up on work I've missed while hanging out with the guys or with Margot. I know the bookworm would've helped me out if I asked her to but I didn't want to burden her with my problems. She's got enough on her plate.

Before I left last night, I said goodbye to Arden, not knowing how much longer he was staying or if I'd see him again. We shook hands, and he gave me that look that said *hurt her and die*. I leveled him with my reply. *I'd take that punishment freely*. He seemed to accept that response and gave me a pat on the back for good measure.

Margot had walked me to the door and I finally got that kiss I'd been jonesing for all night. It wasn't sexy but it was intimate and sweet. It was Margot and I would've loved for a thousand more to grace my lips before I had to leave.

I am happy to see her in our usual seats for class and I plop right next to her. Without glancing in my direction, she hands me the pen she is using, already ready with a spare for herself.

A woman who anticipates a man's needs is sexy as hell. Even if that need is just a writing implement for class.

"Alright, everyone. It's that time again. Speech time," Professor Walker announces at the top of the room. I feel Margot stiffen beside me. I would've thought with the podcast she would've felt a little bit better about public speaking but it seems from her stance that that's not the case.

The professor continues, "Next week, you will take into consideration everything we've worked on so far and you will present a speech about your goals and ambitions for the future after college. And don't get complacent. If you went last the first time, expect to go first this time around."

That meant Margot was likely to be in the first group of presenters and I was in the last. It didn't make a difference to me. Public speaking had never really been an issue of mine, a skill required for running a frat house. I'd made plenty of speeches in my day and not batted an eye.

Margot, on the other hand. Her eyes were shifted, looking back and forth without actually noticing anything. She was completely panicked.

The topic of the speech did startle me, though. A speech about my goals and ambitions for the future? Fuck me.

Margot and I didn't really have a chance to unpack the information I dropped on her at dinner last night so I'm not surprised when she glances sideways at me with worry.

After the professor dismisses class, neither of us move from our seats. The room empties out around us. Margot waits for me to speak.

"When I was a kid, I used to say I wanted to be in the NBA."

Margot breathes out a laugh and I nudge her with my elbow.

"Hey, I was the best shooter on my eighth grade team."

"I'll bet you were," she says with a smile. She's giving me her full attention, which I appreciate but it also scares the shit out of me. I suddenly realize I don't want to let her down.

"In high school, that was when my dad started to really prepare me for entering the family business. My extracurriculars fell to the wayside so I could spend afternoons and weekends at the shop, following in his footsteps.

"When I came here to TU, I started undeclared. My dad didn't give a shit what I majored in. All he wanted was for me to graduate with a degree from his alma mater and then come back home to work at the company."

Margot continues to listen, her hand resting softly on my arm that's resting on the desk in front of me. Her thumb is tracing light circles against my skin, the feeling keeping me grounded in the room, in the conversation.

"In sophomore year, I had to declare something so I just went with whatever classes I thought I would enjoy the most. I started my exercise science major and I really did like the coursework. And many of my fraternity brothers were in my classes."

"Exercise science makes a lot of sense for you," she says softly, with a gentle smile.

"It doesn't matter. A degree in exercise science doesn't mean a damn thing to my father. But as I've taken all these classes these past three years, I've genuinely started to love it. There are so many things I could do with an exercise science degree. I could become a personal trainer. I could own my own gym with training classes. Hell, I could even be a P.E. teacher if I wanted."

Margot laughs, "I'm trying to picture you teaching kickball to a bunch of kindergarteners."

I join in her glee. "Yeah, that one's probably not for me." I grab the hand she has on top of my arm, squeezing the fingers lightly. "But you could actually imagine me as a trainer, can't you?"

"Yeah, I can."

"I can, too," I sigh, leaning back in my chair. I pull my arm out from her grip to run my hands through my hair. "But how can I make a speech about my dreams of being a trainer when I know that I'm never going to be one?"

"Well, you don't know that. What if you talk to your father? Explain to him that you have your own dreams in life?"

I huff out a harsh laugh. "Try explaining that to Oliver Prescott. The man lives only for himself and his business. He doesn't give a shit what I want. Or what Drew wants either."

Thinking about my father always makes my blood boil so I hop out of my seat rather than take my anger out on Margot. I grab my bag and head for the door. Margot follows, rushing on her little legs to catch up to me.

"But you're a man now, you're not a boy he can boss around," she says, slightly out of breath as she catches up to me.

"Oh, but he can."

"But why? What could he do to you if you just say no?"

"It's not what he could do to me. I don't give a shit what he does to me. It's Drew that would suffer from my insubordination."

Drew, my baby brother who has done nothing but support my father, having been the only living parent he's ever really remembered. It's a begrudging respect but respect nonetheless. I swore when we suffered that attack, I swore that I would always protect him. And I always will.

Margot nods. "Okay." She lays her hand in mine and I grip it, interlacing our fingers immediately. "I get it."

I sigh, honestly shocked at how she's able to calm me down. Letting out a breath, I rest my forehead against hers, closing my eyes to relax. And then I open them when I realize we're standing like this in the middle of the quad.

When I look up, there's not an eye in a hundred foot radius that's not trained on us. Margot squeals slightly when she realizes it as well.

Quickly, she pulls her hand out of mine. And I let her. We both step back and look at each other.

What are we doing? This very public display is not something I'm known to do. My reputation precedes me at this school, and I'm not exactly known as the "boyfriend" type. It seems like Margot is having the same mini panic attack as I am. We're both silent for a few minutes, staring wide-eyed at nothing but each other.

"We need to talk," we both say, in unison. Then we both turn and walk right to our Monday afternoon study room, as if on auto-pilot. Instead of sitting on the same side of the table, we sit opposite. As if on a date. Or in an interrogation. *Cue the harsh overhead lighting.*

Margot has her hands clasped on the table and mine rest on the tops of my knees. Neither of us are relaxed. I have no idea how this conversation is going to go. I try to think of what I want to say but Margot, bless her, speaks first.

"I like you, Alex."

She's said this to me before but it doesn't stop my heart from swelling. I'm about to agree with her when she cuts me off, continuing.

"But I understand that you've got a reputation. One that you enjoy. One that I imagine you want to keep so–"

"Hold on–"

Margot speaks over my interruption. "I just don't want you to think you owe me anything. You don't. I've really enjoyed getting to know you these past few weeks but I don't want you to feel pressured to give me more than you're willing to give."

I close my mouth. It was a very practical way of thinking. Very Margot thought-process. And it's given me a chance to really think about what I want. Margot stays silent, allowing me time to form a thought-out response as hers.

But as it turns out. I don't need to think. I've known since the moment she propositioned me about the podcast, the moment I realized I'd be spending so much more time with her.

"I'm willing to give whatever you're willing to take, sunshine."

Margot's eyes bolt to mine but she doesn't speak.

"I've never had a girlfriend before, not for lack of trying on the girls' parts." Margot rolls her eyes. "But," I laugh at her reaction, reaching across the table to grab both her hands in mine. "But, I'm ready now because I know you're the one I want to be with."

"How do you know that?"

I blink. *How* do *I know that?*

"Do you know why I call you sunshine?" Margot only shakes her head. "The first time I met you, that night at the party, there was this glow around your head. I know it was just the lighting from the porch but to me, you looked like the sun."

Margot draws in a breath but I continue.

"Then the next time I saw you, in the library. Same thing happened. This time with the actual sun behind your head. Just reinforced the name for me. Also reinforced the fact that I had to know you. Because if a girl who radiates sunshine could have even a small desire to spend her time with me, I am lucky for it."

Margot, again, is quiet. I've seen her silent before but I never thought I would silence her. I guess I better finish my thought before she runs for the hills.

"I like you, Margot. I would be honored if you would be my girl-friend."

"Holy shit," Margot whispers.

I chuckle. "Okay, sailor." Margot's eyes are as wide as a full moon, her pupils completely dilated. "Got anything else to say? Anything...positive?" I ask, giving her hands another reassuring squeeze.

She blinks but remains quiet still. Suddenly, I start to second guess myself. What if she didn't actually want a relationship? What if she just wanted to keep things casual? Fuck. But I don't want to keep things casual. The thought of another man touching her drives me completely insane. Even when I saw her with Ryan, I wanted to–

"Alex, you're crushing my hands," Margot squeals, and I immediately loosen my grip but don't let go. If she's going to let me down easy right now, I'm not going to let her go until the very last second.

She takes in a very, very deep breath and then nods her head once.

"What is that?"

"Okay," she simply says.

"Okay what?"

"Okay, I'll be your girlfriend." I jump out of my seat and make to grab her face but she speaks again. "On one condition." Deflated, I slump back into my chair, arms at my sides while I wait for her to continue.

"You have to let me help you figure out how you can become a personal trainer."

"Sunshine, did you hear a word I said back there?"

Margot stands and rounds the table, leaning against it closer to me. She places her hands on my shoulders, pulling my eyes to hers.

"I did and I understand what's holding you back, I truly do. But I think we can figure this out. Together. We can find a way to secure Drew a safe future and provide you with the one you want all at the same time, just...let me help you."

She runs her hands down the back on my neck, tugging gently on the hair there. The look on her face is one of fierce sincerity. I know she feels like she can really make a difference here and I love her for it but I know my father. I know there's nothing on this Earth that will make him change his mind. Still, it would be interesting to try and if I get to call Margot mine in the meantime, I'll take that deal any day.

"Fine. We can *try* to figure it out. Together."

The concerned expression on Margot's face immediately morphs into pure joy. She reaches down just as I reach up and our lips connect in an earth-shattering way. Within seconds, she's opening her legs wider and I'm taking that to my advantage as I pull her onto my lap, straddling me. Margot falls gracefully into the new position, worming her hips around in an agonizing way. Our lips never disconnect but I groan as she continues to move her butt on my lap.

Grabbing her hips to steady her, I break the kiss. "If you don't stop moving down there, we're going to have a very big problem on our hands."

"*Very* big, huh? I'll be the judge of that."

She's got a shit-eating grin on her beautiful face and I swear if I didn't love her before, I might now. I would do anything this woman asked of me. Go anywhere as long as I have her by my side.

Margot trails kisses down my neck toward the front of my throat. She licks from my Adam's apple up toward my chin and then moves toward the other side of my neck. It is taking a concerted effort not to explode right then and there. I'm still gripping her hips but that notion hasn't deterred her. If anything, the contact has spurred her on.

"I'm not kidding, sunshine. You keep moving like that and I'm not going to be able to hold back much longer."

"So don't," Margot whispers into my ear, biting my lobe before she pulls away completely and leans back against the table. Her eyes say "fuck me" but I know her heart. This isn't the way she wants her first time to be. I've fucked a lot of girls, something I'm not necessarily proud of anymore, and if this was any other girl, I'd already be buried deep inside them, not a care in the world. But this isn't any other girl. This is my girl.

Using the grip I have on her waist, I hold her in that leaned back position. "This isn't it. You know that."

Margot sighs, halfway in annoyance, halfway in relief and that's how I know I've made the right choice. "Normally I would rail against a man telling me what's best for me but in this case, you might be right."

I flick her nose for good measure. "Of course I am, sunshine. I think you'll find the longer we stick together, the more you'll be saying that."

Margot rolls her eyes and uses her arms to push herself off my lap and onto the table in front of me. The sight of her sitting there, almost spread out completely for me, sets my libido right back into high gear. All I want to do is push up her skirt, rip off her panties and feast.

She tries to move her leg around me to jump off the table but I grab it before she can, leaving it open. "What are you doing?" she giggles, not yet understanding my intentions. We didn't need to go all the way in a library study room, Margot deserves much better than that. But this...this I deserve.

"That door locks automatically, right?"

Margot cocks her head, squinting her eyes in bemusement. It takes her a moment to understand my intentions but when she finally does, she mutters the word I've been waiting to hear. "Yes."

The minute that word escapes her plump lips, I pull her legs to rest on top of my shoulders, then push her skirt up to her waist.

The only window in the room is shuttered and leads to a back alley behind the library. There's no chance of anyone seeing us and if she's quiet, no one will hear us either.

"Alex," she squeals but doesn't stop me. I know she's nervous but she has to know that I would protect her at all costs. No matter what.

"Do you trust me?"

Margot nods vigorously, her eyes wide again. This time in wonder and excitement.

"Good girl," I growl before diving in, moving her underwear to the side for full access. Margot has been ready and waiting for me for a while based on this slickness and I savor her unique taste on my tongue as I devour her.

After a few seconds, I look up at her, not stopping my lapping movement. Her eyes are shut tight but her mouth is open in a gasp. I take a mental picture of the way I'm making her feel, keeping it in a lockbox in my mind.

It doesn't take long for my salacious actions to push Margot over the edge. Her pants start to get louder as I keep up my repetitive motions, knowing that if she's close I need to keep doing exactly whatever it is that's about to push her into ecstasy. Margot grips my hair and I smile against her, not stopping until the absolute last second. She starts to moan louder, louder and suddenly I'm not so sure how sound proof these walls are.

Without stopping my work on her core, I let go of the hand on her hip, my arms thankfully long enough to cover her mouth while I keep driving her completely insane. She groans my name against my palm and the sound almost makes me lose it myself but I finish her off, lapping up the last of her before I pull away, wiping my mouth with the back of my hand.

Once I'm sure that she won't scream, I release the hold I have on her mouth. Margot lets out a breath and falls back onto her elbows onto the table.

"That was…"

"Unforgettable? Extraordinary? Remarkable? Amazing?"

"Hot."

Chuckling, I stand, pulling her up to meet my eyes. "My girlfriend: the wordsmith." Margot places a light kiss on my nose. Resting my forehead against hers, I'm satisfied that this is the best decision I've made in a very long time.

Chapter Thirty-Four

Margot

WE SOMEHOW SPEND THE next hour planning the podcast for Saturday, although how we got through it, I have no idea. I was in an orgasmic coma for at least a good fifteen minutes after Alex showed me—with great enthusiasm—so much of what I'd been missing out on in adulthood. The rest of the time after that either Alex's hands wandering up and down my thighs or his lips were roaming around my neck. It was deliciously distracting and I'm sure I'll have to redo half of what we wrote up but I don't care in the slightest.

Alex drops me off at home with a kiss and a promise to meet up on campus for lunch tomorrow and I shuffle upstairs to fawn over the details of the dream-like past few hours of my life. I'm itching to tell my roommates about Alex and my new relationship and I enter the apartment still floating on cloud nine.

"I am back and I have *big* news," I shout from the doorway. I'm not sure if Arden is still here but he might as well hear this news, too. As I step into the living room, my smile falters slightly at the sight in front of me.

Danika and Sydney are on the couch, both looking at me with solemn expressions. "What is it?" I ask, looking back and forth between them.

"Have you checked instagram lately?" Sydney asks, her voice soft as if speaking to a toddler on the brink of a meltdown. I shake my head, rounding the couch to sit on the coffee table. Before I can even open my phone, a call from Alex comes in.

Danika takes the phone from my hand and puts it down beside her on the couch. "Look," she says, showing me her instagram feed. Story after story of Alex and I touching on the quad. *Okay, it doesn't seem so bad. People are just surprised.* I gear up to breathe a sigh of relief and tell them it's okay...until I see the captions.

I didn't know Alex would slum it with a junior. I would've shot my shot.

Guess this is why he's been doing that podcast. Easy lay.

A rags to riches story in the making. Can you say gold digger?

Each comment was more heinous than the next. Girls calling me ugly and poor. Guys saying I must be an easy lay and wondering when they'd get their turn. After one such comment about how "hard" I must work to keep Alex interested, I shove Danika's phone back in her hand, disgusted.

My own phone continues to vibrate on the couch and I know it's Alex but I need to process before I can speak with him.

"People are going to be assholes, that's how people are made," Danika says. "You can only control how you feel about what they say."

"Well, right now, I'm feeling like shit and that's a very hard thing for me to control." I purse my lips and stand up from the table, pacing back and forth in front of them.

Sydney grabs my arm as I pass her. "What's your big news, Mar? Maybe that'll help."

I stop and level her with a look. "Alex and I are officially in a relationship." That sentence should've been announced with the popping of champagne or the twisting of a beer cap. Not with a stone cold expression of worry and concern.

Still, the girls do muster up some happiness for me. Sydney jumps off the couch, smothering me in a tight embrace. "That's amazing!"

Yes. Two minutes ago, it was amazing. Now, I don't know what it is. Danika grabs my hand, pulling both Sydney and I onto the couch in an embrace.

"Don't let the assholes ruin this for you. You deserve this, Mars."

I settle into her hold and Sydney cuddles up behind me. They're right. This is just jealous people letting off steam because they want what I have and what I have is Alex. The kindest, funniest, most authentic man who cares about me. Not anyone else. Me.

My phone buzzes again, now underneath me. "Let me let the man out of his misery," I sigh, answering the phone. "It's okay," I say in greeting.

"Margot, don't look at...wait. It's okay?"

"It's okay. I'm not going to let anyone ruin what we have. Let them be petty on their own. Once they realize that we're not caring, they'll stop caring, too," I say, pretty proud of myself for how bold I'm being. Danika winks at me.

Alex's sigh of relief is like an air horn into the receiver. "Thank fucking god. You're a rockstar, you know that?"

"Oh yeah, lead singer vibes all the way."

Alex laughs. "Nah, quiet but insanely hot bass player, that's you." I join in his laughter.

"I'll call you later, okay? After I tell my roommates every detail of this afternoon."

"*Every* detail?" Alex questions, a slight hint of nervousness in his voice.

"Okay, maybe not *every* detail," I reply. After saying our goodbyes, I hang up the phone, throwing it behind us on the couch.

"Okay, now I want *every* detail," Danika demands. Sydney hops over the couch to put a bag of popcorn in the microwave and grab some water bottles from the fridge. Danika grips my shoulders, placing herself in my line of sight. "And don't even think about leaving anything out. Because I'll know."

Rolling my eyes, I am shaken by Dani who levels me with a serious expression. "I will tell you—mostly—every detail!" I swear, whispering a choice word but Danika will have none of it. The two girls spend the next hour wringing every bit of information out of me that they can, but I do manage to keep one thing a secret between me, Alex and the table in Study Room G6.

"I hope everyone rests up over Thanksgiving break. Come back ready to chase that lead!" Jessy's inspirational speech falls on deaf ears as most of us are barely listening anyway. I've been trying to finish this article on the new quad sprinkler system but I just can't find the right hook to make it interesting. *Because it's not.*

"Margot," Jessy plants her butt on the edge of my desk. I finish typing the word "cafeteria" and then look up at her. "You're staying on campus this weekend right?"

"Yup," I reply, popping the p.

"Cool. I was thinking it would be compelling to do a piece on how Tomlin supports international students or students who just don't go home while the campus shuts down for breaks. Interested?"

"Yeah, I'll work on that." Jessy gives me a smile before sauntering away just as quickly as she came. That topic does sound interesting but I can hardly think about it right now. I've had my stomach in my throat ever since I sent in the write up and the first few episodes of the podcast. I know I should be hearing from the *New York Times* people soon.

Just as I'm about to pull up the thesaurus to find a better word than "wet", my email pings with that *you've got mail* sound. While typically I ignore most emails that come into my newspaper account, mostly because they're just Jessy telling me to make changes on a story or sending me memes about cats drinking coffee, this time I immediately click onto the email landing page. My lunch threatens to make its way out again when I see the email is from *Editorial@nytimes.com.*

Preparing myself for utter defeat, I open the email, reading the contents out loud to myself.

"'Dear Ms. Davis, we received your admission for the internship contest and are pleased to inform you'–YES!" I screamed at the very top of my lungs, happy tears forming in my eyes.

"Jesus, Margot," Jessy says as she runs back over to me. "What's going on?"

"I made it to the final round of the internship contest!"

"YES!" Jessy's scream matches my own and she pulls me in for a quick shoulder squeeze more leaning over to read the rest of the email.

"'You've made it to the final round in this competition. You are one of fifty contestants that have made it this far. We admire your journalistic creativity in this endeavor and are eager to see more of it in the coming weeks. Please submit your last write up and podcast episodes by December fifteenth and we should have the results on the winner before the holiday season.' Oh my god, Margot, this is amazing!"

I'm full on crying now and there's nothing I can do about it. I can't believe I pulled it off. I can't believe *we* pulled it off, Alex and I. The urge to call him and tell him the news is overpowering.

"Thanks, Jessy!" I reply, wiping my face and grabbing my bag from the floor. "Have a good Thanksgiving!" I yell as I run out the door, phone in hand already to call Alex. As I burst out of the door, I run smack into the man himself.

"Sheesh, sunshine. Where's the fire?" Alex takes a step back, laugh-lines bracketing his mouth. But his mood instantly shifts when he sees my tear-stained face. "What's going on? Why are you crying? Who do I have to kill?" He looks over my shoulder, possibly expecting to see someone chasing me with a knife.

I grab his face in both my hands, pulling his attention back to me. "I made it to the final round."

At first he's confused and possibly still thinking I'm in danger so I roll my eyes with a giggle and pull up the email on my phone. Alex skims it ever so briefly before his eyes light up and soon he's hoisting me into the air, spinning me around like a rag doll.

"You did it, sunshine!"

"We did it!" I laugh into his neck, swatting at him playfully to put me down.

Alex is shaking his head before my feet even touch the ground. "No shot, sun. This is all you. I'm so fucking proud of you." And he means it. I can feel the pride radiating off of him like a heat wave. I want to grab his face and kiss him until we're both a puddle on the floor but we're in the middle of campus and already starting to form a crowd based on the initial outburst.

"What were you doing when I ran into you, by the way?"

Alex runs his hand through his hair. "I was actually coming to look for you and see if you wanted to grab lunch before your next class."

"I don't think I could possibly eat anything right now. All this excitement has my stomach completely in knots."

Alex laughs. "Would you rather go to the library and pour over the podcast website for a bit?"

"Yes, please."

"Let's go, sunshine," he replies with a chuckle, grabbing the sleeve of my jacket and pulling me toward the library across the quad. How could he possibly be able to anticipate my every need before I even know I need it? If I'm not careful, I'm going to fall head over heels for this man. *More than I likely already am?* Yep. I'm in serious trouble.

Chapter Thirty-Five

Margot

"I'M PICKING THIS TIME," Alex says, using the remote to scroll through the streaming apps that Danika downloaded onto our TV. It takes him about ten minutes to find something for us to watch and when he finally lands on one, I sigh loudly.

"*Role Models*? Again?"

"If you can watch *Pride and Prejudice* over and over, I can watch *Role Models* as much as I want," Alex counters, pulling me into his side as the movie starts. I've seen this movie now more than a handful of times with him and while I do find it occasionally hilarious, it's never my go-to movie night option.

Just as Seann William Scott pulls up in a giant medieval cow suit, Danika bursts from her room.

"The dicks are going to Vermont."

Alex pauses the movie as we both stare up at her.

"Excuse me?"

"My family," she huffs, sitting in the chair by the TV. "They're making us go to Vermont for Thanksgiving. My mom got an Airbnb for all of us."

"What's so bad about that?" Alex asks.

"I don't want to go to Vermont. I want to go to South Carolina. I want to be *home* for Thanksgiving. And it means I have to stay up there for my birthday, too."

"Well, we're definitely celebrating your birthday when we get back anyway. And if it makes you feel any better, I'm not going home either," I say, shrugging my shoulders.

"You're not?" Alex turns, looking right at me.

Danika sighs. "This sucks," she groans, heading back into her room and closing the door.

"Why aren't you going home for Thanksgiving?"

I go to unpause the movie, but Alex holds the remote out of my grasp. "Just can't swing the ticket this year. It's not a big deal."

"Sunshine, if you want to I can—"

I lift my hand to cover his mouth. "Don't even think about finishing that sentence. I don't need any money from you."

Alex kisses the hand covering his mouth and then pulls it off gently. "Of course, I just wanted to help you if I could."

"And I appreciate that, but Thanksgiving really isn't a big deal to my family. I just saw my brother when he visited. I'll see everyone else at Christmas." I shrug, hopping off the couch to grab some water and a snack. Alex follows me into the kitchen.

"So, what are you going to do instead? Stay here alone?"

"Yeah. I've got so much work to catch up on. I've fallen way behind with the podcast and everything," I reply, grabbing two water bottles and a family size bag of chips from the cabinet.

"You should come with me," he says.

"Come with you where?"

"To Thanksgiving. At my house."

I halt in my tracks. "Come to Thanksgiving dinner. At the Prescott house."

Alex hesitates. "Um, yes? Yes, come. Please, come."

"Are you asking or begging?"

Alex smiles. "I'm not above begging if that'll get you to say yes."

I narrow my eyes at him for a moment before moving around him and landing back on the couch. "Are you sure? I don't want to impose..."

"Yes, I'm positive. In fact, the more I think about it, the more positive I feel. This would be a perfect time to introduce you to my family. I want you to meet my baby brother." Alex kisses the top of my head before sitting down next to me on the couch. At the very least say you'll think about it."

"No," I reply, popping a chip in my mouth.

Alex draws back a fraction of an inch. "No, you won't think about it or no, you won't come."

"No, I don't need to think about it. Clearly it's important to you and I want to meet your family so yes, of course, I'd love to come."

Alex lunges across the couch and plants his lips on mine. I can't stop the giggle that bursts through my lips. It's like I just told him his favorite basketball player was coming to teach him some pointers on free throw shooting.

Once he settles back on the other side of the couch, I still can't get that grin off my face. I'm just lucky his face matches mine completely.

———ᴡᴡᴡᴧᴡᴧᴡᴡᴧ———

The ride to Alex's house is much shorter than I thought it would be. If I lived this close to campus, I would be home visiting my family almost every weekend. Shoot, I might even stay home and save money on an apartment. But I know why Alex chose not to stay home for college and it had less to do with being a Kappa Alpha and everything to do with his father.

From what he's told me about Oliver so far, I'm expecting to show up, have a pie smashed in my face and get booted right out the door. And if my life were a sit-com, that would probably happen but unfortunately my life isn't split up into hilarious twenty minute vignettes. Nope, instead I'm going to have to sit through a Thanksgiving meal where a grown man talks down to his adult and teenage sons, pressuring them to commit to a life they don't want to live, a future they don't want to have.

When I look over to the driver's seat, Alex's face is stoic, as if he's thinking about the same exact thing as me. Reaching over, I grab his hand, setting it in my lap and squeezing tightly. If there was anyone I would subject myself to an uncomfortable meal for, it was Alex Prescott, the amazing man who has been showing me that, at least, *my* life can be what I make it, even if his can't be.

Chapter Thirty-Six

Alex

I'VE NEVER LOOKED AT my house from an outsider perspective. It's always just been where I've grown up. Where I've played basketball in the driveway. Where I went swimming on a hot summer day. Where I exercised in my home gym or shot some enemies in my gameroom with Drew. I never really thought twice about it. Until I saw it through Margot's eyes.

Her pupils were perpetually widened the entire time I walked her from the car, into the foyer, past the grand staircase and into the dining room where my dad had set up our little Thanksgiving meal. By Dad, I mean our chef Rosa and by little, I mean extravagant. There were place settings, multiple pairs of utensils, candles and decor that matched the season. This is par for the course for my father, but I realize that Margot might not be used to the opulence.

Interlacing our fingers, I pull her hand up to quickly kiss the palm. "Thank you for coming with me."

Margot looks up at me with wonder in her eyes. "Are you kidding? Why aren't we eating here every night?" She asks with a grin. And then the door sounds from behind us, alerting us of my father's arrival. "Ah, right," Margot says, squeezing my hand a little more tightly.

I had given her a long-winded warning about my father on the car ride here. I wasn't about to let her walk into the lion's den unarmed. I know she's strong enough to take on whatever rude thing my father says to her. Because I'm sure he will. But it'll be something smooth and unassuming. A backhanded compliment that actually put her down.

"Alexander?" A stern voice calls from the front door. My father's voice.

"In here," I answer, bending down to get Margot one more quick kiss for strength.

In walks Oliver Prescott. His suit pressed firmly as if he'd just picked it up from the tailor instead of wearing it all morning at the office. Of course Oliver works on Thanksgiving. There are very rare days of the year that he doesn't go into the office. Drew and I spent many years celebrating holidays by ourselves, waiting for him to get home from work. I don't miss those days.

Giving Margot a once over, he turns to me. "Where is Drew?"

"Dad, this is my girlfriend, Margot," I say, ignoring his rudeness. Margot, the ray of sunshine that she is, reaches a hand out to grasp him, the smile on her face undeniable. Except apparently to Oliver Prescott because he looks at her hand, at her face, and then turns to me.

"Would you get your brother, please? I'd like to get this dinner over with quickly so I can head back to the office." He clapped me on the back and then headed into the kitchen.

I didn't even get a chance to apologize profusely to Margot like I wanted to. She turned to me immediately, putting her hand over my mouth.

"It's fine. I'm tougher than I look," she says, dropping her hand but putting her arms out to show off her muscles. I laugh at the silly expression on her face. Only my sunshine could have me laughing in this house.

"Might as well go do what the man said," I sigh.

Margot follows me as we head upstairs toward Drew's bedroom. It's at the end of the hall, near my father's primary suite. My bedroom is one floor up. The *penthouse* I used to call it. No one was allowed up there while I was living in it. But that doesn't mean I'm not surprised that Drew hadn't moved up there the second I left for college.

Knocking twice on his door, I swing it open to reveal my brother sitting in his gaming chair, headphones on, control in hand.

"Go. Go, go, go. FUCK." He shouts, not noticing our presence. I put my finger over my mouth to motion Margot to be quiet and I sneak around his back. Grabbing his headphones, I shout, "Drewster!"

My baby brother jumps, the control flying out of his hand. I can't control the laughter that erupts out of me and I can tell that Margot has joined in the revelry.

"What the fuck, Alex," Drew yells, grabbing the headphones from my hands and the controller from the floor. "I was just about to clutch that!"

"I'm sure you were. Drew," I pull Margot deeper into the room. "This is my girlfriend, Margot."

Having apparently learned her lesson from my father, Margot offers Drew a small wave rather than a hand shake.

"Hey, Margot. You're hot. Surprised you're dating my dickhead brother."

I smack him in the back of the head. "Manners, dipshit." Margot is biting her lip to hold back a chuckle and the sight is equal parts adorable and arousing.

Drew rubs the back of his head. "Sorry." He holds up his hands. "Surprised you're dating my charming, non-violent brother," he amends. Margot lets out that laugh after all.

"Yeah well, that makes two of us actually," she admits.

"Hey!" I groan. I know it took a lot for us to get to where we are but she was just as much a part of the decision as I was. *Rude, sunshine.* "Let's go. Dad's downstairs and he's itching to eat."

"I'm sure he is," Drew mutters, shutting off his gaming device and storing his equipment in its appropriate charging stations. "How did he react to Margot here?"

"Oh, the usual. Ignorance."

Drew sighs. "Classic Oliver." He leaves the room, giving Margot a nod as he passes by. She's looking at me in a curious way.

"What?"

"You guys have really had it rough, haven't you?"

I walk up to her, slinging my arm around her shoulder as I guide her to the door. "Well, as Cherry Valence once said 'Things are rough all over'."

Margot squeezes up closer to me as we both exit the room and head back downstairs for the meal of a lifetime.

We sit at the table and I realize we each have designated spots. We've been eating meals at this table for my entire life and every time Dad sits at the head and Drew and I flank his sides. Margot sits at my side and I move my chair a little bit closer to hers to present a more united front.

Dinner starts as most do, with boring small talk. Dad asks Drew about his grades and he mumbles something about needing a tutor for physics, which my father promptly ignores. The Prescott men do not ask for help. Ever.

After that discussion dies down, Oliver finally turns his sights over to me. "So, Alexander. How are *your* grades this year?"

"My grades are fine. Actually, my best class of the semester is public speaking that I have with Margot." I reach for her hand over the table but she pulls it away. I know she's not trying to push me away, she just wants to play it cool for my dad.

"Is that so," he says, taking a long sip of his whiskey. "And Margot. What is your major?"

The room is silent for a moment and just when I think she's too shocked to speak, Margot clears her throat. "I'm a journalism major."

"So you're the reason that my son has been messing around with this little podcast thing."

I open my mouth to protest but Margot simply says, "Yes, sir. He's doing me a great favor by helping me out with this. I couldn't have done it without him." Now she lets me grip her hand and I hold on for dear life.

"So, what you're saying is, you're using my son to help yourself, correct?"

"Dad," I warn.

Margot just continues as if it's a normal conversation and he wasn't insinuating that she can't do anything successful on her own. "I wouldn't say that. When I told him about the project, he agreed to help." Margot shrugs, taking a sip of her water. She squeezes my hand. "I mean if anything, he should be thanking me for getting him even more campus fame with this podcast."

I cough back a laugh as I drink my water. She's doing everything she can to stand up to my father and I love her for it.

Oliver scoffs, shaking his head. "Right. Campus fame." He takes a large bite of his turkey. The entire spread on the table was to die for. Our chef, Rosa, never fails to produce an amazing meal. I'll have to make sure to thank her after we finish. And take plenty of leftovers back to campus with me. I'll make sure Margot's fridge is full as well. Perks of having a boyfriend with a chef's kitchen.

"Have you decided what college you want to go to, Drew?" Margot asks my brother.

He shrugs but opens his mouth to respond and is immediately cut off. "He'll be going to TU like Alex and myself."

Margot glances toward my father for a brief second and then back to Drew. "Is that where you want to go?"

Cutting aggressively into his lean meat, Dad says, "Doesn't matter what he wants. He's going to TU."

"It doesn't matter what he wants?"

Okay, I'm all for Margot defending herself but she's about to stick her nose in a place she doesn't want it to go. Oliver doesn't back down to people questioning him. Especially people he deems to be beneath him. I squeeze her hand for a second to tell her to back down but she only pulls hers out of my grip. *This isn't going to be good.*

After the conversation we had about me following my dreams and helping Drew follow his, I think Margot might've taken it a bit too seriously. No one talks to Oliver like this. Not even me.

"Drew wants to follow in his father and his older brother's footsteps. Isn't that right?" He looks over at my brother who's looking sheepishly at his plate.

"Yep," he says, noncommittally, but my dad nods in satisfaction.

"Let's just say for argument's sake, you don't go into the family business. What would your dream job be?"

"Margot." Now I'm warning *her.* But she'll have nothing of it.

"What? It's just a question," she says, raising her hands defensively. She looks back and forth between all of us but finds one mute, one enemy, and one reluctant ally. "Fine, forget it."

Margot sip her water and takes a small bite of her mashed potatoes. The room is pregnant with awkward silence. I'm not sure if I should offer a change of subject or just let the silence continue.

I feel like such a coward that I can't support her in her defiance of my father but when you're lived under the man's thumb for as long as I have, I've learned it's very difficult to speak your mind without risking the consequences. Whether that be a cut off of family funds or a swift smack, neither of which I was keen on. Looking over at Drew's forlorn expression, I know he feels the same way.

"I feel lucky that I get to follow my dreams of being a journalist. Back home in South Carolina, my brother's working in a factory to help sustain our household."

I'm not sure what prompted her to say it and I've never, never, ever been ashamed of Margot from where she's come from—in fact, I've openly and endlessly admired her for it—but I could see the bullet she just shoved into her own chest when my father grinned a shit-eating smile.

"So, you're poor. That's why you've latched yourself onto my son."

Margot chokes on her water. "Excuse me?"

"This is all finally making sense. You coerce my son into doing this podcast with you so you can get in his good graces, make him fall for you and then steal his fortune. A gold digger. I should've smelled it on you."

"What the f—"

I shove away from the table. "Margot, let's just go." Margot looks up at me from her seat and the expression on her face breaks my heart. She wants me to stand up for her. And I want to. There's nothing on Earth I'd rather do. But if I stand up to him, he's not going to take it out on me. No. He'll take it out on Drew. I can't leave my brother here defenseless. This has gone on long enough.

Taking her hand, I pull her from the table. She lets me. Margot drops her napkin on the table before following me to the door. I have her car door open before she can say another word. Walking around to the other side, I sit in the driver's seat and pull out of the driveway before someone comes out to change my mind.

Our ride is silent and if I know Margot, I know she's got a battle going on in her head. She wants to fight me but she also wants to commend me.

"Just say it," I sigh, pulling onto the highway.

"You cannot let that man control your life."

"It's not like I want him to."

Margot lets out a frustrated breath. She looks out the window, then back at me, then out the window again. "Out with it," I prompt her again.

"Now that I see what he's really like, we need to go full steam ahead with this plan. We need to get Drew as far away from him as possible, and you need to pursue your own goals."

My knuckles are white on the steering wheel. What a dream. I would love to do both of those things. But she doesn't understand how vindictive Oliver can be. When he sets his mind to something, there's nothing that can change it.

Margot is looking at me and when we stop at a traffic light, I meet her gaze. Her eyes are daggers as she keeps mine and then she utters two words I never thought I'd hear her say.

"Fuck. Him."

The sound of the expletive leaving her lips makes me want to pull the car over right then and there and have my way with her. She clearly cares a lot about my future and I have to thank her for that.

"Do you want to get away with me? I mean, I know we're away now but this weekend, do you want to go some place? Just you and me?"

Margot reaches across the car, placing her hand on my upper arm. "Yes."

If we had bags packed, I'd go right now. But we didn't plan to stay at my father's house. So, I drive Margot to her apartment, assure her I'd be back in thirty minutes and then I go to my house.

Kai and Keith are watching TV when I come in. Their parents live across the country so they don't usually travel on these holidays. In fact, in the past few years they've been coming to mine for Thanksgiving but neither were upset when I said I was bringing Margot instead.

"Hey, man, how was—"

Their greeting gets cut off as I take the stairs two at a time. I have a bag packed and ready to go in twenty minutes and I'm heading back downstairs when I hear a knock at the door. Unless they ordered delivery, there's only one person that could be right now.

Keith rounds the corner and I yell for him not to open the door but it's too late. Oliver steps into the entryway, his hands full of tupperware containers. He spots me on the bottom step immediately.

My father raises the containers. "Thought you might want some leftovers."

Sighing, I try to walk past him out the door but he grabs my arm, stopping me. Kai and Keith are on red alert in the entryway. *Oh good, an audience. Oliver's favorite.*

"Get in the kitchen," he whispers harshly into my ear. "Do not play with me right now."

Ripping my arm from his grasp, I stalk back into the house. I give the boys a nod, and they cautiously head back into the living room, Kai lingering just a bit longer with a curious expression on his face.

Oliver comes behind me, putting the tins in the fridge. When he closes the door, a long sigh escapes. "I apologize for dinner."

"I'm not the one you should be apologizing to."

"Alexander, you cannot be serious. This girl is nothing compared to you."

I want to roar.

I want to scream.

I want to rip his throat from his neck.

Who the fuck is this man to tell me who Margot is. He doesn't even know her. She is one thousand times a better person than I am. She cares more, worries more, loves more. She is every bit of the goodness in this world and I am lucky to have even the tiniest place in her life.

I want to say all of it. I want to shout from the rooftops how much Margot means to me. But instead, all I do is whisper. "She is everything."

Turning on my heels, I ignore my father raging for me to come back inside. Shouting a goodbye to the twins, I run out the door, into the car and head right to Margot's apartment.

She's waiting outside, just like I told her to and luckily I'm only a few minutes late.

"I thought you forgot about me," Margot laughs as she slides into the passenger seat. I reach across the car and grab her by the back of the neck, placing a rough but intimate kiss on her lips.

"Never," I say as I break our lips apart, resting my forehead on hers.

"Everything okay?" She asks, sensing the shift in my mood even after everything that's happened at dinner.

"It is now," I respond, pulling away from the curb and starting toward the highway. I'm not sure where we're going but as long as we're together, we're going to be alright.

Chapter Thirty-Seven

Margot

I WAKE TO ALEX'S soft whisper in my ear. "Wake up, baby. We're here."

Blinking a few times, I give my brain time to adjust to what's going on. Right, okay. Disastrous Thanksgiving dinner at Alex's house, spontaneous trip to who knows where. Looking out the window, the first thing I see is black meaning it's still nighttime, we must not have traveled too far, then. The next thing I see is an ocean and next to it, a little bed and breakfast called the Oceanside Inn. *Oceanside, New Jersey?*

"Where are we?" I ask, groggy from my car nap.

"We're at the beach. My favorite place." Alex unbuckles my seatbelt and I slide from the seat.

"That's nice," I say, still sleepy. Would it be bad if I just want to crawl into this B&B bed and sleep for twelve hours? *Probably.* After grabbing our bags from the back seat, Alex grabs my hand, leading me toward the door.

"Checking in for Prescott," he says to the receptionist, his voice commanding. Sexy. The sound of it wakes me up a bit.

"Oh you late reservers!" The older lady croons. "I always like to pay close attention to the people who book the day of." She taps a few keys on the keyboard then whispers dramatically toward us. "You're not running from anything, are ya?"

Alex laughs. "No, ma'm. Just wanted a nice getaway for the weekend."

"Well, you've come to the right place!" She cheers again. Her name tag says Susan.

"Thank you, Susan. We're excited to be here," I smile at her and she returns my grin. Susan tells us that we're staying in room four and that breakfast starts promptly at nine am.

"And happy hour is at four, you don't wanna miss that," she winks at me and I hold in my giggle.

"We wouldn't dream of it," Alex says with full sincerity. I swear, the way he is with people makes me care for him more and more every day. He's so genuine and kind. I have no idea how Alex turned out the way he did with his father in charge but I'm eternally grateful that he did.

After insisting three times that we can carry our bags, Susan shows us our room and wishes us a good night. When I turn the light on, the first thing I notice is the bed. A huge four-poster with a canopy and curtains rests in the middle of the room, taking up a large majority of it. The sheets are a pale pink that match the pink wall and pink towels on the dresser.

"Very..." Alex starts.

"Pink," I finish. "How did you find this place?"

Alex sets our bags down and goes to investigate the bathroom. "A quick google search. I knew I wanted to come to Oceanside, I just didn't know where to stay."

Sitting on the bed, I feel the firmness of the mattress underneath me. "And why Oceanside?"

Alex pauses in the doorway from the bathroom. He leans against the wall, deep in thought. "When we were kids, we used to come on vacation here. Some of the best times of my life have been spent on this beach." His mouth closes and I know the things he's not saying. *Some of the worst times too.*

I walk across the room to meet him, shuffling over and placing my hands on his upper arms. "I'm excited for you to show me the beach tomorrow." Reaching up on my tippy toes, I place a kiss on his nose.

Alex sighs against me, gripping my waist tightly. He rests his forehead against mine and breathes me in. "Did you know you smell like coconut? All the time?"

"Do I?"

Quickly, I mentally catalog all the skincare, hair care and body wash I use and none of them include coconut as an ingredient.

He takes another big whiff. "You smell like the beach." Alex leans back and meets my eyes. Then he kisses me with a force I didn't expect but am very welcome to. He moves his hands from my hips to circling my waist and he walks us backward toward the bed as his kiss deepens. When the back of my legs meet resistance, I know we've hit the mattress.

"Alex," I say against his lips. "You know I—"

He stops immediately. "Of course, I'm sorry. I'll slow down." He starts to pull away but I grab him tighter, bringing his lips back to mine for a brief, heated moment.

"No, that didn't mean stop. That meant: be gentle with me."

He kisses me lighter this time and I can already tell he's slipping away, wanting to stop this. But I don't want to stop this. I want to keep going. I want to go all the way. I keep his lips against mine but open my mouth wider to allow his tongue access.

"Margot, wait," he protests as I sit on the bed, pulling him down so he's bending to reach me.

"No. No waiting." Moving back more center onto the firm mattress, I motion for him to join me.

"Are you sure?"

In a moment of desperate vulnerability, I answer truthfully. "I've been sure about you for longer than I ever even admitted to myself."

The tether that was holding Alex to his moral high ground snaps and he launches himself onto the bed, meeting our lips together again. I love the feeling of his full pout against mine. Like we were molded to fit each other.

Laying back, I take Alex's t-shirt with me over his head and he makes quick work of the button down shirt I'm wearing, each button quicker than the next. I don't want to think about how much practice he's had with removing girl's clothing. Or his expertise at every sex position known to man. Or the fact that his dick has been in—

"Here, baby." Alex takes my chin in his hand and moves my face so our eyes are linked. "Get out of that beautiful head of yours and look right here." He nods and I do, too. Once satisfied that I'm fully locked in, he continues to pepper my neck with kisses as he moves his body south down mine. With my buttoned shirt wide open, he has access to every inch of my torso not covered by my bra. And when he gets there...

"A front clasp? Nice," he cheers, making quick work of that as well. I get no moment to be self-conscious of my bare breasts out on display as he immediately takes one in his mouth and massages the other. The feeling is like nothing I've ever felt before.

I throw my head back and bite my lip to keep the sounds from escaping. Alex pinches my chin to release my bottom lip.

"Oh, no. Let it out. I wanna hear you."

I look down and see Alex's body raised above mine. God, he is so hot. The type of hot you daydream about. Not the type you actually get to have. With a feral grin, I pull his face to mine and kiss the ever-loving daylights out of him. He moves to unbutton his jeans and slide them off as we kiss. My breath draws as he pulls away, grabbing the condom from this front pocket before throwing his jeans to the floor.

Alex sits back on his heels and looks at me. It takes everything I have not to cover up my chest. "You are so beautiful," he says, placing a gentle kiss on my lips. "Are you sure about this?"

"Yes. I'm sure about you."

Alex kisses me again and then makes quick work of my own pants and underwear. Once I'm laid out bare in front of him, it all becomes beautifully, terrifyingly real. I want this man more than I want my next breath but I'm also so scared of that feeling. The feeling of wanting something so badly.

Alex makes his way slowly down my body, kissing every inch of bare skin he comes in contact with. When he gets to that apex of my thighs, he stops. His breath is hot on my center and the feel of that alone almost causes me to be undone. He kisses me there and I see stars, planets, galaxies in my eyes. I've never known anything to feel so good. With his name on my lips, I explode into a supernova.

Quickly, as my heart rate softens down to above average, Alex fumbles with the condom. He places himself directly at my center and then props himself up with his hands on either side of my face. He places gentle kisses on my nose and then sighs deeply.

"You absolutely sur—"

Before he can finish the word, I thrust up, connecting our bodies in the ultimate way. Pain skyrockets through me and I stifle a yelp at the unknown intrusion.

"Woah, sunshine." Alex says as he moves ever so slowly, keeping us connected and allowing my body to get used to the fullness.

Once the pain subsides into pleasure, I moan my reply, the sound furthering his enjoyment. Alex continues to thrust, the movements quickening, quickening until he stops suddenly, a groan rocking through him. He shifts one more time and then collapses to my right, landing on his side and immediately pulling me against him, nose to nose.

"Are you okay?"

"I'm more than okay."

"You are incredible."

A cheek-splitting grin forms on my face and Alex matches it. We lay like this, staring into each other's eyes, for an unknown amount of time. It's Alex who eventually breaks the silence.

"You need to pee."

Narrowing my eyebrows, I reply, "How did you know that?"

He laughs, shifting us so that we're ready to come off the bed. "No, I mean after sex. You need to pee or else you risk the chance of getting a UTI."

"Look at you, sex expert."

Sliding off the bed, I grab my shirt and underwear and head toward the bathroom.

"I'm not a sex expert," Alex shouts from the other side of the door. When I come back inside, he's disposing of the condom in the garbage before heading to the bathroom himself and completing the same task.

I button up my shirt, put my panties back on and sit on the bed. "How many people have you had sex with?" I ask Alex once he steps back in my line of sight.

He freezes, his hand half-way up to his face. "You really want to know that?"

No. Yes. "Yes."

"Why? Is that important to you? I never claimed to be a saint before I met you."

"I know that. I just want to know. I mean, you know mine."

Alex chuckles and sits next to me on the bed. "I suppose that's true." He sighs before continuing. "I used to get a lot of attention from women. In high school. In college. I mean, I still do. And for a while, it was really hard to turn down. Losing a mom and having a dad that ignores you, I was begging for some attention and I would welcome it at every turn, even if it came from random girls that just wanted to get into my pants for the *prestige* of it all.

"So, yeah. It's a high number. I'm not even sure I know the exact amount but let's just say, it's not something I'm particularly proud of."

Grabbing his hand, I pull it to my mouth to place a kiss on his palm. "You are an incredible man. Anyone with half a brain would see that. Those people were lucky to have had anything to do with you. And now they're unlucky since they'll never get their chance again."

"Is that so?" Alex laughs, pulling me onto his lap and wrapping his arms around my waist. I murmur in the affirmative but I'm starting to lose focus from the way his body feels under mine. He's definitely hard again, that I can tell for sure but I am surprised by how ready I am too. He's going to make me a sex maniac after all.

Rocking back and forth a bit on his lap, I rub his arms up and down for good measure.

Alex groans, "You, my sunshine, are going to be the death of me."

A grin. "A very, very, very good death." And then I attack.

The smell of salt water permeates my senses as Alex and I walk along the water. After spending much of the night wrapped in each other's arms, we decided a morning walk along the beach would be nice. Obviously we bundled up since it was almost December and more than mildly freezing outside. The beach is empty though, so that is a plus.

"How often did you come here?" I ask as Alex snuck his fingers between mine.

"Not a whole lot. Mostly before Mom was gone. Dad never took us on any vacations after that."

I squeeze his hand in mine. I wish I could go back in time and erase all the bad memories he's lived through. I wish I could meet that little boy and tell him that one day he's going to turn into an incredible man and that all the worries he has right now will fade away. I wish that were true but even still, Alex was still worried about Drew before himself. I doubt that feeling would ever go away for him. I wonder if that's what Arden feels about me.

A melody drifts by us as we continue walking down the shore. A soft, jazz like rhythm. Looking to my left, I notice it's coming from a speaker attached to a little cafe on the boardwalk.

"I know this song." Alex shifts and before I know it, he's pulled me in front of him, his hands at my waist, mine on his shoulders. "My dad used to sing it to my mom while she would cook."

Alex sways us back and forth for a few beats before he starts humming the song along with the speaker. I start to recognize it. *Dream a Little Dream of Me.* Resting my head on his chest, I let him move us side to side. "He'd pull her in. Just like this."

Alex tightens his hold on me, placing his chin on the crown of my head.

We probably look ridiculous, dancing on the beach in the middle of the morning, but I couldn't care less. There's no place on this entire planet where I'd rather be.

Once the song ends, Alex takes a step back and smiles, taking my breath away. For real. I have to catch myself for a moment before I can fall back into step with him. There's something about his face and this place we're in together. Something about the way that he's taken care of me and shown up for me even when we were merely just co-hosts on a silly little podcast. The feeling burns deep inside my gut, in my heart, and I think I know what it is. But I don't dare say it. How could I possibly? We only just started dating. There's no way...

"Sunshine?" He asks as he looks back and notices I've stalled out on the beach. "You okay?"

I nod, quickly. Too quickly. I need to process all these emotions before I go and tell him what I'm feeling. What if he doesn't feel the same way? He's been with plenty of girls. He's had feelings way more advanced and more often than me. He'll probably think I'm a fool for feeling this way about him so fast.

Alex kisses my forehead. "Out with it. I can see the wheels turning in there." He points to my head.

"It's nothing," I say as reassuringly as possible. "Just thinking about the breakfast. I hope they have french toast."

Alex laughs and drapes his arm across my shoulders. "I hope so too, baby."

Chapter Thirty-Eight

Margot

THEY DID HAVE FRENCH toast. And scones. And croissants. And pancakes. And every type of egg you could imagine. And it's a very good thing that Alex and I returned for breakfast because it seems as though we are the only guests at the Oceanside Inn and were then expected to devour everything that was cooked–even though it was really made to feed a small army.

"Susan, you better give that chef a huge kiss for me," Alex says, shoving his mouth with a forkful of strawberry pancake.

Susan laughs as she refills our coffees. "Will do. I love kissing my husband, so that really isn't any trouble."

"You guys own this place together?"

"Bought and opened right out of college. We were just a couple of crazy kids back then but look at us now. Been up and running for twenty-five years and our marriage has been just as successful." She smiles down at us before heading back into the kitchen.

"That's such a nice story," I say, wiping some stray syrup from the corner of my mouth.

"Mhm," Alex agrees, his mouth still full. After swallowing and taking a sip of coffee, he continues, "It's pretty inspiring."

"Does it inspire you?"

"To open an inn? Not really," Alex jokes.

I put my coffee mug down on the table. "No, to live out your ambitions. It seems like Susan and her husband started from nothing and they've built this incredible thing together. It's just so…"

"I know, sunshine. Living out my own dreams is obviously what I'd want to do in a perfect world but the world isn't perfect."

"I just don't understand why you won't even entertain the idea of *trying* to figure your dreams out. Drew said it himself, he doesn't want to go to TU. If we can help him find a college he loves with a program he enjoys on the west coast, it'll be much harder for Oliver to get to him."

"Margot—"

"And if you stick to your convictions and actually cut him out, you'll be able to live out your dreams as well. This is possible, Alex. Why can't you see that?"

He puts his napkin on the table and leans back in his chair with a sigh. "You want me to cut out the only parental figure I have left?"

"Oliver is hardly a parental figure. To him, you're just another dollar sign."

Alex looks at me and I realize I've gone too far. This is his family. His life. I need to back off before he gets really upset. Reaching across the table, I grab his hand and relax a bit when he lets me hold him.

"I'm sorry, I didn't mean it like that. It's just that he doesn't seem to give you the fatherly love you deserve. And you deserve so much."

Alex kisses my hand. "I know." He smiles sadly. "I know."

With a sigh, I drop the heavy topic. This isn't the last he's going to hear from me about living out his dreams but for the rest of our getaway, I will keep my big mouth shut.

⌇⌇⌇

Seagulls caw as we walked up the boardwalk toward the restaurant. We'd spent the afternoon alternating between taking in the touristy sights and popping into little shops on the main street. When Alex suggested we have dinner in a restaurant he dined in with his family as a child, I jumped at the chance to gain another piece of him. I loved getting these pieces of his life–I hoped the puzzle would never be completed.

"Reservation under Prescott," he said at the door, surprising me. I nudged him in the side as the host walked us to our table.

"A reservation, huh?"

Alex pulls out the chair for me to sit and then moves to the other side of the table. "You just never know with this place. My dad always makes a reservation everywhere we go, just in case."

The waiter arrives and Alex takes the opportunity to order us a bottle of red wine to share and some appetizers.

"You know, you've talked a lot about your dad but are there any things that you like about him? Positive things you can say about him?"

Alex thinks for a long moment. "For my tenth birthday, he dropped Drew off at a friend's house and he took me to the driving range. I remember I didn't want to go at first because I didn't think hitting golf balls would be a particularly exciting afternoon for a ten year old."

"Fair," I reply, chomping into a breadstick the waiter had left on the table.

"But, it ended up being one of the best afternoons I'd ever spent with him. We hit balls off the top deck and he taught me the difference between all the clubs. Then he said I was doing so well that one day he'd invite me to play with him and his buddies on the real green."

Alex leans back in his chair with a sigh. "Still waiting for that invite."

I place the half-eaten breadstick down on my plate. "It really kills me to see you so upset by him."

Alex nods absent-mindedly for a moment and then seemingly snaps out of his trance. He reaches across the table and grabs a breadstick, devouring it in two bites. The waiter takes that opportunity to pour us a generous serving of wine and place our appetizers down on the table.

"Do you want to talk about your mom?"

I pause with the wine glass halfway to my mouth. "There's nothing to talk about. She had Arden. She had me. She left. That's all I know."

Alex nods but doesn't speak. He's allowing me space to continue and I love him for that. "My dad is the sweetest man you'll ever meet. He's kind, funny, a true southern gentleman. From what I gathered, my mom was a selfish narcissist who wrung him out for all he was worth and hung him and us out to dry. Once his mama's health started declining, he took extra shifts at the factory to help keep us all afloat."

I finally take that much needed sip of my wine. I want Alex to know about me as much as I want to know about him. It's just that these conversations are never easy to have.

"One day, my dad got hurt on the job. Some machine malfunction. Now he's paralyzed from the waist down and needs just as much taking care of as my memaw, although he'll never admit it. Anyway, Arden took over the work and it was agreed that since my grades were better and I got a full scholarship to TU, I'd go get my degree and then I'd get a fancy pants job in a big city and help them out at home.

"And I want to. So, so badly, I want to help the people who have been there for me no matter what. Who have always cared for me. I need to help them."

"That's a lot of weight to carry on your shoulders."

I give a small smile. "No heavier than your burden. I guess we're both destined to take over the family business, so to speak."

I try to enjoy the mozzarella stick in front of me, but my appetite is suddenly gone. I haven't been thinking about my family much lately. No, I've been too busy running around with Alex and partying with my friends. My eye has been so far from the prize, I'm surprised I can even see it anymore.

I need to finish this podcast. And I need to win this *New York Times* internship competition so I finally start helping my family instead of just being a hindrance to them.

Dropping the cheesy stick, I brush the bread crumbs from my hands. Time to get back to business.

"Alex, any interest in taking a short break from our very romantic vacation to look at our next podcast script?"

He smiles widely. "There's my girl."

Of course I brought my laptop on our getaway. They can pry that thing from my cold, dead hands at my funeral. Even though we skipped out on most of our dinner, Alex convinced the waiter to let us cork the bottle of wine and take it with us.

"Small towns, huh," he winked as we walked out the door with it.

Once we got back to the hotel, Alex poured us each another glass and I pulled out my computer.

"I've only just glanced at the comments on last week's post so this is going to be a doozy."

"I'm ready, sunshine." And he was. When I looked over at Alex, he was sitting cross legged across from me on the bed, a look of determination on his face. He wasn't even upset that I had ended our fancy dinner early to go and do work. In fact, it was his idea to leave right then and there. He held my hand the entire time we walked back to the inn. He kissed my cheek when I walked past him holding the door open. He wants to help me succeed.

"I love you."

I smack my hand across my mouth so fast, as if the force could shift the words back into my mouth. *He didn't hear that. He didn't hear that. He didn't hear that.*

Alex's features morph into shock for the briefest of moments and then he smiles like he just won the most coveted prize in the entire world. "What was that, sunshine? Speak up." Alex pulls my hand from my face and the grin covering his own gives me the confidence to repeat myself.

"I love you."

"Finally, I'm not the only one." Alex launches across the bed, cutting me off completely. His lips find mine in a kiss that rivals Romeo and Juliet, before the dying part. He cups my cheeks in his palms, cradling my face like it's the most precious thing in the world. He's kissing me and I lose track of time. He's kissing me and he steals my breath away. He's kissing me and I realize...he didn't say it back.

"I love you too, sunshine. Been loving you for a while now, if I'm honest." Alex breaks the kiss long enough to say the sweetest thing I've ever heard and then he leans in again and I'm lost to his emotion matching mine.

He loves me.

This beautiful, confident, sweet man loves me.

I could leave this Earth happy knowing I've been loved by the man who brought me out of my shell and won't let me back in again. Alex makes me a better person and I can only hope that I do the same for him.

Our kisses turn more fervent as Alex moves his body on top of mine. *The podcast can wait.*

Pulling his shirt over his head, Alex breaks our kiss long enough for the fabric to pass over his face and then he's back on me again, his plump lips stealing my breath away. Moving down toward his belt, I slide the leather through the loops, opening the clasp and pushing his jeans down as best I can from my laying position.

"My girl is a fiend," Alex smiles against my lips. Before I knew him, I might've withdrawn from a comment like that, drew back against the hidden shadows of the wall. But Alex has taught me to be bold and brave, just like him.

"Only for you." I run my fingernails down his back. "Well, for now. I mean, I don't even know what it's like to be with anyone else so–"

With a growl, Alex pulls my neck up to push our lips tighter. His punishing lips draw my breath and I grin at my victory. "And you'll never know. You're mine forever."

"Forever, huh?"

Alex kisses me again, softly, lovingly. "Forever."

He pulls up my dress, revealing the lack of underwear I have on underneath and I silently applaud myself when his breath catches. Sheathing himself with the condom from his pocket, Alex sinks into me slowly, as if I'm breakable.

Intent to show him that I'm not, I hoist myself up, pushing him into me completely. Alex hisses through his teeth but allows me to take control. I move my hips up and down, up and down. Alex lays paralyzed above me, his lips on my neck, my shoulders. His arms are barely holding him up above me.

"Baby, you keep doing that, I'm not going to last very much longer."

With a devilish grin, I move my hips faster, finding that the motion is causing sensation to build up in me as well. With a few more powerful thrusts, Alex and I both explode, my eyes pinch shut as Alex collapses on top of me, making sure to not hit me with his full weight, even in the throws of ecstasy. Alex rolls off of me, pulling his arm underneath my neck to cradle my head.

"Can you say that thing again?"

"What thing?" I ask.

"The thing you said before I rocked your world."

"Oh, that I'm interested in comparing sex with you to sex with some-one—" Alex pinches my arm and I swat him away. We both lean on our sides to we're face-to-face, nose-to-nose. "I love you."

Alex closes his eyes, softly rubbing the tip of his nose against mine. "Never stop saying that, okay?" He opens his eyes again.

"Okay."

We lay like this for a while before Alex demands I use the bathroom while he cleans himself up. After a pee and a very quick body shower, I'm curled up in my pajamas with my laptop open to the podcast page.

"Ready to dive in?"

Alex nods, running his towel through his wet hair. Alex had showered after me even though he begged for us to "save water" and shower to-gether. As much as he may wish after this weekend, I'm really not the sex *fiend* he thinks I am. Alex slides into the bed next to me, placing a quick kiss on my temple before looking at the laptop screen.

The questions are mostly similar to the ones we always get. Questions about Alex's sexual experiences. Comments about wanting to hook up with Alex—some of which include phone numbers. Even questions about me and my sexual escapades. *People are disgusting.*

We laugh and groan as we scroll until we come across a question that causes us both to pause.

"Are you guys dating?"

Alex looks at me. "Let's just come out with it. I don't really understand why we haven't already told people. Like it needs to be some big secret."

"It doesn't need to be a secret but Alex, you and I are treated very differently on this campus. I'm just nervous how this news is going to be received by your...adoring fans."

Alex sighs. "If anyone actually cared about me, they'd be happy that I'm happy."

"But that's just the thing. These people don't care about you. They care about your social status. They want to be with you for the prestige it comes with. They don't know the real you."

Alex blinks. "What do you think the response will be?"

I sigh, pushing the laptop away. "Well, based on the comments I've gotten so far, I'm sure people will jump at the chance to call me a gold digger again. Also, they love to say you're out of my league. Oh, and another good one, I'm just a charity case to you."

"Why do you even look at these hateful, ridiculous comments anyway?"

"It's my job."

"It's shit," Alex says, taking the laptop into his lap. He types the question into our script and then types some bullet point responses. When I go to look over his shoulder, he moves the screen away from my view. "No peeking."

I raised my hands in surrender but I knew I'd look when he wasn't around. He knew it, too. After a few minutes, Alex closes the computer and takes his phone out, opening to instagram. I watch as he posts a new picture, taking one from the recent album in his photos and adds a simple heart emoji as the caption.

After he hits the publish button, my phone vibrates in my pocket. I pull it out to see an instagram notification. Narrowing my eyes, I look at him as I open the app but my eyes widen when I see the photo in full view.

It's a picture of me at the beach yesterday looking out at the water. You can see my profile and my eyes are closed in bliss. I remember this moment. We had just gotten to the water's edge and the wind smelled like salt. I wanted to bask in that moment for as long as I could. A slight smile lit up my face. I looked happy.

"You didn't have to post that." And tag me in it.

"There's no reason not to."

Alex tries to swipe my phone from my hand but I see an unread text from Jessy. She probably just wanted to wish me a happy thanksgiving. Without looking at the message, the phone drops it onto the mattress next to us. Placing a light kiss to my lips, he rests his head against mine. "I don't want to hide the amazing person you are from the world. Everyone deserves to see you shine."

My eyes catch him and there's nothing but genuineness in his expression. This boy. He gives me the confidence to be more than I ever thought possible. Kissing him again, we lose ourselves in the passion of being young and in love. If only the feeling could last forever.

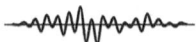

Because Alex whisked us away for a romantic weekend getaway, all the homework I had planned to complete got pushed to the wayside but that didn't stop me from ensuring that Alex and I wrote our speeches before we left New Jersey. I wrote mine in record time but for me, it was easy. I've known I wanted to be a journalist ever since I saw a copy of the *New York Times*. I always found it so fascinating when people ask the hard hitting questions, the rude and uncouth ones, just to get a story. I wanted to be like that. I wrote my speech about my goal of winning the *New York Times* internship contest and my aspiration of being a journalist.

When I showed it to Alex, he sang my praises, of course, but I knew he was struggling with his own.

"Just tell them what you told me. That you want to be a personal trainer."

"That seems like a cop-out," Alex sighs, closing my laptop. He leans toward me on the bed to try and get me to kiss him but I move out of his reach.

"Uh uh, no distractions until you finish this speech," I say, pushing the laptop toward him as I move slightly out of his way.

Alex pouts but opens it up again. "What if I write about what I'm actually going to do once I leave here."

"You want to make a speech about working for your dad? That's neither your goal nor your aspiration."

Alex rubs a palm down his face. "You're right." He lets out a breath, pulling the screen closer to him. "I can do this."

"You can do this. I'll make more coffee," I say, moving off the bed and padding toward the little coffeemaker on the desk in the room.

"Thank you, baby," Alex says absentmindedly, his eyes now glued to a blank document. I hear the typing begin on his laptop and I smile to myself. Even if it's not what his father wants him to do, Alex deserves to have dreams of his own.

Chapter Thirty-Nine

Alex

IF THERE WAS A way to stay in Oceanside forever with Margot, I would've done it. Unfortunately, we had a semester to finish and one more podcast to film before she submits her final project to the *New York Times* internship contest so rushing back to campus was a necessity. Dropping Margot off at her apartment, I gave her a lingering kiss before she slid out the door with a promise to see me tomorrow in class. Who knew that public speaking would become my most anticipated class of the year.

General noise of frat brothers settling back after a long weekend hit my ears as I walked into the house. A beer comes flying toward my head and I catch it with my non-bag holding hand.

"It's not even cold," I remark to Devon who laughs as he meets me in the entryway. He grabs my bag, throwing it toward the stairs.

"Don't whine. That's fresh from the Narragansett brewery, as requested."

I nod in thanks, opening the room temperature beer and taking a sip. Even warm, my favorite beer always hits. "Good break?" I ask as we walk into the living room. Two juniors vacate the couch as we enter and we take their empty spots.

"Not bad. My little sister is a real dick," Devon remarks, taking a sip of his own beer.

I choke out a laugh. "Dude, she's like six."

"Yeah, a six year-old dick."

I shake my head, grabbing for the remote but it's swiped from my hand before I can reach it. Keith gives me a shit-eating grin as he holds the remote above my head.

"Hey, fuckers," he says, pushing us to the side to sit between us. Him and Devon wrestle for control of the space and I look around for his brother. With everything going on, I haven't really had a chance to sit down with Kai and help him through his troubles. I hope that being home helped a little bit.

"Where's your brother?" I ask as the room remains empty besides us.

Keith only shrugs his shoulders like he has no idea but also doesn't give one crap. I place the beer on the table and head upstairs, grabbing my bag on the way up. Kai has been my best friend for too long for me to let this trouble bring him down. He needs to know that I'm still here for him, new relationship or not.

After tossing my bag in my room, I shut the door and head toward Kai's, hearing the sounds of ACDC flooding down the hall. I enter without knocking, not that he would've been able to hear me anyway. Kai startles when he sees me walk in but then he sighs, as if he knows he's in for a long conversation.

Kai uses a remote to lower the music and then it's just him and I and this big obstacle between us.

"How was your break?" I ask, starting slow.

Kai nods. "Yeah, it was good. Yours?"

I nod. "Good. good."

Kai nods again. "Good. Cool."

Sighing, I plop down on the foot of his bed. "Have you been able to sort out this whole paying-for-school issue?"

Kai's quiet for a minute. "I'll get the money. It'll be fine."

"How? How are you gonna get the money? Because I swear, Kai, clearly this gambling shit is what got you in this mess in the first place. It's not going to be the thing that gets you out."

"Fuck," Kai mummers. "You think I don't know that?"

"I think you're a fucking idiot."

Kai stands, ready to defend himself and his honor but he doesn't make it two steps before he admits defeat. Running both hands through his thick black hair, he looks up at the ceiling for far too long.

"You don't have to do this alone. I can help you. Any of the guys in this house would help. Hell, does your own brother even know what the hell is going on?"

"He knows," Kai says quietly. He walks toward the window and I follow him. We look down at the street, watching a girl walk by with her dog. "For the record, he also thinks I'm a fucking idiot."

I huff out a laugh. "Well he knows you best. And so do I. Get your head out of your ass and let us help. There's a world of opportunity out there for you. You gotta use the advantages you're given."

It comes to me in an instant. A real way for me to help him get the hell out of this situation. Set him up good and proper for the future. It would take a little convincing but I could probably manage it.

I clap Kai on the back and he jumps, not expecting the contact.

"I have an idea and a couple calls to make but let me sort it out and get back to you." Turning to leave, I hear Kai call my name and I shift back.

"Thanks, man," he says, reaching out to shake my hand. I take the hand and pull him in for a hug, too.

"That's what brothers are for."

—⁓⁓⁀ᴡᴧᴧᴧᴧᴡᴧ⁀⁓⁓—

Margot jumps in her seat as I plant a kiss on her cheek.

"Geez, every time," she mutters, handing me a pen.

I laugh. "You know I'm coming and yet you always jump." She levels me with a look but can't retort as Professor Walker calls the class to attention. Since the professor mixed up the names this time, Margot and I are both presenting today. I'd like to say I'm not nervous but for some reason, I really am. Not about talking in front of a group of people, I could do that in my sleep.

For some reason, this speech feels even more personal than the first one and that speech mentioned a topic I've only told a handful of people. There's something about talking about the future I want versus the future I have to look forward to. It's daunting in both regards.

Two freshmen go before me and Margot squeezes my hand when the professor eventually calls my name. I grab my note cards from my backpack and head down to the stage. With a deep breath, I begin.

"There are two questions that should have similar if not the same answers. Those questions are 'What are your goals and aspirations' and 'What are you going to do after college'. If you had asked me those questions at the beginning of this semester, the answer would have been the same. But ever since an influence entered my life and threw it completely off its axis, those answers are not even in the same category."

I flip my card over and then stuff it inside my pocket, realizing I'm not even looking at them. No, there's a pair of deep blue eyes I can't take mine off of.

"When I leave college, there's an office waiting for me in the head-quarters of Prescott Cars. An office with wall to ceiling windows, a desk with nothing more than a computer and a sad plant. An office that will suffocate me slowly for the next fifty years of my life."

Margot nods.

"That might be someone's goals and aspirations but it's certainly not mine. No, my goal is to be happy. My aspiration to be fulfilled. I'm no psychic but I can see far enough into my future to know that neither of those things will happen if I sit behind that desk at Prescott Cars.

"If I could have it my way, I'd be a personal trainer when I left this place. But, how often do people get to have their way?" With that, I give a final nod and then exit the stage, reclaiming my seat next to my beautiful girlfriend.

"Well done," she says with a nudge on my elbow.

"Thanks," I grin before turning my attention back to the other presenters.

Chapter Forty

Margot

"I WANT TO BE a journalist for the *New York Times*."

Even after these weeks in class and our podcast, I still wasn't fully comfortable in front of an audience. It was getting easier though, especially with Alex in my corner. Like now, it was only when Alex placed a firm but reassuring hand on my thigh that I was able to calm down.

I try as best as I can to not read from the cards but I found that looking into the crowd was a much scarier feat.

"There's a contest to win an internship. My goal is to win that contest so that I can fulfill my aspiration of being a full-time reporter. I want to chase the story. I want to break the news. I want a front page headline that reads: *History Was Made* written by Margot Davis."

I emphasize each word of the by-line with my palms out flat in the air. When I glance over toward Alex, he is beaming from ear to ear. The sight causes me to smile as I continue.

"When I was young, my father instilled in me the principles of hardwork and patience. He said, 'it's not the work that's hard, it's the time spent waiting for the results'. I take those principles with me to class each day. I take them to the newsroom. I take them to the recording studio." Alex winks and I try my hardest to hold in my blush.

"*When* I win this contest, it'll be because I worked hard and I had patience. And *when* I am successful, I will know that it's because of what I do best. My best."

A loud whoop comes from the center of the room and I see Alex standing up from his seat. I can't control the redness that burns my cheeks as I leave the stage and take my seat again.

"Sit your ass down," I whisper, loudly, pulling his arm down by the sleeve. Alex kisses my cheek as he takes his seat again.

"You crushed it, sunshine!" He whisper-shouts into my ear as I slide even farther down into my seat. I'm glad to be done with it but I'm starting to feel the residual embarrassment. Alex is still beaming as he turns his attention to the next few presenters. I'm just glad to be finished so I can focus on this last podcast taping.

—⁓⋀⋀⋁⋀⋀⋀⋀⋀⋁⋁⋀—

Since we already planned our last podcast recording over the weekend, I use that time to pop into the newsroom and see if there's an article Jessy wants me to work on.

When I enter the chaotic environment, I take a deep sigh in, readying myself for the noise and confusion. I see Sydney at her desk, hard at work on something on her computer screen so I chose not to disturb her, heading toward my editor's desk instead.

"Hey, Jess. Have a good weekend?"

She continues to type on her computer, not giving me a glance. *Damn, she must be working on something important.* I guess I'll go look at the announcement board and see if anything catches my eye. As I turn to walk away, Jessy's voice stops me.

"How's that article about students staying on campus coming along?"

Immediately, I pinch my eyes shut. I totally and completely forgot about that. *Damnit.* But there's no way that Jessy wouldn't know that I didn't stay on campus this weekend. Unless she...

Jessy holds up her phone, showing Alex's instagram picture of me on the beach. "Great pic. Doesn't really look like it was taken on campus, though."

"I'm so so sorry, Jessy. I completely dropped the ball on that one. I'll make it up to you. Give me any story. I'll work on it right now."

Jessy shook her head, standing from her desk to grab some papers from the printer. "You know, Margot, I'm really happy for you that you're doing well on this podcast but I didn't know that that success would come at the expense of your attention to the paper. This is your job, too. I know you get work-study to be on the paper, that's why I try to give you as many bylines as I can."

"I know," I reply softly.

Jessy takes the paper and lets it drop to her side. "More than that, you're a good writer. I've missed your insightful voice this semester. You've just been... I don't know...distracted."

I know she wants to blame Alex for this. Hell, I want to blame Alex for this. But there's no one to blame but myself. I dropped the ball. I need to be the one to pick it up.

"I won't let you down again, I swear, Jess. Please...give me any story. I'll start right away."

Jessy softens a bit. She knows this is out of character for me. I'm usually incredibly meticulous about all of my work, especially the paper because I love it so much. These past few weeks, my attention has been elsewhere, but that's not going to happen anymore.

"There's nothing really going on right now but I could use some help looking over the articles that were written over the weekend. I got a little behind while I was home."

"Say no more," I reply immediately, already making my way over toward my desk. "Send them over, boss."

Jessy lets out a chuckle and some tension releases from my chest. "Will do," she says as she makes her way back to her own desk. As I sit, my phone vibrates with an incoming text.

Lunch?

Can't. Working at the paper

I feel the vibration of another text but I put my phone face down before reading it. It's time to concentrate. Focus. Get back to the reason I'm really here. And I'm going to show Jessy that she *can* rely on me. Even if I have to prove it to myself first.

"Delivery."

A brown bag drops down on my desk, startling me. When I look at the delivery man, I'm shocked to see Alex standing over me, a dazzling smile on his face. I chance a quick look in Jessy's direction before grabbing Alex's arm and pulling him out into the hallway.

"What are you doing here?"

Alex looks confused and slightly hurt. "Figured since you can't come to lunch, I'd bring lunch to you."

"You can't just show up here whenever you want. I'm working. I need to focus."

Alex squints his eyes. "I didn't mean to distract you, I just thought I'd help..."

"Alex, this is important to me."

Alex's voice is quiet, hurt apparent on his face. "I didn't realize I was pulling you away from what matters."

I sigh, placing my hands on either side of my face. I squeeze my eyes shut. "You're not pulling me away. It's just, this time we've been spending together, while it's amazing, it has been very distracting for me."

Alex grips my hands, pulling my palms away from my face. "I get it. Sorry, I've just...never had a girlfriend before. This is all new to me."

"It's new to me too." A small smile greets me when I look up at him. He kisses me briefly on the nose before dropping my arms and stepping back.

"We'll figure this whole relationship thing out," he says assuredly. I nod. "In the meantime, get back in there. Get the scoop. Follow the lead. And all that other stuff."

I huff out a laugh and Alex's face lights up. Reaching on my toes to kiss his lips, I linger for longer than I should to savor him before turning on my heels and heading back to my desk. While I'm almost done with the articles that Jessy asked for help with, I still have to start my final paper for my Investigative Journalism class. And then I need to get my head in the game for this internship contest. The deadline is close and Alex needs to move to the back of my mind so I can shift my priorities to the front.

Chapter Forty-One

Margot

SYDNEY HANDS ME ANOTHER steaming hot cup of coffee and I mutter a thank you, not looking up from my psychology textbook. I'm trying not to panic but I truly cannot believe how far I've let myself fall this semester. I'm holding onto my GPA by a thread that's getting thinner by the minute.

"Are you sure you're okay, Margot? I haven't seen you this focused since spring finals week freshman year."

"A dark time for us all," Danika chants from my doorway.

"I said I'm fine," I reply, still not making eye contact. How could I when I need to memorize five key concepts of the mind by tomorrow afternoon?

"You're not fine," Danika mutters. Before I know it, she's snatched the book out of my hands, holding it up over both our heads. If I wasn't so angry, I would've been impressed by her strength—that's no small feat.

"What the hell, Danika. Give it to me," I yell, attempting to reach it but she's always had some height on me.

"You want it?" Danika taunts. "Go get it." She tosses the book haphazardly behind her into the living room. I gasp, hoping it's not ripped. It's a rental. Before I can go get it, Syd and Dani form a united front in my doorway, their folded arms blocking my exit.

"What is wrong with you two? I'm just trying to study."

Danika sighs. "You've been locked in this room studying for two days. Have you even talked to Alex?"

A grunt of frustration erupts from my chest. "I don't need to talk to Alex! I need. To study." Pushing past them, I force my way into the living room.

Even though I displaced them when I barreled through, they only form the wall again on the other side of my bedroom.

"I saw him at the gym. He asked me about you," Sydney says, her voice small.

"He shouldn't be asking you about me. I'm fine. He knows I'm busy. It's almost finals week." Sydney nods but her face is crestfallen.

I pick up the book, thankfully still intact, and sigh heavily, letting it fall back down onto the couch. "I'm losing it, guys. I don't know how I got so behind this semester but I'm struggling to catch up."

"I know this podcast thing has kind of taken up a lot of your time," Danika says, rubbing her hand on my back like she does when I'm not feeling well. The sisterly touches always make me feel better. "Why don't you let us help you?"

"Help me study psych?" I ask, hopefully.

The girls laugh. Danika holds out her hand. "Hand over the study cards you've got in your back pocket and nobody gets hurt."

Hesitantly, I pull a stack of completely filled index cards and place them on Danika's waiting palm. "Atta girl," she says. "Such a nerd," she whispers to Sydney. I give her a hip check as we all land on the couch, Sydney grabbing my textbook and opening to the page I left off on.

After an hour and another completed stack of index cards, we decide to call it a night. I didn't mean to ignore Alex this week but he has a tendency to make it hard to focus and I really just needed time to myself to get reoriented. Remember why I'm here in the first place.

After brushing my teeth, I lay down in my bed and pull up Alex's contact information. I know he'll answer me even though it's late. At least I hope he does. I hope he's not mad I didn't reach out earlier.

With quiet trepidation, I hit the call button under his picture–one I took of him laying on the bed on our impromptu thanksgiving getaway.

"Sunshine?" He answers after the very first ring.

Just the sound of his voice calms my frayed nerves. "Hey, frat boy," I sigh in contentment. He sighs, too, seemingly relaxed.

"How are you? I've been missing you."

"I miss you, too. Sorry, it's been a crazy couple of days. I just needed to catch up on some school work."

I hear the sound of sports slowly fade away in the background until a door shuts and then silence. "And did you? Catch up?"

"Mostly. I've still got a few papers to write and finals to study for but I feel okay for now."

I wonder if Alex is laying on his bed the same way I'm laying on mine. I wonder if I should ask him if he is.

"What have you been up to?" I ask instead, a little intimidated by what his answer to that other question might've been.

"Nothing crazy. Working out, caught up on some work myself. Oh and I've been talking to Kai. We're trying to figure out a way to get him back on track, ya know."

My heart swells. Not only that he's helping out his friend but that he's comfortable enough to tell me about it. "That's great, Alex. I'm really happy to hear that."

"Yeah, it's good." I can hear the smile in his voice. And the sleepiness. I'm sure he can hear it in my voice, too.

"Alex?"

"Yeah, baby?"

"I think if I don't go to sleep in the next four minutes, I might pass out on the phone." I laugh but it's muffled by a yawn, only proving my point. My eyes start to shutter closed but I force them to stay open. I don't want to miss this time with him but the exhaustion of the last few days has finally hit me all at once.

Alex laughs. "That's okay, sunshine. You sleep. I'll be here when you wake up."

My eyebrows perk up. "You will?"

"If you want me to."

I nod, sleepily, even though I know he can't see me. "I love you, frat boy."

"I love you too, sunshine." The last thing I hear is Alex humming *Dream a Little Dream of Me*.

"Are you ready for another question, Alex?" I ask, pulling up my note-cards. Alex and I had started the recording session the same way as all our previous ones, with our signature greeting and Alex's embarrassing antics that always make me blush.

I still can't believe that this is our last episode ever. Once I submit this to the *New York Times*, we'll have no reason to continue on. We aren't letting the viewers know that though, still wanting them to view and comment on the videos. It also takes some of the pressure off of having to record a "grand finale." If the audience doesn't know it's ending, there's no need to do anything extra for the final episode.

"I'm ready, Margot." Alex winks at me this time instead of the camera and a warmth spreads through me. This incredible man loves me. And I love him.

"Sam K wants to know what she should do if her family doesn't approve of her boyfriend." It was a question we debated answering but ultimately decided it was important enough to try and tackle. Most of the questions we receive are silly or flirty but through the cracks there are some real, meaningful problems that are asking for sincere solutions.

Alex glances down at his notes but I know he already knows what he wants to say. "That's a tricky one, Sam, I'm not gonna lie to you. It's difficult on multiple levels. Do you take your family's side and leave the relationship or do you stay with the person and risk losing your family? I wish I had the answers, Sam but not every situation can be judged in a vacuum."

Alex sighs before continuing. "I feel like this probably isn't advice you get often but, Sam, in this case, I think you need to be selfish. I think you need to put yourself first and think, if you absolutely had to choose, which choice would make *you* happiest.

"Who supports you more? Who helps you flourish? And who will be there for you in your darkest times? That's the person I would pick." Alex really has a way with words and I don't know if I'll ever get used to how eloquent he can be.

"I completely agree." I wonder if his words are penetrating his own mind or if he's just thinking about this faceless viewer. While his father isn't giving him an ultimatum to choose between him or me, he is forcing him to do something that he doesn't necessarily want to do. Alex should take his own advice and be selfish.

I pose another question from a viewer about pooping at a friend-with-benefits' apartment and Alex takes off running with his advice. His smile is breathtaking as he makes a joke. His perfect smile reminds me of how his teeth grazed my inner thigh. How his hot breath coasted up my leg toward that very sensitive part–

"Right, sunshine?"

"Huh?"

"Do you agree?"

"Oh, um. Yes." I can't stop the blush from erupting on my cheeks and I know, based on Alex's smirk that he knows exactly what I was thinking about. The smirk that also says he'll be more than happy to live out that fantasy once we finish recording.

Shaking myself back to reality, I glance at the last notecard I have, ready to finally end the show on a bang.

"It's time for our final question."

Alex's gaze hits mine and he nods with a megawatt smile. "Can I ask the question?"

My smile matches his. "Go ahead."

"The question is, dear viewers, is 'are Margot and I dating?'. To which the answer is," Alex reaches out, pulling the notecards away and then connects his hand with mine, interlocking our fingers so there's no room for misinterpretation. "Yes. Yes, we are."

The instinct to shy away rages inside me but I resist, allowing myself to take pride in this moment. I deserve to show off my relationship. A relationship I worked hard for. If Danika were here, she'd tell me to take what I want and I'm finally doing it.

Giving our connected hands a loving squeeze, I turn toward the cameras again and confirm his answer with a brilliant smile. Beside me, Alex lets out a contented sigh.

"Yes, folks, I finally wore her down."

I can't help but roll my eyes but this time, at least it's in a teasing way. Alex pulls our hands up and kissing my knuckles, not looking away from my eyes.

"And I'm a lucky man," he says quietly, as if just for me.

Our fingers stay locked throughout the rest of the show and continue that way all through the parking lot directly to the car door. Alex kisses my nose before opening the passenger side door.

"Are you sure you can't hang out? I've barely seen you all week," he asks as he slides into the driver's seat. As much as I want to spend time with him, we were coming up on finals week and I've been slammed with work. I need to stop shirking my responsibilities and allowing Alex to distract me.

But when I look over at him, the puppy dog eyes have me faltering. "I need a few hours to edit the podcast and work on my finals but come for dinner. We can order in."

Alex smiles, appeased by my compromise. "Sounds perfect, sunshine."

He pulled away from the curb toward my apartment after he all but demanded he drive me home even though I know he's just going to turn right back around and go to the gym. The man is incorrigible, in more ways than one.

Chapter
Forty-Two

Alex

WEIGHTS CLANG AROUND ME as I wipe my towel across my forehead, mopping up the sweat. It feels good to be back in the gym after a weekend away and the rest of the week filled with finals preparation. Not to mention not seeing Margot for most of the week and her needing to do more school work after the podcast taping. Yeah, I needed to blow off some steam.

Last weekend still feels like a dream to me. Margot, the girl I've been working with all semester, the one who constantly has my back, encourages me to follow my dreams–maybe a little too fervently–the one who continues to surprise me with her courage and dedication. My sunshine. Loves me. And now everyone knows we're together.

I've never been loved by a woman before. That's not to say I haven't had girls tell me they love me before–you can't help what comes out of your mouth in the heat of the moment. But I've always known they didn't mean it and I've never said it back. Because I've never meant it. Never felt it. Not until now.

Margot helps me see things that I didn't think were even possible. Even though she's seen the worst sides of things, of me, she never wavers. She's headstrong. My brave girl. I still can't believe I get to call her my girlfriend, claim even just a little piece of her. Even if my future is locked up, it's a relief to know she'll be there weathering the storm with me.

A splash of water breaks me from my reverie. After I wipe my face, again, Kai and Keith's shit-eating grins come into view.

"What are you daydreaming about? Your girlfriend's tits?" Kai teases but drops the smile the second he sees my face. Kai has seen me pick up grown men and chuck them out onto my porch for less reasons than objectifying my girlfriend.

For good measure, Kai takes a step back, raising his hands up in surrender.

"Come on, man," Keith pats my back once. "I'm starving."

We head toward the locker room to shower quickly before leaving. Ever since I ran into Margot after the gym and she told me, in no uncertain terms, that I reeked like ass, I always make sure to clean up before I leave.

Shortly after, the twins pile into my car and we head home.

"Should we just order pizza for dinner? The fridge is empty and we're actively driving away from our campus meal plan."

"You fuckers can do whatever you want. I'm going to Margot's for dinner."

"You coming back for the party tonight? Last one of the semester" Keith asks as we pull up to the house. I idle outside, not even putting the car in park, anxious to see her now that I'm so much closer.

I shake my head. "Probably not. Gonna be a bit busy."

Kai laughs. "We'll be sure to display your balls on a very special place on the mantle. After Margot releases them, of course."

Before I can smack him in the back of the head, Kai and Keith leave the car, laughter following in their wake.

I couldn't care less what these assholes thought of me and my relationship with Margot. I'm finally happy and there's nothing that can bring me down.

As soon as she opens the apartment door, Margot is hoisted up into my arms. She giggles as I kiss the crap out of her, latching herself around my hips and neck.

"Hi, there," she breaths against me, a grin forming on her face.

"Hey, sunshine. Got dinner plans?"

"Nope, I've been working on my ASL final." I put her down and she falters back a step, like a baby fawn walking on freshly grown legs. When she backs up, I finally get a good look at her.

"What's all over your face?"

Margot narrows her eyes then looks down to examine her hands, noticing red and blue painted across her fingertips, matching the scattered smudges on her cheeks. "Oh. Ink," she laughs, licking an un-inked finger and wiping the stains from her face. She doesn't get it all but I don't tell her, she looks adorable.

"Are you ready for a break? We can order something. Whatever you want."

Margot's face shifts for the briefest moment and I catch a glimpse of hesitation before she schools her features back into delight.

"Yeah, I can break for a little. Let me just check my portal one more time. My investigative journalism final paper grade should be up by now," Margot says as we walk into her bedroom. "It was the earliest one I submitted this week." Margot sits at her laptop, pulling up her online student portal to check her grades for the umpteenth time, I'm sure. I settle onto her bed, making myself comfortable.

She types for a few minutes and I'm about to pull up my food delivery app when a small gasp escapes her lips.

"I got a C," she barely whispers.

I shift up on my elbows. "Ah, shit, sunshine. Maybe you can ask for extra credit?"

"You don't understand." Margot hasn't turned around to look at me. Her eyes are glued to the screen. "I don't get C's. I get A's. I get A's because A's help me keep my scholarship. I don't get A's, I don't keep my scholarship. I don't graduate on time." Margot stands and starts pacing the room.

"Woah, slow down. It's one C."

"It's more than one C, Alex. It's one C and a missed article for the newspaper. Next it'll be a missed class. Then I'll lose the internship contest. Then—"

"Sunshine, slow down," I jump up and grip her shoulders but she immediately pushes me off, still not looking me in the eye. Not looking at anything, really. Her blue eyes glazed over.

"I can't afford to mess this up, Alex."

"I understand that. But this isn't the end of the world."

Margot turns her head and finally looks at me. "Maybe not to you. You don't even care about your grades. Or college at all, really. I don't have the luxury of coasting through life like you do."

The dig hits me square in the chest.

I've never been shy about my family having money but I've certainly never flaunted it, especially not with Margot. She knows more than anyone that I've got no choice in my future. She can go out into the world and do whatever she wants while I'm being pushed through a Prescott Cars shaped door.

I know she doesn't mean what she's saying. She's taking her frustrations out on me.

"Everything was going fine. I was on track. I was reaching my goals. And then, you—"

"Margot, what?"

"You. You burst into my life and even since then, I haven't been able to think straight. You've taken me off my path. You've distracted me."

For a moment we're both silent. I have no idea what to say. On one hand, she's not wrong. We've been spending a lot of time together. Time, I guess, she would've spent on her schoolwork and newspaper job. But I wasn't the one who asked to work together. She came to me at the start of all this. It's not my fault that we fell in love in the process.

And she has no right to blame that on me.

"Let me help you. We can figure this out."

She's not listening to me, lost in her disappointment. I know her asking me for help at the start of all this was a struggle because she didn't know who I was. I never thought after all this that she would still be struggling to ask for help.

"I can't do this. This...is too distracting." She's gesturing wildly and I just need her to calm the fuck down. The words she's saying right now are threatening to shatter me. Margot is spiraling. I've seen this spiral before. A bead of sweat glistens down her brow. Her eyes are wide with shock and confusion. *She's about to drive us into a lake.*

"This?"

"This." She's silent for a beat. "You. Us."

She's taking in deep breaths as if all the oxygen hasn't just leaked out of my lungs.

Shaking my head, I try to make sense of everything she's saying but she's moving a mile a minute and I can't keep up. Even if I could say anything to appease her right now, she wouldn't listen.

Flashes of memory burst into my eyesight. My mom and dad, laughing in the kitchen. The next thing I know, I'm underwater fighting for my life. I couldn't save her. She killed herself because she couldn't care for me. I might as well have pulled her under the water myself. And damn if I'm going to do the same to Margot.

I'm nodding. I'm nodding and speaking before I even know what I'm saying. "You're right. I've been pulling your focus away from what's important. That's not fair to you."

Margot stops pacing and looks at me, tragedy in those deep blue eyes.

"You asked me to help you with the podcast but you never asked me to take over your life."

"Wait–" I hold up a hand to stop her. If she says anything now, I'll lose my steam. I need to do this. For her.

"When people get together, they're supposed to make each other's lives better. But ever since we've gotten together, you've endured internet bullying, frat row drama and now you're at risk of failing your classes. That doesn't qualify as *better* and that's my fault."

She's silent. I want her to contradict me. She wants to contradict me. But she can't. Because we both know that I'm right.

A lone tear escapes her eye and I reach out to wipe it away. "I can't fail, Alex."

"I know, sunshine." My hand drops from her cheek. "And I can't be the reason you do."

More tears fall and it takes every ounce of willpower I have not to pull her against my chest and hold her. Wipe away the tears and make everything clean and new again. But you can't fix something that was broken from the start.

There's a piece of me lost at the bottom of that lake. A piece I need to be whole and able to love without fear of ruining someone else's life. Walking out of Margot's life right now is the only way to save her.

Without another word, I take the most challenging step I've ever taken in my life. A step away from Margot, toward her apartment door. Leaving her crying behind me, I walk right out of her room, out of her apartment, down the hall and out the front door. It's not until I get to my car that I realize.

She's not the only one crying.

The very last thing I want to do is have my house filled with drunken assholes but there's no escaping it. I could leave, but where would I go? Can't go back to Margot's apartment, even though everything in me is screaming to run back and apologize. Beg her to forgive me. Beg her to take me back.

But I can't do that.

Leaving Margot is the best thing I could do for her. Even though it's tearing me apart one vein at a time.

Opening the fridge, I stare inside, looking at the contents but not really seeing.

"Hey man, didn't expect to see you back here tonight," someone says next to me. I don't even blink. Can't.

"Alex?" the voice says again. I keep staring. *What have I done?* Suddenly, my arm is ripped away from the fridge handle and I'm staring at

Kai's confused face. Once he sees my expression, his face sobers. "What happened? Is Margot okay?"

"She's..."

Gone.

I can't say it. I can barely think it. I pushed her to her breaking down and she pushed me away. And I let her. Because I love her more than I love myself. I want to see her succeed more than anything else in this fucking world. And she can't do that if I'm standing in her way, begging for her attention.

I need to be stronger than that. I will be stronger. For her.

Kai shakes my shoulders, pulling me out of my thoughts again.

"What the hell is going on?" By now I see Keith and Devon have joined up behind Kai, all three of their faces mirror images of concern.

"We broke up."

"You—"

A glass shatters in the living room and I finally blink. I can't be here. I need to fucking go. Now.

Ripping my keys out of my front pocket, I run out the front door, ignoring the sounds of my brother's calling behind me. Getting in the car, I put the key in the ignition and drive away. Before I realize what I'm doing, I'm pulling up to the front door of my father's house.

My brother's door is ajar and the sounds of clicking intensifies the closer I get. Drew is muttering curses to himself and he pushes the over ear headphones off of his head right when I walk in the room.

"Jesus Fucking Christ, Alex. Are you trying to give me a heart attack?" he yells as he jolts out of his seat. I can't help but laugh at his apparent fear...until I realize it's the first time I've smiled since I walked out of Margot's room and then the grin fades.

"Sorry, I didn't mean to scare you." I walk further into the room, taking it in for the first time in a long long time. Behind me, Drew settles back into his gaming chair. A glance in his direction says he's wondering what my motive is for being here. I don't blame him. I haven't just dropped by the house to say hi in...never.

"What are you doing here? Doesn't your fancy pants frat throw ragers on Friday nights? Why aren't you there?"

"Couldn't be there," I mutter. I'm pretty surprised to see Drew has a bookcase with a not insignificant amount of books. Glancing at the titles, I see some fantasy, some graphic novels, a few comic books. A few books on cars.

"Since when are you interested in cars?" I ask, pulling out the copy of *Engines for Dummies!* Drew rips it from my hands. I hadn't even realized he'd left his chair.

"I'm not. Just have some books." He chucks the book back on the shelf. "What are you going here, Alex?"

With a sigh, I sit on Drew's unmade bed, pushing aside a pile of clothes. "I was looking for dad actually. He's not here, is he?"

Drew shakes his head. "Some business dinner."

"Shocked," I deadpan.

Drew looks at me questioningly. "Why do you need him?"

Finally selling my soul to the devil. Since I can't make Margot happy, can't give her what she needs, I might as well make someone in my life happy. Even if that person is Oliver. Even if that means, come graduation, I'll be waking up everyday to a life that I hate. Something good has to come out of this hole in my heart.

I came to tell my father that I'm ready to stop fighting him.

My eyes shift from Drew to the desk behind him, cluttered with old soda cans, empty potato chip wrappers and behind it all, a photograph. A framed photograph. My legs move without permission and I pick up the frame, analyzing it closely.

It's the three of us. Drew, myself and our mom. She's hugging us closely, she's grinning, her eyes closed. Drew and I are smiling too. It's a beautiful picture.

"I've never seen this before," I murmur to myself.

"Dad got it framed for me a few years ago."

"He did?" Now that shocks me. Setting it back down, I push some garbage out of the way so that it can be featured more prominently. "What do you remember about mom?"

I have no idea why I'm bringing her up right now. We never talk about her. It's an unspoken rule in our household. But for some reason I can't explain, I'm dying to know. He was so young when she did what she did. When she died. I need to know what he knows about her.

"I really don't remember her at all." Drew's voice is sad and his eyes are even sadder. "I wish I did. You have no idea how much I wish I could recall something but there's just nothing. I don't even remember what she did to us. I just know what you've told me."

For a minute, I'm relieved to know he doesn't remember almost drowning in that lake. The memories of that day have weighed on me my entire life. It's a comfort to know that my little brother isn't burdened by that, too.

But then I remember my mother's smile. My father singing to her in the kitchen. Our impromptu adventures. Drew doesn't remember any of that either. And that's a damn shame.

"You know what I do remember though?" Drew asks, breaking me from my memories. Drew spins around in his chair and I lean back against the desk, settling in a bit more comfortably.

"I remember that time that we built that fort in the backyard in the dead of winter and Dad said we couldn't sleep out there or we'd freeze to death." Drew laughs. "You brought out every single blanket, pillow and sheet in the entire house and told Dad that we'd see him in the morning."

I chuckle at the memory. Of course I remember that. We did almost freeze to death, woke up in the dead of night, shivers wracking our entire bodies. We had grabbed our blankets and both slept in my bed, curled up for warmth.

"I remember that."

"Oh, and that time we went to the beach and I wouldn't go in the water."

"Because of the sharks," I roll my eyes.

"Because of the sharks but you ran right in and started splashing around."

"To scare them away."

"And eventually I did go in because you convinced me that there were way too many people around for any sharks to come by anyway but you stayed by my side the whole time, just in case."

The beach had been packed with people. There was hardly any space to swim in the water let alone get bitten by a shark. I had grabbed his head and shoved him under the water so he could see the shark-free landscape himself and he had splashed me real good on his way back up. Dad was on the boardwalk, phone to his ear.

"And when Dad made you quit the basketball team so you could go work after school at the dealership, you kept practicing on that hoop in the driveway, even though you didn't need to improve your game anymore."

"I still liked playing. And you used to come and play with me sometimes."

"I remember," Drew says. "I don't know much about our mom, and maybe even less about our dad but I know a lot about you."

My throat catches but I don't want to spook him with too much emotion. We've never spoken this openly before. Oliver doesn't care for emotional conversations and by the time Drew was old enough to have any, I was out the door running toward Tomlin University and my freedom.

I hadn't realized Drew had been watching me so much growing up. Noticing things I did for him. Remembering how I protected him. Guided him. I had always wanted him to know that he could do anything he wanted to do, if he set his mind to it. Even though I wasn't able to follow my own advice sometimes, I would burn this world down if it meant my baby brother could live the future he dreamed of.

Drew's hazel eyes glisten slightly and it's like I'm seeing him in a new light. *I never realized how much he looks like mom.* I want to reach out and give him a hug but I know he's probably reached his breaking point of sappy emotional talk so I settle instead for a pat on the shoulder closest to me.

"You're alright?" I ask.

Drew nods. "Yeah, I'm good. Are you?"

I can't return the sentiment. Not yet. But I'm finding myself at least happy with one decision I made tonight and that was to seek out my father. Because it led me here. A place I never thought I'd be.

Chapter Forty-Three

Margot

HOVERING OUTSIDE THE DOOR, I wonder if I've made a terrible mistake coming here. This has always been my study room, my safe haven from the chaos of a college campus. I never thought that bringing Alex here would ruin it for me forever. But now, the very air reeks of him.

Maybe if I close my eyes...

Sliding the key into the door, I squeeze my eyes shut before swinging the door open, stepping inside and letting it close behind me. Only then do I look around. The room looks exactly the same but somehow, completely different. The chairs are tucked into the table. The table where we wrote our podcast scripts. The chairs we sat in a little too close to each other to be *friendly* but neither of us moved away. How could I possibly sit in the room where Alex and I shared ideas, laughs, and even pleasure, one I try very hard not to recall.

I want to be strong enough to do this but, as it turns out, I'm not. Especially when I notice the etching that Alex left in the table. Could that only have been weeks ago? Feels like another lifetime. I run just the tips of my fingers over the letters, fighting back the tears that threaten to fall.

Nope. Can't do this.

Running out of the room as if it was on fire, I bolt up the stairs, practically throwing the study room key at poor unsuspecting Edith. I don't need her concern right now. Her pity would break me.

Sending a quick text to Sydney, I resign myself to sit by the gym and wait for her to finish her workout and take me home. I can edit the podcast from my desk in my bedroom. As I settle onto the bench outside the fitness center, pulling out my book to distract me, a cacophony of male voices pulls my attention.

Then I see them. A crowd of KA guys, led by Kai and Keith, walking toward the gym, water bottles and gym bags in tow. I've never prayed before but now seems as good a time as ever. *Please, don't notice me. Please, don't notice me. Please, don't notice me.*

"Margot?"

This is why I don't pray.

Glancing up, I feign shock. "Oh hey guys, didn't see you there. What's up?"

Some guys wave as they walk past me into the gym. Eying the group, I try to hide the fact that I'm very obviously looking for someone.

"He's not here," Kai says, matter-of-factly. "He went home for the weekend."

"Home?"

"Something about seeing his dad."

I narrow my eyes. Spending time with Oliver Prescott is the very last thing Alex would want to do. Something must be wrong. Sydney, and her incredible timing, exit the gym before the boys can say anything else.

"See ya around," I say as a goodbye and then I pull Sydney toward her car, the look on my face telling her all she needs to know.

I knew editing the final episode of the podcast would be difficult but I didn't know it'd be rip-out-my-heart-and-stomp-it-into-the-ground difficult. Every look, every touch, every laugh burns as if a physical flame is being set to my skin. I need to get this over with as fast as humanly possible.

It feels disingenuous to post a podcast recording all about how much Alex and I love each other when in fact, our relationship barely lasted the length of an entire episode. I can't even think about the reaction this is going to have on campus but I also can't bring myself to care.

In two weeks, finals will be over and everyone will go home and forget this podcast ever existed. *Ask Alex* will fade into Tomlin University obscurity. A whisper of what used to be. And that's perfectly fine with me. I never meant to cause the stir I did on campus, I only meant to make a big enough splash for the *New York Times* to notice.

Still, posting this episode now...it makes me feel like a fraud. Like this whole thing was just for show. Like I'm everything the mean girls in the comments said I am. A pick-me, an attention seeker, a phony.

"How's it going, champ?" Danika asks, bringing me my third cup of coffee. I've been at this for an hour and it hasn't gotten the slightest bit easier. Every time I think it can't get worse, I notice Alex glancing at me with a look of love that drops my heart out of my chest.

"I'm almost done."

"Do you want help?"

God yes. "I'm almost done," I repeat. As much as I would love to pass this task off to someone else, this is my competition piece at the end of the day. I'm responsible for how it turns out. Alex and Nathan both have been huge helps throughout and I couldn't have done it without them, but this I need to do on my own.

With a solemn nod, Dani leaves the room, closing the door behind her.

Another thirty minutes and a few shed tears later, I'm finally finished. While typically I'd wait until Monday afternoon to publish the podcast, I can't bring myself to think about this for one more second.

Surprise, Alex fangirls. You're getting your podcast one day early. But I'll bet you won't be pleased with the contents.

Don't worry, neither am I.

I grip the pen in my hand. The extra one I always give Alex. He's sitting seven rows behind me and I'm gripping the pen like it's my only lifeline. It's pure instinct that I'm even holding it, so used to him trying to steal mine.

You would think there would be a speech as a final for this class but Professor Walker has been surprising us all semester, she's not gonna stop now. After an hour, she dismisses us, collecting the test packets and wishing us all a happy winter break.

Somehow in the rush of everyone leaving, I end up directly behind Alex in the hallway. I want to talk to him. Touch him. Hear him call me *sunshine*. But I know I can't. He doesn't want to be my distraction. He wants to live his own life. Without me.

I resign myself to a silent walk until I remember the fact that his friends said he was with his dad for the weekend and I can't stop the words from slipping out of my mouth.

"Alex?"

Alex turns to me, looking like he's seen a ghost. "Yeah?"

"Is everything okay?"

"What do you mean? Of course, it's not."

The comment stings. "I know you went to your dad's this weekend. Just hoped all was well with your family."

"Oh. Yeah, I went to tell him that I'm ready to take the spot at Prescott Cars. Looking forward to it, even."

The shock is apparent on my face. "You told him that?"

"Yes. No. But I will. I'm going to." Alex turns to leave but I can't stop myself.

"Why? Why are you giving up on your dream?"

He turns back to me, his eyes heavy with sadness. "What dream, Margot?" I try not to die inside when he calls me by my first name. He walks away and this time I let him. You would think it would be getting easier for me to let him walk away but as it turns out, it hurts more every time.

Leaving the building after him, I try to give us a wide berth so we don't run into each other walking through campus. As I wipe an errant tear from my cheek, I swing the door open and run smack into a blonde girl, both of us tilting backward from the assault.

"I'm sorry, that was my fault."

"No worries," she says. She glances at me once, then double takes, staring at me much more intently. I've been getting looks like this for weeks, ever since the podcast started but there was something different about this one. Something more intense.

"Oh my gosh, wait. Are you Margot?" she asks, her eyes widening.

I nod politely in response, ready to continue my way through the doors but her next question stops me in my tracks.

"So you and Alex Prescott are really dating?"

My chest caves in. The tears I was holding in threaten to rush down my face. "I—"

"Yep." Alex says from behind the girl. I hadn't noticed him stop on the walkway until I heard his voice. He walks over and puts his arm around my shoulder, pulling me tightly but I know him, it's not tight enough.

Clearly caught, the girl gives us a cute little smile before walking past me into the building. Alex immediately lets go of his hold on me and I feel the absence like a bullet to the heart.

When I face him, he has his hands stuffed in his front pockets. "Let them think what they want for the next few weeks. Once we get back from break, we can tell them the truth."

I can only nod.

It's a very nice gesture. One I'm not shocked he's making.

Alex nods too then turns and walks away.

Yep. Harder and harder every time.

Chapter Forty-Four

Margot

AT SOME POINT OVER the next week, I write up my final entry for the internship competition and I send it, along with the link to the podcast episodes, over to the *New York Times*. I also study for my finals, finish all the papers I was working on and write an article for the paper about students protesting on campus. Between all that, I make a very important phone call that will hopefully help at least someone be happy in the future. I do all of that without a heart in my chest because it had fallen out and rotted away on the floor of my apartment Saturday night.

Another week passes and I can feel a shell forming around myself, a protective cover guarding against outside forces that could hurt me. Because I can't stand to be hurt again, I won't survive it. Sydney leaves for winter break, giving me a kiss on the check and reassuring me that things would get better.

Danika drops her duffel bag on the couch in a huff.

"That's all you're bringing home?" I ask, wheeling my small carry-on suitcase into the living room.

"Are you kidding?" Dani walks back into her room for a moment and when she returns, I can barely see her over the size of the massive suitcase she's pushing.

"I am not helping you put that giant in the overhead bin," I huff.

Danika only scoffs. "You already know I'm checking this bad boy," she says, giving the suitcase a couple pats for good measure. I would've laughed but the joy has drained out of me these past couple weeks. I haven't had it in me to feel anything but hopelessness. "You ready to go?" She asks, pulling up her Uber app to call a cab to the airport.

I nod, grabbing my coat and my sneakers. When I bend down to put on my shoes, my phone falls onto the floor face up, a flurry of notifications on the screen. I've been avoiding looking at that thing since the last podcast episode went live, putting it mostly on do-not-disturb. I have absolutely no desire to read the comments about mine and Alex's "relationship".

Reaching down to grab it and silence the noise once again, a particular email notification catches my eye. An email from *Editoral@nytimes.com* with the subject: "Internship Competition".

Immediately I want to puke.

Here it is. My true failure. The one thing I set out to do this semester to all but guarantee my future as a journalist. A simple email that will say "sorry, but you suck." I squeeze my eyes shut. *I can't do this right now.*

"Mars?" Danika looks down at me and I hadn't realized I'd sat right on the floor where my phone had fallen. She catches a glimpse of the email my finger is hovering over and gasps. "Oh my god."

The contents of my stomach threaten to emerge but Danika is jumping up and down on top of me and I can't catch my breath.

"Open it! Open it!" she's shouting but I can't make my finger do anything but float above the screen. "Margot, I swear to god—" The knowledge that she's just going to snatch the phone and click it herself propels me forward and I use all the courage I have to open the email notification.

I don't want to read it out loud. I can't have Danika look at me like a failure. I can barely look myself in the mirror, I don't need my best friend's pity on top of all of this.

Fortunately, I don't have to read too much to know the contents, the news is apparent from the very first line.

"I won," I whisper.

Danika draws in a huge breath.

"I won!"

Danika screams at the very top of her lungs and I can't help but join her. Before I know it, we're jumping up and down on the couch, my excitement reaching beyond what I ever would've thought.

"You did it!" Danika shouts, pulling me in for a bone crushing hug. We bounce down onto the cushions, catching our breath. "I mean, I always knew you would but you really fucking did!"

"I really fucking did," I sigh, dreamily. And then it hits me. "Well...we did. Me and Alex." The moment of joy has quickly turned into a moment of turmoil.

"Are you going to tell him that you won?"

"Should I?"

Danika hits me with her empathetic look. The look that says, "I wish I could tell you what to do but you need to decide for yourself."

Nodding, I resign myself to thinking about that decision the whole way to the airport and even on the ride home. But for now, I need a few more blissful minutes of happiness. Because, I didn't fail. I finally won.

Chapter Forty-Five

Alex

As if enduring the holiday break at the Prescott house isn't bad enough, I don't even have Margot with me to make everything better, the way only she is able to. I spend the first weekend at home spending as much time as I can with Drew, playing basketball, watching baseball and even playing whatever auto-themed game he's into. It's nice to have this time to spend with him, especially after knowing the effect our time shared has on him.

I guess I should've realized that Drew would look up to me. I certainly set a better example than our father at being a nice person. But I never really thought about how much he looks to me as a role model. And the entire time I've been home, I can't help but feel like I'm letting him down.

A text from my father has me making my way to his office. He doesn't often summon me unless it's to talk business, of which I was never in the mood, least of all now.

I find Oliver behind his desk, clicking away at his computer, a phone to his ear. He looks up at me when I enter the doorway and puts up one finger, asking me to wait. I haven't spent a lot of time in this office, it never really sparked a lot of happy memories so there was no reason to want to come in here. As my dad talked to whoever about whatever, I took a chance to look around, notice my surroundings as an adult rather than a child.

His bookcases were full of old-looking books. Merely for decoration, I'd imagine. I've never seen that man read a day in my life. There were art pieces on the walls. A globe in the corner. All the things you'd picture in a successful businessman's office.

The only thing missing was...him. There was nothing in this office that had any shred of humanity. It might as well have been scooped right out off the cover of Bloomberg Businessweek.

I sigh, content to wait outside, until something catches my eye. A picture. The same framed picture that Drew has on his desk. The picture of Mom smiling, holding onto Drew and me. Oliver has it displayed on a bookshelf but I notice it's on a lower shelf, eye level if he's sitting at his desk, which he always is.

My dad hangs up the phone. "Hello, Alexander."

"You looking for me?"

"Yes." Oliver stands, pushing in his chair. "Care to go for a drive?"

I narrow my eyes. "To where?"

He nods his head toward the door. "Let's go."

"Why did you bring me here? A little morbid, don't you think?"

After asking a few million questions on the way, I slowly started to quiet down once I realized where he was taking me. Parking the car directly next to the bridge, he gets out without a single word, urging me to follow.

We walk down to the edge of the lake, close enough to smell the fresh water but not in any danger of accidentally falling in. I've done my time in those germ-infested waters, I have no intention of ever going back in there.

"What's your last happy memory of her? Of your Mom?"

"Why are you asking me this?" Had he overheard my conversation with Drew last week? My father never talks about my mom. Ever.

"Just indulge me, please."

For a moment, I'm quiet. Looking behind me, I spot a flat patch of grass and sit down on it, shocking my father who then surprises me by joining me on the lawn, stretching his legs out in front of him.

"A trip to Oceanside. We stayed at some shitty resort, where we all shared one room." Oliver gives me a glance as if to scold me for my language but ultimately resists. I continue on. "Early in the morning, Mom woke me up and snuck me out of the room while you guys were sleeping. We walked along the beach until the sun rose and she told me about all the things I could do with my life."

Oliver sighs heavily. "What kind of things?"

"I'm not sure the specifics but I remember some of them being pretty outlandish. Like an astronaut or a king," I laugh at the memory.

"A king," my father laughs with me, as if remembering a thought of his own. "Yes, she always had the craziest ideas."

I fall silent again, sensing that father is not done speaking. In fact, it feels like he's just beginning.

"Your mother was my greatest joy," he starts. "And she was my greatest pain."

He pauses but I know better than to interrupt him right now. I'll give him as much time as he needs to get through this.

"On her good days, she would radiate positivity and light. Adventure after adventure. She'd dress us all up, drag us around town. She loved showing you boys off to the neighbors. It was like nothing I've ever seen, her love for you boys. Brought me to tears more than a few times.

"And that made it all the more difficult on her bad days. Tantrums and shouting. She'd lock herself in our room and not let me in for hours, and I'd pace back and forth hoping to god that she wasn't hurting herself.

"The day that she..." his voice trails off. "When she died, I felt like a piece of me died right along with her. For years, I collapsed into myself."

"I know," I said, unthinkingly. I don't mean to make him feel bad but I can't ignore the need to tell him how his reaction affected me and Drew. "We know."

My dad runs a hand down his face. "None of this was supposed to happen. She was supposed to love me and you boys. She was supposed to take care of us but instead, she let her demons get the better of her.

"And I...I did the same. I pulled away from you. I let you raise Drew because I didn't know if I could do it properly without her. I pushed you toward a career with me because I thought having you at work would bring us closer. Bond us. But I know you don't want that, Alex. I've always known."

Oliver looks over and for once it's like he's looking at me rather than through me. It's the most honest we've ever been with each other and I hope beyond hope that it's a turning point in the right direction.

"Why didn't you ever tell me that?"

"It's hard for me to talk about her. To talk about the ways I failed you."

"You haven't failed me, dad. I understand. I was going through it, too."

I want to reach out and grab his hand or pat his back—something to let him know I'm here and I'm listening—but I keep my hands folded on my lap. This seems like a breaking point, the most emotional we've ever been with each other. I need to speak up. If I can't speak up for myself and push back against my father's control, then I couldn't possibly be the man Margot needed me to be, anyway. If I can't have a say in my own future then I don't deserve to be a part of hers.

It's now or never.

"Dad," I start, taking a very deep breath in. "I don't want to work at Prescott Cars."

"I know. You don't want to work with your old man."

"Is that what you think? Dad, it has nothing to do with working with you. I have no interest in working in an office at all."

He looks at me, his inquisitive brow perked. "What do you want to do, then?"

Looking back at the lake, a ray of sunshine glinting off the water catches my eye. "I want to work in fitness. I want to be a trainer or own a gym or something like that."

It is the first time I said it out loud to anyone other than Margot. And I am saying it now to the last person I ever thought would want to hear it. Oliver is quiet. For a while the only sounds we hear are the birds chirping in tree tops above. Suddenly, after a sharp breath in, my dad breaks a decade long silence.

"You're a man now, Alex. You have every right to make your own decisions about your future."

"Are you saying..."

"Your mom would've wanted you to be happy doing whatever it is you're happy doing. I want you to be happy, too. So, go. Do what makes you happy. For both of us."

A tear threatens to escape my eye and I let it. "Thank you, dad. You know I've missed Mom all this time, but not half as much as I've missed you." Dad reaches across the empty space between us, gripping my neck and pulling my head over for him to kiss roughly before releasing me.

"I've missed you, too, kid."

"Not that I'm not happy about this breakthrough but, where is this all coming from?"

My dad gives me a coy look. "Margot called me."

"She–"

"She called me and boy did she give me a piece of her mind," he laughs.

I'm in shock. Not only that she would call him but that he would even speak to her. And he's laughing about it? Have I stepped in an alternate dimension?

Shaking off the weirdness, I picture Margot calling him after that brief conversation we had at the end of speech class. Did she tell him that we weren't together anymore? She must not. I need him to tell me every single detail of the conversation but I can't seem too eager or he'll catch on that something is off.

"What did she say?"

"She's a stubborn one, your girlfriend." *Keep it together.* "She told me that I've been holding you back from being the man you were meant to be. Or something to that effect. She said you had your own passions and none of them included working at a 'car factory'."

Oliver Prescott is a very proud man. He does not take kindly to disrespect. But when I look in his eyes, there's a playfulness there that I don't think I've seen since I was a child.

"She didn't really give me much of a chance to respond. She told me to watch some of that podcast if I really wanted to 'get to know the real Alex.' Direct quote."

There was never a doubt that I am still very much in love with her but the feeling is intensifying tenfold.

"So, I watched a random episode. And then another one. And then I went back and watched them all from the beginning. I just...it was nice to see you like that. Happy. I haven't seen you like that in, well, seems like years."

I can only nod in response. I was my happiest doing that podcast with Margot. But that's gone now. She's gone. *Don't dwell. Take this moment for what it is.*

We sit in companionable silence for a few more minutes before the honk of a passing car breaks us from our reverie.

We head toward the car, both of us feeling much lighter than we were before. Dad opens the driver side door as I slide into the passenger seat.

"I guess I gotta put out an ad for an intern to fill your spot for this summer," he mutters.

"Actually, I had an idea about that."

When my dad looks at me, I'm smiling from ear to ear.

Chapter Forty-Six

Margot

"Are you sure you have to go to New York?"

"I'm sure I have to go to New York." I smile as I take Memaw's plate into the kitchen. She follows me, her steps slower than they used to be.

"But that place is so scary."

I laugh, placing the dishes in the sink and start to wash them. "I'll be okay."

"Yeah, Memaw, Margot can handle herself out there. I raised her tough like that." Arden grabs the wet dishes from the drying rack and starts to dry and put them away. We work in tandem, Memaw sitting at the kitchen island behind us.

"Just don't go out at night. And don't get on those dirty trains they have there and don't—"

"Memaw, it's going to be alright," I say with a huff. "I'm only there for two weeks and I'll be staying near the *New York Times* building so that's probably a nice area."

Memaw shrugs. "Nothing about that city is nice," she mutters under her breath.

Arden rolls his eyes and hits my hip with his. "Imagine the day when Margot lives there and we have to go visit her."

"I ain't never going up to that loud place," Memaw says, slowly standing from her dining room seat to go and settle in for the night on her living room arm chair. "They got newspapers in South Carolina, you know," she shouts as she goes.

"Just as prestigious, I'm sure," Arden says in my ear and I hold in my giggle. We keep working in silence as the dishes dwindle down. After a few moments, Arden speaks up.

"So, you've been home for a week now. Are we going to talk about the Alex thing or what?"

I close my mouth for a moment. Maybe I should just play dumb. "What Alex thing?"

"Mars," Arden says, seriously. The tone of his voice causes me to look in his eyes. Can't play dumb with the one person who knows me better than anyone else. "Let's talk."

Arden gestures toward the now empty kitchen table and we sit in the same seats we just sat at for dinner. "The last episode of the podcast featured you two lovebirds making googly eyes at each other and now you haven't mentioned him, haven't talked to him once since you've been home. What gives?"

"It's nothing."

Arden rolls his eyes. "It's not nothing. I met the guy. Anyone with eyes could see you were crazy about each other. He didn't hurt you, did he? Cause I'll—"

"He didn't hurt me. Not physically anyway. I just...we decided we weren't right for each other, that's all."

"*We* decided?"

All I can do is nod.

"But why, Mars?"

I want to tell Arden about everything but, knowing him, he'd just see a boy hurting his little sister and there wouldn't be much stopping him from going up to his house and taking matters into his own hands. I can't have that. I need to control the situation like I've been doing. I need to keep my calm and just tell Arden to mind his own business.

"We just weren't going to work in the long run. I need to think about my future and I don't think he fits into it."

Arden quietly narrows his eyes at me. He knows I'm lying but he seems to be choosing not to press me on it. I appreciate him for that. More than he knows.

I need out of this conversation before I start sobbing.

"Gotta go finish packing," I say, hitting my palms on the table and standing up.

Arden nods but doesn't follow suit. "I'm here for you. You know that, right?"

"Of course I know that."

As I walk by, I grab his shoulder, pulling his face down so I can plant a kiss on his cheek. I wish I could tell him everything but this is one battle that I need to fight on my own.

Memaw was right about one thing. New York is loud. And busy. And hectic. But it's also brilliant, electric, and exciting. Everything about this place buzzes with importance and prestige. If I am able to live here one day, I will never shut up about it.

The *New York Times* building is smack in the center of Times Square and every time I step out of my hotel to walk to the office, I am faced with another incredible thing about this city. From the billboards to the people to the atmosphere. There's even still some confetti on the floor from the New Year's Eve celebration the weekend before.

It's only been three days and I've already learned that you must walk on the right and you must walk fast.

I love it here.

The building itself is gorgeous. The first thing you see when you walk into the lobby is a huge orange wall. I was floored the very first time I saw it and still am every time I walk in.

Flashing my badge to security, I am let in and grin from ear to ear as I ride the elevator up to the fourteenth floor.

"Morning, Lulu," I say enthusiastically to the expressionless girl who sits behind the receptionist desk. She doesn't look up from her phone but gives me a hum of acknowledgement as I walk by.

"Morning, Mr. Baccus." My manager for the duration of my internship. He's not much older than myself and has insisted over and over that I call him Paul but I can't bring myself to do it. I am a professional after all.

"Hey, Margot. Just in time." He stands from his desk and starts walking down the hallway. I already know that means I have to follow him and I do, quickening my pace to keep up with his hurried strides. Everyone is always moving in this place and I absolutely love it. I'm already sad that this journey has to end. I wish I could stay here forever.

Paul stops and I take the opportunity to hand him the coffee I brought for him. He thanks me as we take a seat in a conference room. Paul sits at the table but my chair is slightly on the outside of the group, signifying my inexperience. I'm okay with it though, that just means it'll be more meaningful when I do actually get a seat at the table.

The meeting starts and I take copious notes on every single thing that the editor says to his staff. I don't think I've lifted my pen from the paper once in the entire hour meeting and by the end, my hand is cramping.

"You got all that?" Paul asks as we leave the room and head back toward his office.

"Yes. Do you need me to run anything back for you?" When I look up from my notebook, Paul is smirking at me. "You're teasing me."

Paul laughs. "Only a little."

I smile and we both take our time a little bit as we walk down the hall.

"You know, I watched your podcast."

"You did?"

"Yeah, the judging committee showed it to me when they told me you'd be shadowing me. It was very good, actually. You and that guy have great banter."

"Yeah, we did," I reply quietly.

"Did? You're not going to continue it?"

I shrug as we get to his office and I take my place in the seat in front of the desk. "I already won the contest. There's really no reason to keep it going anymore."

"Well, did you enjoy doing it? It certainly looked like you did."

I grin at the memories. "Yeah, I did."

Paul takes his jacket off and slings it around the chair. "Then, I say keep it going. There's nothing you can lose from it."

I look down at my empty hands. Nothing to lose that hasn't already been lost.

"I can't believe I already have to leave."

"I'm glad this was a good experience for you, Mar. You deserve it," Sydney says on FaceTime as she makes herself lunch. Danika is laying on her couch watching whatever reality television show she's into this week. She's sporting a lovely double chin through the camera lens.

"It was so incredible. I can't believe how much I've learned in just two weeks." I sigh as I lean back in my chair. Paul has gone out to lunch as he typically does, leaving me an hour of peace which is much appreciated after being in that hectic environment all morning.

"What are you gonna get for lunch," Danika asks, her mouth full of popcorn.

"Probably just a burger and some—"

A notification at the top of my phone pulls my attention. It's from YouTube. Our Ask Alex podcast channel just posted a new video.

"Hello?" Dani calls my attention and now they're both staring at me intently.

I bolt up in my seat, clutching the phone to my hand. "I just got a notification that a new video was posted to the Ask Alex channel."

"Aren't you the only one who has access to that account?"

"Nathan does too. And I guess Alex, I told him the credentials once but I didn't think he ever signed into it."

"Well, what are you waiting for?" Sydney shouts. "Watch it!"

Just as I'm about to hang up, Dani shouts even louder. "Hold it, hold it! Stay on the phone and watch it on your laptop. Just in case."

I nod, running across the office to grab my computer from my bag. It takes me a couple seconds to log in and pull up the website and my heart is in my throat the entire time.

A new video was posted twenty-four seconds ago. It already has over two hundred views and the thumbnail is just Alex sitting there alone. Each of our episodes has a title that coincides with one of the topics we discuss during the video. This video is titled: Distraction or Destiny.

"I can't play it."

"Why? Is it not loading or something?"

I blink, my eyes holding back tears. I have no idea what this is going to say but based on how we left things, what we said to each other, what we didn't. I have a sinking feeling this is only going to destroy me further.

"I'm afraid."

Danika sighs. "Don't be scared, Mars. Whatever it is, we'll help you through it. But you need to see first before you jump to conclusions."

Taking a huge breath, I let it out as slowly as I can. "Okay," I say, propping my phone up on my lap so they can see the screen in realtime. I take another breath before clicking the big red PLAY button on the video. *He looks so handsome,* I can't help but think.

The video starts and it features Alex sitting in his same seat that we always sit in for filming. He hasn't moved to the middle, he kept himself on the right and my seat on the left is noticeably empty.

He doesn't start the video with our catchphrase, either. Instead he sighs and says, "You might notice an empty seat next to me. The person that typically fills this seat is currently in New York City fulfilling a lifelong dream of hers and I couldn't be happier for her. I wish I could be there with her, supporting her but unfortunately, something happened that's preventing that."

I pause the video. "Wait, how did he know I won the contest? I never told him."

Danika and Sydney are uncharacteristically quiet, until Sydney bursts. "I told him!" she yells, shame threaded in her voice. "I'm sorry. I felt like he had a right to know. And Margot, feel free to yell at me all you want later but right now you better play that damn video, we're dying over here!"

On the screen, Alex continues.

"So this isn't going to be a typical episode of Ask Alex. I am going to be answering a few questions but they're not sent in from viewers. No, these questions are ones I've been asking myself. Some for a while now and some more recently. So buckle up, folks and Margot, if you're watching, please listen closely."

"Holy shit," Sydney comments on FaceTime and I had almost forgotten that they were there. I quickly pause the video and pull their faces back to mine.

"What do I do?" I ask, frantically.

"Press play!" Both girls shout and I immediately put them back in position and unpause the video.

"The first question is: What happened with me and Margot? That's a very simple question with a very complicated answer."

I draw in a breath and I know that Sydney and Danika are holding theirs too.

"What happened between us was magic. It was power, confidence, and determination. It was creativity, drive, and enthusiasm. Margot and I had love. Have love. Because no matter what she might think, I will never stop loving her. And no matter what happens between us, I will never give up the fight for her. I know it might seem like I have given up, Margot, but I swear I haven't. I just needed to sort out a few things in my life before I could be the man I need to be for you and I've done that now. This time apart has made me realize, there's never been something I've wanted more in this life than Margot Elaine Davis and I will do whatever it takes to get you back."

My phone falls down on my lap causing a loud mix of girly shouts and angry yells to erupt. I pause the video and pull my phone back up. I know my jaw is on the floor and it matches my roommates' expressions, as well.

We blink at each other and then I put them back and press unpause. No hesitation required.

"The second question is: What do you see yourself doing in the future? Well, before this week, I would've said I'd see myself as the future Vice President of Prescott Cars. I'd see myself earning millions of dollars, busy as hell, and absolutely fucking miserable. I'd see myself worn out, lonely, and probably addicted to some substance or other. But, ever since an enlightening conversation I had with my father and my best friend who also happens to be a business major, I can say with the utmost confidence that in the future, I see myself being confident, independent, and happy. Because I am going to follow my dreams. Finally."

My eyes fill with tears and I don't even try to blink it away as they fall down my cheeks.

"The third and final question is this: What happens now? Well, if everything goes according to plan, I am currently waiting outside the *New York Times* building in Manhattan. And if Margot decides to give us another chance, she'll come down from her swanky office and give me the biggest show-stopping kiss she can muster. But if she doesn't want to try again with me then I guess I'll just be catching the next flight out of here. The choice is yours, Margot. Which will it be?"

I'm out the door before he even finishes the question. I hear a faint sound of cheering from my phone as I click it closed and shove it in my back pocket. The elevator is my best friend at this moment because it's ready and waiting for me and when I get to the lobby, I'm almost out of breath from running.

My heart is in my throat when I open the doors to the street and I see him there.

Waiting.

Chapter
Forty-Seven

Alex

SHE'S SOFT IN MY hands. Her hair is clutched in my fist and I'm holding her against me like it's the very last time I'll ever do so. Except it's not the last time. So far from the last time.

"What are you doing here?" Margot asks as she tries to pull herself out of my grip but I don't let her. I need to hold on longer. Her coconut scent hits my nose and I hold on tighter. "Alex?"

"God, I've missed you so much."

She grips the back of my shirt. "I've missed you, too." I let her go, reluctantly. "What's going on? Your dad, Kai? I don't understand."

"My dad and I finally had a real talk. He understands that me being at Prescott Cars would be the worst thing for me. And, after some slight convincing, he offered Kai my intern position, even offering to help pay for his last semester of school if he interns for the whole year instead of just the summer." She takes in a surprised breath and I kiss her forehead.

"I'm sorry we left things the way we did. I just saw life spiraling out of control and I didn't want to bring you down with me."

"There's nowhere I want to be if it's not with you. It might've taken me a minute to realize it but I can manage my time *and* have you in my life. I know I can."

"I know. And I can help. I won't be a distraction."

Margot grips my forearms, her eyebrows pinching in. "Alex, you're not a distraction. You're everything."

When I kiss her, it's like the very first time. Our lips touch and everything else fades away. No honking cars. No bike bells. No angry tourists. Just us and this moment together. I never want to let her go and from now on, I never will.

Epilogue

Alex

WHEN WE HEAD BACK to campus a week later, I can officially confirm that Margot and I are one hundred percent together. Everyone knows it. Everyone is getting used to it. I get to hold my girl's hand on campus and not worry about how people are going to treat her. Even her roommates have warmed back up to me.

We decide to continue doing *Ask Alex* episodes because...why not? It was the most fun I've had and it made sure we spent time together every week, especially since we had no classes together during the spring semester. There was only one change I requested when we brought the new podcast to air, which of course met with reluctance but eventual acceptance. We even got a banner to put behind us during the taping. One displaying the new title: *Ask Alex AND Margot* (yes, the 'and' is capitalized).

Margot is full of confidence after that internship. Ready to take on the world with me and I wouldn't have it any other way. Just one more thing first...

"What's going on? Why aren't you guys having a party? It's Friday night," Margot asks as she looks around our empty living room. No kegs, no red solo cups, no DJ blasting music far too loudly. She looks over at me, perplexed.

"Decided no more parties for the rest of the year," I replied, shrugging my shoulders nonchalantly. When she turns back around, I wink at Devon over her head, giving him the signal.

He nods his head and whistles. Margot whips her head in his direction but the damage is already done. The confetti pours from the ceiling fan and falls all over us. Margot looks up in astonishment.

"Get pranked, sunshine," I say through my laughter. Margot chuckles as the confetti falls on her head and mine.

Her smile is wide when she says, "Grow up, frat boy." Then she kisses me. Her coconut scent, her soft lips on mine, the confetti falling around us. It all makes me feel like I've finally won the future I deserve.

Acknowledgements

There are so many people to thank for this book. I don't even know where to begin.

To Tara, this book would not be what it is without you. From initial brainstorming ideas to paperback format design, you've been with me every step of the journey. Thank you for always answering my crazy plot idea texts at all hours of the day or night. Thank you for being critical when I needed you to be. Mostly, thank you for always being your supportive, awesome self! Can't wait to bother you again with the next book.

To my editor, Kathleen, thank you for showing me that my first draft had more plot holes than a brick of swiss cheese. It's not easy to hear criticisms about your work but Kathleen's feedback was friendly, constructive, and entirely necessary. Much of this story is in thanks to her.

To my cover artist, My Lan, words cannot describe how indebted I am to you. This cover is beautiful. I'm awed with the way you brought the characters to life. Can't wait to work on the next with you! (and the one after that, and the one after that...)

To my betas, you showed me all the ways my book could be better and I thank you endlessly for that. You also definitely toughened my skin and I begrudgingly thank you for that, too.

To my discord writing crew (you know who you are), if we didn't do that month together, this book would not be here today. Thank you.

To my husband, Eric, thank you always supporting my "I gotta go sit at a cafe for 1 to 5 hours, see ya later" habits. Your help with this book has been greatly appreciated–even though romance isn't your genre of choice, I still love you anyway.

To my friends–reading and writing and otherwise–and my family, I love you all. Thank you so much for the unwavering support. I couldn't do this without you.

Emily R. Bellas is happiest when she's writing. Or reading. Or lounging. Or drinking coffee. Or wine. (Imagine all at once). *Ink & Ambition* is her fourth novel and she's excited to keep working on this series. She resides in Brooklyn with her husband and their four year old puppy. Check out her website and mailing list/substack for more info!

WEBSITE   SUBSTACK

ALSO BY
EMILY R. BELLAS

friends with
benefits
(gone wrong)

enemies to
lovers

romantic
suspense

www.ingramcontent.com/pod-product-compliance
Lightning Source LLC
Chambersburg PA
CBHW020015120726
47903CB00004B/1302